Praise for Sharon]
Mys... ..._

Magick & Mayhem

"Magic, Merlin, and murder are a great mix for this debut cozy. Up to her ears in problems, both magickal and mortal, Kailyn's a fun and adventuresome heroine I loved watching. Crafting a spell, summoning a familiar, and solving a murder shouldn't be this hard—or this fun."
—**Lynn Cahoon,** *New York Times* and *USA Today* best-selling author

"Pape has a sure-handed balance of humor and action."
—**Julie Hyzy,** *New York Times* best-selling author

"Sharon Pape's *Magick & Mayhem* is spellbinding, with magical prose, a wizardly plot, and a charming sleuth who, while attempting to protect a cast of sometimes difficult and always surprising characters, has a penchant for accidentally revealing her own powers and secrets to exactly the wrong people."
—**Janet Bolin**, Agatha-nominated author of the national best-selling Threadville Mysteries

"*Magick & Mayhem* is a charming, must-read mystery with enchanting characters. A fun and entertaining page turner that I couldn't put down."
—**Rose Pressey,** *USA Today* best-selling author

Other Books by Sharon Pape

Magick & Mayhem*
That Olde White Magick*
Sketcher in the Rye
Alibis and Amethysts
Sketch a Falling Star
To Sketch a Thief
Sketch Me if You Can

*Available from Lyrical Press, an imprint of Kensington Publishing Corp.

MAGICK RUN AMOK

An Abracadabra Mystery

Sharon Pape

LYRICAL UNDERGROUND
Kensington Publishing Corp.
www.kensingtonbooks.com

LYRICAL UNDERGROUND BOOKS are published by

Kensington Publishing Corp.
119 West 40th Street
New York, NY 10018

All Kensington titles, imprints, and distributed lines are available at special quantity discounts for bulk purchases for sales promotion, premiums, fund-raising, educational, or institutional use.

Special book excerpts or customized printings can also be created to fit specific needs. For details, write or phone the office of the Kensington Sales Manager: Kensington Publishing Corp., 119 West 40th Street, New York, NY 10018. Attn. Sales Department. Phone: 1-800-221-2647.

Lyrical Press and Lyrical Press logo Reg. U.S. Pat. & TM Off.

First Electronic Edition: May 2018
eISBN-13: 978-1-5161-0059-0
eISBN-10: 1-5161-0059-X

First Print Edition: May 2018
ISBN-13: 978-1-5161-0060-6
ISBN-10: 1-5161-0060-3

Printed in the United States of America

For the guy with the aqua eyes.

"A little magic can take you a long way."

—*Roald Dahl*

Chapter 1

"I'm going to be a pariah. A pariah!" Tilly wailed. "People will avoid me like I've got the plague." She'd come into Abracadabra through the door that connected her shop to mine. Merlin was right behind her, like an odd shadow. Since it was not yet nine o'clock, she found me at my desk behind the counter, paying bills online. She shuffled up to me in ancient slippers she refused to replace, because the soft fabric had stretched to accommodate her bunions and arthritic toes.

"Nonsense, Matilda," Merlin said sternly. "There is naught to be concerned about. On that I stake my substantial reputation. You will never become a nasty little fish! Besides, if it were to happen, I would immediately change you back to your dear sweet self. Kailyn, please tell her that. She refuses to take my word for it."

"I said *pariah*, you old fool," Tilly muttered, "not *piranha*. As if I don't have enough to deal with right now." She turned to me. "What am I to do?"

"Why are you worried about becoming a pariah?" I asked, figuring she was back to her original plaint. "Everyone in town loves you."

"They won't once they realize I'm the angel of death," she replied miserably.

"Hold on. You want to catch me up?"

"I had a premonition about yet *another* murder." Her voice trembled. "First, I stumble across Gary Harkens' body, then Amanda's and now this new murder—well, psychically anyway."

"What did this premonition tell you?" I asked, coming from behind the counter.

"Just that someone else would be killed."

"No images of the victim, no location, no time of the murder?" She shook her head. "Aunt Tilly," I said, "please sit down and listen to me." Tilly settled into the chair I kept there for bored husbands and exhausted shoppers. "You have things a little muddled. First of all, I'm the one who tripped over Gary Harkens. You fell on top of me."

She perked up. "You're right! *You* found him."

"Secondly, both you and Beverly discovered Amanda at the same time. And this premonition of yours is probably nothing more than a…a hunch, a bad dream, a figment of your imagination. It could be just another glitch in our magick."

"What a blessing you are," Tilly said, popping out of the chair as if she were reborn. She pulled me to her and hugged the air right out of my lungs. "I'm off to bake some of your favorite Linzer tarts," she chirped. "Traditional raspberry or tangy apricot?"

"I believe I'd like some traditional," I said.

"Then it's settled. I'll make both."

"I am in your debt as well," Merlin whispered, before following her back to Tea and Empathy. He graced me with the modified bow he'd adopted in deference to his age and a growing tendency to fall on his face if he attempted a deeper one.

Sashkatu had been watching us from his private loge on the window ledge. He rose, stretching his sinewy feline body, before he descended his custom-built steps and accompanied the wizard back to Tilly's place, the home of fine aromas and finer tastes.

When I looked at my watch, it was ten past nine. I hurried to open the shop for business. Bronwen and Morgana, my mother and grandmother, would have frowned at my lack of punctuality, although there was no one beating down my door in urgent need of a cure or a spell. My progenitors agreed on very little, but on this subject, they were united. I could only hope they hadn't noticed, but of course they had. My grandmother's cloud of energy popped out of the ether first, my mother's a moment later. Both were calm and white. Maybe I'd be spared a lecture after all.

My grandmother Bronwen spoke first. "You did an admirable job of quieting your aunt's fears," she said, "but there is something you need to know." I was pretty sure I didn't want to know what she was about to tell me.

"At least a few of our ancestors were remarkably talented at predicting death."

And I was right. "Did they have the ability from the time they were young or did it come on later in life?" I asked, looking for a loophole to crawl through.

"I believe it's happened both ways," Morgana said, dashing my hopes.

"But this premonition was very vague," I pointed out. "For all we know, it wasn't a premonition at all." I felt like I was pleading my case before a panel of judges.

"The details may fill in over time," Bronwen said. "Or they may not." I was rooting hard for the *may not.*

"If it doesn't come to pass this time, can we assume she doesn't have the ability?"

"That would be nice," my mother agreed, "but I'm afraid it's not that simple."

Of course not, why would it be? "I don't suppose there's any way to turn off or blunt this particular talent?"

"None I've ever heard of," Bronwen said, "but I'll ask around." Ask around? Was there a bartender or a manicurist beyond the veil who *knew* things? A guy on a street corner who could get you information for a price? Before I could ask what she meant, Morgana said they were being summoned and promptly vanished.

"Don't forget that punctuality is a sign of respect for your customers," Bronwen managed to stick in, her voice trailing behind her as she too winked away.

While waiting for customers, I finished paying my bills and caught up on some dusting, trying not to dwell on the havoc my aunt's nascent ability could cause in our lives. I wasn't successful until the bells above the door jingled to announce the day's first customer. The woman looked about thirty, petite and pretty enough to forego makeup and still turn a man's head. She seemed to be blown into the shop by a cold gust of wind, along with the last of the shriveled oak leaves that skittered across the hardwood floor. She had to put some weight into closing the door behind her. "It's awful out there," she said, shuddering in a jacket that was more suited to early September than mid-October.

"Welcome," I said. "It's the sun that tricks you into thinking it's a nice day to be outside. Are you from around here?"

"Sort of." She extended her hand. "I'm Jane Oliver."

"Kailyn Wilde," I replied, briefly taking her hand. It was overly formal for a shopkeeper and a customer, but hey—I'd been taught the customer was generally right.

"I moved to Watkins Glen two years ago. I guess by now I should know what the weather's like this time of year, but I go from the garage where I live to the garage where I work and hardly ever poke my head outside."

"What brings you to New Camel today?" I asked.

"Your shop. I'm on a mission to find a good moisturizer and everyone raves about your products."

"Word of mouth is our best advertisement," I said. It was nice to hear that a customer made the trip to town specifically to visit Abracadabra. In many instances, my shop was an afterthought, a let's-peek-into-the-magick-shop, after the tourist had already bought pounds of candy at Lolly's, skeins of wool at Busy Fingers, or lunch and a shake at The Soda Jerk. My mother had been pragmatic about it. For her, commerce was commerce no matter how it came about. But I got a kick from knowing the shop was the primary reason someone came into our town.

"Let me show you where to find the moisturizers," I said, leading the way to the second aisle. I pointed out a shelf at eye level. "There are quite a few, so take your time. Feel free to ask questions."

"Thanks." Jane sniffed the air. "Where is that incredible smell coming from?" She was doing a pirouette, trying to pinpoint the source. "Do you have a bakery in here too?"

I laughed. "It's coming from next door. The owner is not only a renowned psychic, but also an incredible pastry chef. You can have a glimpse into your future and then enjoy an authentic English tea."

"The tea sounds great," she said, "but I don't believe in psychics or any of that paranormal stuff. I'm a scientist from the bottom of my feet to the top of my head."

I tried to keep my smile from wilting and in the politest of tones, I reminded Jane that she was standing in a magick shop.

"I know," she said. "It's a cute gimmick."

I didn't like it when people shrugged magick off as a children's game, a trick worthy of snide remarks. I understood that being circumspect was for our protection, maybe even for our survival, but it still chafed.

When Jane came up to the counter a few minutes later, she was holding two jars. "I can't decide which would be better for me," she said.

I pointed to the one in her left hand. "That one is better for really dry skin." Jane charged the purchase and went on her way, blissfully unaware how lucky she was that my family never dabbled in black magick.

Only two more customers stopped in during the morning, locals who needed health-related items. One was desperate for a lip balm that would actually work for her kids, and the other bought my last bottle of cough medicine for her husband, an early victim of the flu. I wasn't aware I'd run through my entire stock of it, until she pointed it out. The slow morning instantly turned into a boon, giving me time to whip up more of the three different formulas I sold.

It had been a whole lot easier to keep up with demand and still run the front of the shop when my mother and grandmother were alive to share the workload. But I found that if I left the storeroom door open and didn't listen to music, I could easily hear the chimes marking someone's arrival. That worked well for simple formulas. The more complicated ones required me to add ingredients at specific intervals in the process or complete the recipe without interruption. I had to leave those for afterhours. It made for longer workdays and a glower of cats unhappy about their delayed dinner hour, but I didn't collapse from the longer day and they didn't starve from waiting an extra hour or two to eat. If it wasn't an elegant solution, it was at least an equitable one.

Fortunately, I had all the ingredients I needed on hand. The basic honey, lemon, coconut oil mixture was number one on the hit parade. It always sold out first. The thyme tea only appealed to those who enjoyed the flavor of the herb, but those who did were rabid in their devotion. The ginger peppermint syrup was favored by people who preferred a little zip to the taste of their medicine. They were all somewhat effective in easing coughs. The game changer was the addition of the spell my mother created decades ago. It drew its strength from the power of three. It required three candles, three oils (myrrh, mint, and sandalwood) and three pieces of quartz. I anointed each of the candles and quartz with each of the three oils. Then I placed a candle and a piece of quartz together at each point of an imaginary triangle with three equal sides. The words of the spell were deceptively simple, but repeating them three times imbued them with power if the practitioner came from the right bloodline.

Magick mend and candle burn
Illness leave and health return.

I printed out the labels and was applying them to the bottles when I checked the time and realized I was late. I ran out of the storeroom, set the I'll-be-back clock to one-thirty, put it in the window, and bundled myself into my down coat, gloves, and scarf for the two-block walk. No amount of lousy weather was going to discourage me from meeting Travis for lunch. As I hurried to The Soda Jerk, I noticed that most of the shops I passed were decorated for Halloween, their windows filled with images of pumpkins, witches, and skeletons. My family always steered clear of decorating our shop for holidays, believing that true magick isn't seasonal. Not even at Halloween.

I wasn't surprised to find The Soda Jerk less than half full. Folks who didn't need to leave the warmth of their snug homes hunkered down on days as raw as this one. I looked around to see if Travis was waiting at a table. He was usually punctual, but this time I beat him there even though I was five minutes late.

I didn't know any of the other patrons, but I could tell by their uniforms they were deliverymen, cable guys, and a lone mail carrier. For those who worked outside year-round, a warm restaurant was a welcome refuge from the cold.

The wait staff at The Soda Jerk was back to its post summer numbers, one busboy and the two waitresses I'd known all my life. Margie spotted me first and whisked me off to her section, which was fine with me. Her counterpart was often brusque and stingy with a smile.

"There are only two people you'd come out for in this weather," Margie said, seating me at a booth away from the draft of the door. "Who is it today—Elise or Travis?"

"Travis," I said with a grin. "I'll bet you know all the secrets in this town, don't you?"

"Who me?" she said with a wink. "How about I whip you up a cup of hot cocoa?"

"You twisted my arm, though to be honest, it didn't take much twisting."

"One cocoa, double whipped cream coming up."

The door opened and Travis walked in, making my heart trip into the little jig it reserved for him. I waved and caught his eye, but no acknowledging smile lit his face as he headed toward me. He got to the booth as Margie was setting the cocoa in front of me. She must have seen his eyes widen at the sight of it. "Can I get you one too, Mr. TV?"

"Another time, Margie, I'll stick to coffee, thanks." He slid into the booth across from me, looking harried; his thick hair was wind-tossed and stubble darkened his cheeks. "Mind if we order right away?" he asked me, before Margie could leave.

"No, that's fine." I knew the menu by heart anyway. "Grilled cheese and tomato soup combo."

Travis handed Margie the unopened menus. "Make it two." He usually engaged in a little banter with Margie, but today he was all business. It derailed me.

"I'll put a rush on it," Margie said. She didn't seem the least bit surprised by his behavior. She'd waitressed enough years that she could read people and situations better than most psychologists.

"What's wrong?" I asked after she left.

"A friend of mine's gone missing," he said, raking his fingers through his hair the way he did when he was worried or puzzled.

"Oh Travis, I'm so sorry. Are the two of you very close?"

"I've known Ryan since high school."

I sensed there was more to it, but I didn't want to press him on it. "Have you notified the police?"

"The police won't act on a missing person's report for an adult, until the person's been gone for at least forty-eight hours."

"That's crazy," I said.

"Not really. Can you imagine what it would be like if you could call the police and send them searching for everyone who's late arriving somewhere? Or isn't answering their cell? Besides, there's a fine line between protecting people and keeping tabs on them."

"I didn't think of it that way," I said, still far from convinced that forty-eight hours was a reasonable amount of time to wait.

Travis's coffee arrived by busboy. While he was adding sweetener, I took a sip of my cocoa. When I looked up again, he was smiling. "A white moustache is a great look for you." I grabbed my napkin and wiped it off. "Way to win a girl over with compliments." The moment of levity felt good, but it couldn't last beneath the weight of Travis's distress. "You're certain Ryan is missing?"

"Yes, if you knew him, you'd understand. He digs for stories that might be better left unearthed. Stories that can get him killed. And he has a bad habit of trusting the wrong people. This wouldn't be the first time he's needed to be rescued."

"We needed a little rescuing ourselves not too long ago," I said, thinking of our last case. "Things aren't always as dire and hopeless as they seem."

"But we had a secret weapon—he doesn't."

There was a time when the idea of real magick sent him running from me, and now my family's magick had become his secret weapon. Talk about zero to sixty in a flash.

Margie arrived with our lunches, gooey cheese and steaming soup. "Enjoy," she said, off to the mailman who was beckoning her. I took a bite of my sandwich; Travis took two, polishing off half of his.

"When did you start looking for Ryan?" I asked.

"Six p.m. yesterday," he replied between spoonfuls of soup. "We were supposed to meet for an early dinner in Watkins Glen. He never showed. Doesn't answer his cell. I started with all his usual haunts—nobody's seen him. I've been driving around in widening circles, checking everywhere the road drops off, every place his car could be hidden in woods or dense brush."

I nibbled on my sandwich, no longer hungry. "Have you slept or eaten since then?"

"I catnapped in my car for an hour or two before the sun came up. And I had a couple of donuts and lots of coffee." He looked up at me. The naked pain in his eyes made my heart ache. He managed a lop-sided smile. "Don't worry," he said, "I'm fine. Believe me. I've survived on less." He checked his watch and stuffed the last of the sandwich into his mouth.

"Go, it's okay," I said. "Lunch is on me. Just please be careful."

He gulped down the coffee, then reached across the table for my hand before turning it over to plant a lingering kiss on my palm. As kisses go, it was a lot more effective than I would have thought. He ran his finger along the side of my face, and I wanted to grab his hand and hold him there a little longer. "I'll call you."

"You'd better," I said, "or *I'll* be out there searching for *you.*" I'd meant it to sound playful, to lighten his heart for a moment, but my voice cracked. "Good luck and stay safe," I murmured as he walked away.

Chapter 2

"You're back!" Merlin said, swooping down on me as I returned from my abbreviated lunch. I peeled off my cold weather gear and stepped behind the counter to stow my purse.

"Make haste, make haste," he urged me a good seven times before he added, "It's Matilda. She is in dire need of you."

"Why didn't you say that *first?*" I yelled, running for the connecting door to her shop. I had visions of her on the floor, stricken with a heart attack or stroke, a broken hip or horrible burns. I was so geared for disaster that it took my brain a moment to reboot when I nearly collided with her. There wasn't a drop of blood on her, not a red curl out of place. She was beaming at me, a doily covered tray of Linzer tarts in her hands.

"You scared me half to death!" I snapped at Merlin when he caught up to me, panting like he'd run a marathon.

"Well…ah…hmm…" he stammered. "You see, Tilly, dear woman that she is, wished to present you with this gift of her love and gratitude. She was waiting and waiting for you, after standing on her poor aching feet for hours baking these magnificent confections."

Tilly rolled her eyes. "Poppycock, he was distraught when I told him he couldn't have a tart until you did. As you are aware, his highness is sorely lacking in patience."

Not what I wanted to hear, since I was uncomfortably stuffed from lunch. I must have been caught up in Travis's nervous energy, because I'd bolted my food too. I felt like half of it was still stuck in my throat. As beautiful and tempting as the tarts were, they would have to wait a few hours. But Merlin looked so eager for one I didn't have the heart to make him wait any longer. I sat down at the elegant tea table my aunt had set and selected a tart with raspberry jam. Tilly and Merlin took apricot ones, after which Tilly poured her homemade ginger peach tea.

I sipped my tea and told my aunt about the cold weather patrons at The Soda Jerk. The wizard didn't take his eyes off me. He was like a vulture waiting for its next meal to finish dying. Tilly must have warned him not to eat until I did. There was no way around it. I took a dainty bite of the buttery cookie with its mantle of confectioners' sugar. At any other time, I wouldn't have been able to stop until it was gone. But at that moment, I was having trouble swallowing the tiny piece in my mouth.

"Never better," I murmured once I'd gotten it down. "Perfection."

Tilly was looking at me, one eyebrow arched skeptically. "Something's wrong. No need to spare my feelings," she said, squaring her shoulders, but already sounding hurt. "I'd prefer you tell me, Kailyn, so I can correct whatever it is the next time."

"I swear to you, there's not the tiniest thing wrong with it. I just had too much lunch. I'd like to save it till later when I can really appreciate it."

"Okay," she said, although she didn't seem convinced. Meanwhile Merlin had made quick work of his and was reaching for another. Tilly slapped his hand away. "You may have a second one, but after that, not one bit more. Do you understand me?"

"Of course I understand," he said indignantly.

"And don't try your sad, puppy dog eyes on me. It won't work."

We sounded like a good old dysfunctional American family again, the way we had when Morgana and Bronwen were alive. Apparently even magick isn't capable of changing family dynamics.

"Have you heard what our resident wizard is proposing to do?" Tilly said, no doubt trying to move past anymore discussions of tarts.

"Not yet." What new can of worms was about to explode in my face? Merlin had chosen a raspberry tart this go-round and didn't seem to be listening.

"Merlin, what's this new plan of yours?" I asked reluctantly. The sooner I found out, the more time I'd have to prevent or moderate the consequences. Even so, ignorance seemed like the better option.

He sat up straight with pride, forgetting his tart for the moment. "To right a wrong, as any nobleman of my time would."

Something about the way he said it, made Don Quixote pop into my mind, along with a deep sense of dread. "What wrong would that be?" I sounded impressively calm for someone whose stomach was trying out for a gymnastics event.

"I intend to make a run for the vacant seat on the town board," he said grandly. "And when I win, I shall call for a vote to reestablish the proper name of this town and adopt a more appropriate emblem for it."

There were so many problems within those sentences; I had trouble deciding which one to address first. I finally went with, "You have to be an American citizen and a resident of this town to run for the board."

"Says whom?"

"The people who made the laws. Since you didn't enter the country, not to mention the state, the county or the town, legally, you are not a legal resident."

"Then tell me how to remedy the situation."

"There is no way." Fast and blunt, a ripping-off-the-Band-Aid approach. I hoped it might deter any further discussion. I should have known better.

"I see," he said. I waited in silence while he pondered the problem. Tilly and I shared empathetic glances. "How is one recognized as a legal resident?" he asked finally.

"You would need a birth certificate stating you were born in this country as well as a social security card and that's just the beginning. If you tried to use phony documents, you would wind up in prison, if not in a psychiatric ward." Merlin went back to eating his tart, but I could practically see the gears turning in his head.

* * * *

Dinner time came and went, without my appetite making an appearance. I fed the cats, who had no such problem, worked on the computer, and watched TV. At ten o'clock, when I looked at the tart sitting on the kitchen counter, it finally looked inviting to me. I wasn't going to save it for dessert, though. It was going to be dinner. I enjoyed it thoroughly and was still licking the homemade jam off my fingers when I called Tilly to extol its virtues. She lapped up the praise the way her big Maine Coon lapped up whipped cream.

I listened to the late news before climbing into bed. There was no mention of Travis's friend, but then it wasn't yet forty-eight hours since he'd gone missing. I was worried about Travis driving around again all night with no sleep, staring into the dark for any sign of Ryan or his car. I tried to keep Tilly's premonition of death from wandering into my thoughts, but it was like piling sand bags to stop a tsunami. I didn't know I'd fallen asleep until the phone woke me. "I found him," Travis said.

"Is he all right?" I asked, hoping it was just fatigue that made him sound so empty.

"He's dead."

Chapter 3

The roads were empty and a little eerie. The street lights seemed farther apart and the darkness more impenetrable than I remembered from other times I'd driven there. I knew it was all in my mind, because I was once again headed toward death. Travis's voice over the Bluetooth was comforting, but his directions were sketchy at best.

He told me to take Grand Avenue west from New Camel. It was one lane in each direction, divided by a double yellow. It might have lived up to its name when it was new, but it was old now and in disrepair. Holes pitted the macadam in so many places it was impossible to avoid them all, especially at night. I bumped along it through a small town that had faded until it was no more than a gas station and mini-mart. The newer road that bypassed the town had hastened its demise. Although New Camel was still thriving, with more tourists every year, I couldn't help wondering if it might someday face a similar fate. Everything had its time; nothing was forever. A chill flashed through me that wasn't from the temperature outside, but I turned up the heater anyway.

With virtually no landmarks to go by and a navigation system that required a specific address, Travis had to be creative about the directions he gave me. "After you pass the old gas station," he said, "make the first right you come to after the speed limit sign."

I saw the street at the last minute and turned sharply, my wheels spewing gravel as I fishtailed onto it. If the street had ever had a name, there was no longer a sign post on which to display it. One street light flickered on and off farther down the road. Travis's disembodied voice made me feel like I was stranded in a maze, getting vague directions from another lost soul.

"What do I do next?"

"It gets a little tricky now," he said. "There aren't any street signs and I don't remember exactly how many roads I drove through in this area before I found Ryan's car. My best guess is to take the first left after the second right. It should be about a quarter mile down from where you are. I'll leave my headlights on for you to home in on. They're just about the only light around."

How had he remembered even that much? He'd been searching for hours on no sleep, randomly turning left and right. I had a better idea. I told Travis I'd call him back in a few minutes. He wasn't happy about it, until I explained that a little magick might help me find him more quickly. Before he let me go, he made me promise to keep my doors locked and windows up. I was about to remind him that my car was covered by protective wards, but that would only waste time. It was easier to promise.

I looked for a good place to park for the few minutes I needed. I didn't want anyone calling to report a strange car in front of their house. Such a call would bring the police and they'd stumble upon Travis and the missing journalist before I did, making my trip there pointless. The few houses I could make out along the road were totally dark. Not a single outside light among them. It was impossible to know if the occupants were asleep or the houses were abandoned. I chose a spot between two houses and pulled over onto what seemed to be the edge of the road, but where the gravel and dirt ended and the dirt and weeds began was hard to determine.

I didn't know a spell to find a person, but I had one for finding missing objects. I changed a few words to better fit the situation and figured it was worth a shot. I had a hard time clearing my mind with so much going on in it. I'd finally reached a Zen-like state, when Travis called. "Is everything okay?" he asked. "Why didn't you call me back?"

"I was doing fine, before you interrupted," I said. "But I need to have my mind under control if this has any chance of working. I won't forget to call you back."

"Sorry," he said sheepishly and hung up.

When I regained my focus, I envisioned Travis and began the spell:

Moon, Sun, and Earth,
Air, Fire, and Sea,
He who is lost
Return him to me.

I repeated the spell for the third time and opened my eyes, not sure what to expect. I was still in my car at the edge of the same road. I called Travis. "I don't think it worked, but don't worry, I'll find you."

I rode up and down streets, Travis telling me to try one turn or another. At the ten-minute mark, I made a unilateral decision to listen to my instincts instead of him. After that epiphany, it wasn't long before I saw his headlights. The spell had worked after all. I just had to trust myself enough to set it in motion. I pulled up nose to nose with his car. We both got out and met in the middle of the road. Travis pulled me to him. His hands were ice cold, even through my warm jacket, not surprising given the temperature and the fact that his friend was lying dead at the bottom of the embankment.

"Thanks for coming," he murmured, his cheek pressed to mine. We stayed like that for a full minute. "It looks like Ryan lost control, went over the edge, and into a tree," he said after releasing me. "I want you to see the scene before I call 911. After the cops are here, they won't let anyone get near it. I need your input—I'm not objective enough. I'm going to position my car for the headlights to light up the crash scene." While he was doing that, I walked to the edge of the road and looked down. His headlights were already helping to illuminate the drop-off. It wasn't as steep as I'd imagined, but Ryan's flight down the hill had put him on a collision course with a tree large enough to win handily in any combat with a car. I turned away and searched the nearby roadway for evidence that Ryan had slammed on his brakes, burning rubber, when he realized what was about to happen.

Travis joined me there, catching my hand in his and weaving his fingers through mine.

"I can't find any tread marks," I said.

"Yeah, there aren't any."

"Could he have been distracted by his phone until it was too late and he was hurtling down the hill?"

"I'd like to say 'no', but he was bad that way. Usually kept the phone on his lap when he was driving."

I wondered if Travis was also *bad that way*. It was a subject that would have to wait for another day. He let go of my hand and hooked his arm through mine instead. "Are you ready?" His voice wobbled a bit as if he were asking himself the same question. He'd been down there once, so it wouldn't be the shock it was the first time, but that didn't mean it would be any easier. His emotions were ripped up and raw.

"Ready," I said, clenching my jaw against the cold that was biting its way through my jacket and the anxiety over what I was about to see. We started slowly down the hill. The vegetation underfoot was slick with dew. I was glad I'd taken the extra time to put on sneakers before leaving the house. Even so, halfway down my foot slipped. If Travis hadn't been holding on to me, I would have tumbled all the way to Ryan's car.

When we reached the bottom, I saw the accordion of twisted metal that had been the front end of the car. Although his airbag had deployed, it hadn't saved his life. Or had it? It was possible he survived the crash, only to lie there unconscious in the cold with no one around to render help. It would take an autopsy to answer that question and many others.

"How did you ever see his car down here in the dark?" I asked.

"A flashlight. If I'd been lucky enough to drive by here during the day, it would have been a hell of a lot easier."

"What do you want me to do?"

"Examine the car and its contents, so I can be sure I didn't miss something important. But don't touch anything, not even with your gloves on. If this wasn't an accident, you could destroy evidence.

"Evidence?" I said. "How could this be anything but an accident?"

"I'll explain after you take a look."

I followed him closer to the car. He pulled a small LED flashlight out of his jacket pocket to better illuminate the car's interior. Ryan's upper body was suspended by the seatbelt just above the airbag. He looked like a macabre marionette, waiting for its puppeteer to return.

"Tell me everything you see, even if you don't think it could have played a part in his death. It's our one chance before the police take over." He handed me the flashlight and took another one from his pocket.

It was hard to see the entire front compartment without moving Ryan out of the way, which was clearly not an option. I did my best to view it from every window, every angle. I felt like I was at a movie theater straining to see the screen around the NBA player in front of me.

There was a half full to-go cup in one of the two cup holders. If there was a straw or lid, I couldn't find it. They probably wound up under the seat from the impact of the car hitting the tree. The cup was plastic, the kind used for cold drinks, not the pressed paper used for hot drinks, since Styrofoam's fall from grace. There was a box from a burger joint on the floor between Ryan's feet, a partially eaten burger hanging out of it.

I looked in the back of the car on my way around to the other side. An umbrella, an ice-scraper, a Chinese takeout menu, and a pair of ratty old sneakers – things you might find in any car. I continued to the front passenger window. There was nothing on the seat. I looked down at the floorboard. I didn't see the cell phone, until the flashlight glinted off the dark screen. I described all of this to Travis, who was either examining the ground for clues or trying not to keep staring at his friend's body. I figured it was the latter.

I completed my circuit of the car and turned my attention to Ryan, himself. I was relieved that his eyes were closed, but my renegade mind still wondered if he'd seen death coming. When I moved the flashlight down his face, my stomach recoiled. I had to look away and take a couple of deep breaths before I could focus on him again.

Travis was instantly at my side. "Are you okay? You don't have to go on if this is too much for you."

"I'm good," I managed to say without my voice wobbling. "I'll be fine." I had to be fine for his sake. I trained the light back on Ryan's face, willing my stomach to stay put. There was the residue of something caked around his mouth and clotted on the front of his coat. The burger? That's when I saw all the bloody scratches on his neck, his mouth, and his chin. Some of the scratches were so deep they were more like claw marks. Had he choked to death on the burger?

"Check out his fingernails," Travis said.

Ryan's left hand was hanging down between his body and the door, impossible to see. The right one lay in his lap, where I could easily see that his nails and cuticles were caked with dried blood.

"He did that to himself?" I knew the answer, but couldn't keep the words from spilling out as my mind tried to come to terms with the horror of it. I stepped back from the car, my knees rubbery. It was a relief to look away from Ryan.

Travis put his arm around my shoulders and I leaned into him, until my legs felt like they could bear my weight again.

"How are you holding up?" I asked him.

"I don't feel much of anything right now. Shock, I guess."

He linked arms with me and we made our way back up the slippery hill to the road. "Come on, we'll talk in the car." He'd left the engine running for the headlights and the heater. It was blissfully warm inside.

"Okay," I said. "What did you mean about it not being an accident?"

"You saw the hamburger box and the mess on his face and jacket?"

"Yes." I'd probably take the image to my grave.

"He wasn't eating the hamburger, Kailyn, because he's been a committed vegetarian since he was fifteen."

"No chance he could have slipped?"

"Not Ryan. Not once. When he was in his early twenties, he ordered vegetable soup at a restaurant. The menu didn't mention beef stock in the description of the soup. He was sick for two days afterward. His stomach couldn't even handle the stock anymore."

"Could the burger have been vegetarian?" I asked to cover all the possibilities.

"No, I thought of that too. The place it came from only makes beef burgers. Like I said, there's no way Ryan was eating that burger of his own free will. If the ME attributes his death to choking on the burger, it was no accident. It was murder. Someone force-fed him that meat."

It took me a minute to wrap my mind around the possibility that he'd been murdered. Travis broke into my muddled thoughts. "Thank you for coming," he said, reaching for my hand and squeezing it. "You have no idea how much it means to me. But you need to leave now so I can call the police."

He walked me back to my car. "Let me know when you get home," he said. "I won't call them, until I hear from you. I don't want to take the chance a cop on his way here might see you and wonder what you're doing out and about at this hour. Do you remember the way back to Grand Avenue?"

"Sure," I said, not at all sure. He had more than enough on his mind. If my spell didn't work in reverse, I'd set my GPS to take me home.

Chapter 4

I shut the alarm on my bedside radio. I was too tired for the time to be right. I pulled up the covers, hoping to fall back to sleep, but the memories of the night flooded back into my head. Travis—he'd sent me home, but he must have been up the rest of the night with the police. They wouldn't care that he'd been without sleep for over forty-eight hours. They would take him back to headquarters in Watkins Glen, where Detective Duggan would question him relentlessly. I grabbed my phone on the nightstand and was about to click on his number when I stopped myself. As much as I wanted to find out how he was, I didn't want to risk waking him if he was finally asleep. I settled for texting him.

My troubled thoughts turned to Tilly. If Travis was right about how Ryan died, her prediction of another murder had come true. At least she hadn't known the victim, location or cause of death beforehand. However, if my mother and grandmother were right, her unenviable talent might expand to include those things. Maybe Merlin knew a spell to prevent that from happening. Or maybe he would only succeed in making matters worse.

I dragged myself out of bed and down the stairs to feed Sashkatu and the band of would-be familiars I'd inherited along with the house and magick shop. Once they were settled, I took a hot shower and pulled on a sweater, jeans, boots, and a down vest. But I couldn't seem to shake the chill in my bones. I didn't have time to brew coffee, so I promised my stomach coffee and something more substantial from the Breakfast Bar.

As soon as Sashkatu and I walked into the shop, he made a beeline for his window ledge that was already warmed by the morning sun streaming in. I gave him fresh water and cleaned the litter box I kept in the storeroom. I was about to step through the connecting door into Tilly's shop to say "hello," when I heard her arguing with Merlin. I made a quick U-turn to avoid being dragged into their drama and headed for the front door and breakfast. I realized it was cowardly, but I was bone-tired and brain-fried.

The Breakfast Bar was a recent addition to New Camel. It was a mother/daughter enterprise that only served breakfast and was open from 8 a.m. to 3 p.m.—the hours Beth Lee's kids were in school. Her mother, Diane Kim, was the chef. Beth ran the business end. The Bar was an immediate success with both locals and tourists. Diane was always open to suggestions for new dishes. If it was a hit, she added it to the menu and named it after its creator. My aunt Tilly was the only one I knew who didn't like The Bar. She maintained that the women were encroaching on her territory. Logic held no sway with her. It didn't matter that their menu was completely different from the items she served at her high teas or that psychic readings were the mainstay of how she made her living.

Beverly Rupert was walking out of The Bar as I was walking in. I nodded, counting myself lucky for missing her, until she stepped back inside to chat. "Did you hear about the reporter they found dead in his car? They say he must have lost control, because the car went off the road and slammed into a tree." She added a theatrical shudder. I knew her well enough to be certain it was only for effect. And she didn't mention the reporter's name in an obvious attempt to scare me, to make me worry it was Travis who had died.

"The reporter was Ryan Cutler," I said, watching the disappointment register on her face.

"Well, thank goodness it wasn't your Travis," she said, clapping her hand to her heart.

"Exactly. Now if you'll excuse me, I should put in my order." My stomach was grumbling for an egg and cheese Panini.

"Of course, of course," she said. "Nice to see you."

I should have said, "Nice to see you too," but the words seemed stuck to my tongue. Instead I wished her a good day. I returned to my shop, breakfast in hand, and sat down at the desk to eat it. Sashkatu opened one eye and sniffed the air. Though he was generally a fan of eggs, that morning they couldn't compete with the sunlight. Seconds later he was snoring away.

I was finishing the last bite of Panini when Tilly marched into my shop from Tea and Empathy. Her cheeks were nearly as red as her hair, which meant she was either embarrassed or furious. There was nothing ambiguous about her facial expression though—fury won by a landslide.

"Do you know what your wizard friend did?" she demanded as if I were somehow responsible for his crimes.

"Aunt Tilly," I said evenly, "how would I know? *You're* the psychic in the family."

"Of course I am. The question was purely rhetorical."

"What did Merlin do now?" I asked, dreading the answer. He already had an impressive list of priors, each more novel than the last.

"He wantonly destroyed one of my favorite muumuus. And they don't come cheaply. It doesn't seem to matter to Evelyn that we've been friends since the fourth grade, she's never given me a penny's discount." It was a complaint I was treated to every time she received the seamstress's bill. And it was likely to continue, because Evelyn had created the pattern for Tilly and her work was unassailable, even if her pricing wasn't.

"Why would Merlin do something like that?" I asked to refocus her on Merlin and the tale of the ravaged muumuu. When she was upset, she tended to ramble off topic. Before she could answer me, Merlin came through the connecting door, the contested garment rolled up in his hand.

"Has Tilly told you about my banner?" he asked, his chest puffed out with pride.

"Merlin," I said sternly, "you can't take what isn't yours just because you want it."

"And you certainly have no right to ruin it!" Tilly added.

"I had a far better use for it," he said. "Does that not count for anything?"

"No!" we said in unison.

"Aha—so there's a conspiracy afoot. Mayhap, young Kailyn, you should see the evidence before you choose with whom to align yourself." He unfurled the banner and pulled it taut. There was no denying that he'd done a fine job of it, given his limited resources. The banner depicted a highly stylized, golden lion rampant on a field of emerald green muumuu. Of course it no longer bore any resemblance to Tilly's dress, but only the three of us would ever know the truth of it. Unless Tilly got chatty.

Both Merlin and my aunt were looking at me, clearly awaiting my verdict on the matter. "As beautiful as the banner is, Merlin, you stole what belonged to Tilly and nothing can justify that. You should have asked her permission or requested she buy you some fabric for your project."

"I loved the way that color set off my red hair," Tilly said, still bemoaning her loss.

"I bet Evelyn can find more of that fabric and make you a brand new one," I said to console her. "You could even have her add some sequins or beads to the neckline this time."

"Oh my, that *would* be stunning, wouldn't it?" Tilly said, brightening. "I think I'll give her a call right now." She headed back to her shop with a lighter step than when she'd arrived.

"All's well that ends well," Merlin declared triumphantly. But he didn't seem to be in any hurry to follow her back to Tea and Empathy. He ambled around my shop for a few minutes, picking up this and looking at that without any apparent interest.

"Everything okay?" I asked, though it didn't take a psychic to figure out what was bothering him.

"Ah...do you think...I mean... Dear child, might I impose on your good graces to remain here a while longer?"

I had to bite my lip to keep from laughing. "Is it my aunt?"

"There is a chance, a wee chance, that sweet Matilda may harbor some lingering resentment."

"In that case," I said, "you may want to hang out here until the new muumuu arrives."

Chapter 5

When I opened Abracadabra the next morning, I still hadn't heard from Travis. By then I was better rested, but starved for information. It wasn't likely that Duggan threw him in jail without probable cause. And although Travis had to be fifty miles past exhausted, how long could he sleep? If he didn't call or answer my texts by noon, I intended to call him.

I was helping my elderly neighbor, Maddy Nelson, find a cure for her indigestion, when the door chimes jingled. I poked my head out of the aisle to tell the newcomer I'd be right with them. Seeing Travis there did more to lift my spirits than St. John's Wort or Golden Root ever could. "I'll be with you in a minute," I called as if he were just another customer. I preferred to keep my private life private. It made me a troglodyte of sorts in the age of uncensored social media, but through the millennia, my family has always needed to conduct their lives differently from the rank and file of society. Our ancestors learned the hard way to stay in the background and exercise caution in order to survive.

I went back to Maddy and her indigestion. She was squinting at the label on one of the jars I'd pointed out, looking overwhelmed. "There are too many choices," she said, turning to me. "Ginger, chamomile, peppermint. I don't even know what fennel is. How's a body to choose? Maybe you could just choose one for me?" she asked with a hopeful smile.

"I have a better idea. I have samples of them. Brew one at a time into a tea. If the first one doesn't work or you don't like it, go on to another one, until you find the one that's right for you."

Maddy's eyebrows drew together. "I'm afraid buying the three samples would be too costly. Like those travel size toiletries that always seem to cost more. I'm on a fixed income, you know."

"The samples are free," I told her. "How else can I expect my customers to decide what to buy?"

"Well, aren't you a thoughtful young woman," she said. "Morgana and Bronwen would be proud. What a pity they're gone."

Not as gone as you might think, I said to myself. "Give me a minute and I'll grab those samples for you." I'd been spending the shop's slow hours making up sample packets of the various products and remedies I sold. The idea had immediately caught on. Everyone loved being able to try things out before purchasing a larger amount. As word of my sample policy spread through town and into surrounding areas, I'd noticed a definite uptick in business. People I'd never seen in my shop were venturing in, taking samples and, in most cases, coming back to buy more.

I found Maddy at the counter, making small talk with Travis. She thanked me again and slipped the sample packets into her purse. "This is the place to come if anything ails you," she said to Travis. "Don't be put off by the magicky decor and stuff. It's just for show." I saw her glance down at Travis's hand before adding, "And if you happen to be in the market for a lady friend, you won't find a finer one than Kailyn Wilde." I felt the heat rise from my neck to my cheeks. I hadn't blushed like that since my early teens. Maddy's remark made me wonder what I'd done with the spell my mother created for the problem back then.

"I promise to keep that in mind," Travis said, escorting her to the door and holding it open for her.

"I was going to call," he said, coming back to me, "but then I decided I'd rather see you up close and personal."

"It happens I'm a big fan of up close and personal."

"I'm glad we agree." He put his hands on my waist and kissed me, but it seemed perfunctory, as if his mind was somewhere else.

I pulled back. "I know you've got a lot going on with your friend's sudden death, but I get the feeling it's more than that. What am I missing?"

"Can the Q and A wait until later?" he asked. I was taken aback by his tone. He'd never been so short and dismissive with me. My reaction must have been written on my face, because he immediately tried to make amends. "Sorry. I didn't mean it to sound like that. I swear I'll answer all your questions, but there's something I need to take care of first and it can't wait. To be honest, I came to ask for your help."

Not the best way to go about it, I thought, but I held my tongue until I could figure out what was going on with him. In any case, I didn't want to be excluded from whatever he was up to. "Sure," I said, "count me in."

"Once you hear what I want you to do, you may change your mind."

"Okay then, talk me out of it."

"Ryan was renting a month by month in Watkins Glen to investigate some story in the area that had him all revved up. He was like a blood hound that's picked up the scent of trouble. After Duggan let me go, I ran by his place. Unfortunately there was already yellow tape across the door and a cop on duty."

"If Ryan's death was accidental, do they have a right to search his home?" I asked.

"No. All they can do at this point is protect the scene in case the ME finds evidence of criminal involvement. If he does, Duggan can get a court order to tear the place apart for clues and the first thing his guys will take is Ryan's laptop. I need to get in there before that happens and find his thumb drive."

"In order to do some investigating of our own?" I asked soberly. Although I'd never met Ryan, he'd clearly meant a lot to Travis. And that meant a lot to me. I wanted to respect his loss, which meant no overt enthusiasm over a new case.

"We've already collared two killers before Duggan could—which brings me to my request. I need a diversion if I'm going to get past the cop on duty there."

"I'm your girl," I said, turning the shop's OPEN sign to CLOSED before the words were out of my mouth. I glanced at Sashki on the window ledge. He was snoring away on his pillow, blissfully unaware of the woes that afflict humankind. If he wanted for anything while I was gone, Tilly and Merlin were a mere yowl away.

We drove the 45 minutes to Watkins Glen lost in our own thoughts. I spent the time working on a way to distract the officer. Breaking the law came with real consequences, so it required the most foolproof plan I could devise. I considered the spell of invisibility, but quickly discarded it. The spell only worked for the person casting it. I thought of and rejected half a dozen other spells for the same reason. I'd never realized how many spells worked that way. By the time we reached the outskirts of the county seat, I'd finally come up with one that could work. Hardly the sure thing I'd been aiming for, but at least it gave us a shot. Maybe we should have taken Merlin along. He could have made Travis appear to be someone else, maybe even Duggan. Then again, he might have changed him into another species entirely. And forgotten how to change him back. For better or worse, my magick would have to suffice.

Chapter 6

We were able to park a couple blocks down from the three-story apartment building where Ryan had been living. Travis turned to me. "We need a plan. What about damsel in distress. It's an oldie, but a goodie."

"Does anyone fall for that these days?" I asked. It made me think of a girl tied to railroad tracks by a man with a handlebar mustache and a fiendish laugh.

"I don't know, but I think if I heard a woman crying for help, I'd at least investigate."

"I suppose if I heard a man crying for help, I would too."

A wry smile tugged at his lips. "I assume you have a better plan?"

"I have a spell that should work," I said. It was one of Bronwen's spells. I'd watched her cast it a few times over the years, though I'd never tried it myself. "It's all in the bloodlines," she used to tell me when I hesitated to try something new. "The blood of the Wildes runs through our veins. Your only enemies are lack of confidence and fear of failure." And Detective Duggan, I would have added.

Travis shook his head. "'*Should* work?' Damsel in distress is sounding better by the minute. I think we'll keep it on deck just in case."

"I don't intend to fail," I said firmly and got out of the car. I must have been convincing, because he seemed a bit more at ease. At least one of us was. In a best case scenario, I would have been able to try the spell once before casting it. But we were out in public and I didn't know how to downsize the spell to produce a tiny image that wouldn't bring the fire trucks roaring to save the day. They'd be receiving a call soon enough.

Travis locked the car and joined me. "Exactly what does this spell do?" he asked as we headed north on Franklin Street.

I zipped my parka against the headwind and stuffed my hands in my pockets. "It creates a temporary vision."

"You mean it makes people see things that aren't there?"

"Yes."

"What vision do you have in mind?"

"Fire. We need the cop on duty to leave the apartment unguarded long enough for you to slip in, find the thumb drive, and slip out again. Fire is our best bet."

"The fire station is only a few blocks away," Travis said, frowning as he considered it.

"The cop will call it in and evacuate the building. I'll have to be in and out of the apartment in less than five. Not easy, but doable. I think I remember where Ryan kept the drives. How long will the vision last?"

"Ten minutes," I estimated. I'd never clocked Bronwen's visions. "But it will start to deteriorate before then."

"Just to be clear, there isn't any chance of a real fire?"

"No, it's all about tricking the brain. Of course you'll have to keep reminding yourself it's not real. You'd be surprised how hard it is to run into a fire even when you know it can't hurt you." I spoke from experience, having tried it as a child.

When we reached the apartment building, a police cruiser was parked at the curb. We'd been walking quickly, but before opening the outer glass door of the building, we both stopped and inhaled deeply as if girding ourselves for our first foray into crime. If anyone happened to be watching, our little routine probably looked choreographed.

"You've got this?" Travis asked me.

"I've got it." Failure could mean jail and a criminal record, so it was simply not an option. We walked in, passed through the second glass door, and emerged in the lobby, which was mercifully warm and windless.

"Anyone who sees us is a potential witness," Travis whispered. "Don't make eye contact. If we act like we're having a serious conversation, most people will respect our personal space and look away."

"Are you a reporter or a psychologist?" I whispered back.

"You'd be surprised what you learn in this business."

The elevator was straight ahead of us, but Travis took my arm and steered me to the right where a door was labeled STAIRS. "Taking the elevator could be risky," he said. "If there are other people on it, they'll have time to get a good look at us. And they'll see where we get off."

"Stairs it is."

When we stepped out of the stairwell, Travis opened the door to the third floor as quietly as he could and peered out. "The hallway's clear. How close do you have to be to cast the spell?"

"I don't have to be all that close, but I need to get a peek at Ryan's apartment, at least the door, in order to visualize it properly. After that I can do the rest out of sight."

"It's going to be a challenge.We don't want the cop on duty to see you while you're getting your peek. Fortunately, the hallway turns a corner before we reach the apartment. We just have to hope the cop is facing the other way long enough for you to poke your head around the corner and see the door. Will that do?"

"It has to." I gave myself a silent pep talk. *Believe in your power; fear nothing.*

"Okay, let's go." Travis took the lead. I followed close behind him.

At the corner, he turned to me. "There's no sense in us both risking a look. It has to be you."

"What if he's looking right back at me? Shouldn't we have a plan for that?"

"Sometimes you have to stop thinking and just act."

"Right." It was now or never. I moved my head as close as I could to the corner of the wall and took a quick look. I drew my head back so fast I slammed into Travis, who'd inched up behind me. When I turned around, he was holding his nose, his eyes watering from the pain. "Sorry, I'm so sorry," I mouthed. "Are you all right?"

He nodded, but I was pretty sure he just wanted to keep me from going on about it. He was already retreating to the stairs. "Well?" he asked, once we were safely behind the door.

"He didn't see me. He was doing something with his cell phone. He wasn't anyone I knew either. But I did get a good look at the door. It's beige and could use a new coat of paint. The apartment number was black wrought iron and there was a peephole. Details help. Should I start the spell?"

"The sooner the better."

I closed my eyes, focusing on the image still fresh in my mind.

Fire crack and fire leap,
Fire hiss and fire sizzle.
Smell the smoke and see the flame.
Trick the eye and fool the brain.
No harm come and nothing burn.

When I'd repeated the spell for the third time, Travis stepped into the hallway to listen for sounds of activity. He ducked right back inside. "Sounds like the cop's running down the hall, banging on doors to get people out. They'll all be using the stairs. You need to go now and wait in the car like we planned."

"Good luck," I said, hating to leave. What if something went wrong and he needed me? "Maybe—"

"*Now, Kailyn!*" He cut off my argument by making his way back into the hall as the first tenants were rushing into the stairwell. I started down the stairs with them. Grim-faced men and nervous women holding on to young children, carrying babies, as well as assorted cats and dogs and birds in cages. I wished I could tell them not to be afraid, but they wouldn't have listened anyway. At the second-floor landing, we were forced to slow down as more tenants piled onto the stairs. The sirens of approaching fire trucks mixed with those of the police and emergency vehicles, stoking everyone's fears and thrusting them into overdrive. Someone stepped on the back of my shoe, causing me to stumble. I would have gone down and knocked over the person in front of me, if I hadn't been holding on to the banister—a domino cascade with live dominos.

When we reached the lobby, everyone ran for the outer doors. I ran with them, afraid if I took my time strolling out of the building, I would attract attention.

Firefighters brushed past us, racing into the building in full gear, axes in hand. Outside others were hooking up fire hoses to hydrants. Now that the tenants were outside and out of danger, the urgency was gone. They were milling around, phoning loved ones, talking to neighbors, trying to comfort children and pets. Some were crying, silent tears streaming down their faces, no doubt worried about what would become of their homes and possessions.

The police were telling everyone to move away from the building for their own safety and to let the firefighters do their job. I worked my way around them feeling more awful by the second. I told myself it was a good thing it was the middle of the afternoon on a weekday. At least many of the residents were at work, most of the children still in school, but I didn't feel any better about it. What had we done?

I walked down Franklin, past the looky-loos. Running now would only make me appear suspect. The wind was at my back, pushing me along as though complicit in my escape. By the time I reached the car, I was alone on the street. I unlocked the door and slid inside. My heart was pounding. What was I thinking? I'd only wanted to help Travis investigate Ryan's death. He'd been so devastated by it. But in retrospect, I was guilty of a major lapse in judgment. Although no damage was done by the conjured fire, a lot of people were suffering fear and anxiety. Children would have nightmares. I'd failed to consider the wider ramifications of my actions. And I had no one but myself to blame for it. I'd pulled the wool over my own eyes.

Minutes later Travis opened the car door and slid beneath the steering wheel, interrupting my mental lashing. He held up Ryan's thumb drive. "Mission accomplished." There was no joy in his words, only relief.

I couldn't muster up any enthusiasm. "We should never have done this. Did you see the faces of the people who ran out of the building? Did you hear the kids crying?"

"I know," he said evenly. "I did some second guessing about it too. But it was the best way for me to get the disk. It could be the single most important clue to finding Ryan's killer."

"The ME released his report?" I couldn't believe he hadn't told me right away.

"No, but the more I thought about how he clawed at his throat, I'm sure he choked to death."

I didn't know what to say, so I just nodded. That thought had certainly crossed my mind as well. But there were too many unanswered questions for me to buy into his certainty and I didn't want to argue the point. Besides, he was entitled to his theory, until it was proven right or wrong.

"One thing I know for certain," I said hoping to end the discussion on neutral ground, "Ryan couldn't have asked for a more devoted friend."

Travis didn't say anything for a minute and when he did, his words were heavy with emotion. "I haven't been completely honest with you. Ryan wasn't just a friend, he was my brother."

Chapter 7

"I don't understand," I said. Travis had never mentioned a brother. When he'd talked about his childhood and his family, it was always his mom, dad, and him. Plus Ryan's last name was Cutler, not Anderson.

Travis was staring straight ahead through the windshield. "It's complicated."

"If you don't want to go into it now, that's okay," I said, though my Nancy Drew alter ego was kicking me in the shins.

He turned to me. "I've been avoiding the subject, because I'm not exactly the good guy in this story."

So that was the reason he'd avoided telling me about it until now. I put my hand over his on the console between us. "It can't be harder than it was for me to admit that I'm not your typical girl next door and that my family has more in common with the Addams Family than The Brady Bunch."

"Yeah, and remember how well I took that news."

"I promise not to run," I said. "In fact I dare you to scare me off."

His mouth curved up in a rueful smile. "Well, when you put it that way, how can a guy resist?"

"C'mon, give it your best shot."

"Okay, here's the unvarnished story." He looked down at our joined hands as if it was easier not to face me. "Up until my freshman year in high school, I was a happy, slightly spoiled only child in a middle-class household. Ryan was a freshman in the same high school. We had a lot of classes together, but we ran in different circles. Never clicked as friends. There was this silent kind of rivalry between us that I don't think either of us signed up for. I bested him academically; he beat me out for quarterback. Stupid high school crap. One afternoon he's called out of class and he doesn't come back. We're all wondering what kind of trouble he's in. Was he suspended? Expelled? That night my mom tells me his parents died in a car crash. One minute Ryan has a family and the next he's all alone."

"No siblings?" He shook his head. "No grandparents or aunts and uncles?"

"Nope, not a one. So Ryan winds up in the foster system. Enter my mom, social worker extraordinaire with friends in all the right positions to bend a few rules and overlook a few others. She knew the Cutlers casually from school functions and was heartsick about Ryan's circumstances. The next thing I know, we're his foster family."

"Did your mom run it by you?" I asked.

He shook his head. "I guess she had to run it by my father though, get him to sign some papers and be approved."

"Wow" was all I could think to say.

"Yeah," he said wryly. "Mom is a steamroller when she has a cause."

"I take it the transition wasn't easy for you."

"To be fair, it was harder on Ryan. But that wisdom was a long time coming. I felt like my home, my whole life had been invaded. I tried to be cool about sharing my room, my parents, my world, but most of the time I know it came across as grudging."

"You were fourteen for goodness sake. I don't know if there could have been a worse time for that to happen. For both of you. How did he handle it?"

"He was stoic. I never saw him cry. Made me think he didn't even appreciate what my family was doing for him. What I was giving up for him. My mother tried to help me understand. She said he was numb. When pain is too difficult to bear, the psyche copes by repressing the emotions. 'What about my pain?' I asked her. 'What about what I've lost?' It took me years to recognize how selfish and crappy that was."

"So at some point your parents adopted Ryan?"

"Fast forward to May of our junior year—May tenth to be exact. The day is etched into my mind. They told him they wanted to adopt him, make him their son in the eyes of the law. It was like lighting the fuse to his emotions. He blew up, said he didn't want any part of it. He was proud of the name Cutler and it had been left to him to see that it survived."

"He could have hyphenated the names."

"My mom told him that. She said he didn't even have to change his name. He thanked my folks for everything they'd done for him, but he'd had wonderful parents too and he refused to think of anyone else in that way. I could tell my mom was disappointed, but she said she understood.

To me it was the final insult. Which made no sense, because I'd been against the idea until he turned them down.

Anyway, Ryan and I muddled through the last years of high school, living as separately as we could under the same roof. I knew it saddened my parents, but I didn't care. The whole damn thing was their fault to begin with." Travis paused to look up at me. "Ready to run yet?"

"Not even close," I said softly, not wanting to interrupt the flow of his words.

"Man, I couldn't wait to go off to college and be done with him. My grades got me a free ride to Duke. He was offered a football scholarship to Penn State. Distance didn't make our hearts grow fonder. I dreaded going back home for the holidays. Summers, Ryan found jobs so he could stay in Pennsylvania. I was thrilled. At least I expected to be. The longer Ryan stayed away, the more I found myself thinking about him, which irritated the hell out of me. The first time he didn't come home for Christmas, I finally had to admit that I missed him. My small family had been more than enough for me all the years before Ryan joined it, but somewhere along the way, in spite of myself, he'd become an integral part of it. I could tell my folks felt the loss too, but to their credit, they never blamed me. I think they took it as their failure, which only made me feel worse."

I was so engrossed in Travis's confession that I nearly went airborne when the theme from *Star Wars* rang out. He pulled out his cell and listened to the caller for all of twenty seconds. "Got it," he said before clicking off and turning on the engine.

A groan almost escaped my throat, but I managed to swallow it. I was learning to dread the music. Whenever I heard it, Travis had to leave. I was Pavlov's dog, minus the all-important reward. I didn't say it to Travis, not even in a joking way. News happened when it happened. It didn't run on a schedule. If I wanted him in my life, I had to learn to live with the interruptions and sudden changes in plans. The way he was learning to live with magick. "What's happening?" I asked as he pulled away from the curb. I doubted it could be as important to me as the story of him and Ryan.

"The ME is going to release a preliminary report on Ryan's death at four."

"That's fast. Doesn't it take longer for the toxicology results?"

"Maybe he found something he doesn't want to hold back until then."

"I guess I can watch on my phone," I said, thinking out loud. "Unless I have a customer."

"Not a problem. I'll call you as soon as I'm off the air. If you don't answer, I'll leave a message."

"My very own breaking news report. I must really rate."

"Don't let it go to your head," he said, hitting the gas. "I'll just have time to drop you back at your shop and make it to the press conference. Listen, I wanted to let you know that Ryan's wake is tomorrow evening; the funeral's the next morning. It's in Huntington, out on Long Island, so I don't want you to feel obligated to attend."

"I'd like to be there for you," I said. "Besides, what will your folks think of me if I don't come at such an important time?"

"They know you have a business that would have to close if you were out of town. And they know you never had a chance to meet Ryan. My mom actually made me promise I would tell you to stay home and take care of your business. She said it's ridiculous for you to travel so far. But she and my dad would like very much to meet you someday in the near future."

"That's very thoughtful of her," I said, "especially when she has so much to deal with."

Travis shrugged. "She's pragmatic, always has been. She deals with life head-on."

"But what about you? Don't you need some emotional support?"

"The best thing for me is to get back to finding the killer. That's my way of honoring Ryan. And you've already done a lot to help."

"If you change your mind, all it takes is a phone call and I'll be there."

"I know you would."

"By the way," I said a minute later, "what type of business do your parents think I own?"

"I told them it was a magic shop, but when they asked if you sold magic kits and tricks for kids, I didn't correct them." He stole a glance at me. "I'm sorry. I'm not quite ready to enlighten them."

"You did the right thing," I said. "My family prefers to reveal ourselves to the least number of people possible." Besides I didn't want to scare his parents off before I met them.

Chapter 8

I couldn't recall a weekday in the late afternoon when I'd ever been so busy. None of my customers seemed to care about the four o'clock press conference. Then again, they probably didn't know about it. The only reason I knew was because I was dating a reporter. I could have tried to watch some of it on my phone, but I didn't want anyone to think I was rude or not sufficiently interested in their patronage.

Most of the customers who came in at that hour were locals who'd run out of the products they used. They didn't require anything of me, beyond the financial transaction. I would have preferred to be swamped with questions, anything to keep me from dwelling on Travis's confession and the press conference I couldn't watch. I almost kissed Milton Hagadorn when he marched up to me and said he needed help.

He came in occasionally with his wife Dara, but I'd never seen him here alone. They were a strange couple. Opposites are supposed to attract, but they stretched the theory to its limits. They were both in their forties. Milton had the manner and style of a much older man, while Dara dressed and acted like a girl of twenty. She babbled nonstop; he was miserly with every word that passed his lips. She loved to dance; he was married to the history channel and reading nonfiction. Yet something had bound them together for over fifteen years. If I could bottle that essence, I'd be a wealthy woman.

"Can you be a little more specific?" I asked, coming from behind the counter.

Milton glanced around us like a spy worried about being overheard, then leaned closer to me and whispered, "My hemorrhoids are killing me. Dara told me to come here for something natural."

I whispered back, "I have just the thing. Wait here and I'll get it for you." When I returned to the counter, I found Milton squirming in the customer chair trying to find a comfortable position. I handed him the bottle. "This has several natural components. Most people find relief with it." Or so my grandmother had claimed before she shuffled off, leaving hemorrhoids and other human woes behind.

Milton hauled himself out of the chair, issuing an elderly sort of grunt. I scooted around the counter to ring up his purchase. "How is Dara?" I asked, putting the bottle into a mini tote.

"Same bundle of energy as always," he said. "She's at the gym as we speak." He shrugged, as if to say *beats me*, and ambled off.

At four-twenty, Travis called from his car. He didn't sound happy. "That was fast," I said.

"The ME spoke for all of two minutes. He said his preliminary findings were consistent with accidental choking. But he stressed that he was still awaiting the results of lab tests. Translation—he was covering his ass in case he turns out to be wrong. The scuttlebutt is that Mayor Tompkins and Police Chief Gimble requested the quickie press conference to allay the public's fears of another killer in their midst."

"It's understandable, given that this little town has had two murders in a few months."

"There's only one little problem—he's wrong."

"Look at it this way," I said, "if the police believe Ryan choked on that burger, they'll call off their investigation. You and I will have freer rein."

Travis's tone lifted. "True. I just don't like the way they're sweeping Ryan's death under the carpet in order to ease the mind of the public."

"They probably don't even know he was vegetarian," I pointed out.

"They would if they bothered to talk to anyone who knew him. Listen, I'll swing by your house later, unless you have other plans."

* * * *

Later proved to be after eight o'clock, because he was needed back at the newsroom first. The cats had eaten on time, but I was famished by then. I ordered Chinese, far too much of it. When I'm that hungry, everything on the menu seems critical to my survival. I added the dishes Travis liked, in case he hadn't eaten yet. I brewed tea, Tilly's special tummy-tamer blend. It cuts right through greasy food like magick.

Travis and the delivery boy arrived at the same time. From what I could gather, Travis must have intercepted him and paid for the order, because when I opened the door, he was the one holding the food—a whole carton of it. I was baffled for a moment, until I saw the delivery car pulling away from the curb.

"I was going to call for Chinese when I got here," Travis said, stepping inside and planting a hello kiss on my lips. "You must have read my mind."

"Not I—Tilly is the family psychic. I can barely read my own mind." I followed him into the kitchen, the aroma of the food so dense and rich I felt like I could take a bite out of the air itself. I pulled paper goods out of the pantry.

"You have no idea how relieved I am to hear that," he said. "The idea of my girlfriend poking around in my head would be disturbing and more than a little embarrassing." He set the eight containers of food on the table and dropped the carton onto the floor.

"Embarrassing? Just what do you have going on in that brain of yours?" I poured the tea and brought the mugs to the table.

"That's none of your business," he said with a grin. "But if you play your cards right, you might find out one day."

"I can hardly wait," I said. I took the chair beside him and helped myself to a spare rib. While we ate, I brought Travis up to date on the latest happenings in New Camel. I told him about Merlin's campaign to change the name of the town and the flag he made from the purloined muumuu. Merlin's exploits were always good for a laugh, until they blew up in our faces. I described Lolly's new dark chocolate cranberry fudge for the coming holiday season. "I've been thinking," I said, after we pushed our plates away. "I should have a copy of Ryan's disk. It would make the investigation more efficient. Besides," I added, in case he felt proprietary about it, "I helped you steal it."

He wagged his head. "I don't know, Ryan entrusted it to me. He showed me where he kept them because he was concerned something might happen to him. Giving them to you would be breaking his trust."

I felt my hackles rise. "Seriously? Have you forgotten we're partners? Not to mention, I could have gone to jail for what I did?"

"Oh wait, that must be why I've already copied it for you." He stood up and pulled the thumb drive out of the pocket of his chinos. He handed it to me with a "gotcha" grin.

"You're incorrigible."

"On so many levels," he said, pulling me into his arms.

"Whoa, I believe you still owe me the rest of the story about you and Ryan."

He let me go with a sigh and followed me into the living room, where we sat on the couch, our legs so close they might have been tied together for a three-legged race.

"Okay, where did I leave off?"

"When Ryan didn't come home that Christmas, you realized he'd become part of the family in spite of your worst intentions."

"Right. So after the holidays, I took a trip to Penn State to hunt him down. I apologized for being a jerk and asked for his forgiveness. I half expected him to haul off and punch me in the face. I deserved that much and more. But he didn't. He said, 'Whatever man, don't sweat it.'"

"That was it?"

"I know, surprised the hell out of me too. Don't get me wrong, it wasn't like we became instant buddies after that. It took time, but over the years, little by little, we found our way to a real friendship, a brotherhood."

"Your parents must be devastated by his death," I murmured.

"They are. They don't believe it was accidental either. But as much as they want justice for Ryan, they're against me getting involved in the investigation."

"You have to look at it from their perspective," I said. "They're afraid of losing you too."

"I get that, but how do I walk away like he meant nothing to me? And after we'd finally found our way to each other?"

I had no answer for Travis. I empathized with his parents and worried for his safety. But I also understood his need to find Ryan's killer. "Tell me about your brother," I said. "I'd like to know more about him if I'm going to be part of this quest."

"I think this will give you some insight into him. A couple of years ago, we were hanging out, watching football, drinking beer and somehow or other the conversation got around to his folks. Before that I'd avoided the topic, because I didn't want to upset him. But he brought it up himself. He said his parents' sudden deaths tore away the ground beneath his feet and reshaped his outlook on everything. If life was so risky and random at its core, tip-toeing carefully through it, afraid of your own shadow, wouldn't buy you an extra hour, an extra minute."

"That helps explain the career path he chose. It's interesting that you both wound up in journalism."

"In very different ways," Travis said. "I followed the conventional route, scrabbling up the network ladder. Ryan didn't want anyone telling him what to do or how to do it. He went strictly freelance. He chose what stories to investigate and always had takers for his 'Beyond the News pieces'—that's what he called his investigative reports. There were bidding wars for a couple of them; he won awards too."

"Do you think he was still competing with you?"

Travis shook his head. "Judging by the crimes he dug up, the type of people he antagonized and made enemies of, it was more like he was competing with death."

Chapter 9

The next morning I was up before the sun and the rest of my household. Curiosity about the contents of Ryan's disk had pulled me from a disjointed dream in which Merlin and Ryan were beta testing a time travel machine. If Travis was right, the disk could tell us what his brother had been working on and it might even point us in the direction of his killer. Given that Ryan had been living in Watkins Glen for the past month, it seemed likely that the subject of his investigation was somewhere in the greater Glen area. Not even Travis had been privy to more details than that. He said his brother observed a strict code of silence about his investigations, until they appeared in print or on the air. Ryan claimed it wasn't a matter of trust. It was simply human nature that people with the best intentions often let information slip.

As I emerged from my warm cocoon under the quilt, the air pricked my skin like the spray of a cold shower. My grandmother Bronwen had had the heating system updated decades ago, followed by new windows guaranteed to stop the continuing loss of heat. They didn't. Morgana had tried caulking and having extra insulation blown in. And when that still didn't fix the problem, we had a parade of experts troop through, all of whom concluded that old houses were leaky as sieves. One went so far as to cavalierly suggest tearing the place down and rebuilding it the right way. He was shown the door with the help of a magickal push that made him stumble over his own feet. Morgana took the matter into her own hands and spent most of her free time trying to create a spell that would resolve the problem. Five years ago we thought she'd finally succeeded, but it turned out the spell made the house so airtight that we all nearly suffocated in our sleep. If not for Sashkatu sounding the alarm, the Wilde family and its magickal bloodline would no longer exist. At the time of Morgana's death, the problem had yet to be solved. I continued to make do with thick quilts, warm robes, and lots of Tilly's hot teas. There was never any question that the house would remain inviolate for future generations of Wildes.

When I'd crawled under the covers the previous night, I'd made the tactical error of leaving my robe at the bottom of the bed. Now there were two cats curled up on it. If I woke them, they'd start thinking about breakfast and I wanted to spend the quiet time before dawn on the computer. I exchanged my nightgown for an ensemble of ratty old sweats on the floor of my closet. I'd been meaning to throw them out, but they were handy and warm. If I fussed about for something more stylish, I'd probably wake all the cats.

I pulled on thick socks and padded into the smallest of the four bedrooms that had been used as a home office as far back as I could remember. I'd kept everything pretty much the way Morgana and Bronwen had left it, with the exception of installing a computer there. I plugged in Ryan's thumb drive. There was only one file on it. He probably used a new drive for each investigation. I clicked on the file and found a meaningless list of dates, locations, and names. Although Ryan would have understood his notes, to me it was like staring at a jigsaw puzzle without a picture on the cover to show me what the puzzle should look like in the end. My phone beeped with a text from Travis, asking if I was up yet. Perfect timing, maybe he could help me make sense of it. I called him back.

"I'm not only awake," I said," I'm stumped."

"Tell me about it," Travis said. "I just looked at his disk."

"Do you happen to speak Ryanese?"

"Not a word, but it's a starting point. We have to find out what these people have in common."

"Did you notice that the dates are months, even years apart?" I asked.

"Yeah, whatever Ryan was hunting happened over a relatively long period of time."

"Maybe he saw a pattern involving these people," I said, thinking out loud. I was so thoroughly engrossed in our conversation that I was startled to find myself staring into Sashkatu's face. He parked himself on the keyboard and eyed me balefully. He must have climbed up the bookshelf and walked across the window sill to reach me. The others wouldn't be far behind. Dawn was breaking and stomachs would soon be grumbling for breakfast.

"Let's start with the names and see what that nets us," Travis said.

"Okay, I'll try to find out if the list refers to people who are alive or dead." Google and Facebook should be good places to start.

"Let me know what you find. I'm going to be chasing down a story about political corruption in Albany."

"That doesn't sound like much fun," I said.

"Depends on how you look at it. I have a lot of fun receiving the paychecks. Especially when a stack of bills comes in." Sashkatu started to chatter at me and batted at the phone in my hand. His gang of five chimed in. "What on earth is going on over there?" Travis asked.

"A feline uprising," I said as another cat scrambled onto my lap.

"I'll let you deal with the mutiny. We'll talk later."

I powered through my morning routine, intrigued by the clues and where they might lead. But it was hard not to dwell on the sobering fact that Ryan's death lay at its core.

* * * *

"Kailyn," Tilly called as she came through the connecting door. "Oh dear, oh my, Kailyn." The timbre of her voice was the perfect soundtrack for hand-wringing. I was restocking products in the second aisle. I set down the jar I was holding and intercepted her on her way to the counter. She was wearing the turban she used for dramatic effect when giving a reading. Paired with her bright sneakers and bedazzled muumuu, she looked like the one who flew over the cuckoo's nest.

I gave her rouged cheek a kiss. "What's up, Aunt Tilly?"

"Mayor Tompkins is threatening to have Merlin arrested."

"For what?" Maybe this *was* a good time for hand-wringing.

"Election fraud, forgery—"

"Wait, is this about his bid to run for the town board?"

"Yes, that's how I understood it."

"Where is Merlin now?"

"In my shop watching TV, but Tompkins told me to come back to discuss the matter at three o'clock."

"I'll go with you," I said, which immediately calmed her. Too bad it didn't ease *my* mind. If Merlin was arrested, the whole issue of his status in New Camel and the country would come under scrutiny. He might even be deported, if they could figure out where he belonged. The truth was he didn't belong anywhere in the present. When the news outlets picked up the scent of this problem, things would go from bad to worse. Merlin would become national news. From there it was a short hop, skip, and jump to international notoriety, courtesy of social media. The man who came from nowhere. Whenever things went haywire with modern technology, Bronwen would bemoan the loss of the "olden days." I used to tease her about being old-fashioned, but I was starting to realize there was something to be said for a simpler, Little-House-on-the-Prairie life.

At ten to three, we all piled into my car for the short journey to New Camel's town hall. The building occupied an old white clapboard house with forest green shutters and a weather vane that straddled the sharply pitched roof. The second floor was off limits, deemed unsafe as far back as I could remember. In any case, the main floor was adequate for the town's purposes. The mayor's office was in a small room off the public area. There was no mayoral residence. Tompkins lived in the house where he'd grown up, although now with his wife and children instead of his parents.

We walked into his office at precisely three o'clock. He had three chairs waiting for us. Either he'd guessed that I would accompany my aunt and Merlin, or three was the room's normal complement. Tilly had talked Merlin into wearing his best jeans and a sweater. She'd lassoed his unruly hair with a rubber band. He could have passed for an eccentric artist, a mad scientist, or a hippy leftover from the seventies.

Once we were all seated, Tompkins reached across his desk to hand me a form that was several pages long. The heading at the top of the first page read "Petition to Run for the New Camel Town Board." Signatures filled all the lines below it. I flipped to the next page and the next. There were a lot of signatures. I looked more closely at the names that were both printed and signed. I recognized most of them as belonging to local residents. So far so good. My first clue that all was not as it should be, came with the signature of Jim Harkens who'd been dead for the last few months. Another problem popped up a moment later when I found Tompkins's signature. Oh Merlin, weren't there *any* laws back in your time? Or were you exempt from them because of your status and close relationship with the king?

Tompkins was glaring at me when I looked up from the papers. "Do you understand why I asked your aunt to come back to discuss this matter more fully?" His expression dared me to shrug it off.

"I apologize, Mayor Tompkins. What can I say? As you're aware, Merlin is a bit different and often doesn't understand the right and wrong of such things. My aunt and I promise to be more vigilant about keeping him out of trouble. We'd be so very grateful if you could find it in your heart not to turn this over to the police." Boy, did I hate begging him. I wanted to go home and wash my mouth out with soap.

"There is a remarkable aspect to your cousin's disregard for the law," Tompkins said, breezing over my plea. "He forged my signature so perfectly not even I can tell the difference. I checked a lot of the other signatures against documents in our files that were signed by those individuals. Merlin forged them all with uncanny accuracy. How do you explain this ability?"

I went with the first thing that came to me, though it was far from a perfect analogy. "*Rain Man.*"

Tompkins frowned. "Excuse me?"

"The Tom Cruise, Dustin Hoffman movie from the late eighties?"

"Are you trying to tell me your cousin is an autistic savant?"

"How else could he do such a thing?" I said, hoping it didn't occur to the mayor that Merlin couldn't have memorized all the signatures, because he'd never seen most of them before.

"In-ter-est-ing." He drew the word out as though dissecting the possibility. "That would explain a lot," he concluded.

"You know what?" Tilly piped up. "I would love to bake a pie or cake for you. Name your favorite. Why don't we make it a different one every week for a month? Six months? You deserve it for your trouble."

Tompkins sighed. "You don't want to be bribing me, Matilda." He looked at me, shaking his head. "Kailyn, please take your family home before they break every law we have in New Camel."

"Are you going to bring this to the attention of the police?" I had to know if there was a knife hanging over our heads.

"Not this time. Just go—with my sympathies."

* * * *

"How did you forge all those signatures?" I demanded of the wizard once we were in my car and headed back to our shops.

"With magick of course, silly girl." He was in the front passenger seat, having called *shotgun* as we emerged from town hall. It was anyone's guess where he'd learned that expression. I was having a hard time keeping my anger in check. Any minute steam might pour from my ears and eyeballs. "You promised not to use magick unless one of us okayed it."

"I was merely following the instructions on the form," he replied blithely. "If they are incorrect, the person who wrote them should be reprimanded." He turned his head to address my aunt. "Tilly, dear lady, might you still have one of the blank forms?"

I heard my aunt rummaging in the depths of the oversized tote she called a purse. "Aha," she exclaimed, "there it is." She held up a small plastic bag containing a partially flattened jelly donut with the jelly oozing out. "I couldn't find this for the life of me yesterday."

"I'll take half," Merlin said, although she hadn't asked for volunteers.

I parked in front of my shop. "Aunt Tilly, do you have a copy of the form?" I hadn't paid particular attention to the instructions on the one Tompkins showed me.

"Yes, yes," she said, dividing the donut in half. She handed Merlin the larger piece. Then she dove back into her purse and came up with a folded sheet of paper that she handed to me:

Petition to Run For the New Camel Town Board.
Interested parties must present the signatures of at least one hundred legal residents of the town and file said petition with the town clerk before the first of December, 2018.

"You can see for yourself that there is no mention of *how* one should obtain the signatures," Merlin said. "Was I expected to ring every doorbell in this town and ask if the people living therein were legal residents? What do you think the result of such an effort was likely to have been?"

He had me there. The instructions were not specific about how to obtain the signatures. Merlin knew only a handful of people, primarily the shopkeepers. More likely than not, everyone else would have slammed their doors in his face, if they even bothered to open them in the first place. But there were important points he'd chosen to ignore.

"First of all," I said, "it is assumed that anyone applying for the position is aware that forgery is illegal. Secondly, it is also assumed that applicants know they have to be legal residents of this town."

The wizard was absorbed in plucking bits of jelly out of his beard and licking it off his fingers. "Mayhap they are too quick to assume such things."

"Trust me, Merlin, you do not want to give any branch of the government cause to look into your background or ask for your ID. It would mean a quick trip to a prison cell or, in your case, a hospital for the insane."

"Then I will find another way to restore the town's original and proper name," he said clearly undaunted. We'd reached a temporary impasse and I had a business to reopen. Tilly and he climbed out of the car and headed into Tea and Empathy. I unlocked Abracadabra, Merlin's avowed mission weighing heavily on my mind.

Chapter 10

After a quick sandwich of turkey, cranberry sauce, and coleslaw from the mini-mart, I sat down at the computer, ready to begin our investigation into Ryan's death in earnest. I knew Travis wasn't going to rest easy until we found his brother's killer.

I accessed the coroner's report for the first name on the list. The public part of the report provided only the basics. Martin Frank of Watkins Glen was forty-six at the time of his death on March tenth, 2011. His death was attributed to multiple stab wounds to his torso. To get a broader sense of who he was, I tried looking him up on Facebook, but there were a lot of people with that name. In any case, the odds were his account had been deleted years ago. Since his death was ruled a homicide, I also checked back issues of the local newspaper for articles about his untimely end. Authorities believed he was the victim of a botched burglary. The murder weapon was never recovered and the killer was scrupulous about cleaning up after himself, because no DNA was ever found. Martin was survived by his wife, Nina, and their two sons. There was a family photo of them all dressed up and smiling. Anything else we learned about him would have to come from interviewing members of his family.

The next name was Calista Gonzalez of Hassettville. She was listed as deceased on February twenty-eighth, 2012, at the age of seventy. Cause of death was a cerebral hemorrhage, most likely the result of a fall. I found her account on Facebook where her brother, Max, had posted a goodbye to her. There were a few other acknowledgements of her passing, but nothing that provided more useful information about her.

According to the coroner, Axel Stubbs of Burdett was twenty-four when he died July third, 2014, from a drug overdose. A dozen people had posted on his Facebook page, many of the comments along the lines of *It's about time* and Axel *who?* His obituary in the local paper said that he was survived by his father and two sets of grandparents.

I only had two names to go, but as much as I wanted to continue, the words were swimming on the page and I was sure I fell asleep for a few seconds with my eyes open. I'd heard it was possible, but it was unnerving enough to send me upstairs.

When I walked into my room, the cats were already fast asleep and covering a good portion of the bed. Even my pillow had been usurped. I didn't want to disturb them and set off a game of musical cats, so I lay across the width of the bed, curving my body around and between them and using an afghan blanket Bronwen had made in her one attempt at crocheting.

Travis called the next morning as I was stepping out of the shower. I asked him to hold on while I wrapped myself in my terry cloth robe. Morgana had added a neat little spell to it that allowed me to warm it to any temperature I desired. Almost everything in the house tied me to one family member or another. It was like living inside a hug.

"What's going on there?" he inquired when I got back on the line. "Is someone there with you?" Before I could answer, he barreled on with wry indignation. "I knew it. I've been gone one day and you've already replaced me with another man."

"Men are way too much trouble for me to start breaking in a new one," I said. "The truth is you got me straight from the shower and I needed my robe, before I froze to death."

"Oh, then I guess you're forgiven."

"How's it going in Albany?"

"Turns out corruption and kickbacks aren't all they're cracked up to be. Have you made any progress on Ryan's notes?"

I updated him, adding that I'd check out the last two names later in the day. A busload of tourists was scheduled to descend on New Camel at ten and I wanted to make sure every bottle and jar was sparkling clean. Travis wished me a profitable day and said he'd check back later.

Bus tours at this time of year were far less frequent than in the spring and summer. When the temperature dropped and snow, sleet, and ice came to town, day-trippers were replaced by skiers, for whom après-ski took second place and shopping came in a distant third. All the shopkeepers were looking forward to an uptick in business from this busload of tourists. We were bent on making their experience one that would lead to return visits and favorable word of mouth.

Tilly was already deep into her baking by the time Sashkatu and I arrived at Abracadabra. She had a full slate of customers for the hours of the tour, thanks to the company's revamped website that urged people to make reservations in advance for the town's restaurants, as well as her readings. By ten o'clock, I was high on the sugary aromas wafting into my shop from hers. It felt like I was gaining weight by simply inhaling the air.

My first customer of the day was a young mother with a toddler boy and a girl who looked about seven. The mother seemed to be entranced with the shop from the moment she walked in. The little girl was clearly on watch-your-brother duty. She was glued to his side, taking his hands away whenever he tried to reach for something. Why wasn't he strapped safely into a stroller? I wondered. Or home with a babysitter? I felt sorry for the girl, who was too young to bear the sole responsibility for her whirlwind of a brother. The mother never even turned around to see what was going on with her children, although her daughter kept saying, "no no, Joey, no touch."

The mother came up to the counter to pick up a shopping basket, then went back to browsing as if she were on her own for the day and the kids belonged to someone else. I was about to tell her I was concerned about the safety of her children, when words became inadequate. The girl had paused for a moment to look at a display of amulets. That was all it took for the toddler to start scaling one of the wooden shelving units, knocking glass jars off to shatter on the floor. If he fell, he could be slashed by the shards of glass below him. If that wasn't worrisome enough, the whole unit started wobbling, on the verge of throwing him to the ground and toppling onto him. Before I knew what I was doing, I was whisking the boy off the shelf. After I'd carried him out of harm's way, I reached out with my mind to pull the whole unit upright again. I struggled against gravity, my powers failing. Defeated, I watched the unit wobble and then... stand straight up again? I was bewildered, until I saw Merlin duck out of sight at the back of my shop.

"What is all the commotion?" the mother demanded, finally dragging herself out of the aisle to see what was going on.

When I thought about the incident later, I realized that the only way I could have reached the toddler in time was by teleportation. That would help explain why the girl looked awestruck. And why she told her mother that the shop lady had to fly so fast to save her brother that she became invisible. Maybe all my practicing was finally starting to pay off. Teleportation was still leaving me drained, but not unconscious like my first successful attempt.

"Shop ladies can't fly, Bella," her mother said sharply. "You've been watching too many cartoons." She took the toddler from my arms without so much as a *thank you,* grabbed her daughter's hand, and stormed out of my shop with one parting remark. "This store is dangerous for children. You're lucky they didn't get hurt."

"I'd say we both are," I replied tightly. I couldn't help myself. Sometimes the customer isn't even close to being right.

I took a minute to poke my head into Tilly's shop and thank Merlin for his strategic help. My aunt was involved in a reading, but Merlin was sitting in the kitchen area where the clients couldn't see him. I waited for him to look up from his new iPad and motioned for him to join me.

"Thank you," I whispered when he met me in the hallway.

"You are most welcome, mistress. I felt your energy surge, then plummet, hence I came to see if my help was required." Under the circumstances, I couldn't bring myself to blast him for using magick without our permission. After all, he had kept the shelving unit from crashing and possibly taking down the next one and the one after that like a line of dominoes. Had that happened, the kids' mother could have been badly injured.

I closed the shop as soon as the bus pulled out of town. There had been no time for lunch, so I was tired and hungry. Thankfully the trouble with the first customer was the only speed bump of the day. Everyone else who came into the shop was friendly and well-mannered. They bought beauty products for themselves and others on their Christmas lists, as well as healing teas, crystals, and amulets. It was going to be a very magickal holiday for dozens of people.

Since it was early for the cats' dinners, I walked down the block for a slice of mushroom pizza. Travis had introduced me to what he called "real pizza" when we were in Brooklyn investigating our last case, but when you're as hungry as I was, New Camel pizza hit the spot. I stopped back at the shop for Sashkatu, who ignored my cajoling to come down from his window sill. The steady stream of people in and out of the shop had apparently disturbed his daytime napping cycle and he was busy catching up. Words held no sway with him when he'd made up his mind about something, but since he was quite portable, I picked him up and carried him home to the accompaniment of his outraged yowls. I figured that some salmon in his dinner kibble would make up for any real or imagined indignities he'd suffered and restore me into his good graces.

Chapter 11

I had just parked myself at the computer to look up the last two names from Ryan's notes, while stroking a never-ending parade of cats, when Travis called. He wanted to know how my day went and if the bus tour met my expectations.

"It was a financial success," I said. "A good day all around, except for the toddler who nearly wrecked the shop." I spent a couple of minutes recounting the details. "How are things going up in Albany?"

"I actually had a couple minutes free, so I checked the public records to see if they were also deceased."

"Didn't they ever teach you in journalism not to bury the lead?"

"I must have cut class that day," he said. I could hear the grin in his voice. "Now, would you like to know what I found?"

"By all means. You have the floor, sir."

"Okay, Chris Dowland, from Montour Falls, died on January third, 2015, at the age of thirty-seven from blunt force trauma to the back of his skull."

"I didn't think the public records listed the cause of death."

"They do if one has a friend with the right connections."

"Say no more. Moving along, what about McFee?"

"Ronald McFee, from Hassettville. He was forty-one when he died on June sixteenth, 2016, of carbon monoxide poisoning."

"Four men, one woman, all different ages, and from different towns," I mused aloud. "Two were clearly murdered, though by different means."

"The names on Ryan's list have only two things in common," Travis said. "They were all from Schuyler County and they're all dead."

"So Ryan's file is a list of decedents. That's not much to go on. If I picked five people at random, I'd probably find they had more in common than these five seem to. I can't imagine what piqued Ryan's interest."

"He had a sort of sixth sense about these things," Travis said. "'A nose for news' as they say. And I think his so-called *accidental death* is proof he was getting too close for the killer's comfort."

"We're going to need a lot more information than the handful of names Ryan left in his notes if we're ever going to figure out what he was investigating and why. I get that he didn't like to talk about an investigation he was working on, but it seems as if he didn't want anyone, including you, to figure out what it was. I don't know why he bothered telling you where he kept the thumb drive. It's close to useless without a Ryan Rosetta Stone to decipher it." I heard the petulance in my tone and immediately regretted it. *Nancy Drew would have been ashamed of me.* "Sorry, Travis. It's been a long day."

"No apology necessary. I understand how frustrating it can be to have information that's useless. Ryan was always a private kind of guy, but after his folks died, he got worse. He became secretive about the most ridiculous stuff. I figured it was because he couldn't count on anything or anyone to have his back. I certainly didn't help him feel welcome or safe in my family. As Ryan got older, I remember thinking he might be borderline paranoid. I asked my mother what she thought, but she wouldn't discuss it with me. Anyway, she told me not to worry; she was on top of things. After we reconciled, I tried to talk to him about it, but he always put me off by joking. 'Hey, just because I'm paranoid, doesn't mean there aren't people out to get me.'"

"But then why keep investigating the kind of people who really *would* come after him?" I asked. According to Travis, he'd made a career of tweaking some extremely dangerous noses. "It's like poking a stick into a pile of rattlers to see if they'll strike."

"Look at it this way," he said. "There are two ways to deal with paranoia. You can either hide under the bed or you can dedicate your life to exposing the bad guys. Ryan chose not to hide and that's probably why he's dead."

"Given how little he left us to go on, we'll have to talk to the families of the deceased to try to find some other commonalities."

"Questioning family members who have lost someone is not my favorite investigative tool," Travis said soberly. "It feels wrong, no matter how kind I try to be."

"Something my aunt Tilly told me helped a lot in the last case."

"Silly Tilly?" I pictured one of his eyebrows arching.

"Turns out there's a wise side to her I never got to know when Morgana and Bronwen were alive."

"I'll take your word for it," he said. "Lay some of that Tilly wisdom on me."

"She told me that it's more uncomfortable for us to raise the topic of the deceased than it is for the one in mourning. The grieving person usually finds solace in talking about their lost loved one."

"That does make me feel a little better about contacting the families," Travis said. "Maybe Tilly should add dispenser of wisdom to her resumé."

We divvied up the list so I had three names and he had two. "I can handle all five if your real job needs you," I assured him.

"I appreciate it, but I want to do some of the legwork in this case even if it means losing my beauty sleep. Besides you have a business to run too."

* * * *

Elise Harkens came by the shop the next morning before opening, armed with a bag from the Breakfast Bar. Seeing her gave my spirit and my stomach a lift. I knew something was up the moment she walked in wearing makeup and high-heeled boots under serious pants, the kind you wear to church or an upscale restaurant. Or a job. "Do you have two minutes to talk?" she asked, dangling the bag under my nose as bribery.

By way of reply, I hiked myself onto the counter and patted the space beside me. Elise hopped up and set the bag between us.

"I've missed you," I said.

She opened the bag and handed me a coffee and a bear claw. "That's why I'm here. If we don't catch each other up more often, we'll need a month to do it."

I removed the lid from my coffee and breathed in the heady aroma before taking a sip. "Is there a job I don't know about?" I asked, too curious to wait until she brought it up.

"It sort of happened by accident," she said. "You know I've been toying with the idea of going back to work. I don't want to deplete my resources, and the money for the boys' education has to remain sacrosanct." She took a nibble of her pastry. "When I was up at the high school the other day, because Zach forgot his homework again, Lois Frame saw me and stopped to chat." Elise read the question on my face and added, "She's vice principal now. She said I saved her a phone call. It seems one of the English teachers went on maternity leave and her replacement quit the day before she was due to start. Some kind of family crisis. Lois asked if

I might be interested. Since it was only for three months, she thought it would be a great way to ease back into teaching."

"It does seem like a win-win," I said. "If you enjoy it, you'll know for sure you want to get back into teaching. If not, you only have to hang in there for three months while you contemplate other options. Seriously—what other job can you test drive?"

"That's what I thought, so I said *yes*. I don't start with my classes until tomorrow. Today is all the paperwork and a crash course on the curriculum, the school's principles of education and teaching, yada, yada. I don't have to be there until ten." She sounded excited, but jumpy.

"Jitters over tomorrow?" I asked.

"Jitters on steroids. I haven't been in front of a class in fifteen years. Plus Zach hates the idea of my working there even though I won't be his teacher."

"You wouldn't be home in time for Noah if you had to commute to another high school."

"He knows that, but he's a teenager; he lives in the land of me, myself, and I. Communications with Earth are spotty at best."

"I'm proud of you for not caving."

Elise sighed. "Go me." We were quiet for a bit, eating our bear claws and drinking our coffee. She broke the silence first. "You wouldn't happen to have a little spell, something to prop up my confidence and make me fearless for the big day?"

There were a number of spells for courage and composure, but the spell to make one fearless was universally eschewed. Too many practitioners had tried it and wound up dead. A healthy dose of fear is a good thing, in spite of how uncomfortable it may feel. "The best spell I can give you is a calming spell," I told her. "You already have more than enough courage and confidence; your nerves are simply blocking your access to them. Once you're calmer, you'll see that I'm right."

"Do I need to write it down?"

"No, it's really simple. Just look at the palm of your hand and repeat after me: 'As I focus on my palm, I become relaxed and calm.' Continue chanting it and looking at your palm until a feeling of peace comes over you. It's a riff on repeating the sound *ohm* in meditation."

"It'll really work? Sorry—stupid question," she said sheepishly. "You wouldn't have given it to me if it didn't work."

"It does depend to a great degree on your input, your belief that the magick works."

"I should know that by now," she said, shaking her head.

"You do. You just need some centering." The past five months had been hard on her. I don't know if I would have handled things as well as she had.

"I'll get there," she said with her usual grit. "You're up now, lady. What's new? What's going on with that handsome reporter of yours?" One of the things I loved about Elise was the honest interest she took in her friends no matter how deeply mired she might be in her own morass. As I ran through the investigation to date, her eyebrows cinched together. I knew that look. She was trying to tease something more from the few facts I'd laid out for her.

"Elise, you're going to be late," I said, suddenly noticing the time. Jolted out of her thoughts, she hopped off the counter, pulled on her coat, grabbed her purse, and was out the door in less than a minute. Too many appointments were casualties of our time together. We really had to start setting an alarm on our phones or get a good old-fashioned timer with a blaring bell.

Chapter 12

An influx of guests from the ski resort took up most of my lunch hour. They arrived as I was hanging the I'll-be-back clock in the window. I couldn't afford to close my door on that much possible revenue and word-of-mouth, so I set the clock aside and unlocked the door. They were a lively, raucous bunch who'd spent the morning on the slopes and were looking for a diversion before a second go-round in the afternoon. Most of them had clearly thrown back a hot toddy or two by the fire, before hitting Main Street. Their faces were red from a combination of the cold and the alcohol. They spent freely on gifts for the holidays as well as on products for their own consumption.

By the time they departed, I had ten minutes left. Grab lunch or try to set up an interview with a family member of one of the deceased? The phone call won. Since memory can fade with time, I'd decided to start with Martin Frank, the victim who'd been gone the longest. I wanted to speak to his family before their memories of the event deteriorated any further. Finding the phone number for his wife was harder than I anticipated and probably for the same reason I'd chosen the Frank family—six years had passed since his murder. There was no listing for Frank online. It was possible the number was unlisted. It was also possible that Martin's wife and children had moved away or that she was now Mrs. Somebody Else. I used up my ten minutes with nothing to show for it. Since no one was beating down my door to come in, I stopped into Tilly's shop before reopening, to ask if she had any ideas on how to locate the family or at least a working phone number.

"White magick won't help you," she said, picking up the plates from her last high tea. "It boils down to an invasion of privacy." I wasn't surprised by her answer, but I was disappointed. I took the teacups and utensils and followed her into the kitchen. Merlin was on his kitchen stool engrossed in a game on his iPad.

"A few twists and tweaks have been known to change black magick to a dark grayish hue," he said without looking up.

"No black magick," Tilly and I said in unison. Opening that particular box was reputed to be as fraught with danger and evil as the one in Pandora's keeping. I, for one, had no desire to test that theory.

"There is a more mundane solution to your problem," Tilly said. "You could ask Paul Curtis for his help."

"I can't. He's got a crush on me and I don't want to manipulate him that way."

"It's not like it would be the first time," she murmured, walking past me to finish clearing the table.

I was taken aback, realizing Tilly set me up to see how I would react. It was particularly unsettling, because she'd never been judgmental of me in the past. Maybe she felt obliged to assume Morgana's role now as the eldest living member of our family.

"I still feel guilty about using him," I said, partly to show my aunt that I'd learned from my mistake and partly because it was the truth. "He's too nice a guy to treat that way. He could get in serious trouble if someone found out he'd bent the privacy rules. He might even lose his job."

Tilly returned carrying the teapot and a plate of leftover pastries, which Merlin lifted deftly as she went by. She didn't miss a step. They had their routine down pat. She emptied the last of the tea into the sink and turned to face me. "My last suggestion is for you to speak to Beverly Rupert."

I groaned. No one in my family liked her. "How can Beverly help?"

"She's a hairdresser. If she doesn't know the Frank family, then she probably knows someone who does. Or that person knows someone who knows someone and on down the insidious grapevine of gossip."

"But then my interest in the Frank family will become the next topic for the grapevine," I protested. Three options and not one of them decent.

Tilly had turned on the water and was hand washing the delicate china she used exclusively for her teas. "In life you've got to pay to play," she said, raising her voice over the noise of the running water. I thanked her for the suggestion and as I passed Merlin, I plucked a miniature éclair from the plate in his hand. What's good for the gander is good for the goose.

Between customers, I called Beverly. She said she didn't know the family, but she thought her cousin did. She'd call back when she had an answer one way or the other. I didn't doubt it, because that's when she'd take her pound of flesh.

* * * *

Morgana popped in while I was making the cats' dinner. I heard the electrical crackle preceding her appearance before I turned around. Her cloud was slate blue, heavy on the gray, the dismal color of rain clouds and sadness. "Kailyn," she said solemnly, "please extend our condolences to Travis. We just heard and we're very sorry about the loss of his brother. We hope you're successful in finding justice for him." It wasn't the first time I was struck by how weird it was for the dead to be expressing their sympathies on another's passing. Wouldn't it be more comforting for them to say something upbeat like "no worries —we'll keep tabs on Jack or Jill until you get here?" Maybe that simply wasn't allowed. Beyond the veil, there seemed to be any number of rules regarding how the deceased were permitted to interact with the living.

"Where's Bronwen tonight?" I asked, since they seemed to hang out together the way they had in life.

"Taking what you might call a course in humility," my mother said. "More than overdue if you ask me." I wondered why my mother wasn't taking the course with her, but I held my tongue. Who knew what courses I'd need when I got there?

I was heading up to bed when Beverly called. Ordinarily, if I saw her name come up on Caller ID at such a late hour, I'd let it go to voice mail. A dose of Beverly at bedtime was not conducive to a good night's rest. But I was too curious about what she'd discovered to ignore it.

Chapter 13

After a detailed five-minute monologue, listing every call she placed to this relative and that friend, Beverly was proud to report that she had the information I'd requested. I made a big fuss about how much I appreciated her diligent work on my behalf.

"You're welcome. Not many people would go to such lengths for someone who was barely a friend," she added pointedly.

I knew exactly where she was headed and decided to get it over with, so I could go to bed. "How can I ever repay your kindness?" I asked, sounding like a hammy actress in a bad soap opera.

Beverly didn't seem to notice. She must have been focused on the word *repay* to the exclusion of everything else. "If you really mean that," she said, "I would welcome a gift certificate for your shop, assuming you're no longer having problems with, how shall I put it…quality control?"

It was uncanny how she always managed to say something irritating or downright obnoxious. "I haven't had any complaints," I said, trying to keep sarcasm out of my tone. I had no intention of telling her that Merlin's arrival seemed to have stabilized our magick to a great degree. "I'll put the gift certificate in the mail tomorrow."

"No need," she chirped. "I'll stop by for it and do some shopping while I'm there."

"That works." Now I just had to figure out the amount of the gift certificate. Too much and she'd be fawning all over me and bragging about it to everyone in town who might then expect a similar gratuity for any sort of help they rendered. Too little and I could forget about ever asking for her help again. Beverly was one of those what-have-you-done-for-me-lately people. I settled on fifty dollars, thinking I might throw in a few extra free items when she came to the register, depending on how she behaved.

* * * *

The first thought to pop into my head when I awoke at seven a.m. wasn't about dreading Beverly's visit. It was about making the phone call Beverly had made possible. The number she gave me was for Nina Frank Lewis. Nina had married a divorced podiatrist, barely a year after Martin died, and moved into his house in Watkins Glen. According to Beverly, there was some talk about Nina being the reason for the foot doc's divorce. Leave it to Beverly to get all the dirt.

Common courtesy demanded I wait until at least nine o'clock to call someone who didn't know me. To pass the time, I puttered around the house, fed the cats, drank two cups of coffee, and read the news online without absorbing a single word of it. I wasn't able to concentrate on paying bills, returning emails, or any one of a dozen chores that required my attention. I finally dressed and roused Sashkatu from his post breakfast nap and went off to Abracadabra to wait out the second hour.

I'd already decided not to open until I'd made the call. I didn't see how it could last very long. Either Martin's widow would be receptive to talking about her late husband and his brutal murder or she wouldn't. I didn't allow myself to dwell on the latter.

I cheated the clock and made the call a few minutes early. The phone rang three times. I was formulating the message I would leave on her voice mail, when she finally picked up with a cautious "hello?" Curiosity must have won out. But if I wasn't careful, she could still hang up.

I explained that I was a private investigator looking into a number of unsolved homicides in the county and that I was hoping she could spare a few minutes to meet with me at the time and place of her choosing. "I don't know," she said, "I've tried to put that awful time behind me." I didn't push. No high-pressure sales pitch. She sighed, clearly on the fence. "I suppose I owe it to Martin to do everything I can to pursue justice for him." She didn't say anything for a few seconds, probably wishing I would speak up and tell her she was doing the right thing, the decent thing.

"There's no right or wrong decision," I said, "but most people want to know who killed their loved one and why. It helps them find peace." I had no actual data to back that up, but it seemed like a logical conclusion. With only five names to pursue, Travis and I couldn't afford to let even one slip through our fingers.

"Okay, yes," Nina said finally. "How is tomorrow at ten?"

"You're the boss." At least I wanted her to feel that way. If she thought she was in control, she was more apt to speak freely.

"At my house."

"I'll be there," I said, "thank you." I thought she would insist on a neutral location, anywhere *but* her home. She didn't know anything about me. For a woman in her fifties, Nina didn't seem to have much common sense. Maybe it was a product of having lived her life in an area that, until recently, had known little violent crime. Investigating two murders had opened my eyes to the potential dangers lurking in the most peaceful of places and in the minds of the most benign-looking people.

* * * *

The Lewis residence was on a tree-lined street that was no doubt beautiful in summer, but in autumn the trees were leafless and skeletal. Had I been in charge of the town's landscaping, I might have gone with evergreens. The house itself was a stately brick colonial with crisp white trim and a circular driveway. Although I had no idea about Nina's circumstances when she was married to Martin, she seemed to have done well for herself the second time around.

I rang the bell and Nina ushered me inside with a smile that kept twitching on and off like a faulty light bulb. The house was well-appointed; the hardwood floors gleamed and the light fixtures sparkled. She led the way into a formal living room, where pale fabrics indicated that no young kids resided there. She offered me a seat and after I chose one of the tufted side chairs, she perched on the edge of the couch as if she might change her mind about the interview at any moment.

"I want to thank you again for agreeing to meet with me," I said, when she didn't initiate the conversation.

She gave a wobbly laugh. "To be honest, I'm not sure why I did. I recently spoke to a reporter too—that poor man who skidded off the road and into a tree. I'll ask you what I asked him—'If the police failed to make headway in Martin's case back when it happened, why do you think you can six years later?'"

"My partner and I are looking at your late husband's murder from a different angle, as part of a larger case. I can't guarantee we'll be successful in finding his killer, but we believe it's worth our time to take another look."

"Who hired you to undertake the investigation?" she asked. "I'm sure you're not just doing it out of random curiosity. Someone must be footing the bill."

"Someone is," I said, "but they prefer to remain anonymous, at least for now." If I told her we were doing it for free, I was afraid she might not take me seriously.

"This all sounds very mysterious, but if there's no fee involved and there's a chance to find out who killed Martin, I'm in."

I took out the list of questions Travis and I had compiled and opened the record app on my phone. Before starting, I asked Nina's permission to record our conversation. She was reluctant, but finally agreed.

Most of the questions were not the standard ones you hear on every cop show on TV. The police would have covered those back when they were working the case and it clearly didn't net them the killer. Travis and I were looking for a common thread that linked all the names on Ryan's list. Until we knew what they had in common, we weren't going to find the killer. "Tell me about your late husband," I said instead. If allowed to speak freely, I hoped Nina might reveal things that more specific questions might fail to elicit.

"Let's see—he worked for Horizon Cable. He came home every night for dinner, then he'd skim through the paper, mostly the sports section, and watch TV until he fell asleep. He didn't gamble. The most he ever drank was a glass of wine with dinner or a couple of beers watching TV and never on the same night. He was a good man. Our lives weren't exciting, but we were content."

"What sort of things did he like to do on the weekends?"

Nina took a moment to think back. "He liked to tinker with cars. If he hadn't gotten the job at Horizon straight out of high school, he probably would have been a mechanic."

"Did he read a lot?"

"No, he used to complain that his eyes were too tired at the end of the day."

"Did he have any regrets in his life?" Nina wriggled farther back on the couch as if to put more distance between her and my question.

"He wasn't much of a talker," she said finally, "especially when it came to emotions and stuff. In other words, a typical man. One thing I do know is that he regretted never going to college. I could see it bothered him when someone asked where he went to school. And he was passed over for promotions a number of times in favor of younger men with college degrees."

"Was he vocal, argumentative when it came to politics or religion?"

"He definitely had his opinions on politics," she said as though she hadn't agreed with him, "but he didn't bother much with religion." The more she told me, the more I suspected she hadn't known Martin very well in spite of nineteen years of marriage. Their connections didn't seem to run deep, but who was I to judge? My only experience of marriage was my mother's and grandmother's, along with glimpses into Tilly's union and discussions I overheard between the women in my family. And when the marriages failed, I was only privy to the women's points of view. My takeaway was that men should not be counted on, because sooner or later they would leave. By the time I was in my teens, I had no interest in marriage. I was never that girl who fantasized about her wedding day.

"Did he belong to any fraternal or charitable organizations like the Elks?"

Nina shook her head. "Neither of us was much of a joiner. I have to say, your questions sound a lot more like a survey from *Good Housekeeping* than an investigation into my husband's death."

"I did say we were going about it differently."

She looked at her watch. "Will it take much longer?"

"We're almost done," I assured her. Five minutes later, I heard the front door open and close, followed by footsteps coming our way. Nina didn't appear surprised, but a frown flitted across her brow. It was gone by the time a young man came through the living room doorway and headed toward her. I saw his resemblance to Nina immediately.

"Hey, Ma," he said, kissing her on the cheek. I wondered if Nina's question about when we'd be finished had anything to do with her son's arrival. Had she been hoping I'd be on my way before he got there?

"Jeremy, this is Kailyn Wilde, the woman who's looking into Dad's death. Ms. Wilde, this is my older son."

He acknowledged me with a head bob and turned back to his mother. "You never told me you were actually going to meet with her," he said with barely veiled contempt. I felt like waving my hand and saying, *Hello, I'm right here. You may want to have this discussion after I leave.* I could only imagine how appalled Nina had to feel about her son's behavior.

Jeremy appeared to have no such concerns. He peeled off his parka and threw it onto the far end of the couch. When he finally turned to face me, his eyes were narrowed and there was a challenge in his tone. "My mother said you were looking at my father's murder as part of a larger case. Exactly what kind of larger case?" If Detective Duggan ever needed an assistant, Jeremy could probably wrest a confession from any perp he skewered with those eyes.

"That's correct," I said, determined not to let his attitude derail me, "but I'm not at liberty to go into more detail at this time."

"Of course not," he said with mock gravity. "You listen to me, Ms. Wilde, my mother seems to have forgotten about all the scam artists we had to deal with after my father was murdered. Phony psychics who swore they could contact him to find out the name of his killer, financial advisers who scared my mother into making risky investments, and the list goes on. There's no way I'll let that crap ever happen again. Is. That. Clear?"

"Jeremy, please, this is nothing like that. I apologize, Ms. Wilde." Nina sounded mortified. I could see why she might have hoped to avoid this encounter.

"Not everyone is out to profit from your loss," I said.

"Yeah, well until I come up with a way to tell the scam artists from the saints, I'm going to protect my family the best I know how. For starters, this little interview session is over *now*." I could see by the expression on Nina's face that she wasn't going to argue with him. To spare her further embarrassment, I excused myself.

She hurried over to walk me to the door, apologizing again for Jeremy's attitude. "You're lucky to have your son looking out for you," I said.

"Family," she said wryly, "you know how it is."

Chapter 14

Driving home I was lost in thought about Nina and Jeremy and forgot to turn off onto the back roads, until it was too late. I was stuck in the traffic snarl at the construction site of the new hotel. I'd expected the novelty to have worn off by now, but I was wrong. Everyone still slowed down to see what progress was being made. It was going to be a long, long siege if people considered a foundation all that interesting.

The flagmen compounded the problem. They were constantly stopping traffic to allow construction vehicles and workmen to enter and leave the site. Travis had laughed at me when I complained about the situation. "You are one spoiled country sorcerer. This kind of traffic would be a welcome change on the streets of New York City." He was right of course. Bronwen used to say, "Life is all a matter of perspective." I preferred Mary Chapin Carpenter's more colorful version: "Some days you're the windshield, some days you're the bug."

I chafed at being the bug. I'd been gone from Abracadabra longer than I'd intended. I consoled myself with the thought that the traffic would ease up once I made it past the construction site. But even after I'd passed the construction, I was still moving at a crawl. When I finally saw the reason, I almost jumped out of my car in the middle of the street. Common sense prevailed. I pulled into the next parking lot I came to and ran back to the block where Merlin was parading up and down the sidewalk carrying a sign like a doomsday prophet. With his wild white hair, ragged beard, and burlap pants he even looked the part. Odds are everyone would have ignored him and his sign if all it predicted was the end of the world. It was the message on Merlin's sign that was stopping traffic:

All ye Fools

Wake to the Truth

Your town began as New Camelot
Merlin was flipping the sign around to show the message on the back
as well:

Learn the Truth

Sat. 2PM at the Library

Free Refreshments Served
People had to slow down if they wanted to read both sides. Merlin knew
his audience. If curiosity didn't grab their attention, "free refreshments"
would. Unfortunately some people took exception to being called "fools"
and sitting in traffic only made them angrier and more vocal about it. Car
windows were opened and epithets hurled in Merlin's direction, along with
a host of other things, including empty beer cans, a takeout coffee cup,
and a rotting tomato, the latter by a motorist who clearly traveled well-
prepared to express his opinion. So much for trying to keep Merlin out
of the public eye. I had to shut him down before a camera crew arrived.
But it wasn't easy. He fought me off as valiantly as he did the garbage
raining down on us. He didn't cave until I threatened him where it hurt.
"For every minute you stand here arguing with me, you're going to lose a
week of TV." He thought about it for several seconds, before following me
back to the car, muttering and grumbling into his beard until I deposited
him at Tilly's shop.

"Oh thank goodness!" she exclaimed. "I was doing a reading and didn't
realize he was gone until five minutes ago. I was frantic. You weren't here
and I didn't know where to begin looking for him. I didn't know whether or
not to call the police, because…" She'd run out of breath and was about to
collapse onto a chair that wasn't there. Merlin ripped into action, shooting
a chair across the floor. It arrived beneath her without a second to spare.
He looked at me like a puppy expecting a reward.

"Okay, fine," I said, both grateful and defeated. "We'll call it a wash."
He walked away grinning, headed no doubt to scavenge for leftovers in
the kitchen.

Once Tilly's breathing quieted and her color pinked up, I showed her
Merlin's sign and explained what he'd been doing. "Do you know if he
actually arranged for the time at the library?" I asked.

"I… I have no idea."

"Don't worry, I'll find out." The minute I opened Abracadabra, the bells over the door jingled and Beverly marched in. "You know there's no point in having a clock sign that says when you'll be back, if you don't honor it," she said huffy with indignation. "I was beginning to think something dreadful had happened to you. I tried to ask your aunt, but she wouldn't unlock the door or answer the phone."

"When she's doing a reading, she doesn't allow interruptions," I said.

"Well, this is my third time back here today. It's wreaked havoc with my schedule. Now I'll have to spend part of tomorrow doing laundry." Flexibility had never been one of her strong suits.

"The circumstances couldn't be avoided. I'm sorry you were inconvenienced," I said in a tone that wasn't the least bit apologetic.

She seemed to be debating a comeback, but then she must have decided there was nothing to be gained by antagonizing me. "I'd like to redeem my gift certificate," she said. I opened the register and presented it to her. Judging by her neutral expression, she was neither amazed nor disappointed by the amount, the exact middle ground I'd been aiming for. "Thank you, Kailyn," she said formally.

"Take your time and let me know if you have any questions."

"I can't take my time, since I wasted it by waiting for you." She grabbed a basket and headed off to the first aisle. Maybe it hadn't occurred to her that the giver of the gift certificate could just as easily rescind it. And after the Merlin incident, I was already close to the end of my rope.

"You should have called to find out if I'd returned," I said sweetly. I realized I was burning a bridge I might one day need to cross again, but at that moment it felt awfully good. If Beverly wasn't hooked on our beauty products, I think she would have turned on her heel and walked out, slamming the door shut behind her. All things considered, not the worst thing that could happen.

She'd only been gone a few minutes when Lolly walked in. I came from behind the counter to chat with her near the door. She liked to keep an eye on her shop ever since the candy thief struck. Until then she hadn't felt the need to watch it so closely if she ran across the street for a few minutes. But the week before Halloween of last year, she'd come to give me a sample of her new eggnog fudge. When she returned to her shop, she found she'd been robbed—entire trays of candy gone. She was more upset about the wasted hours on her feet making the candy than the actual loss of revenue. And she was irked, because she didn't even catch a glimpse of the thief for the police report.

Since that day, we chatted at my door, where she'd be able to see anyone entering her shop. "Beverly popped in a couple of times today," Lolly said after we hugged, transferring a bit of fudge from her cheek to mine. She pointed it out and offered me a tissue from her purse.

"I bet it was every time she came back to look for me."

"The first time, she seemed so upset I gave her a piece of candy." Which explained why she didn't want to just call to see if I was back yet. You don't get free candy that way. "The second time, she was more agitated. When I didn't offer her another candy, she had the nerve to ask for it. 'I felt so much better after that piece of chocolate you gave me earlier,'" Lolly said, doing a great imitation of Beverly. "'Considering the circumstances, do you think you could spare one more?'"

I groaned. "Please tell me you didn't give her another freebie."

"I said, 'Yes, if you can spare a dollar. I'm given to understand that's how commerce works.'"

I clapped, delighted. "And?"

"She pulled a dollar out of her purse and slammed it down so hard on the display case I thought the glass would break. "She said, 'I'll take another dark chocolate covered caramel' and stormed out of the shop."

"Think she'll ever come back?"

"Lord, I hope not," Lolly said, laughing. "But with that sweet tooth, I suspect she will. Listen, I had another reason for coming to talk to you."

"What's up?"

"A number of locals who came into my shop today were talking about your cousin Merlin and his sign."

"You're not smiling," I said. "Why aren't you smiling?" When Lolly was this serious, it was generally due to well-founded concern. And Merlin plus "serious" added up to trouble.

"Mostly they were talking about his eccentric appearance and whether or not his sign was correct. Chances are nothing will come of it, but I thought you should know in case it snowballs into something more."

"Thanks, I prefer not to be ambushed." I'd never told Lolly the truth about Merlin and how he'd arrived here. She believed our story that he was my eccentric cousin from England. Though I felt a little guilty about it, we needed to keep the secret limited to as few people as possible. Tilly, Elise, and Travis were the only ones who knew as much as I did.

"Caleb Winston was one of the locals who came in today," Lolly continued. I knew the name, but couldn't immediately put it with a face. "The town historian," she added in response to my puzzled expression. "He must be a hundred by now. I hadn't seen him in ages."

I'd forgotten all about Caleb. The picture that came to mind was dredged up from my childhood. Even then he was an impossibly old man with a cane, his eyes all but hidden in the deep shadow of his brow. No child wants to dwell on old age while they're still feeling immortal, and I'd been no different. "What brought him out?" I asked, although I was pretty sure I knew the answer.

"Merlin and his sign. Caleb's in a wheelchair now, not at all the imposing figure he was in his prime. According to his aide, Louise, they were coming home from a doctor's visit when they were caught in the traffic jam. Caleb insisted on stopping in town to find out what it was all about. Louise decided if she had to stop, it was going to be at my shop."

"What did you tell them?"

Lolly shrugged. "That I knew as much as they did. But as it happened, Caleb knew more. He claimed the town's name never had anything to do with camels. It had to do with sorcery. Then Louise bought a quarter pound of Forbidden Fudge and a praline toffee bar and off they went."

"Could it just be dementia talking?" I asked, hoping people would dismiss his words. I didn't want the issue debated by the whole town. No good could come of that.

"I don't think that's a concern. As old as Caleb is, he still sounded clear-minded to me."

"Maybe we should ask the current town historian," I said. With any luck, he or she would render the issue moot.

"We don't have one," Lolly said. "As far as I know, it's always been an informal position created by some ancestor of Caleb's and tolerated by the board as innocuous. Caleb never had children, so…"

"No younger town historian. Did Caleb or any of his family members keep notes or diaries?"

"It wouldn't matter if they did, the Winston family homestead burned to the ground in the early twentieth century. Nothing escaped the fire, but the people and their dogs."

Although the thought of learning more about the Wilde family in America was intriguing, I told myself that it was all for the best. Without proof that New Camelot was the original name of the town, talk about it should quiet down in spite of Merlin's efforts. Travis and I had a murder investigation on our hands. We didn't need additional distractions.

Chapter 15

Tilly made her hearty split pea soup for dinner the next night. The cold weather had kick-started her annual parade of soups, and she believed it would be easier to set Merlin straight about his recent behavior with his belly full of split pea in a bread bowl. If not, at least it would fortify us for a battle of wills.

I kept checking my watch during dinner. Travis had texted that he'd call about eight to discuss Ryan's case. I didn't want to miss his call for a variety of reasons, not all of which had to do with the investigation. Merlin guzzled his soup plus two more servings in the same amount of time it took Tilly and me to eat our single portions. It was quickly apparent he could benefit from a tutorial on how to eat soup in the company of others, but that would have to wait its turn.

When he finished eating, Tilly insisted he go into the bathroom and rinse out his beard in the sink. A sunken ship had less barnacles attached to it than the amount of soup detritus clinging to his facial hair. He returned to the table reasonably clean and asked what was for dessert.

"Dessert will have to wait until after we discuss something," I said. "How many times have we told you that drawing attention to yourself will end in disaster one day?"

"I have never kept count," he said. "Was I expected to?"

"Well no, that's not the point. Merlin. Why do you constantly flout the rules meant to keep you safe?" I repeated the usual litany of horrors that can befall someone without ID or any means of securing it. He brought up his objections. I shot them down. He suggested magick and I forbade it. We were left in a veritable stalemate as usual. Tilly had spent the time clearing the table and setting up for dessert. At seven forty-five she brought in her dark chocolate peanut butter pie with a pint of vanilla ice cream and resumed her seat. She fixed Merlin with a beatific smile that made her look like an overgrown Hawaiian cherub.

"Aren't you going to serve dessert?" he demanded when she made no move to cut the pie or scoop the ice cream.

"As soon as you and Kailyn settle your dispute," she said.

"Good woman, that's blackmail," he sputtered.

"Nope—my pie, my rules."

He lasted another three minutes. "All right," he grumbled, "what must I do to be allowed dessert?"

"It's simple," I said, "stop making a spectacle of yourself."

"How else is one supposed to bring about change in your democratic system? If this were the kingdom of Camelot, all I'd need do is talk to the king, we were very chummy, and he would accede to my wishes. Clearly a better system."

"Maybe for you, but not for the average citizen," I pointed out.

"So what is it you would have me do?"

"Nothing," I said.

"But then nothing will change." He seemed appalled by the concept.

"Precisely."

"Kailyn," Tilly said, "Would you like some pie?"

"I'd love some. With ice cream, please."

Merlin watched her slide a piece of pie onto a plate and scoop up a big ball of ice cream to set beside it. As she handed me the plate, it passed directly under Merlin's nose.

"Ready to agree, Your Loftiness?" Tilly asked sweetly.

"No," he said, rising from his seat. "There comes the hour when a man of worth must take a stand against injustice, and this be mine." He strutted away from the table as if there were a golden halo of virtue atop his head, leaving Tilly and me with our mouths agape.

"I know his game," my aunt said finally. "He intends to wait until I'm off to bed, and then sneak down to have his fill of dessert."

I laughed. "You're probably right. Maybe I should take it home with me."

"Yes, indeed."

I was pulling on my coat when the doorbell rang. It was after eight, an odd time for someone to come by unannounced in our little town. Tilly peered through the peephole and immediately flung the door open. Travis stepped inside and gave her a hug that made her giggle. I was happy to see Travis, but not particularly surprised. He had a habit of showing up when I least expected him.

"You'd better keep tabs on this one, Kailyn, he's very free with his affections," Tilly said.

"Not guilty," he protested, turning to fold me into his arms. "It's some kind of magick you Wilde women have over me. Although I have to admit," he said, giving Tilly a wink, "I've always been attracted to red hair."

"Ah," she said knowingly, "is your mother a redhead?"

"No, but growing up I did have a fabulous Irish setter named Maggie." We all laughed, my voice all but lost in his coat. When he finally released me, Tilly handed me my purse from the bench in the foyer. She handed Travis the pie and the pint of ice cream. "Hey, you even come with dessert," he said. "Am I a lucky guy or what?"

Tilly shooed us out the door with a promise to let me know what happened when Merlin discovered his plot had been foiled.

Back at my house, Travis declined my offer to make him dinner. I could hardly blame him. I hadn't been grocery shopping in a while. It came down to a choice between pasta, eggs, or PB'n J. "What's wrong with chocolate peanut butter pie and ice cream?" he asked with all the innocence of a child. I couldn't come up with a valid answer. So we sat at the kitchen table while he ate, and I gave him the lowdown on my visit with Nina Frank Lewis.

"Her kid's got issues," he agreed. "Could be a variety of things from his father's passing, to his mother's remarriage, to being the one who killed his dad."

"Do you really think that's a possibility? It crossed my mind at the time, because his reaction had seemed over the top, given the years that had passed. I could tell that Nina was distressed by it, but I don't think she was surprised."

"If all the victims on Ryan's list had something in common, I doubt it was Martin's son. But let's keep him on the back burner for now."

"I scheduled an interview for tomorrow with Max Gonzalez, Calista's older brother," I said, "but I can postpone it until after you leave."

"Actually, I'd like to come along and get my feet wet in the case."

I was all for it. "Max wasn't the least bit reluctant to talk to me," I said ready to launch into a full synopsis of our conversation along with my first impressions of the man.

"Can't it wait till morning?" Travis asked, carrying his plate and fork to the sink. He turned around, leaning back against the counter. "I'm bushed. If I try to input one more byte of data, my brain is going to crash."

"Yes, sure," I said. I chucked the empty ice cream container into the garbage and stowed what was left of the pie in the fridge where the cats couldn't get at it. When I passed Travis, he reached out, hooked a finger into my belt loop and pulled me closer. You didn't have to hit me over the head with a rubber mallet. Even before moonlighting as an investigator, I was pretty good at understanding non-verbal cues.

Chapter 16

Max Gonzalez was as pleasant in person as he was on the phone. At seventy-five, he was Calista's older brother, but he had a ready smile and an agile stride that carved years off his appearance. He answered the door promptly and led us into the kitchen where his wife, Esmeralda, was brewing a fresh pot of coffee. Although she acknowledged us politely, I could tell she wasn't happy to have us in her home. Max was surely aware of it too, because he didn't give us time to dawdle there before continuing into the adjacent family room. The house had been built with an abundance of oversized windows that bathed every room in sunlight and made the house feel like a joyful place. In contrast, the furnishings were heavy and ornate. Maybe Max and Esmeralda were worried that the light-filled house might up and fly away without such means of anchoring it to the ground.

Seating in the room was limited to a large sectional couch that formed a semicircle around the largest wall-mounted screen I'd ever seen outside of a movie theater. It was a perfect arrangement for watching television, but awkward for conversation. Travis and I sat at one end of the sofa and Max sat in the center. In order to face each other, we had to sit at an angle that made it impossible to lean back.

"I must confess," Max said, "I don't really understand the purpose of your visit any more than I did Mr. Cutler's." At Travis's request, I'd made no mention of his personal connection to Ryan. As far as Max knew, we were simply continuing the investigation initiated by our fallen colleague. "I'd like to extend my condolences," Max added. "I was sorry to hear about his passing. Far too young. When something like that happens, you're reminded of how fragile life is and how easily snuffed out." We both nodded and I saw Travis's jaw tighten. I'd done the same thing to stave off tears when the loss of my mother and grandmother was still an open wound.

"Thank you. Ryan believed there might be an underlying link between several deaths in the county over the past five or so years," I said to give Travis an extra moment to compose himself.

"I know," Max said, "but Calista died of a cerebral hemorrhage, and when I asked Ryan if the others died of a similar problem, he said they hadn't."

Esmeralda entered the room carrying a tray with three mugs of coffee and the fixings. She set it on the wood and wrought iron coffee table and walked out. "Please, help yourselves," Max said. I'd learned that accepting refreshments often moved things along more quickly than refusing them. No need for the host to ask: "Are you sure? Would you prefer tea or a cold drink? Please let me know if you change your mind." Travis must have come to the same conclusion over time, because we each took a mug and murmured "thank you."

"Unfortunately Ryan never told me much about his investigation," Travis said, picking up the dialogue, "but he was an award-winning journalist and if he suspected a link, we believe it should be explored."

"To honor his memory," I added, "as well as to uncover the truth for the families involved."

"I'll tell you," Max said, "my wife is a religious woman and she thinks we should let Calista rest in peace. After all, we were satisfied with the coroner's report until Ryan showed up. I guess I have a curious nature. If there was more to my sister's death, I want to know about it."

Travis took a sip of his coffee. "Did she have any physical condition, any illness that could have produced the hemorrhage?"

"She never discussed her health with us, or much of anything else," Max said, pouring a packet of sweetener into his mug. "She lived alone. When we couldn't reach her by ten that night, we drove over and let ourselves in. Calista and I had keys to each other's houses in case of emergency." He shook his head. "Not that it did my sister any good. We found her at the bottom of the stairs. Esmeralda called 911, while I gave her CPR, but it was too late. The EMT confirmed that she was gone. The coroner's report said that the bleed could have been the result of falling down the stairs or it could have precipitated the fall."

"Is there any reason to believe Calista might have been pushed down the stairs?" Travis asked.

"The police didn't find any evidence of forced entry, and as far as I could tell, nothing was missing. Could someone have pushed her on purpose or by accident and then fled the scene? It's possible, I suppose."

"Did she ever confide in you about regrets she had in her life?" I asked, thinking of my interview with Nina and her hesitation with that question.

Max shook his head. "If she had regrets, she never told me. I doubt she ever let anyone inside."

"Was she ever married?" Travis asked.

"Once, about thirty years ago, but it lasted less than two years. No one was surprised. Calista was not an easy person to live with. Even when we were kids, I thought of her as prickly."

"A curmudgeon?" I said.

"I suppose, but not the kind with a heart of gold like you see in the movies. How do two kids grow up in the same house with the same parents and turn out so differently? I once asked a psychologist friend who knew us both. He believed Calista suffered from psychiatric issues. But in spite of all the difficulties between us over the years, it broke my heart that she died alone." Tears welled up in his eyes and he tried to blink them back. Travis and I busied ourselves with our coffees to give him time to settle himself.

"I imagine you have some more questions for me," he said moments later with only the slightest hitch in his voice.

"If you don't mind," Travis replied.

"At my age you don't put off for tomorrow what you can do today," Max said wryly, "so you'd best get your answers while you can."

When we were back in the car, Travis asked if there was anything I'd heard so far from Nina or Max that stood out to me, a similarity that might have drawn a killer's attention. "No, and we're two down, three to go *if* they all agree to speak to us."

"They will," he said. "We need to think positive."

"Right there with you." Travis's phone rang through the car's Bluetooth. I'd never heard the news director's voice before. It was intense, the words clipped as if he could barely afford them. "Another probable homicide. Outside Watkins Glen. Sending the address now. What's your ETA?"

"Twenty minutes," Travis responded. That seemed a little optimistic to me.

"A news van's en route. Stafford covering."

"On my way." The call ended and Travis glanced at me. "I'm sorry—I don't have time to drop you off. I have to get over there."

"I'll see if Tilly can open for me," I said. I hated to miss an entire day's sales, but his sudden tension was palpable. It crackled in the air between us like static. I'd be lying if I said I didn't mind how easily he dismissed my livelihood in favor of his own. After all, the director said there was a van on the way with a covering reporter. But truth be told, I wanted to go to the site of this latest murder myself.

"Thanks," he said, staring straight ahead, his foot heavy on the accelerator. I looked at the speedometer. We were barreling along at nearly twice the posted speed limit. I didn't say anything, afraid to distract him. Instead I pulled out my cell phone and called my aunt. I reached her at home in a whirlwind of baking for back to back teas the next day.

She answered the phone with a wary, "Are you okay?"

"I'm fine. Why are you asking?"

"Another death," she said with a sigh. "It crept into my mind hours ago and even my baking marathon hasn't dislodged it."

Sadly I'd have to confirm her prediction, but that could wait until I got back home. "I was hoping you could open Abracadabra for me even if it's just for a few hours. Travis has to get to the site of some breaking news and can't drop me off."

"Not to worry," Tilly said. "The last batch of scones will be done in ten minutes, and then I'll scurry right over there. It'll be a nice break in my day." Not only did she try to help whenever possible, but she always made it sound as though I was doing *her* a favor. "It'll be good for Merlin too. The man's been staring at one screen or another since his eyes opened this morning."

"You're the best," I said.

She chuckled. "An easy title to win, since I'm all you've got."

Chapter 17

We arrived at a mobile home in the middle of nowhere. If you took away the police cars, the ambulance, forensic unit and coroner's vans, the yellow police tape and the four news vehicles with their crews, there was little else to see. The only view from the trailer's windows would have been dead, matted vegetation and winter-bare trees. The occasional fir provided the only pop of color in the dreary landscape. The mobile home was old, the kind you'd see in movies of the 1940s or 50s. It must have looked sharp when it was new, sparkling white with turquoise trim. Now the white was the color of nicotine-stained teeth and the turquoise was faded and chipped like a bad manicure. The trailer was unhitched from an old black pickup that appeared to be equal parts metal and rust. Whoever resided there, did so without benefit of a water or electrical hookup. The thought of living under such conditions made my skin crawl.

Travis stopped the car as close to his network's van as he could, without mowing down a couple of newscasters and cameramen. He threw the car into park and jumped out, without a word to me. Was I expected to remain in the car? Did the police tolerate the journalists' presence, but draw the line at anyone else who happened to be along for the ride? I debated getting out and testing the waters, but decided to wait a bit and see how things played out. Ten very slow minutes ticked by. Travis was standing with a younger reporter, who I presumed was Stafford. Neither of them looked happy, but Stafford seemed more disappointed than anything. He'd probably raced to the scene believing this was going to be his first break.

I noticed a young man standing between the trailer and the police line corralling the reporters. He was wearing jeans, a parka, and hiking boots.

There was a knapsack on the ground at his feet. Had he come upon the cabin during a hike, caught the smell of decay, and called the police?

The trailer door opened and the victim's body was wheeled out in a black body bag that reminded me of the trash bags people fill with leaves and debris in the fall. No one ran after the gurney, distraught and sobbing. If the victim had family or friends, they hadn't heard about his passing or didn't care. Detective Duggan came out of the trailer, followed by Paul Curtis, both looking grim and official. The more time Paul spent with the detective, the more he was adopting his expressions and mannerisms. I doubted he was even aware of it.

Travis and the other reporters shouted questions at the two as they emerged from the trailer. Duggan stopped abruptly in his tracks and rounded on them. Curtis, who'd been at his heels, crashed into him, knocking them both off balance. They teetered back and forth on the brink of falling as if they were learning a new dance move. After a performance lasting several critical seconds, they both managed to stay upright. The detective cast his displeasure on Curtis, then glared at the media as if they too were to blame for the impromptu vaudeville act.

"A middle-aged man by the name of Henry Lomax was discovered dead of multiple stab wounds inside this trailer," Duggan said. "We need to let the ME do his job. Until his report is ready, I have no further comment." Despite his statement, the reporters kept throwing questions at them, Stafford as vocal as the rest. Travis abstained, loping back to the car instead. "It's important to know when to advance and when to retreat," he'd once told me. This was plainly not the time to antagonize the detective. He wasn't free to say anything more.

"I can take you home before I head back to the station for the evening news," he said, spinning the wheel in a tight U-turn. Ten minutes passed before I surfaced from my thoughts. Ten minutes without a word from Travis. "Stafford didn't seem thrilled to see you," I said to break the silence.

"He's hungry and he sees me as easy prey. That's why I had to get down there. I'm becoming a household name in the immediate viewing area, but I'm still building my brand." So he was worried about his career. Boy, could I be dense sometimes! Although he'd never mentioned his career concerns to me, he was a man and men aren't big on talking about those things. Especially when they're trying to impress a woman. I may not be Tilly, but I should have realized what was going on. "You're definitely a household name in *my* house," I said to tease him into a lighter mood.

He gave me a wink. "You're biased, because you get perks. It would be exhausting to try to promote myself that way. Maybe if I were younger…"

"Don't even think about it," I said. The air in the car already felt lighter and easier to breathe. "I knew the dead guy," I said, causing Travis to look at me in surprise. "I guess *knew* is stretching the definition. It was more like everyone around here knew about him. His hobby was setting fires."

"You're kidding—an arsonist? Did he ever do time?" Travis asked.

"From what I remember, he got off once or twice. But then he set a fire that killed a man. Even then I don't recall him being gone for very long. All the kids at school called him Hermit Henry and made up horror stories about him."

"Assuming his death is part of the same string of murders we're investigating, it's awfully soon after Ryan was killed," Travis said. "Maybe the killer knows we're on his trail and he's feeling pressed for time. That could mean he has a specific agenda to get through."

"And up until Henry, all the deaths were different," I pointed out. "This is the second stabbing. It seems like the killer didn't take the time to plan this murder properly."

"I think you're right," Travis said. "He's rushing to finish his mission, whatever it is. Maybe he'll get sloppy and start making mistakes."

"Unfortunately it's also brought the police back into the investigation. They brushed off Ryan's death as accidental, but they can't do that with a stabbing."

"Hey, they aren't cherries if they don't have pits," Travis said dryly.

I laughed. "I never heard that one before."

"That's because I made it up. In my line of work, you have to be good on your feet."

Travis deposited me at my shop a few hours before closing time. I didn't expect to see Sashkatu on his ledge, snoring away. I hadn't asked my aunt to go to my house and bring him along, because I was concerned that he'd give her a hard time. He was always moody when I left him home and he hates being in a car. But Tilly being Tilly, she wouldn't consider it optional.

I found her behind the counter, chatting with a local acquaintance who'd never stopped in before. The middle-aged woman was holding one of our large totes with her purchases. Tilly was a great sales lady. It was the rare person who could resist her open, embracing personality. She could chat a bald man into buying shampoo for dyed hair. Not that she would, unless he really deserved some comeuppance.

Her latest conquest thanked her for all her help, nodded at me and left the shop with a bounce to her step. "There were two other customers," Tilly said, coming out from behind the counter. "And they bought even more." She always sounded amazed by her own sales prowess.

I hugged her and sent her home to rest her feet. After hours of baking and covering my shop, she had to be suffering. "Not to worry," she said, "I'll have Merlin give me one of his magickal foot rubs." I let her go without asking for more details. Some things are better left unsaid.

In the hours that remained, only one more person came in. He was big and broad shouldered, wearing a battered leather jacket open over a T-shirt with a skull motif. Tattoos peeked out of both sleeves of his jacket and from the neck of his tee. He was wearing jeans and combat boots and carrying a biker's helmet under his left arm. His hair was spiked and the stubble on his cheeks had the look of a permanent two-day growth. Tilly referred to men like him as *biker dudes*.

"How you doin'?" he asked before I could greet him.

"I'm well, thanks. How are you?"

"Good, good," he said, nodding like a bobble-head doll as he gave the shop the once over. He turned back to me. "I was just passing through, you know? And the name of your shop hooked me in."

"Are you interested in magick?" I asked him.

"If you're talkin' magic like in magic shows, nah, except for when I was kid. Now if there was such a thing as *real* magick, sure—I'd be all over it, who wouldn't be?"

I laughed. "True enough."

"So what is it you have goin' on here exactly?" he asked as he started browsing down the first aisle.

I raised my voice so he could hear me. "Natural products for what ails you, beauty aids for the skin and hair, candles for aroma therapy…"

He exited the aisle at the other end and instead of going down the next one, he headed back to me, clearly not interested enough to finish his self-tour. "It's quirky, cute," he said, words that sounded odd coming from a biker dude's mouth.

He shifted the helmet from his left arm to his right like he was settling in for a while. "New Camel's definitely small-town America. I'll bet you know every soul and every rumor makin' the rounds."

If I'd been a dog, my ears would have pricked. For someone just passing through, someone who'd walked into my shop on a whim, why was he so interested in my acquaintances? It might be idle conversation, but I was investigating a potential string of murders and I couldn't afford to dismiss any offhand remark by a stranger. "You'd be surprised," I said, morphing out of casual shopkeeper mode and into wary investigator in a split second. "My shop and this whole town are geared to the tourist trade. I do know many of the locals, but certainly not all of them. And if you're talking about Watkins Glen, I probably know less than thirty percent of the residents there. Are you from a big city like New York?" Two can play the question game.

"I travel a lot," he said, his eyes flitting around me for someplace to land other than my face. He spotted Sashkatu on the window ledge and grinned, showing off perfect white teeth. A man of the highways and byways who flossed and brushed regularly. "Cool detail, the cat," he said. "What do they call the cats that help witches?"

"I think you mean 'familiars.'"

"Yeah, that's it." He picked up a candle from one of the little display tables near the counter, turned it over, sniffed it, and put it back down. "I stopped in Watkins Glen to grab a burger for lunch. Everyone was talkin' about the guy who was found dead in his mobile home. I heard some folks say he deserved whatever he got. Guess he wasn't liked much."

I shrugged. "I wouldn't know."

"You don't expect to hear stuff like that up here. In a city, yeah, but here in quiet-ville?"

"There are bad people everywhere. For all we know, the killer was just some guy passing through," I said pointedly. He looked me squarely in the eye, and I had a smile all ready for him.

"A waitress was makin' a wager with the guy at the next table," he continued after a moment. "She bet the 'Wilde girl' in New Camel would catch the killer before the cops again. You know who that is?"

"I'm Kailyn Wilde," I said, pretty sure he already knew that, since he was standing in my shop.

"You really that good at findin' criminal types?"

I shrugged. "People like to exaggerate. I've probably just been lucky. Right time, right place, you know." If he was involved in crime, murder specifically, there was no sense in giving him reason to eliminate me first.

"Nah, I'm mostly in the wrong place at the worst time," he said chuckling at his own wit. He glanced at his watch. "I gotta hit the road. Good talkin' to you, Miss Wilde. You stay safe."

"I intend to," I said. Over the years, my family and I had dealt with every sort of person, but not one of them had left me feeling as unsettled as this guy. I breathed a whole lot easier after he walked out and I heard the rumble of his motorcycle fade into the distance.

Chapter 18

The next day, before going to my shop, I stopped at the Dorothy Tippin Library. It was located one block off Main Street in the old Dutch Colonial Dorothy had bequeathed to the town for that purpose back in the 1950s. According to my grandmother, when the library was named after its patron, there wasn't a single objection, which in our town was akin to a small miracle. Having been a woman of insight as well as foresight, my grandmother's words, the bequest included funds for converting the house into a library. On the first floor, walls were removed to create a large open area with ample room for shelving units and a circulation desk. In more recent years a bank of computers was also installed. The second floor was off limits to anyone but staff. It held a small kitchen area and additional storage to accommodate the overflow of materials from the first floor.

I went directly to the circulation desk where Donna De Marco was working. When I was in middle school, I'd volunteered at the library over a couple of summers and we'd developed a nice rapport. "Kailyn!" she said, coming out from behind the desk to embrace me. "One of the wonderful folks I don't see as much, since computers have taken over the world."

"Guilty," I said, sheepishly. "Life gets busy and we forget simple pleasures."

She smiled. "Like the smell of old books. You used to love camping out in the stacks and searching for what you called 'treasure.'"

The memory glowed in my mind. The slightly musty smell could instantly whisk me back to my childhood in the way an old song could. "Whenever I found a book I hadn't read from one of my favorite mystery series, it did feel like I'd discovered a treasure."

"I know exactly what you mean," she said. "But I'm sure you didn't stop in just to chat about the past. How can I help you today?"

"I'm actually here to try to help you if I can."

Her forehead wrinkled and for the first time I noticed she was no longer the young woman of my childhood. "That sounds cryptic," she said. "I guess you're still a fan of mysteries."

I laughed. "Some things never change." I told her about my eccentric cousin, Merlin. I'd repeated the story so often that it was beginning to feel like the truth. "Would you know if he booked the library for a meeting on Sunday?"

"Not as far as I know, but he might have talked to Abigail. Let me check the computer to be sure." She went behind the desk and tapped at the computer keys for several seconds. She looked up, shaking her head. "No one's reserved the library for anything on Sunday."

It was too soon for a sigh of relief. "It's possible he thinks he can just show up, with half the town in tow."

"I'm afraid you've lost me," she said. I explained about Merlin parading around with his sign. "You're kidding. I saw him that day, but I didn't know who he was and I definitely didn't see the back of his sign."

"I'll do my best to shut him down, but I wanted you to be aware, just in case."

She chuckled. "Well, if nothing else, it will shake things up a bit around here." I was reminded of one of the reasons I loved her—she was unflappable, the exact opposite of the prim, tight-lipped head librarian who'd preceded her.

"If he out-maneuvers me and walks in here, I'd really appreciate it if you could hold off calling the police, until I have a chance to wrangle him myself."

"I'll do what I can," she said, "but with cell phones these days, any patron in the library can call 9-1-1."

And there was my challenge in a nutshell: keeping a famous sorcerer from the Middle Ages a secret in the Age of Technology.

Back in my shop, I had just enough time to make a phone call before opening. Since the day Lolly mentioned Caleb Winston, I'd wanted to speak to him. I had questions only he might be able to answer and my window for asking them was getting shorter by the day. I looked online and found the town historian listed along with the other town officials. Next to the names, there were extensions to use after you reached Town Hall. Next to Caleb Winston's name was an entirely different number with the notation that it was his home phone. At his advanced age, and with no progeny to take over from him, he was clearly hanging in there for as long as he was able. I couldn't afford to keep putting off my call.

A woman with the lilt of the Caribbean in her voice bid me a cheerful *hello.* I introduced myself and asked if she was Louise. She said she most surely was and what could she do for me?

"I wonder if Mr. Winston is able to speak to me for a few minutes. I have a couple of questions regarding New Camel's history."

"I don't see why not," Louise said. "He's feeling pretty chipper this morning, don't you know." She asked me to hold on. A good three minutes went by before I heard Caleb's voice. It was frail and thin as if all the years of talking had worn away his vocal chords.

"Louise tells me you have questions," he said. "Let's hope I still have some answers."

"Thank you, Mr. Winston. I appreciate the opportunity to speak to you."

"You'd better get on with it—I could go at any time," he said, causing himself a brief fit of laughing and wheezing. I didn't know whether or not to laugh along with him. Gallows humor is tricky. I decided to skip over the problem by posing my first question.

"Mr. Winston, is it true that New Camel wasn't always the name of this town?"

"Quite right. The original name was New Camelot." I wasn't surprised to hear that Merlin's research was correct. From the moment he'd first told us, it had felt right to both Tilly and me.

"Do you know when it was shortened to New Camel?" I asked. "And why?"

"Well, it wasn't long after the Salem witch trials. This town was still in its infancy—not much of a town at all. There was your family's magick shop, a general store, and a small church with a fire and brimstone preacher due to take over the pulpit. One morning, in advance of his arrival, the town awoke to a new name. Overnight the last two letters of Camelot had disappeared from every sign, map, and document," he said with a dramatic flourish to his words that brought goose bumps to my arms. "To this day, no one knows how that was accomplished. Unless perhaps *you* can shed some light on it, Miss Wilde?" Despite his age, he was as canny as a younger man.

"I'm afraid not," I said, "that's why I came to you looking for answers." I thanked him and wished him well. When Louise returned to the phone, I asked her what sweets they liked best. Without hesitation she said they both coveted Lolly's fudge, especially the dark chocolate peppermint. I told her to expect a package from Lolly's with my thanks.

As soon as there was a lull in business, I scooted over to Tea and Empathy. Tilly was cleaning up from her last tea of the day. Merlin was helping, as usual, by consuming the leftovers so there was less to be put away.

"I had an interesting talk with Caleb Winston, the town historian," I said. "Come sit a minute, both of you, this is important." When we were clustered around one of the small tea tables, I repeated the story Caleb had told me.

"Aha!" Merlin said, slapping the table for emphasis. "So it would seem I am vindicated!"

"Yes, but to be fair, Tilly and I never doubted you. We were simply trying to keep you and your situation out of the news." Tilly nodded vigorously, her red curls dancing in agreement.

"Then it is up to *you* to spread the word," he said. "*You* must bear the standard and remedy the error."

"We don't have the right," I said.

Merlin opened his mouth to object, but Tilly told him to *shush*. "Give her a chance to explain, old man."

"It seems our ancestors changed the name of the town to protect themselves and their descendants from persecution. You might think we live in a different sort of world now, but hatred is still very much alive. We need to respect the wisdom of our ancestors. New Camel stays New Camel. Within the family, we'll pass the truth on to future generations. It will remain our secret."

"It seems I need to cancel my speech at the library," Merlin said with a sigh. "And I was so looking forward to the brownies Tilly was going to bake for the occasion."

"What brownies?" she asked. "You never said a word about it to me."

"I was waiting for the right time, dear lady. But as it happens, brownies would also go a long way to easing the pain of my disappointment."

Chapter 19

"Not interested," Austin Stubbs said after I introduced myself and explained the reason for my call. Not five minutes earlier, I'd congratulated myself on how easy he'd been to find. He still lived in Burdett, in the house where he and his wife had raised their son, Axel, only to lose him at the age of twenty-four. I wasn't surprised that his father refused my request. He wasn't looking for justice, because he was satisfied that he knew the reason for Axel's demise. But I kept coming back to Ryan's death. Knowing it was not an accident, I couldn't dismiss the possibility that Axel's death might not be as clear cut as it seemed either.

I decided it might be worth a trip up to Burdett to try to talk to Stubbs in person. The only problem was that I couldn't give up another day's business. It would have to wait until my aunt was free and willing to cover for me again. I worried that I expected too much of her, but since Morgana and Bronwen were no longer able to pitch in, I didn't have much choice. My ever-ready conscience balked, reminding me that I could solve the problem easily enough by sticking to my day job and leaving crime to the police and Travis. But being a shopkeeper didn't get my adrenalin flowing the way pursuing a killer did. Had my family still been intact, I would have had time off to pursue other interests. But with no one else to share the work, it was me, twenty-four seven. My conscience mocked me. *Poor Dear, being a sorcerer is so tedious and unfulfilling. And teleportation? How humdrum. How can you be expected to cope?* My conscience was sounding a lot like my mother. Too much like her. I spun around and found myself face to face with a little cloud that was pink with satisfaction.

"Mom! How could you?"

"Someone had to," she said reasonably. "I just popped into your head for a moment to say what needed saying."

"You have no right to…to trespass in my mind like that. I deserve some privacy, some respect." I didn't even know it was something she could do, from the other side of the veil no less. "How would you feel if Bronwen intruded in your head that way?"

"You're right—I apologize. It won't ever happen again."

She sounded properly chastened and a little hurt. In any case, I would have to take her at her word. As far as I knew there was no council or board that handled problems between the world of the living and that of the reluctant dead.

"I'll leave you to wallow in your misery," my mother said. She vanished, but not before I heard her grumble, "Plenty of children would be grateful to have their mothers visit from beyond the grave."

"That would depend on their mothers," I grumbled back, in case she was still listening. I spent the rest of the morning in a foul mood. Fortunately Sashkatu was astute enough to understand he didn't get to be the grouch for a while. Whenever I sat down, he climbed into my lap. I petted, he purred, and by lunchtime I was back on an even keel and he was sunning on his window ledge.

I'd been craving pizza for the past few days, so I put the clock in the window to let customers know I'd be back in ten minutes. Racing out the door to buy a slice, I collided with Elise who was coming in with a small pizza box. We fumbled it between us for a few very long seconds before she had it once again firmly in hand.

"Is today a school holiday I don't know about?" I asked as we both sloughed off our coats and tossed them onto the chair.

"It's administrative conference day."

I took a slice out of the box, inhaling the intoxicating aroma. "Works for me," I said, hopping up on the counter on one side of the box. "You brought the pizza, so the floor is yours. How are you and the boys doing?"

Elise planted herself on the other side. "They're doing okay. But me—I don't know. I'm just tired. Tired and bored. I don't miss the cheating louse I was married to, but I feel…I don't know…at odds with myself."

"Do you think you're ready to try to meet someone?" She shook her head. "Then maybe you just need a change of pace," I said, "a little adventure."

"What did you have in mind? Taking into account that I have two kids and a job."

"A little detective work for a day. I have to go to Burdett and try to dig up some information from the local citizenry there. I'd love the company, and you can take your investigative skills out for a whirl. You're always complaining we don't spend enough time together anymore."

"Hold it. Stop," Elise said.

I was taken aback. "Okay, it was just a suggestion."

She started laughing. "No, I meant stop trying to convince me. You had me at 'detective work.'"

"Do you have any more of those conference days?"

"No, but I think I'm coming down with a bad cold." She sniffled. "There's so much going around at school. It's a breeding ground for every imaginable bug."

"That works," I said. "I promise not to tell your kids about the bad example you're setting."

Chapter 20

Aunt Tilly and I worked out a mutually beneficial deal that soothed my conscience. She would run my shop for the day, and I would take Merlin off her hands for the two busy days she had coming up. In my opinion, she got the sweeter end of the deal.

I picked up Elise and we headed to Watkins Glen. From there it was only a few miles northeast to the tiny village of Burdett. With a population of less than 400, it was smaller than New Camel. I'd been there several times over the years with family, friends, or on school outings. It was a pretty area, with Seneca Lake and its rocky bluffs to the west and rolling farmland to the east. Most of the people were farmers. A small percentage owned the businesses that included a bicycle shop, a small variety store that sold groceries as well as greeting cards, newspapers and lottery tickets, and a mom and pop pharmacy that had escaped the attention of the big chains. There was also a bed and breakfast, a bakery/gelato shop, and a few low-end restaurants. In the winter, some of the older shopkeepers closed up and headed to Florida. In spring, Burdett came back to life along with its flowers and trees.

We were fortunate that the main roads were clear of ice and snow. They could just as easily have been treacherous. The last snowfall had been followed by moderate temperatures, but the cold was slated to return after sunset, reasserting itself with a vengeance. Anything still wet would quickly freeze over. So we were aiming to be home before dark.

We pulled into Burdett and rode down Main Street in search of coffee. The only possibility seemed to be a little café. There was no problem parking. I turned into a spot directly in front of the door. The frame building was old, but well-maintained inside and out. The restaurant offered mostly tables with chairs, though there were a few booths in the back. Two elderly women occupied one of them, and what looked like a mother, grandmother, and two young kids were arranged around one of the tables. I caught one of the little boys poking his brother in the ribs, which led to some impressive high-decibel wailing.

We walked up to the counter to order two coffees and a cheese Danish to split. The woman behind the counter was sixty or close to it, a hard-earned sixty. Aside from a short order cook we could hear rattling around in the kitchen, she appeared to be the only one working there, waitress, busgirl, and cashier rolled into one. The plastic tag pinned to her white blouse said her name was Enid. You could tell she was an old hand at her job, no wasted motions. She had our order ready in under three minutes, the Danish cut in half, covered with wax paper, and in individual bags. We fixed the coffee to our liking at a station near the door and were about to leave when Elise nudged me with her elbow. "Why don't we start with her?"

A good question. A better question was why hadn't I thought of that? We walked back to the counter. Enid looked up from emptying the dregs of one catsup bottle into another. "Did you want something else girls?"

"A few minutes of your time, if you can spare them," I said. "We're looking into a number of deaths in the county. One of them was in Burdett back in 2014. We were hoping you might be able to help us out with some information."

"You cops or something?" she asked, narrowing her eyes as if to better judge us.

"No, we're not connected to the police in any way," I assured her. I didn't want it to get back to Duggan that we were passing ourselves off as cops. "I guess we're what you'd call amateur sleuths."

"You're kidding," she said, her eyes lighting up. "Like in the cozies I read?"

"Yes, I suppose so."

She looked delighted. "I'd be rightly pleased to help in any way I can. It's not like these catsup bottles will report me for taking a break." She came around the counter, wiping her hands on the apron around her waist, and ushered us to a table in the corner, from which she could keep tabs on her customers' needs while we talked. "You've got me intrigued. Who was this person you're interested in?"

"Axel Stubbs."

Her forehead bunched. "Axel Stubbs? You may be wasting your time. Everyone knows he died of a drug overdose. Of course some folks think it was," she lowered her voice to a whisper and gave a quick look around as if to make sure no one else would hear her, "suicide. Why are you two interested in an open and shut case like his?"

"We're not at liberty to say at this point," Elise replied, breaking her silence. I'd told her on the trip up there that I wanted her to dive right in with questions and observations, that I valued her input. For a little while, I thought I might have to resort to kicking her under the table to encourage her participation.

"Did you know Axel Stubbs or his family personally?" I asked.

Enid laughed. "If you live in a town as small as Burdett and you work in a restaurant for over thirty years, you're gonna know everyone. I'm not saying you're bosom buddies with everyone, mind you. There are different levels of 'knowing' a person, if you take my meaning." I nodded and let her continue. Travis taught me that interrupting a narrative was a good way to forfeit information.

"Axel Stubbs was a handful straight outta the womb," she continued. "Colicky, moody, barely slept, but Valerie doted on him in spite of it. I never saw a woman more devoted to her child."

"What was he like growing up?" Elise asked.

"Not much different, from all accounts. He was argumentative, sassed his teachers, was suspended more than once, if memory serves. Every incident chipped away at Valerie's heart. When she died of a massive coronary at forty, no one in these parts was surprised. Axel took it hard, crawled inside himself. Could be he blamed himself for her death. The word around here was that his dad, Austin, blamed him too. I know whenever I saw the two of them in town they were either arguing or not speaking to each other. I guess Austin couldn't stand it anymore, because he finally took his son to a psychiatrist. Axel was diagnosed with clinical depression and some other things I don't recall. He was put on medication and even spent a short while in the mental ward in Schuyler Hospital over in Montour Falls. I heard through the grapevine that he was somewhat better after that. Not that it turned him into the all-American boy next door, mind you. But he squeaked by and somehow graduated high school. I always wondered if it was on account of the teachers wanting to get him and his influence out of the building. He left town for a time and supposedly started running with a bad crowd. He wasn't back in Burdett long, before getting himself arrested.

"What was he charged with?" I asked.

She took a moment to think about it. "Selling drugs, if memory serves."

"He must have done time for that," Elise said.

"You would think, but it was a first offense, and his attorney played on the jury's sympathies. Axel was a poor lost kid after his mother died. If he was sent to prison, he'd come out a hardened criminal. The judge sentenced him to community service and psychological counseling."

"What happened after that?" I asked.

"He started working part-time over at Willy's Wheels, that's the bike shop. Things seemed okay for a little while, but then I started hearing that he'd fallen off the wagon and was going back to his old ways. I'm no detective, girls, but it seems to me you wouldn't be asking these questions unless you think someone had a hand in Axel's death. Am I right?"

"It's a possibility we're exploring," I said, "but I want to be clear that we have no evidence one way or the other. At this point it's pure speculation, and we don't want to be the cause of rumors flying." Rather than ask her outright not to gossip about our conversation, I put the onus on Elise and me, hoping Enid would be astute enough to understand what I meant.

"Gotcha," she said, putting both palms on the table to lever herself out of the chair. She nodded at the elderly woman who was waving from the back booth. "'Scuse me, girls, I need to drop a check for them." Since we had to be going anyway, we thanked her for the help and left her a nice tip.

Chapter 21

We decided to talk to some of the other merchants, before starting the trek from farm to farm. First up, Willy's Wheels. I drove down two blocks and parked in front of the shop. But instead of getting right out, Elise and I looked at each other and without exchanging a word, reached for the bags with the Danish. We'd sipped our coffees while we were talking to Enid, but it didn't seem polite to stuff our mouths with Danish even though we had bought it there. From the first bite it was clearly a perfect balance of butter, sugar, and creamy cheese filling.

"Maybe we should have bought two instead of sharing," I said, licking the crumbs from my fingers.

"No way, you promised to stay strong for me, now that I've reached the age when my metabolism isn't as forgiving as yours."

"Sorry. It was so good I lost my head. You know we can't ever tell Tilly about this little piece of baked heaven."

"I disagree," she said. "It wouldn't be the worst thing if she came up here and wangled the recipe out of Enid. That way we could have one every now and then without having to drive up here."

"Wouldn't it be more efficient if we brought one home for her to try?"

"Forget it. You know very well that the second it's in the car, we'll both be pulling pieces from it."

I sighed. "I wish I could come up with a spell to suppress the desire for carbs." Bronwen and Morgana had spent most of their adult life trying to concoct such a spell, without success. What made me think I could succeed where they had failed? The universe had its rules and many of them were immutable. Why not messing with carbs was one of them, I had no idea.

"Ready to tackle Willy?" Elise asked.

"I would have been more ready after a whole Danish," I murmured, expecting a friendly punch in my arm. Elise did not disappoint.

We found Willy behind the counter at the back of the store. When we walked in, we needed a moment to get our bearings. There were bikes everywhere, suspended from the ceiling, mounted to the walls, and occupying nearly every inch of floor space. There was no clear path through the maze to the counter. It reminded me of the layout of department stores. To get from point A to point B, you had to walk between and around a lot of other merchandise. It was a shameless ploy to entice you into buying items you hadn't come for. Personally, it just irritated me, especially if I was in a hurry.

"How may I help you today?" Willy asked when we finally made our way to him through the metallic forest. He was short and thin. If he were a woman, he'd be described as petite. He had a great smile and perfect teeth, although they were blue-ish in the florescent light. He'd clearly overdone the whitening agents in an effort to play up his best feature.

"Hi," I said. "We're not actually here for a bicycle." No need to get his hopes up about making a sale. His smile drooped at the corners. "We were told Axel Stubbs worked here part-time before his passing, and we're wondering if you'd tell us a bit about him from your perspective as his boss."

"Mind if I ask why the interest three years after his death?" His expression had changed from "pleased to meet you" into "what are you up to?"

I gave him my standard reply. He chewed on that for a minute before agreeing to talk to us. I couldn't tell if his decision was based on the merit of my words or old-fashioned boredom.

He stayed on his side of the counter; we stayed on ours as if we were neighbors chatting over a fence. "Sorry I can't offer you seats," he said with no apparent regret, "but space here is at a premium and the merchandise always wins." We assured him we understood. "So what is it you want to know?"

Elise jumped right in. "For starters, why did you take him on after his conviction?"

"I believe in giving a guy a chance," he said. "It's not like Axel was a murderous thug. I liked the idea of helping him to avoid becoming one. Thought of it as a good deed. If we all did more good deeds, the world would be a nicer place, right?"

"I like the way you think," I said.

"How was Axel as an employee?" Elise asked.

He shrugged. "I didn't have any complaints. Sure, when things were slow and he'd done everything I expected of him, he'd sit and play with his phone. He wasn't what you'd call a 'self-starter.' I hear that's often the reality in today's world. But he didn't take any sick days. He was polite enough to the customers and pretty talented at bike repairs. I missed his help the last couple of years."

Elise and I exchanged looks, both of us clearly thinking that bicycle shop Axel wasn't the same Axel of the coroner's report and rumor mill. "Did he ever appear to be strung out on drugs or alcohol?" I asked.

"He'd have a beer with lunch now and then. I would too for that matter. Some days he seemed sharper than others and he could be moody, but I never saw him impaired, if that's what you mean." I wasn't sure what I meant anymore. Who was the real Axel Stubbs?

After leaving Willy of the blue smile, we spent the next couple of hours interviewing other shopkeepers and people at some of the local farms. Their take on Axel was a lot like Enid's. Maybe you had to work closely with Axel to appreciate him. Or maybe if you were the school rebel, it made sense to folks that you'd eventually die an ignominious death. It fit their *Zeitgeist.* They could point to Axel and warn their kids not to be wise-asses and troublemakers or they'd wind up dead like him.

On the way out of Burdett, we came to the turnoff for the Stubbs's farm. Elise knew I wanted to try speaking to him in person. "This is it. What do you think?"

"Nothing ventured, nothing gained," she said. "Wow, I'm really beginning to sound like my mother." We drove up to the white, two story house that was clearly in need of some TLC. The peeling paint made it appear to be shedding its skin like a snake. One of the green shutters on an upstairs window was missing and another was hanging by a nail. We rang the bell. Austin Stubbs opened the door. I introduced myself and he slammed it shut in our faces. The whole encounter took ten seconds—max.

Walking back to the car, I glanced into the backyard, which was mostly dirt and would have benefitted greatly from a camouflaging layer of snow. A big tire that must have come from a tractor was leaning against a tree trunk. Planted nearby was the aluminum skeleton of a clothes line. With no string left on which to hang anything, it was more like a modern sculpture of hard times than a useful device. Rounding out the attractions was a tarpaulin-covered motorcycle, part of its tires visible.

Before heading home, we stopped on the outskirts of town for a couple of quick burgers. "Is it possible Willy isn't a great judge of character and behavior?" Elise asked when we were seated at a table in the corner. "Maybe Axel used those deficits to his advantage."

I took a bite of my burger and my appetite roared back to life. After the Danish, I'd been too engrossed in our mission to realize how hungry I was. "Are you thinking what I'm thinking?" I asked after swallowing.

"That the killer knew Axel's history, figured an overdose wouldn't seem out of character, and helped him get there?"

I nodded, took another bite, and washed it down with some Coke. Elise was eating her French fries like a chain smoker, clearly caught up in the excitement of trying to solve the mystery. "How far do you think the police investigation went after hearing the coroner's report?" she asked between fries.

"Not far enough would be my guess. I'd love to know if they ever questioned Austin and made him account for his time during the hours preceding his son's death."

"There must be *some* way to find out," Elise said, locking eyes on me. I laughed. "Is that supposed to be a subtle hint?"

Elise swallowed her first bite of burger. "Who said anything about subtle?"

I rolled the idea around in my head. Stealing information fell into a very gray area of magick. The reason for taking the information had to be above reproach. Satisfying my curiosity didn't cut it. But if said information could prevent more deaths, the gray was more like dingy white. First I'd have to determine who was likely to hold the answers I needed, and then I'd have to propose the idea to Tilly. But I didn't want her to get into trouble with our progenitors, or more importantly, with higher powers. I explained all this to Elise in general terms while we finished eating.

Not for the first time since my mother and grandmother's passing, I missed their wise counsel. Unfortunately I had no way to summon them. I could only hope they dropped by for a visit soon.

"I'm starting to understand why you love these investigations," Elise mumbled around a mouthful of burger. She paused to drink her soda. "My brain is fired up. I swear I can hear the thoughts pinging from neuron to neuron like a jazzed-up game of pinball."

"I know, but the other half of the job involves confronting the bad guys. That can get scary fast. You're a single parent with two kids to think about, whereas I'm unfettered and have magick at my disposal." Not entirely true. I couldn't leave Tilly adrift with Merlin for the rest of her days and my magick was hardly fool proof.

"Thanks for the reality check," Elise said. "But I'd love to be included in the brainstorming."

We made good time on the drive home. I dropped Elise at her house with a promise to keep her posted. "Before I forget," she said, with one foot already out of the car, "I decided to go up to my sister's for Christmas, but I want to have Thanksgiving here with you and your family. Please pass my invitation on to Tilly and Merlin."

"Are you sure you know what you're signing up for?" I asked wryly.

"It'll be great. And don't forget to invite Travis."

Chapter 22

I found Tilly in the customer chair, eyes closed, rhythmically petting Sashkatu, who was curled up in her lap. They looked so peaceful I hated to disturb them. But before I could, I heard a duck quacking. It seemed to be coming from Tilly's shop. At first, I thought it was on the small TV she kept there to amuse Merlin, but there was no denying that the sound was coming closer. I thought I heard webbed feet. Wet webbed feet squishing on the floor. I didn't have long to puzzle it out, because a duck walked into view from the hallway to the connecting door. It was a typical white domestic duck with an orange bill and feet. Maybe Tilly was duck-sitting for a friend. It wouldn't be the first time she'd cared for a friend's pet. An iguana, a mouse, a llama and a pony were the ones that immediately came to mind.

The duck waddled toward me, dripping water from its lower feathers and leaving wet duck prints on the hardwood. Tilly issued a deep sigh before opening her eyes, as if she didn't want to deal with the reality that awaited her. Sashki leaped to attention, back arched, hissing in a way I rarely heard. He left Tilly's lap for the window ledge and gave me a piercing look that clearly said, "You own this establishment—do something!"

The duck stopped a few feet away and eyed me hard with one of its beady brown eyes. The other one was fixed on Tilly. "A friend's duck you're watching?" I asked hopefully.

"Oh how I'd love to say 'yes,'" she replied.

"I'm not going to like the truth, am I?"

She shook her head. "Perhaps you should look at it this way—in ten years, we'll remember this and have a good laugh."

I leaned back against the counter as ready as I would ever be. "I'm listening."

"Well the best I can figure it, Merlin wanted duck for lunch. When he tried to conjure up the dish, he must have messed up the spell. This is the result."

"Is he an actual duck or does he just look like a duck to the world?" The wizard was capable of making anyone or anything appear to be different, but he could also transmute any living being into another form. We'd seen him do it a few months ago. Thankfully he'd had no problem then and had easily reversed the spell as well.

"I think he transmuted into a duck and I have no idea how to return him to his human form." She sounded hopeless.

"What about the spell to reverse spells. The one Bronwen gave me when Merlin summoned all the woodland creatures?"

"That was the first thing I tried."

I didn't say so, but I was thinking she might not have remembered it precisely enough. "I may as well give it a try too," I said. "The way things have been going lately, maybe something as silly as the timbre of my voice will make the difference."

A spell was cast,
Now make it past.
Remove it here
And everywhere.

I repeated it ten times. Nothing changed. Merlin was still very much a duck. Was our magick so strangely warped that we couldn't even depend on a spell from one usage to the next? It was a scary thought. But rescuing Merlin was a more immediate issue.

Tilly's brow knotted for a moment; then she brightened. "The only thing I remember him saying was a number, but for all I know it was a magickal bar code for duck. Although the man drives me crazy at times, I want him back as he was."

"I know you do, Aunt Tilly. We're going to figure this out, I promise." I was awfully free with my promises. What if I couldn't figure it out? No! I chastised myself. No more negativity!

Bronwen always said, "What you send out into the universe is what comes back to you. Raise your thoughts to a higher level and believe in the light." Thinking of her words lifted my spirit. Even if I couldn't figure out the right spell to restore Merlin to himself and even if I wasn't highly enough born for it to work, there was always the chance that he'd set a time for the spell to lapse.

"You need to create a reversal spell of your own," Tilly declared with absolute certainty. "Morgana was incredibly talented at creating spells, and you are her daughter. You must at least make the effort or you will never know."

My aunt was right. I had to try. The Merlin-duck interrupted my thoughts by stomping his webbed feet up and down on the floor. I thought he was dancing, until I looked at his face. For a second, the sorcerer's countenance swam into focus beneath the surface of the duck's feathered one. As brief as it was, I could see Merlin's frustration and fear. "We're working on it," I shouted, enunciating each word in the hope that he would understand me, like a traveler expecting to be understood in a foreign land by speaking louder and more distinctly. Sashkatu opened one eyelid and sighed, no doubt to remind me there was no excuse for using an outside voice when you were inside where someone might be napping. "Stop complaining," I told him, "at least you get to nap."

Chapter 23

Tilly and I started the night at her house, poring over the ancient scrolls that were spread on the dining room table, in hopes of finding a spell to change the famous wizard back into human form. Although I was still intent upon fashioning one myself, I had no idea how long my creative juices would take to percolate. In any case, a backup spell would be welcome. Deciphering the archaic words was hard enough without the Merlin-duck pacing around the room, issuing an endless stream of strident squawks and quacks at often painful decibels.

In spite of our best intentions, dinner had only made his distress worse. We'd bought him the best duck food on the market and made ourselves omelets, because he wasn't overly fond of eggs. He dug into the mixture of cracked corn, oats, and Milo seed as if he was famished, but promptly spit it out. We offered him ice cream, although we worried it might hurt his duck digestion. He spit that out as well. The weird hybrid he was couldn't or wouldn't eat anything we gave him, until we tried grapes. It took him a while to make it through the first one, but he finally managed to break it up and swallow it. To make the process easier for him, we cut the grapes into pieces. He ate them as fast as we could supply them, polishing off the entire half pound Tilly had in her refrigerator. Once he seemed to have had his fill, I foolishly hoped he'd settle down and sleep. But food only served to refuel him. Without some peace and quiet, we were never going to make headway with the scrolls. I suggested locking him in the bathroom with a tub full of water to swim around in. There was silence for all of ten minutes. In the end, we left him in there to quack himself to sleep, while we drove over to my house.

By one in the morning, Tilly and I had both fallen asleep with our heads on the table. Tilly awoke first, needing a bathroom break, and hearing her moving around woke me. We didn't have much to show for the hours of eye-straining study of the scrolls. Who were we kidding? Even if the scrolls contained an antidote spell, we'd need Merlin to translate it for us. If nothing else, we were in good company. Morgana and Bronwen had never been able to make heads or tails of the archaic language and overwrought writing either.

Tilly didn't want to go home and take the chance that the Merlin-duck would hear her come in, so she spent the rest of the night in the room that used to be mine. I crawled into the cat-laden bed that had been my mother's and was now mine and fell asleep before I could turn off the lamp.

Travis called at 7 a.m., knowing I always set my alarm for that time. I was barely coherent.

"You okay?" he had to ask twice before I processed what he was saying.

I fought my way through the cobwebs in my brain and pushed myself up against the headboard. "Just tired, late night."

"Were you at least having fun?"

My pillow was beckoning with its come-hither softness, but I struggled to ignore it. "Merlin is a duck," I said bluntly. "Not much fun at all."

Travis was silent for a few moments as though trying to get his bearings. "Kailyn," he said finally, "I need you to wake up and talk sensibly. You're scaring me."

I shook my head, trying to rattle my brain awake. I explained as best I could about the wizard's latest disaster and our current lack of success in restoring him to his proper form.

"Whoa, that's awful. That's…I can't…I can't imagine," he stammered with a hint of laughter that he tried to mask by gruffly clearing his throat. "Kailyn, I'm really sorry." He was making a valiant effort to sound properly serious and concerned, but I could still hear the amusement bubbling just beneath his words. How could I be angry with him? If I weren't the one who had to rescue Merlin, I'd be rolling on the floor with laughter. Responsibility was a sobering task master. "Then I guess you'll be busy with that today," he said, sounding disappointed, once he had himself under control.

I had to admit, I felt perversely pleased about disappointing him. But I was equally glad to lift his spirits, no magick required. "Not necessarily," I said. "Tilly and I are stumped, so unless my mother or grandmother drops in with a solution… What were you going to ask me?"

"I called Judy McFee last night, and she said something in passing that could be our first solid lead in the case. She agreed to an interview later this morning."

"That's terrific," I said, buoyed by the prospect of useful information. "What was it? What did she say?"

"She asked if I wanted to hear about the time Ron got arrested, same as the other reporter who came to see her. Listen, I'm getting a call from the newsroom. We'll talk when I get there." I dragged myself out of bed, still feeling drugged. Tilly had brewed some tea to help us sleep last night. I'd have to ask her what she put in it. I didn't wake her. She was going to need all the energy she could stockpile to deal with the Merlin-duck, day two.

I was showered, dressed, and on my second cup of coffee when Travis arrived. I poured him a cup and we settled at the kitchen table. His eyes were as red as mine from lack of sleep, but he seemed wide awake. Finding a clear direction in the hunt for Ryan's killer had to be the reason.

"The other reporter Judy mentioned must have been Ryan," I prompted as Travis added cream to his coffee.

"And if McFee's arrest is what caught Ryan's interest, we may finally have a clear trail to follow."

"We already know Axel Stubbs was arrested," I said, "so you're thinking the other people on Ryan's list also had run-ins with the law."

"Yes, but let's not get ahead of ourselves. Are you up to coming along for the interview?"

"I could use a distraction. Maybe if I give my brain a rest from wizards and ducks, I'll have an epiphany about how to solve Merlin's crisis."

Travis glanced at his watch and jumped up. "We'd better get going." I pulled on my waterproof boots, a heavy parka, gloves, and a woolen hat and left Tilly a vague note telling her not to worry, which was a useless phrase in our family.

The forecast called for freezing rain, sleet and snow—not my favorite driving conditions. But I doubted that even a full-blown blizzard would have caused Travis to reschedule the meeting. I climbed into his current rental, an SUV that looked like the muscular older brother of mine. I was glad to see the shovel, ice scraper, and snow chains in the back seat. We were girded for anything Mother Nature might have in store.

After we'd been on the road for twenty minutes, it was obvious the weather conditions were deteriorating. Tiny ice pellets were pinging the windshield like the stingers of a thousand bees. I called my aunt and told her to go home while she still could.

The McFee residence was part of a cookie cutter development of split-level homes fifteen minutes east of Watkins Glen. Five of the seven houses on Judy's cul-de-sac were white, shutter color the most distinguishing feature between them. Judy's were red. I thought of red as a happy color, the color of love. But it could be argued that it was also the color of rage and bloodshed. Judy was solidly in the second camp. I felt it as soon as she opened the door. Anger was coming off her like a heavy mist, her own special fragrance. From what I could tell, Travis seemed completely unaware of it.

Judy invited us in with a minimum of pleasantries, as if she was having second thoughts about the interview. She led the way into the family room where an old black Lab with a gray muzzle slept under the skylight, probably wishing for the sun to warm him. His front legs twitched as if he was running in a dream.

Judy apologized for the chaos that her kids had left in their wake. "I stopped caring if the house isn't neat as a pin anymore." But if she truly no longer cared, she wouldn't have apologized. When Tilly gave up trying to lose the pounds that accompanied menopause and proclaimed that she no longer cared about it, she never mentioned it again. Tilly didn't do things by half-measure. "The schools are closed today due to the storm," Judy said. "At least when they're in school I get a chance to pick up after them."

"They're very quiet," I observed.

"That's because I shipped them off to the neighbors so we could speak freely. They've had enough trauma to deal with in their young lives. Please sit wherever you'd like."

Travis and I picked our way around abandoned Legos, Barbie dolls, Matchbox cars and a slew of toys I didn't recognize from my own childhood, before reaching a loveseat. Judy took the chair across from us, relocating a mini iPad to the end table. "Do you want to know what I told the other investigator?" she asked, getting right to the point.

"Yes, please," Travis said. He pulled out his trusty pad and pen. "Sometimes old school is just better," he'd told me the first time I saw him take notes that way. "Fits in my pocket better, doesn't need recharging, and can't be deleted by accident." Another reason for my mother and grandmother to love him.

"So," Judy said, "my dear, devoted husband woke up one day and decided he didn't want to go on living. He didn't take into account that he was the sole support of our family or that he was the one who'd insisted I stay home to raise the kids instead of working."

"This happened when you and your children were in the house?" I asked, trying to wrap my mind around the enormity of what she was saying.

Judy shook her head. "The kids and I were away visiting my sister overnight. When we came home the next morning, I knew something was wrong even before we went inside. Shadow was barking in the backyard. We never just left him outside barking, and we always put him in the house if no one was going to be home. About the same time, I realized Ron's car was idling in the garage. But when I looked, the garage door was closed. I told myself it couldn't be what I was thinking. But what else could it be? I told the kids to wait outside while I went into the house. I was shaking so badly I had trouble getting the key in the lock. I ran right to the door that leads into the garage. Ron was in the driver's seat, slumped over the steering wheel. I guess it didn't even occur to him that it might have been one of the children who found him that way."

"Was this in any way consistent with other behaviors he exhibited during the years you were together?" Travis asked

"No," she said. "I never knew him to be depressed or hopeless. Certainly never suicidal. He was an even keel kind of guy. That's what drew me to him. My own childhood could have been a case study in dysfunctional families. Ron showed me life could be good, enjoyable. I learned how to relax." For a moment I heard grief overtake her anger. She took a deep breath and tucked the emotions away. "What I don't understand is why you two and that other reporter are suddenly so interested in his death. It's not like he was some kind of saint or hero. Not long before he killed himself, he was arrested for drunk driving and leaving the scene of an accident. Thank goodness no one was badly injured, but he almost had to do time in prison. If it wasn't for his attorney, he probably would have."

"What was the attorney's name?" I asked.

"Sam Crawford." She turned to Travis. "On the phone you said you were working on a case that could clear up the mystery of Ron's suicide."

"I'm not in a position to talk too much about it yet," Travis said, "but I promise you, I will come back when our investigation is complete and tell you everything." He was using his official anchor voice, heavy on the gravitas. It was hard not to believe him when he spoke that way. Judy accepted his answer and asked if there was anything else we wanted to know. Travis handed her his card. "Give me a call if you think of anything else that could be relevant to your husband's passing." She thanked us, we thanked her, and we were out the door, slogging through several inches of ice, sleet, and snow.

Travis's steadying arm kept me from falling a couple of times before we made it into the sanctuary of his truck. The trip back to New Camel was slow-going. We inched along like a giant steel snail, which was just fine with me. Better slow than skidding off the road into a tree. The image of Ryan's car popped into my head, making me shudder. Travis noticed and raised the temperature in the car, but the cold from that image couldn't be banished by anything as simple as heat.

We were one of the few vehicles on the road, aside from the town plows and salt spreaders. The wind had picked up, driving the sleet into the windshield as if it had a grudge to satisfy. Visibility was down to a couple of feet. We heard one of the big plows scraping and growling, before it appeared beside us in the left lane. Despite the poor visibility, I knew we were approaching the place where the road narrowed to one lane. Between the blades of the windshield wipers I saw the sign warning drivers to merge. Travis dutifully slowed and hung back so he could swing into the left lane behind the plow. The plow slowed too. We were quickly running out of lane. Travis slowed again. The plow dropped its speed and kept pace with us. Travis laid on the horn. I didn't ask if he was thinking what I was thinking, because he was busy enough and I didn't want corroboration anyway. Why hadn't I insisted on taking my SUV? Granted it was smaller, but I'd cast wards around it as soon as I drove it home from the dealership. I was covered by the spell of protection too, but Travis wasn't. I didn't have the materials with me in order to properly place the wards. Maybe the words alone would afford him and his car some protection. My mind was racing. I needed the most general spell. What were the words? *With Earth and fire…no, no—With Earth and water, air and fire—that was it.*

With Earth and water, air and fire
Protect us from all who'd harm us.

The last part was off, but I couldn't remember how it should be. I repeated this version three times, praying it would help anyway.

"What's on my right?" Travis yelled over the noise of the storm and the plow.

"A ravine," I yelled back, "but I don't remember how steep it is here." The road was narrowing by the second. The side of the plow clipped our front fender and sent us spinning off. Travis wrestled with the wheel and kept us on the roadway, but we wound up facing in the wrong direction. If there were other cars on the road, they would have hit us head-on. The white-out blinded us. I tensed, expecting a crash, while Travis whipped the truck back around. The plow didn't get away unscathed. We'd heard it bang and scrape along the cement divider until it came to a stop. Before I could sigh with relief, the plow reversed and slammed into us with enough force to flip the SUV. Travis fought gravity, barely managing to keep us upright as we flew over the edge of the road and into the ravine.

Chapter 24

I awoke to Tilly's worried face hovering over me. "What happened?" I mumbled, trying to kickstart my memory. The last thing I recalled was climbing into Travis's truck for the trip back to New Camel. Yet there I was in my aunt's guest room. I tried to sit up, but the pain in my side quickly changed that plan. Tilly urged me to lie still.

"You were in an accident," she said, her voice fraught with emotion. "I blame myself. If I hadn't been asleep, I would never have let you go out on a day like today."

She seemed to forget that I was not known for following advice or demands, but at that moment I wasn't up to arguing the point. Besides, when Tilly was determined to be upset, you just had to let her ride it out.

"You suffered a concussion and you have two broken ribs from the airbag," she said. "Travis… Is he all right?" I asked, suddenly terrified that I'd lost him.

"He's fine. He's resting on the sofa-bed in the study. He suffered a concussion too, but beyond that he only has bumps and bruises, nothing that time can't heal. And Merlin and I can't speed up," she added. "I mean, *I* can't speed up."

"What about Sashkatu and the others?" I was worried they'd been forgotten in the aftermath of the accident, but I should have known better.

"Taken care of. All is well, although Sashki is nursing something of a snit. I'm sure you'll be forgiven when you get back home." I thought that was overly optimistic. It might take a salmon filet to mend his mood. I once blamed my mother for turning him into a spoiled cat-brat, but I was just as bad.

"Here's what I don't understand," Tilly said, "what were you and Travis thinking, driving around in such horrible conditions? On the TV, on the radio, they were telling everyone to stay home. The County Executive and mayor sent emails. I even got a robo-call about it: 'Stay home, stay safe. The plows can't do their job, if there are cars in the way!'"

Something in her words struck me as important, but I couldn't hook into it with my head throbbing like a bad tooth. I gave up trying. I'd remember when I was ready to or I wouldn't. Had I thought that or had Tilly said it? No matter. I let my eyelids fall closed, since that's what they were determined to do. I didn't have the energy to stop them.

When I woke the second time, my marbles didn't feel quite so scattered. I was starting to remember pieces of the missing time and specific questions were cropping up. I could hear my aunt puttering in the kitchen, talking to Merlin or maybe to Isenbale, because I didn't hear any quacking. I clenched my jaw against the pain from my broken ribs as I maneuvered myself up to sit against the tufted headboard. Tilly loved tufting. She claimed it made everything look richer and more elegant Anything in her home that could be tufted, was. I'd often thought Isenbale, with his luxurious coat, was lucky he hadn't fallen prey to her passion.

At that moment, Tilly came into the room, carrying a bed tray. "You look a little better," she said with an approving smile. She set the tray down carefully, so that its legs rested on either side of mine. The tray held a steaming mug of tea and a plate with a homemade English muffin that bore little resemblance to the store-bought variety. Seeing it there, all buttered and spread with apricot jam, my appetite perked up.

"The tea is a blend of Comfrey leaves to heal your ribs and Ginkgo Biloba to mend your brain," she said. I made a face, recalling the unpleasant brew from a childhood fall from a tree. "I don't care how it tastes," she added firmly. "Just drink it up."

I drank the tea, holding my breath to minimize the taste. As soon as I drained the cup, I dug into the buttery, sweet muffin. My aunt had also brought a little bowl with a sponge she'd soaked in the essential oils of sweet marjoram and sweet woodruff. She set the bowl beside me on the night stand. Smelling them was said to help heal the brain too. I much preferred the scent of the actual plants, but they weren't easy to find that time of the year. The woodruff smelled like newly mown hay, the marjoram like sweet herbs with a subtle undertone of camphor. A pleasant enough mixture.

"Can you stay a minute?" I asked Tilly, who'd come to take away the remains of my breakfast.

"At your service, my dear." She sat down on the edge of the bed near my knees, careful not to jostle me. "What can I do for you?"

"I need answers. My memory is returning and I have a head full of questions."

"I'll do my best."

"Who found Travis and me?"

"Paul Curtis. His shift had ended here and he was heading back home on that road. Along the way, he was keeping an eye out for anyone in trouble. As I heard it, he saw your truck's tail lights blinking in the snow at the bottom of the drop off. He found a place to pull off the road, called for an ambulance, and made his way down to you. Both of you were unconscious when he first got there. He covered you with blankets from his car and waited with you until the ambulance arrived. They said it took a good forty minutes in the storm. Travis came to when they were transferring him into the ambulance. You didn't wake up until you were in the ER."

I tried to imagine myself in the situation she described, but my mind balked. Although I believed her, it was as if she were trying to sell me a story about two strangers. "Schuyler ER in the Glen?"

She nodded. "They kept you there a few hours and tested you every which way before discharging you. By then they were apparently all scratching their heads. They couldn't figure out how you two survived that accident with fairly minor injuries. The truck was totaled." Tilly arched one eyebrow at me.

I smiled. "Yeah, it was a last-minute protection spell I kind of threw together. I'm actually surprised it worked as well as it did."

"Aha! It worked because you have an amazing talent with spells. That's exactly what I've been telling you. As soon as you're up to it, you really need to help Merlin."

"I know. I will." I just had to calm the thoughts ricocheting around in my head first.

Tilly was walking out with the tray as Travis walked in. "Behave yourselves," she called over her shoulder, "you both still need your rest."

Travis looked disheveled, but otherwise surprisingly good for someone who'd narrowly escaped death. I wondered what I must look like.

"It's good to see you," I said. So good that my heart managed a bit of its usual jig in his honor.

"Right back at you," he said, sitting carefully on the edge of the bed, mindful not to jostle it or make it bounce. "It seems a 'thank you' is in order."

I shrugged. "No need. It's just one of the perks of dating a sorcerer."

"So, now that you saved my life, aren't you responsible for looking after me forever?" he asked with a mischievous smile.

"This isn't China," I said, "but I'll do what I can." There was irritable quacking in the hallway, alternating with Tilly's voice in its upper register as if she and the Merlin-duck were having a heated conversation.

Travis wagged his head and smiled. "You sure have problems you don't find in most families."

"It does keep life from getting boring." I watched his smile fade and the laughter in his eyes evaporate. "Is something wrong?"

"Yeah. There can't be any doubt now. The killer intends to get rid of us. Whoever was driving that plow wasn't working for the county."

"Does anyone know what happened to the driver who was supposed to be behind the wheel?" I asked.

"According to a colleague, one of the other drivers found him unconscious in the snow—blunt force trauma to the back of the head. If it wasn't for the cold, he wouldn't have survived."

"Thank goodness. I'd hate to be the reason that an innocent party died. Has he been able to describe the killer?"

"He was hit from behind." Neither of us spoke for a minute. "If you want out, I wouldn't blame you," Travis said finally. "In fact I encourage you to walk away."

"And just how can I keep you from harm if I do that? Wait a minute," I said, narrowing my eyes at him. "Do you have another sorcerer standing by in the wings?"

He chuckled. "Not I. One sorcerer is all I can handle."

"What a happy coincidence; one reporter happens to be my limit too." I reached for his hand, needing the connection. "All kidding aside," I said, "I'm in this with you until we catch the killer. Tomorrow morning I'm going home. I'll contact the victims' families again, like we discussed."

"Good," Travis said, but he didn't sound all that happy about my decision to see the case through. "I intend to sneak out in the next hour or so—if I can get past Tilly. I need to head over to the news bureau and play catch up. I'm going to ask them to pull me from the Albany story at least for now. Wish me luck."

"With your boss?"

"No, in escaping your aunt. For a sweet woman, she turns into a wolverine if you're under her care."

"She's only like that with family," I said. "You should feel honored."

He rose and planted a kiss on my forehead. "Honored but also imprisoned. She made me drink this awful stuff."

I laughed. "Welcome to the family."

Once the storm was over, Travis made his escape with a ride from a colleague. About the same time I eased myself out of bed and went to find Tilly. She was in the kitchen baking homemade duck food.

"I have a spell to try on him," I said and watched her face light up. "Where is he?"

"In the bathtub. Let's go tell him the good news."

"Don't oversell it, Aunt Tilly. I don't want him to get too excited in case it doesn't work.

"No negativity!" she chastised.

The Merlin-duck jumped out of the tub the moment we walked in, perhaps suspecting that something was afoot. He gave himself a vigorous shake, getting us soaked in the process. I still contend he did it on purpose. Focusing on him, I began:

Reverse the spell that Merlin cast.
He never meant for it to last.
Return him to his human form.
In every way restore his norm.

Tilly and I held our breath as the duck began to mutate and change. A beard popped out beneath its bill, then withdrew. Merlin's bony foot replaced one of the duck's webbed ones. Here an arm, there an ear. For a moment Merlin's entire head rested on the duck's thin neck, only to disappear again. After what must have been an exhausting five minutes, the duck was once again intact.

"Give me your hand, Aunt Tilly," I said, remembering my first foray into detective work. "I'm not strong enough to change him by myself." She grabbed my hand, squeezing it so tightly I gasped.

"Sorry," she said, loosening her grip.

"Repeat the spell with me ten times." Again we watched the incredible contortions of man and duck. Again the duck was winning. It wasn't until the tenth repetition that Merlin burst free of his feathered prison. He collapsed on the floor like a shipwrecked man who has finally reached dry land. Tilly screamed her joy. I remained silent, my heart lodged at the base of my throat with the fear that we'd killed the legendary wizard. From where I stood, Merlin didn't appear to be breathing. I moved closer to feel for his carotid artery, but I realized there was no need for it. I could see the barest rise and fall of his chest. His breath was far too shallow, but as I watched, it grew stronger and deeper. With tears of relief, I collapsed on the floor beside him.

Chapter 25

If Ryan had questioned Judy McFee about her husband's arrest, he must have considered it important to his investigation. And the best way to determine that significance was to find out if the other people on the list also had an arrest in their past. With that in mind, as soon as I returned home the next morning, I placed a call to Nina Frank Lewis, the woman whose son had the chip on his shoulder. When I identified myself, she thought I had new information about her husband's death and was clearly disappointed that I didn't.

"I hope to in the near future," I said in an effort to appease her. "It would be a huge help if you would answer just another question or two over the phone."

She sighed. "I'm beginning to think my son was right to throw you out of the house." For a moment I thought she was going to hang up on me. I needed answers and getting them from the next of kin would be the quickest method. I had to win her over, give her a reason to trust me. "Can I tell you something in confidence?" I asked.

Nina hesitated as though she suspected I had a hidden agenda. "I suppose," she said finally. "I mean, I won't tell anybody."

"My partner and I are getting close to the truth. We know this, because there's been an attempt on our lives too."

"Have you told the police?" She sounded horrified, but also more invested.

"No, if the police become involved, the killer will go further underground. I need you to trust me. This isn't our first case. We know what we're doing." I was definitely taking liberties with the truth. It was our third case and we weren't all that sure about our methods. If I'd been Pinocchio, you could have tied a swing to my nose and given a toddler a ride.

"All right," Nina relented, "let me hear your questions."

"Thank you. Was Martin ever arrested?"

"Yes, but I'm not going to discuss that with you."

"You don't have to. Can you tell me the name of the prosecutor in the case?"

"Bradley Epps."

I could hear her distaste for the man in the way she spoke, as if his name curdled on her tongue. "And your husband's defense attorney?"

"Sam Crawford. If you ever need a criminal attorney, he's the one you want."

"Good to know." I thanked her, and she told me to be careful as if she sincerely meant it. I decided to take it in that spirit. I looked at my watch to see if I had time for one more call before heading over to Abracadabra, but I was already late. It was two days since the accident and I was still moving in slow motion, feeling like I couldn't get out of my own way. According to the ER doctor, it takes time to recover from a concussion and I was not to push myself too hard too soon. It was a good thing he didn't know about the exertion required to rescue Merlin or he probably would have had me lashed to a hospital bed, until he considered me fit to be on my own. For Tilly's sake, I'd tried to mask how much it took out of me. She was in such a difficult spot, desperate to help Merlin and afraid to harm me. I was sure the only reason she let me try the spell so soon after the concussion was because she'd convinced herself that my magickal abilities were separate from my physical state.

I searched around the house for Sashkatu, but he wasn't in any of his usual haunts. When I'd first returned home from Tilly's two hours earlier, he'd glared at me, lifted his chin in the air, and disappeared. At least the other cats were happy to see me. I considered taking one of them along to the shop, but which one? The last thing I needed was a jealousy-fueled cat fight. I gave up and was closing the door behind me, when Sashki slipped neatly through the narrowing space between the door and the jamb. Had he timed it any more closely, he might have lost the tip of his tail. He threw me a haughty glance over his shoulder as if to say, "You're not dealing with an amateur here."

The morning was busy with customers. No time to rest. At noon, I put my clock sign in the window so I could catch my breath. Lolly, who didn't often close for lunch, made an exception that day and came to visit. I couldn't turn her away and more to the point, I didn't want to. She wrapped her arms around me in a tight embrace, then held me at arms' length to study me. "How are you doing after that awful accident? When Tilly was filling in for you yesterday, she told me you were on the mend, but that it would take time. I never expected to see you back at work this soon."

"I'm fine," I said with a smile. "And if I'm not a hundred percent, I will be soon."

"Thank goodness. There's been more than enough bad news around here lately. Now if you don't mind, I'll take advantage of that chair to get off my feet for a bit." I followed her over to the chair and saw how gingerly she lowered herself into it. I realized she didn't look well. Her face was flushed and most of her hair had escaped its usually well-secured bun.

"Are you all right?" I asked her.

She wagged her head. "I've started making the chocolate for my special holiday boxes and I'm already done in. The demand has grown tenfold over the years. There are folks who come in and buy fifteen, twenty boxes to give as gifts. I know I shouldn't complain. Lord knows I can use the money, but every year it's harder on me than the year before. There isn't a part of me that doesn't ache."

I'd never known Lolly to be a complainer. She came from the old school of "suck it up and get on with it, and while you're at it slap on a smile."

"I have something that may help," I said.

"You've come up with a cure for old age?" she asked wryly.

"Don't I wish. That would certainly bring in the customers."

"The doctor says it's my arthritis creeping into my knees and back," Lolly said. "Apparently it's no longer content with just my fingers and toes."

"Can you describe the pain?" Morgana and Bronwen had formulated different mixtures for different types of pain.

"It's like winter set up shop in my joints and is gnawing away at them."

"Give me a sec." I went down the second aisle and, after rooting around a bit, found the last tube of the special ointment for chronic pain hidden behind the jars of liniment for muscle soreness. The ointment was infused with a spell for pain relief and another for general wellness. Although it's difficult for magick to completely erase physical pain, this ointment seemed to do the trick for a lot of my customers. I'd have to make more of it the first chance I had. I brought the tube back to Lolly and rubbed some gently into her swollen knuckles to show her how to apply it.

"Well, I'll be," she said, "if that doesn't already feel some better. Thank you." She began to pull herself out of the chair, but then dropped back down. "Believe it or not, I didn't actually come here to complain to you, though I seem to have done an admirable job of it."

"What's up?"

"I remember you telling me about a rough-looking biker guy who came in and asked you some peculiar questions not too long ago."

"Did you see him around here?" I asked, instantly on alert.

"I think he must be the one who came into my shop yesterday, ordered some fudge, and asked about you. He'd heard about the accident the day before and wondered if you were okay."

"What did you tell him?" And why was he still hanging around New Camel? He'd painted himself as a vagabond, a traveler, a man without roots, always on the move. He should have been long gone from our tiny corner of the world.

"I asked him why he wanted to know. He said he enjoyed talking to you and hoped you were doing all right. I told him you were doing fine, but I didn't go into detail." It was more likely he wanted to hear that I was dead or dying.

"Was he riding a motorcycle?" I asked.

"Yes, I watched him from the window when he left. He had it parked at the curb a couple shops up from yours."

"By any chance, did you get the plate number?"

"I tried, but the angle was too oblique for me to see anything. And I was busy looking at the paint job," she added sheepishly. "I'm sorry."

"What was it about the paint?" I asked, trying to hide my disappointment.

"It reminded me of a Harley one of my boyfriends had a thousand years ago," she said with a sigh of nostalgia. "Black on white, the design made me think of swirling snakes with their forked tongues extended."

"What part of the bike had the design?" At least I'd have some means of describing the bike to the police if it ever came to that.

"The gas tank," she murmured, lost in her memories. "Johnny was the bad boy no girl could resist. He would pick me up and off we'd go. He was quite a looker. It all seemed very romantic at the time. My mother hated that bike and Johnny, I suspect. It wasn't until I had my own kids that I was able to understand her fears."

I laughed. "I can't picture you as a wild teenager. I've only known you to be sensible and nurturing."

"Everyone is young at least once," she said. When I didn't smile or say anything, she asked me what was wrong.

"I just don't know why this biker is so interested in me."

"Have you looked in the mirror lately?" Lolly said. "Any man would have to be at least half dead not to be taken with you."

I decided to drop the subject of the biker. There was no point in worrying her, when I might be tilting at windmills. I asked about her grandchildren, a proven method of lightening her mood.

The shop was quiet in the afternoon, as if the local populace had conferred and decided to pile on me in the morning. I took the opportunity to call the other family members. Max Gonzalez didn't hesitate to answer my questions.

"Was Calista ever arrested?" I asked.

"There was an incident a number of years back, but it was over pretty fast as I recall. She had a great attorney."

"Sam Crawford?"

"Yeah, good guess."

"Was the county prosecutor Bradley Epps by any chance?"

"He was… You're on fire."

Next up was Chris Dowland's widow. Chris had had a run-in with the law and hired Sam Crawford to defend him. Once again Epps managed to lose the case. Either Crawford was terrific or Epps was abysmal. Since different judges had presided over the cases, it wasn't likely they'd played a pivotal role in the outcomes.

I called Austin Stubbs, Axel's father, but came away as empty-handed as every other time. He still had an old-school land-line, because he slammed it down so hard my ear was ringing for a good five minutes. I turned to the internet and tracked down an article about Axel's trial that mentioned Epps and the "flamboyant defense attorney," Sam Crawford.

Travis called as I was walking into my house at the end of the day, feeling more dead than alive. The ER doc knew his stuff. In the first seconds of conversation, we established that the concussions had whipped our mutual butts. I gave him a brief account of my phone calls.

"I spent the day trying to dredge up some kin of Henry Lomax's to interview," he said.

"Hermit Henry," I murmured. While most kids across the country were terrified of Freddie and Jason from the movies, if you lived in the greater Watkins Glen area, Hermit Henry was the monster you ran from in your nightmares. I'd never seen a picture of the man, but a child's imagination doesn't need much fodder on which to build its horrors. I pulled myself back to the present. "No luck I take it."

"I have one possible lead. According to a few people in the area, he had an ex and a daughter. The wife was given sole custody of the girl, so it didn't surprise anyone when they left town as soon as the ink was dry on the divorce decree. If the rumor mill is to be trusted, the ex died of cancer maybe ten years ago. No one's heard anything about the girl in at least that long."

"All we need for now is his attorney's name. Try looking online like I did for Axel."

"Will do. Listen, I don't think we can go much further without speaking to at least one of the principals at all these trials."

"I'd start with Epps," I said.

"My thought exactly."

Chapter 26

After a week of wrestling with the aftereffects of our concussions, Travis and I finally began to function more like ourselves. It took Merlin considerably longer. Not only was he much older, but a concussion couldn't be compared to the trauma of a transmutation. Make that two transmutations in just a few days. There was nothing to be found on the internet that addressed the problem and no practitioners of magick more knowledgeable or powerful than what was left of my family, namely Tilly and me. His lingering problems included quacking in the middle of an otherwise normal remark and squawking when he was distressed—a self-perpetuating cycle, since one set off the other. We did our best not to laugh at his predicament, but we weren't always successful.

When Morgana and Bronwen popped in to assure themselves that I was on the mend, they had a front row seat to Merlin's misery. Though they too tried to remain sober, death hadn't robbed them of their sense of humor. Morgana was the first to cave, her energy cloud bouncing up and down in the air with her laughter.

"How could you?!" Bronwen demanded. "Merlin deserves more dignified treatment."

"Precisely," he sputtered. "Quack you, Bronwen, squawk!" That proved too much for even Bronwen to bear. She dissolved into great peals of laughter, her cloud scudding across the room like a sailboat catching the wind. Grumbling and squawking, Merlin took off to the bathroom. A moment later we heard splashing in the tub. The need to immerse himself in water was another of his duck issues, along with an addiction to grapes.

I kept thinking how lucky we were that Tilly hadn't suffered a similar fate when she let Merlin transmute her just a few months ago. Whatever was playing havoc with our magick was completely unpredictable. One day I could rearrange my living room by telekinesis and the next I couldn't send a bowl into the sink without smashing it into a thousand pieces. It was like walking down a familiar road, not knowing when or where the pavement might suddenly collapse beneath our feet. Perhaps the worst part was not being able to identify the cause of the problem. Without a cause, how could we hope to fix it? I tucked the matter back behind the door in my mind where unsolvable questions moldered. We had enough other problems to deal with at the moment.

In the top spot was finding Ryan's killer. There was a good chance that when we did, it would turn out to be the same person who'd killed the five victims on the list, six if we included Hermit Henry. Although Travis and I agreed about speaking to Epps as soon as possible, we were stuck on how to make it happen. Being forthcoming would never work. "Mr. Epps, my partner and I would like to interview you. In what regard, you ask? Well, we'd like to know why you lose so many cases to Sam Crawford." Not a scenario likely to win us the entrée we sought. What could we say that could get us in his door? Although Travis had the experience of an investigative journalist, I was a woman and women tend to have a more cunning turn of mind. "Mr. Epps, we're doing research for a story about defense attorney Sam Crawford. We've talked to a lot of people who sang his praises, but no story is complete without hearing from his detractors as well. You've faced off against Mr. Crawford in the courtroom on a number of occasions, and we've been given to believe that your relationship with him is barely cordial. Would you be willing to provide us with your impressions of the man?"

Epps sounded harried when he finally agreed to take my call, but after I'd run through my little speech, he was able to squeeze us in at four o'clock on Friday. I expected a juicy interview. After all, I'd just handed the man a-once-in-a-lifetime chance for some measure of revenge. If Travis and I worded our questions the right way, we stood to learn plenty about the CP in the process. In case he choked and was reluctant to admit how he really felt about Crawford, I'd found an old spell of Morgana's that might help ensure his honesty. The only problem was that it required thyme, a red candle, and a flat plate on which to put the herb. Since it wasn't possible to use any of those items in front of the man, I'd have to rely entirely on the words of the spell.

Travis and I worked on questions and follow-up strategies over the phone. When Friday arrived, I closed the shop at two forty-five and plucked a testy Sashkatu from his window ledge. "Must you?" his bleary eyes seemed to say. "How would you like to be toted around at another's whim?" Back at the house, I set him on top of the sofa. He grunted his displeasure, before falling right back to sleep. I had Tilly on call to feed him and his brethren if I wasn't back by six.

I raced upstairs and shed my chinos and cowl-neck sweater for more business-like attire. I went all out—the burgundy suit that showed off my curves and a hint of cleavage and high-heeled, black suede boots. I pulled my hair back into what my grandmother called a "French twist" and applied lipstick in the shade of a good Chianti. When I looked in the mirror, I didn't recognize myself.

I was supposed to meet Travis in the lobby of the courthouse where Epps had his office, so we could walk in together like the team we were supposed to be. Travis had been staying in Ryan's apartment whenever he was in the Glen. He'd worked out the same month to month arrangement Ryan had had.

I walked into the courthouse a couple of minutes before four o'clock. Travis was already there. He did a double take when he saw me, but managed to tuck his eyeballs back in their sockets by the time I reached him. We'd agreed that we had to be all business for the interview and it had to start before we even hit the lobby. No hello kisses, not even a friendly peck on the cheek, nothing to indicate we were more than work partners. It was unlikely we'd get another opportunity to speak to Epps, and we couldn't take the chance of ruining this one by appearing unprofessional.

The County Prosecutor's office was easy to find once the woman at the little information desk told us, with a wink, to follow the sounds of the party. The party turned out to be ten people milling around the anteroom of the CP's office, eating chocolate cake. According to the Mylar balloons anchored to the desk by pink foil-covered weights, Travis and I had walked in on a bridal shower. The bride-to-be was the CP's secretary, Lena. She was easy to pick out by the huge smile on her face. Since we were early, we stayed at the periphery of the group until a clock somewhere in the building chimed the hour. Reminded of the time, Lena looked past her co-workers, and saw us. She nodded in our direction and got busy shooing out all the celebrants.

"I hope you weren't waiting too long," she said as she came up to me. Travis had wandered away to look at something.

"Not at all," I said, adding my best wishes.

"I'll let Mr. Epps know you're here." She went to the closed door beyond her desk and knocked. Apparently, Epps wasn't into bridal showers, which made me think of him as churlish and unsociable. Lena opened the door partway and announced us. I didn't catch his response, but she motioned to us. "He's ready to see you."

Travis was standing at the easel with its photo montage of the bride and groom-to-be. He turned when I called his name. "Sorry," he said, joining

Lena and me at the door. "I like your board there—nice way to give people a little bio of your lives."

"Thank you," Lena said as she ushered us in and closed the door softly behind us. The room was small, but not cramped. The desk was utilitarian. It held a computer monitor and keyboard along with a pile of teetering file folders and loose paperwork. A professional-looking photograph of Epps with his wife and two boys occupied a central spot on the wall across from his desk. A handful of framed diplomas and prints of famous paintings adorned the other walls.

Epps pushed back from his desk and came around to greet us with a smile and a hearty handshake—the preeminent politician. He was tall and lean with thinning hair and large ears. Wire-rimmed glasses magnified his blue-gray eyes. He was in shirtsleeves, his suit jacket hung over the back of his chair. I noticed that he'd chewed his fingernails down to the quick and attacked his cuticles, until a couple of them had bled. It seemed the CP had anxiety issues.

"Please make yourselves comfortable," he said, waiting until we were settled in the two chairs facing the desk, before he retired to his own. "Before we begin, I'd like to correct a misapprehension you seem to have about Sam Crawford. He is far from universally lauded or liked."

I was doing a little dance in my head. I *had* gotten to him with my speech. *High five, Nancy!*

"Do you have any objection to the session being taped?" Travis inquired. "It helps ensure that we don't misquote you."

"Go right ahead. If there's one thing I can't stand, it's being misquoted." I couldn't tell from his tone if he was being sarcastic.

Travis placed his phone on the edge of the desk. I launched the interview. "In doing research for the article on Mr. Crawford, we found about two dozen cases over the years in which you were the prosecutor and Crawford was the defense attorney. Does that sound accurate?"

"More or less," he replied.

"How would you describe your relationship with him during those trials?" Travis asked.

"Polite, but heated at times. That's to be expected, given that our jobs are adversarial in nature."

"How would you characterize his performance in the courtroom?" Travis followed up.

Epps took a minute to consider his answer. *"Performance* is actually a good word to describe Crawford's style. Sometimes it seems like he's playing the part of an attorney in a movie. That's not to say he isn't an attorney," he hurried to add, "but he does lean heavily on theatrics."

I was racing through the spell in my head:
Let fear and caution leave your mind.
Fret and worry leave behind.
What is true may now be spoken,
What was hidden be now open.

"I imagine that can get irritating," I said, trying to draw an emotional response from him.

"Sure, it can chafe, especially when Crawford carries things too far, too often. I object, the judge sustains the objection and orders it stricken from the record. Unfortunately, there's no way to strike it from the jurors' minds."

"In other words, he doesn't fight fair."

Epps laughed wryly "Fair or not, lawyers use that tactic all the time. Some judges are more tolerant of it than others. He's been reprimanded on a number of occasions, even threatened with contempt of court. Truth be told, I would have loved to see him thrown in jail in one of those damn custom suits he wears." His words had acquired a vindictive edge, mirrored by the steely blue in his eyes.

Travis gave me a quick "What's-going-on?" look. I hadn't told him about the spell, because I didn't know if it would work. I wasn't even using the props it required. And some people are simply impervious to it. I was afraid worrying about it might throw him off his game. I should have known better. He picked up the interview without missing a beat. "Do you think Crawford's tactics are the reason he's racked up so many acquittals?"

"Can't say for sure. He does know how to charm the ladies, though, and he's partial to seating as many of them on a jury as he can. Look, he appeals to people's emotions and while it may not be politically correct to say it, women are generally more in touch with their feelings." He looked at me, possibly to see if I was offended. I had my own act to play, so I smiled to reassure him. He gave me a lopsided smile in return.

"After a grand jury decides there's enough evidence to send a case to trial, it has to be frustrating as hell to watch a defendant walk free because of Crawford," I said.

"Frustrating sure, but above all worrisome."

"Worrisome?" I asked.

"Let's say the cops arrest a guy for driving in the wrong direction on a highway. He's either drunk or strung out on drugs. If we're lucky he didn't kill anyone. This time. But what happens when all he gets is a slap on the wrist?"

"Wouldn't he lose his license for something like that?" I asked.

Epps wagged his head. "It doesn't matter. You'd be surprised, or maybe the word should be horrified, if you knew how many people go right on driving impaired *without* a license. The cops arrest them, and lawyers like Crawford get them off again. Sometimes they do a little time—never enough. We're like the Department of Fish and Game," he continued grimly. "We have our own catch and release program, only those guys have it easier. Fish don't drive."

"Have any of Crawford's success stories gone on to kill someone?" It wasn't one of our prepared questions, but I had to know. A drunk driver had killed my mother and grandmother. In their case, the cops never caught the guy. I couldn't help but wonder if he'd been arrested before and if Sam Crawford had set him free.

"I'm sorry to say it's happened more than once. If you want more information, you'll have to do the legwork yourselves. It's all in the public records."

Travis and I were both silent for a moment. He recovered first. "It's clear that you're dedicated to your work, Mr. Epps."

"Call me Brad. I must be dedicated, otherwise why would I choose to work for the government, instead of chasing money in private practice?"

"I take it you're referring to Sam Crawford," I said.

Epps leaned forward, his elbows on the desk. "Look, I believe everyone deserves a fair trial in this country, which by definition means they deserve competent legal representation. Do I wish all the defense attorneys were above stretching the rules to serve their clients? Hell, yeah. But without a good win record, they're not going to get the buzz necessary to bring in the big bucks."

"Do you ever think about switching sides?" Travis asked.

The CP sat back in his seat. "Every time I get my kid's tuition bill," he said wryly. "Will I ever? No, I'm not built for it. I have an overactive conscience and I've grown fond of sleeping at night."

"Makes you wonder how Crawford can sleep," I murmured.

"I actually asked him once," Epps said. "You know his answer? 'I sleep just fine, because I know somebody has to do the job in order for the system to work. Why shouldn't it be me?'"

"Too bad superheroes don't really exist," I said, lightly. "They could clean up whatever the courts get wrong."

Let fear and caution leave your mind.
Fret and worry leave behind.
What is true may now be spoken,
What was hidden be now open.

"If one of them happened to ring my doorbell, I'd —" Epps stopped short and shook his head. "Sorry, where was I?"

"Superheroes?" I prompted, though I knew the signs; the CP's shields had finally gone up. I could forget about getting any more uncensored remarks from him.

"What do you think of Crawford as a person?" Travis asked as the silence lengthened and Epps didn't pick up on my cue.

He blinked rapidly and licked his lips before responding. "Now that's… That's a tough question. I don't have any real experience with the man outside of court. We've never gone out for a beer after work or passed a comment about sports or the weather when our paths cross. I can't deny that he makes my life harder on a daily basis, but I doubt he wakes up in the morning and thinks, 'I'm going to squash Epps today.' I'm a small annoyance to him. Most likely he wakes up thinking about how much his stock portfolio is worth or how much he'll make on his next case. Have you interviewed him yet?"

Travis fielded the question, a good thing since I didn't know what to say. "No, we wanted to get an overall feel for the man before speaking to him. You've been a big help in rounding out his public profile for us." In one smooth, practiced move, he rose, scooped up his phone, and reached across the desk to shake the CP's hand. "Many thanks for your time."

"And for your candor," I couldn't resist adding. Epps's brow furrowed as if he wasn't sure about my meaning. Before he could figure it out, Travis propelled me out the door with his hand on the small of my back.

"Was that some magickal footwork you laid on good ol' Brad?" Travis asked as we walked out of the courthouse. The sun was low in the sky, the temperature already dropping. I pulled my coat closed over my suit. "A bit," I said, "just to loosen him up." Travis grinned and pulled me closer to his side. "There's a Starbucks down a bit. Do you have time for coffee before you head home? I'd like to get your take on the interview while it's fresh in your mind."

"Make it a hot chocolate and I'm in."

Chapter 27

Travis set the two cups on the table, mine distinguishable by its crown of whipped cream, and sank down beside me on the little sofa. "Before we get started on Epps," he said, "I took your advice and located an article about Hermit Henry. Guess who his attorney was?"

"It's not really a guess at this point," I said. "But how did he afford Crawford?"

"It seems that although Henry lived like he was destitute, he had a fortune stashed in the bank—generations of family wealth. And he was an only child. Apparently, arson wasn't his only peculiarity."

"So," I said, "what did you take away from our talk with call-me-Brad?"

"For one thing, he's a pretty talented actor himself. Without that spell of yours, we wouldn't have gotten that glimpse inside. I bet there's a deep pit of resentment boiling away in him. You hit a sore spot with the remark about Crawford's popularity. Epps couldn't let it go unchallenged."

The cocoa was too hot to drink right away, but it did a good job of warming my hands while I nibbled on the whipped cream. "But was that resentment enough to make him take justice into his own hands?"

"It's a tough call," Travis said. "Epps spent a good part of his life upholding the law. That can't be an easy one-eighty to make."

"He's got to feel like a failure. I would if I were in his shoes."

"He definitely has a logical motive, but the overriding factor has to be an individual's breaking point. Are there mitigating factors that would weigh in that kind of decision? In his case, there's a wife and kids whose world would be upended if he were caught and sent away. That possibility has to come with its own weighty rasher of guilt."

"What if he hired someone to do the killing for him?" I said.

"That's usually a big mistake. No hired gun is going to have your best interests at heart. And if they're caught, they'll give you up in a heartbeat. Besides, how could Epps afford to hire a killer? That kind of work doesn't come cheap."

"Too bad, it would have been nice to solve the case this quickly." The cocoa had finally cooled enough for me to drink it without risking third degree burns. "Here's another thought, Epps mentioned that people died as a result of Crawford's clients being acquitted. The families who suffered those losses also have motives for going after the person responsible."

"That would mean one person isn't responsible for all the deaths Ryan was investigating," Travis pointed out.

"Since almost everyone on his list was killed by a different method, it does beg the question."

"Maybe, but I still think one wily killer could have murdered them all, using various methods and leaving long lapses between killings to cut down on the chance he or she would catch the attention of the police. Flying below the radar, so to speak. That's the kind of thing that would have occurred to Ryan and piqued his interest."

"Granted," I said, "but we still need to find out who took those innocent lives and talk to the families of the victims. In order to do that, we first have to find out their names."

"I'll do some research on that tomorrow."

"Good deal," I said, getting up. "I hate to drink and run, but it's been a long day and I prefer to drive while my eyes are still open."

Travis pulled on his coat. "Generally the best way." We dropped our cups in the garbage on the way to the door. It was fully dark out, the air colder than it had been half an hour earlier. "I'll walk you to your car," Travis said. "Did you park near the courthouse?"

"Yes, but it's not necessary," I replied.

"Of course it is. Have you forgotten there's a killer out there?"

Chapter 28

The next morning Tilly wanted to hear all about the interview. She bustled into my shop as if she didn't have a bunion to her name. With her sneakers on, she was practically Olympic material. "Give me the lowdown," she said, forgoing the chair. "I have two readings and teas today, so I don't have much time. Plus I left the baking under Merlin's supervision, and you know what that means."

I gave her the basics with a promise to fill in the details later. She was heading back to rescue her pastries, when she stopped and turned to me. "I've been meaning to ask—did you ever find out if Axel's father had an alibi for the time of his son's death?"

"Not yet. I'm open to ideas about how to get that information, if you have any?"

"I don't suppose asking Duggan outright would work?"

"That's about as likely as Merlin refusing pizza," I said dryly.

"What if Officer Curtis happens to win a free reading in a little raffle I hold?" She was beaming as if the idea had indeed been a light bulb moment. "While I'm groping around in his mind, I can look for the answer to your question."

My initial reaction was a big old *no way,* but that didn't deter my aunt.

"As I see it," she said, "the information we're seeking is for a good cause. It can eliminate a suspect or be the first step in bringing one to justice."

"It would still be an ethical non-starter," I said. The thought of Tilly traipsing through Curtis's head was unsettling and a little nauseating. Of course, the nausea might have been a result of the ice cream I'd binged on late last night.

"It's only unethical if the information obtained that way is used for evil purposes." Tilly was digging in her heels. "Should I turn up information unrelated to the matter at hand, I will take it to my grave." I didn't doubt her intentions, although there had been times in the past when her definition of ethical was somewhat broader than mine.

"I need to think about it," I said finally. "You should go rescue your pastries before Merlin devours them all." My reminder sent her scuttling back to her shop. If I couldn't think of another way to find out about Austin Stubbs, I might have to take her up on the idea.

Travis called when I was helping a local resident with a spell to make her garden thrive in the coming spring. I told him I'd call back. "I know I'm a wee bit early to be doing this," Elizabeth said, "but I want to get all my ducks in a row." An image instantly sprang to mind of a disorderly row of Merlin-ducks all sporting the wizard's beard. I had all I could do not to laugh out loud.

I'd known Elizabeth since grade school. She was always determined to stay ahead of things. She stocks up on pet-friendly ice melt in July and starts her Christmas shopping immediately after July Fourth. She drove more than one teacher crazy with her requests to be given all the homework assignments for the semester on the first day of school. Her husband likes to tell the story about how she once set the table for lunch, only to start putting everything away again before they'd eaten. But as Tilly says, "she's good people."

"I have just the spell for you," I said, noting that she already had a pad and pencil in her hands. "You'll need four stones: garnet to symbolize fire, amethyst for air, jade for water, and jet for earth." I waited for her to finish writing. "You'll also need a compass and a green candle." Although there were alternative stones one could use as well as a brown candle, I didn't mention these possible substitutes. I knew from experience that when Elizabeth is presented with choices, she sometimes becomes stuck trying to pick the best one. She doesn't accept the idea that two things can be equally good.

"Using the compass, stake out the cardinal points of your garden and bury each stone as follows: garnet to the south, amethyst to the east, jade to the west, and jet to the north. As you bury each stone, repeat four times, "By the four powers, my garden flowers." Then set the candle in the center of the garden area and light it. Say the words four more times and visualize a healthy white circle glowing around your garden, nurturing it, protecting it. Let the candle burn for a few minutes before blowing it out." *Uh-oh.* I realized my error as soon as the words left my mouth.

"How many minutes?" she asked, pencil poised above the pad.

"My mistake," I said quickly. "Three minutes, exactly three minutes."

"That's not so hard," Elizabeth said brightly. "That's really all it takes?"

"That and properly tending the flowers throughout the growing season." She left as happy as I'd ever seen her—another item checked off her to-do list for next May. After she left, I turned the OPEN sign to CLOSED and called Travis back.

"What did you find out?" I asked when he picked up.

"Hello to you too," he said. "Okay, getting straight to the point—I found two people who lost their lives because Axel Stubbs and Chris Dowland were back on the streets after serving minimal sentences. Of course, that's to date. Who knows what would have happened in the future? The killer must have been thinking along those same lines when he or she decided to eliminate them before they could do any more damage."

"Yeah, except that's not how innocent until proven guilty works in this country."

Chapter 29

According to Travis's notes, Tanya Royce died of the injuries she sustained when Chris Dowland crossed the center line while sending a text and hit her car head-on. It was his second arrest for distracted driving. The first was a year earlier when he'd tangled with a utility pole, knocking out power to hundreds of people. Sam Crawford had gotten him off with a fine and a year of community service. He was still performing that community service when his car slammed head-on into Tanya Royce's. He was sent away for three years. He was released in January of 2015 and murdered two weeks later, supposedly the victim of a botched burglary. The big question for Travis and me—was that really how he met his end or had someone killed him for taking Tanya's life?

I needed a different cover story with which to approach Tanya's husband, Everett Royce. I couldn't very well use the story that I was looking into the death of his loved one in hopes of learning the truth about how she died and who killed her. The who and how of the case were already public knowledge. So I came up with a new story that suited the circumstances of his tragic loss.

After giving Sashkatu and his subjects their dinner and bolting a Spanish omelet for mine, I called Everett Royce. I said I was with a political action group, working to get stiffer penalties in cases of distracted and impaired driving. I didn't say it outright, but the implication was clear—had stiffer sentences been in place, Tanya might still be alive. Royce said he supported our agenda and hoped we were successful, but he wasn't willing to sit for an interview on the subject. Tanya's death, coming mere weeks after their wedding, had devastated him. It wasn't until a few years later that he finally picked up the pieces of his life and started moving forward again.

He'd recently become engaged to a wonderful woman. He didn't want to tear open the wound that had taken so long to heal.

I should have kept pushing him, trying to unearth the anger that could have made him kill Dowland, but I just couldn't. What were the odds that he'd killed Dowland anyway? Or worse—that he'd not only killed Dowland, but made it his mission to eliminate others he deemed a threat to society? Mild-mannered man to super-avenger in one giant leap? On the other hand, how could I dismiss a suspect who might be playing me?

I made a shaky peace with my conscience and asked Royce if he'd be willing to chat with me for another minute or two, nothing formal. He hesitated before grudgingly agreeing. *Would a guilty man have agreed? What say you Nancy Drew?* My muse was as silent as ever.

If the next couple minutes were all the time I'd have with him, I had to be forthright in my approach. I normally relied a lot on a person's expressions and body language to gauge the honesty of their words. There was no point in trying the spell I'd used on Epps, because it only worked when I was in close proximity to the subject. All I had left in my arsenal were blunt questions and a pushy attitude. They might elicit emotional reactions that would be easier to discern in his voice. Given the limits of the situation, it was my best shot.

"What fires me up every morning when I open my eyes," I said, "is the simple fact that people like Dowland are a menace and should be behind bars for a good long time, not behind the wheel where they can take another innocent life. I'm sure you agree with that."

"Yeah, I suppose." Royce's tone was guarded.

I lowered my voice as if I were entrusting him with a secret. "Between you and me, I wouldn't blame you a bit if you were the one who took him out. I'd applaud you."

"Wait—what are you saying?" I heard the spike of anxiety in his words. I'd clearly taken him by surprise.

"I'm saying that Tanya would still be alive if Dowland had given a damn about anyone but himself. Why should that piece of trash get to live his life when she can't? What kind of justice is that?"

"Justice?" Everett gave a contemptuous grunt. I was getting to him. *Stop hiding, Everett Royce. Show me your true colors.* "But that's an old story. You and your group are not the first ones to try to reform the system. I admire your resolve, but if I were you, I wouldn't hold my breath waiting for things to change." He was pulling back.

"It's going to take a groundswell to bring about change," I said. "And it won't happen at all, unless people like you stand up and advocate for victims like Tanya." Everett was silent long enough for me to wonder if he'd hung up. Truth be told, I wouldn't have blamed him if he had. I didn't enjoy the role I was playing. "Everett? Are you still there?"

"Yeah, I'm here. Look—I can't argue with what you're saying, but it's not like Dowland is out there partying and living large. He's as dead as he's ever going to be. One thing my shrink taught me was that I had to let go of the anger if I wanted to heal. I need to concentrate on me now and on the new life I'm building. Miss Wilde, I'd be lying if I said I didn't want to bash Dowland's head in a few years back—I was that angry with the system and with bottom feeders like Sam Crawford. But I didn't do it. I went and got help instead. It was real hard for a long time, but I'm finally in a good place. I'm happy again. There was a time when I didn't think that could ever happen. I can't afford to get involved with your group. I wish you the best of luck though."

I sat there staring at the blank screen on my phone as if it were a crystal ball that could answer the questions buzzing around in my brain. I wanted to believe that Royce was innocent of any wrongdoing and that he would get his happily-ever-after with his new love. But what if he'd gone to the shrink not only to sort out his grief, but also to work through the guilt of having become an executioner?

I headed to the kitchen. I needed a break before I tackled the Caputo case. I grabbed the chocolate peanut butter ice cream from the freezer and filled a dish with two hefty scoops. A mouthful of ice cream bliss goes a long way to soothing the soul—my soul anyway. By the time the dish was empty, I was as ready as I'd ever be. Angelo Caputo was a twenty-four-year-old man who overdosed on tainted cocaine. I reworked my pitch to fit the situation and gave myself a pep talk. All the lying was in the service of finding Ryan's killer and shutting down whoever was hijacking the justice system. I tapped in the number for the senior Caputo's home and talked with his mother. I told her I was working with a group of activists to make the streets of Schuyler County drug-free.

That's nice," she said, "where were you when that little Stubbs weasel was hanging out with my Angelo and getting him hooked?" Her tone was surprisingly neutral, her words without inflection as if she'd been drained of all emotion, an empty shell that walked and talked, but was only going through the motions of a living being. Had the loss of her son stripped her of feeling or had his descent into addiction hollowed her out long before his death? Talking to her unnerved me. I asked if her husband was home.

Michael Caputo was booming. Booming I could work with. I introduced myself and told him why I was calling. "The citizens of this county need to come together and build a grassroots advocacy to drive drugs out of our towns." I sounded like I knew what I was talking about, but if he'd asked me about the finer points of the plan, I would have been left standing there with my mouth hanging open. Luckily, Caputo didn't seem interested in the details.

"Damn straight we do," he thundered. "You just holler if you need some muscle."

"I appreciate the offer," I said. "Forgive my curiosity, sir, but do you share your wife's belief that Stubbs was to blame for Angelo's death?"

"In multiple ways. He got my boy hooked to begin with. We fought like hell to get him into a good rehab facility not once, but twice and both times he came out of there clean. But as soon as he got home, Stubbs slithered back into his life. So we arranged to send Angelo to a rehab in California. My sister-in-law lives out there and she agreed to let him stay with her when he came out. It was a good plan and I believe it would have worked, but Stubbs and the drugs got to him first."

"You must have wanted to go after Stubbs, put an end to him," I said, hoping to fire up Caputo to the point where he would slip and reveal how he'd done just that.

"You got that right. Trouble is, I'd have to pay the price for it and I don't think I could hack it in prison. I was one happy man when I heard somebody else took him down. Far as I know, there's no law against being glad he's dead." I thanked Caputo for his time and he reiterated his offer of *muscle,* though I no longer knew what that meant.

It was ten o'clock when I called Travis. He was half asleep in his Albany hotel room watching an old movie on TV. He came fully awake when he heard my voice. "Hey, how'd it go?"

"Well, I won't be meeting with either of the families. Royce flat-out refused and Caputo's all bark and no bite."

"We're erasing them from our suspect list?"

"I'm not ready to let Royce go yet," I said. "He strikes me as the type who could go off the deep end under the right conditions. I also want to see if I can get the phone number for Tanya's parents. Losing a child often trumps losing a wife."

"I can save you the trouble. They died in a small plane crash a couple years back."

"What about siblings?"

"She didn't have any." I was out of options. "Maybe Everett Royce did bash in Dowland's head and discovered the role of avenging angel suited him."

"Ryan would have figured it out by now," Travis said. I could picture him wagging his head, the loss of his foster brother still painfully close to the surface. It was hard to comfort him over the phone.

"It may take us a little longer," I said, "but I'm absolutely certain we're going to nail his killer."

"I know, but sometimes it feels like we're spinning our wheels, getting nowhere fast. For what it's worth, I'm going up to Burdett tomorrow to try my luck with Austin Stubbs."

Chapter 30

A bad cold snap had swooped down from Canada overnight, and a tour bus was scheduled, both of which made me happy to be spending the day in my snug little shop. The moment I stepped outside, the frigid air smacked me in the face with a wicked left hook. Sashkatu's furry face suddenly seemed more practical than bare skin. I could swear I caught him gloating about it a moment before a powerful gust knocked the look off his face. Together we sprinted from the house to Abracadabra's back door. I hadn't seen the old boy move that fast in quite some time. It cost him though. He was spent for the rest of the day and needed my help to reach his private solarium. At least there was plenty of sun to warm the chill out of his joints.

Next door I could hear my aunt Tilly baking away for the day's appointments. Merlin came in by the connecting door, looking frazzled. "Your aunt is beside herself and that is too much Matilda even for me," he said. "Mayhap you can calm her. I would be ever so grateful."

"What's wrong?"

"She's in a dither about the cold. She thinks folks will cancel and stay home, so she can't decide how much to bake."

I breathed a sigh of relief that it wasn't a more serious issue. "Tell her most people won't cancel last minute because the bus company won't refund their money. Besides, the tours leading up to the holidays are always packed. She just needs to be reminded how great business is in New Camel this time of year."

"New *Camelot*," he said sourly. "If it's going to be our secret, we can at least use the correct name among ourselves!"

"You're right," I said, because I didn't have time for a debate. "I apologize. Now please go tell Tilly I'm sure the bus will be full." Apparently satisfied with my level of contrition, Merlin left to convey my message. Sashki hadn't moved a muscle during the wizard's visit. He was one tired feline if Mr. Catnip had no effect on him.

The bus pulled in right on time. Passengers hit the street at the stroke of ten. They were mostly women over the age of fifty, bundled in winter gear. Since Tilly, Lolly, and I were located at the far end of town it would probably be a little while before they reached us. I didn't want to stand at the door looking desperate or overly eager, so I sat down at the computer to check my email.

When my first customer walked in savoring a dark chocolate turtle from Lolly's, I had an instant craving for one. I promised myself I'd run across to her shop after the bus tour left. My sugar addiction pointed out that Lolly could easily be out of them by then. Okay—maybe I'd run over there when there was a lull in customers.

Travis called at eleven, sounding glum.

"How did it go?" I asked.

"Stubbs knew me right off the bat. I'm usually thrilled to see an uptick in my recognizability quotient, but not in this case. He called me a *troublemaking newsmonger* and slammed the door in my face."

"We can't give up," I said. "If we can link that motorcycle of his with the Biker Dude who's been keeping tabs on me, it could split this case wide open." I had no idea if that was true or even logical, but it was the only thing we had to go on and I wasn't willing to dismiss it.

"What do you suggest?"

I laid out Tilly's offer to poke around Paul Curtis's brain and find out if Stubbs had given the police an alibi for the day of his son's demise.

"Poke around?" Travis said. "There's got to be a better way to describe what she does."

"How does *probe* suit you?"

"Never mind, that makes me think of alien encounters."

"All right, let's not play thesaurus. The important thing is that Paul won't realize what Tilly is doing to him and he won't suffer any side-effects from it."

"Paul?" Travis repeated dryly.

Was that a wisp of jealousy I heard in his tone? "Yes, Paul. We've sort of become friends. He's helped me out with stuff a time or two."

"Stuff, huh?"

"Is there a problem?" I asked.

"You are aware he's interested in you, right?"

I laughed. "Why would he be interested in me?" I said, hoping to nip his speculation in the bud and move on. Big mistake—I wasn't any good at acting coy.

"Don't be disingenuous, Kailyn," Travis said, clearly irritated. "It's not who you are. And I have enough phony crap to deal with in my career."

After our ups and downs, it was nice to know Travis cared enough to be territorial about me, but I felt like a kid caught with her hand in the cookie jar and two cookies already stuffed in her mouth. "I'm sorry," I said. "I do know he's interested in me. He asked me out a couple months ago, but I turned him down." There was silence from Travis's end. "Are you there?"

"Yeah, I'm here," he said finally. "I appreciate the honesty but I don't think I should have to search for it. I want to know I can trust anything you say to me without having to parse your words for hidden meanings. Can we agree on that?"

"Yes," I said, feeling properly chastened. What was I thinking? I've never been a game-player, especially when it comes to relationships. The nature of my lineage alone would have made plenty of men bail and never look back. Travis had wrestled with it, but had eventually come around. I suspected it was still a work in progress. I had no way to know what new straw might be the final one.

"Getting back to Stubbs," Travis said, "your aunt's mind probe—there's got to be a better way to describe it— may tell us if he has an alibi, but what if it doesn't reveal anything about the motorcycle? Who's left to approach the man?"

"I have an idea, but I want to wait until I have the kinks worked out before I tell you." The chimes jingled, signaling the arrival of half a dozen tourists. I told Travis I'd call back later and went to welcome them. Some of the women looked familiar from previous visits. I loved repeat customers. They already knew the quality of everything I sold and were always eager to share their knowledge with the uninitiated. They were walking, talking billboards.

One of the women I recognized came over to say *hello* and ask about Morgana and Bronwen. Had they turned the business over to me entirely? she asked. Were they off somewhere warm and sunny? When I told her they'd passed on, tears welled up in her eyes and she put her hand over mine on the counter. "I am so sorry, dear. What dynamic women they were. What a loss." I thanked her and she went back to shopping, shaking her head.

She'd nearly had me in tears too, until I remembered that I still had my mother and grandmother in my life, along with a lot of the same problems as when they were incarnate. Apparently, death didn't automatically make souls into saints. Maybe that came later in the process. In any case, I didn't have long to dwell on the unknown. I was busy fielding questions, suggesting remedies, and ringing up sales.

A few of the customers requested specific spells. Since it was impossible to prevent everyone else in the shop from hearing me dictate the instructions, I'd come up with what seemed like an equitable solution. I'd uploaded the most commonly requested spells into my computer, so I could easily print them out for those who wished to purchase them. Every spell came with a caveat though. It was imperative that the buyer use a pencil and paper to transcribe the spells when they got home. Failure to do so, could keep them from working properly.

By the end of the day I was beat, but if this first round of holiday shoppers was any indication of sales in the coming weeks, my bank account would be in good shape by year's end. Tilly hobbled in from her shop with her turban askew and crumbs clinging to the front of her muumuu. "You were right," she groaned. "I don't think a single person stayed home. Maybe *you* should be the psychic."

"It was just a guess based on past experience," I said. "Don't you dare think about retiring, Aunt Tilly."

"How could I? Have you seen my grocery bills now that I have a bottomless pit to feed?"

"Speaking of Merlin—how did you keep him out of trouble today?"

"By leaving him home with his favorite electronics and a promise of dinner at The Soda Jerk if he stayed out of trouble."

"And?"

"I've been afraid to call," she admitted. "But I'm maintaining a positive outlook. I've found that ignorance truly can be bliss, at least until reality sneaks in and kicks you in the keister. I'll keep you posted. That reminds me, have you decided to let me hold the raffle?"

"I can't think of any other way to find out if Stubbs gave the police an alibi, so you have my blessings."

"A bit more enthusiasm would be nice, but I'll take what I can get."

"Have you considered the possibility that Paul may not want to participate?" I asked.

"Well…well…" she stammered, "you need to stop sending negative vibes into the universe."

I didn't say anymore on the subject, lest I be blamed for its failure. Instead I thanked her for her ingenuity.

"You're welcome," she said mollified. "Wish me luck. I'm off to see if my house is still standing."

I wished her well and hoped Merlin got to have dinner at The Jerk. I didn't want him to be in a snit in the morning. He was essential to my plan to question Stubbs. That alone should have raised all sorts of red flags for me, but it's easy to ignore what you don't want to see.

I left for home shortly after Tilly, cradling a sleep-dazed Sashki in my arms. Instead of trying to wriggle out of my grasp, he snuggled his head in between my chest and upper arm in anticipation of another gale-force gust.

Chapter 31

According to my aunt Tilly, she came home to a miracle. Although Merlin had managed to get into mischief, it was so minor, so inconsequential that in her relief she took him to dinner anyway and let him have two ice cream sundaes for dessert. When I saw her the next morning in the shop, she explained that the wizard had tried to make popcorn in the microwave the way he'd seen her do it. But instead of putting a small handful of kernels in a brown paper bag, he'd filled half the bag. When he opened the microwave, a flood of popcorn poured out. In no time it was everywhere, courtesy of Isenbale. The Maine Coon didn't like popcorn, but he'd had a dandy time batting the airy stuff around the house. Merlin tried to clean it all up, but the next morning Tilly was still finding popcorn under the refrigerator, beneath the living room couch, and upstairs in her closet.

The cold snap ended two days later, the temperature rising into the balmy thirties. Eager to kickstart her plan, Tilly set off in her can-do sneakers to register the merchants of New Camel as well as Officers Curtis and Hobart and the volunteer fire department for her bogus lottery. She planned to tell them all that it was her way of giving back to the business community of New Camel. She believed that the more people she included in the lottery, the more believable it would seem. She chose not to consider that the more people she registered for it, the more people she'd be tricking. She left Merlin in her shop engrossed in an old TV movie. She didn't have any appointments scheduled and she figured there was less potential for him to cause disaster there with me just steps away. She told him to ask my permission before doing *anything.*

I walked through the connecting door and found Merlin obediently watching his movie. I put it on pause and explained what I wanted him to do.

"Yes, yes, most certainly," he said, reaching to take back the remote. "Whatever you wish."

"Merlin, I need to know the truth. Is it too risky for me?"

"No, it should be fine."

"Should be or will be?" I pressed him.

He sighed. "*Will*, is that what you wish to hear?"

"I wish to hear the truth," I said, losing patience. It might be a simple request for him, but it was a major decision for me. One that could change the course of my life. "You're not getting this remote back until you give my question the attention it deserves."

He swiveled in his chair to face me. "You will be fine, mistress, unscathed. I haven't the slightest doubt of it."

"Now you sound like you're trying to humor me."

"Is there not a single answer that will buy me freedom from your paranoia?" I handed him back the remote. He was right. He could give me every assurance and it wouldn't be enough. Because it wasn't up to him. It would depend on the current vagaries of our magick. The decision to take the risk was up to me and me alone. I spent the next few hours driving myself as crazy as I'd driven poor Merlin. In the end, I decided to go ahead with it and cast my doubts away.

When Tilly returned aglow with the cold and success, she shot me down. I reminded her that she'd done the exact same thing mere minutes after meeting the wizard. "At least now I know how to reverse the spell if he forgets again," I said. "I'll write it down for you just in case." She had no comeback. Travis proved a whole lot harder to convince.

"Are you out of your mind?"

"I think the idea deserves reasonable consideration, not an emotional reflex," I said evenly.

"You're right, it does," he said after taking a moment to compose himself. I explained that the reversal spell would be my fail-safe, but he didn't take comfort from it the way Tilly had. For him it was just more magick that could go wrong.

"I have to be honest, Kailyn, the thought of it just scares the hell out of me. If something goes wrong, then what? You spend the rest of your life looking like a guy?"

"A guy is much more believable than a woman in this situation, especially since I'll be dealing with someone who's old school. Don't worry, nothing is going to go wrong." But I had no guarantees to support my claim. And I could hardly blame him for being worried. He'd been privy to some impressive shortfalls in my family's magick. If only I could transfuse him with a few liters of my innate confidence in it.

"Can you explain it to me again?" he asked. "Slowly this time." He sounded like he was trying to find a way to be more receptive.

"Merlin is going to glamour me so that anyone who looks at me will see a man."

"Wait, I thought vampires glamour people."

"Vampires are pure fiction," I said. "Let's stick to reality, okay?"

"Right. What's that other thing Merlin can do? I get them mixed up."

"Transmutate one living organism into another. Like changing a dog into a cat. It's much more difficult magick, but a couple of months ago you saw first-hand how successful he was at it. And glamouring is a lot less risky." Travis was silent again. "It's the only way I might be able to get Stubbs to show me the motorcycle. If it's the one Lolly described, we'll know that there's a connection between Stubbs and Biker Dude. We have to follow up on every little clue if we want to find Ryan's killer."

"I know, but I don't want to lose you too," Travis said bluntly. "And it's not only me. You need to consider what it would do to your aunt and Merlin and all the people who love you."

"My family is all right with it, because magick is a part of who we are. I hope you can find a way to focus on a positive outcome."

"I will," he said with a sigh. "One way or another, I will."

Chapter 32

Paul Curtis won Tilly's lottery—big surprise. That was the easy part. The hard part was convincing him to accept his lucky win and actually use his prize. He tried to sound grateful when she called him with the good news. She had the phone on speaker so I could listen to the conversation.

"I can't thank you enough," he said, "but I don't know when I'd have time to use it. Maybe you should pick another winner."

"Nonsense," Tilly said, "I'll work with you until we manage to fit it into your schedule."

"But—"

"No *buts* about it," she said brightly. "You won the lottery because it was meant for you." She lowered the pitch of her voice to somewhere between serious and grave. "Paul, there could be something critical you need to hear." It was difficult to cut Tilly down when she was on a mission.

He sort of laughed and coughed. The man was clearly out of his element. "Well then, I guess I'll be seeing you. Thanks again." This *thank you* was considerably less enthusiastic than the first one. Before he could add *goodbye,* Tilly pounced.

"Now is as good a time as any to set a date," she said. "When is your next day off? The reading won't take more than half an hour of your time, unless you'd like to stay for a proper English tea, complete with clotted cream from England."

"I've heard people rave about your teas, Ms. Wilde. They sound terrific, but I'm afraid even a thirty-minute session—"

"Then it's settled. A quick reading and away you go. Are you off on Monday?" He hemmed and hawed, until Tilly wore him down. In the resigned tone of someone scheduling a colonoscopy with a side of root canal, he agreed to ten o'clock and was off the phone before she could rope him into anything else. I felt sorry for the guy.

Travis called, sounding equally unhappy. He was heading back to Albany to continue his coverage of the ongoing corruption investigation there. His boss assured him it was only until something new broke on the Schuyler County murders. The local media had reduced the name to the handy acronym SCM that quickly morphed into the more colorful pronunciation of *scum*. The days after the bus tour, business was slow, but it didn't worry me. Once Thanksgiving arrived, so would more buses, as well as lots of shoppers from surrounding areas. The lull was a good time to take my teleportation skills out for a spin. With all that was going on in my life, I hadn't been consistent in my training. If only there was a teleportation guru on TV like the fitness and yoga instructors. All my motivation had to come from me, although the prospect of taking Merlin back home was certainly an incentive.

Sometimes just thinking about the intensity of teleportation was enough to make me look for other, easier tasks like cleaning out closets, paying bills, doing inventory, and twiddling my thumbs. I always felt guilty after a day of procrastination, my conscience only too willing to take me to task. *Was I a sorcerer or wasn't I? Was I willing to settle for mediocrity when such incredible abilities were mine for the taking?* To shut down the harpy in my head, I didn't go straight home after closing the shop. The cats wouldn't starve if dinner was delayed twenty minutes. Besides, Sashkatu was still snoring away on his ledge.

I went into the storeroom to prevent passersby from seeing me vanish before their eyes. I set an empty glass jar at eye level on one of the metal shelves where I kept additional inventory. It was the kind of jar in which I kept the various plants, herbs, and decoctions in my shop. I'd promised Bronwen I would always try teleporting an object before trying to teleport myself, to be sure my magick was up to par. If the jar broke or developed so much as a crack on landing, teleporting myself was out for that day.

I'd noticed that the more I practiced, the easier it was becoming to gather my energy. It was as if I was wearing a pathway in my brain/body connection where there had once been only virgin territory. That pathway cut down on how long it took me to reach what I thought of as *critical mass*—enough energy to complete a teleportation. Unfortunately, it still took an awful lot out of me. I had no idea if that would ever get better and I had no one to ask. That was the problem with a talent that cropped up once every three or four hundred years.

I started with some deep-breathing to center my mind. When I felt ready, I drew the energy from all the cells in my body and focused it on the jar, chanting:

From here and now to there and then
Attract not change, nor harm allow.
Safe passage guarantee to souls
As well as lesser, mindless things.

I sent the jar to my aunt's shop, because I knew that she and Merlin were at home. I didn't have to worry about it hitting anyone in the head…again. I heard the barest clink of the jar setting down on the hardwood floor. When I went in there to check, I found it intact. I was *go* for teleporting myself, as Mission Control might say.

Back in the storeroom, I had to decide where to go. Teleporting to my house or my aunt's had become boring. *Why not somewhere that could be helpful to the investigation?* I asked myself. Preferably a place where I wouldn't bump into anyone, cause hysteria, and possibly wind up in jail. Epps sprang to mind, or more specifically his office did. Wasn't one of the perks of government work clocking out at five? I went back and forth over it. *You can't take the chance of being seen. But I'm tired of playing it safe. What if Epps is burning the five o'clock oil? You have to take risks if you want to succeed.* Since I couldn't stay there all night arguing with myself, I impulsively took the leap.

I landed in the small lobby of the courthouse. I remembered the smell of old wood mixed with the lavender scent the woman at the front desk doused herself with. The building was dark, except for a couple of security lights. My heart jumped into my throat when I realized belatedly that I hadn't factored a security system into my derring-do. Although I hadn't opened any doors or windows to get inside, there could be motion detectors I might trip. So now what—teleport right back to my shop? I wasn't ready to give up that quickly.

The good news was that everyone was gone for the night or they wouldn't have set the security system. The security lights indicated it was set. In the dim light, I couldn't tell if there were cameras too. And I had no way of knowing if said cameras were programmed to transmit images real time to a security company. This being Watkins Glen, there was a good chance that level of security was considered unnecessary. If I was wrong, someone would have seen my image immediately. Yet the police were not breaking down the door to get at me. There were no sirens in the distance. My heart subsided into my chest and my breathing calmed. At least I had time to weigh my options. The possibility of motion detectors meant I didn't have many. Since I couldn't risk moving from my current position, I'd have to depend on a spell. The invisibility spell wouldn't work with a motion detector. It didn't have the psychological component that left people vulnerable to misdirection. To the best of my knowledge, no one in my family had ever written a spell to turn off a security system. I'd have to come up with one myself. Other impromptu spells I'd cast had performed well.... I could do this. As pep talks went, it wasn't exactly rousing, but it was the best I could manage under the circumstances.

Fifteen minutes later I'd cobbled together a spell that seemed workable, if not inspired. I'd know soon enough if it was adequate:

Disarm alarms, detectors off,
Disable now the circuitry.
Cameras down, transmissions end,
Scrub memory and never send.

I repeated the words twice more, then it was time to road test the new spell. I was a little anxious about it. This slapdash spell could be the end of me—not literally of course. But if it failed to work, I could be sent to jail for breaking and entering. Well, entering anyway, I didn't break anything to get in, except the law. I wondered how they would go about incarcerating someone who could teleport themselves out. I was willing to bet they'd never had to deal with the problem before. All of this was flashing through my mind while I was still standing in the same spot where I'd landed. *Move,* I ordered myself *or go back and feed your fur family!*

I took one shaky step forward and waited a moment before taking another. The silence was undisturbed. I headed for the CP's office to do some snooping. If I'd had my druthers, as Bronwen was fond of saying, I would have had my aunt Tilly there with me. She was sort of a snooping savant. She couldn't seem to control the impulse. If she visited someone's bathroom, she left with a mental inventory of everything it contained. For better or worse, I hadn't yet graduated from teleporting 101. Taking someone with me was a long way off.

The first thing I realized once I was in Epps's office was that I hadn't thought to bring a flashlight. *Nancy, please don't give up on me.* I couldn't risk turning on the overhead light. Someone in the small town who knew it shouldn't be on might notice and call 911. There was a soft splash of moonlight coming through the blinds. I tried angling them to let in more of the light. It helped a little. Or maybe my eyes were getting better adjusted to the dark. I opened the top folder on his desk and took out the first page, but I couldn't make out what was written on it. I was about to give up on my sleuthing when I saw a Post-it note stuck to the frame of the computer monitor. Someone, most likely Epps, had written on it in black marker: Royce - 11/7 - 6:30 - Grotto. Everett Royce? How many Royces could there be in the county? And why would they be meeting the County Prosecutor for dinner?

I was pondering the ramifications of the note when I heard the building's front door open. My heart leaped back into my throat, a place it was becoming all too familiar with. Would the security system show that it had been turned off or had my magick bypassed the usual pathways? I didn't have long to agonize. I heard the tones of the code being entered on the keypad and then the final beep of the system being turned off the way it was intended to be. My spell hadn't left any evidence of tampering, but I wasn't out of danger. If I ran out of Epps's office and through the anteroom where his secretary, Lena, held court, I'd be in the lobby with the intruder. Who was I calling an intruder? If they had a key and knew the alarm code, they must work here. *I* was the intruder.

I briefly considered using the invisibility spell, but I didn't have time to reach the state of mind necessary for it to work. The footsteps were coming in my direction, a woman's footsteps, judging by the sharp tattoo of heels on the old hardwood. I was running out of time. I could hide behind the open door and pray she didn't close it and discover me or I could crawl into the cubbyhole under the desk. The desk won and not a moment too soon. I had to learn to make faster decisions.

The woman came into the office, but didn't turn on the lights either. That could mean she worked there, but wasn't supposed to be there after-hours. At least she'd thought to bring along a flashlight. From my hidey hole, I tried to sneak a look at her, but the bright beam of the LED shrouded her in deep shadows. I heard her rustling through the folders on the desk. She must have found what she was after, because she walked back into the anteroom and after a few seconds I heard the copier running. She came back into the office and it sounded like she was placing papers back in a folder. No one would be the wiser—except me. I was desperate to get a good look at her, but not desperate enough to come out of my hiding place and confront her. I was on pretty shaky legal ground by just being there. She was walking out of the office again, probably ready to leave the building. Last chance. I thumped softly on the underside of the desk, just enough to make her look over her shoulder. In that moment, before she swung the flashlight back into the office, I saw her face. I'd only met the woman once, but the moonlight was all I needed to recognize the CP's secretary, Lena.

Chapter 33

On my return to the shop, I nearly gave poor Sashkatu a heart attack by popping out of thin air inches from his nose. He froze in place, his green eyes wider than I'd ever seen them. He was so stunned that he didn't even fuss when I scooped him into my arms and carried him home. We found the other cats gathered in the kitchen, hungry and clearly miffed. No snuggles and purrs for me. They were standoffish in their greeting and strident in their complaint. I had the uncomfortable sense that I'd interrupted a discussion about making me walk the plank. I felt lucky we were on dry land and that they didn't have opposable thumbs with which to build said plank.

I was so exhausted from my teleporting round trip that after filling everyone's tummies, I ate a banana and crawled into bed. I fell asleep while the cats played a spirited game of tag over and around me. I didn't open my eyes for a good ten hours and when I did, my brain was still foggy. I went downstairs to feed my housemates, who'd let me sleep without a yowl of disapproval. Maybe they'd decided irregular mealtimes were better than no mealtimes. Or maybe Sashkatu had told them to cut me some slack. I put up coffee and called Travis while it brewed, hoping to catch him before he got mired in his day.

"After Lena left the courthouse, I tried to figure out which papers she copied, but there were too many folders with way too many papers and I'd already overstayed my visit." I'd just finished telling Travis about my adventure that had come close to being an utter disaster. He was concerned about the chance I'd taken, but he made his way past that quickly enough, once he heard about Lena's little escapade.

"Unfortunately, without that information, it's hard to know what she was up to," he said.

"I know it's just conjecture at this point, but maybe she was stealing information to help the killer in some way. Then there's also the possibility that she's working with the police to build a case against Epps if they suspect he's the killer."

"You mean she might be a mole? An interesting possibility."

"I don't know," I said with a sigh. "For that matter, I suppose *she* could be the killer."

"Or maybe whatever she came back for has nothing to do with murder," Travis said, playing devil's advocate.

I sighed again, more loudly than I'd intended. "Then I guess we're back where we started."

"Not entirely. Now we know that Lena has some less than admirable qualities, ranging from sneaking back into the office all the way to possibly conspiring in six murders."

Speaking of breaking the law underscored my own recent forays into crime. Between the fake fire in Ryan's apartment and trespassing last night, I was playing fast and loose with gray magick. I couldn't afford to take a misstep over the next line. That thought scared me more than when the snowplow edged us off the road.

"I have some interesting news, myself," Travis said, pulling me away from my gloomy thoughts. "I had a call from none other than Mr. Samuel Crawford, Esquire. He said he's heard about the story we're doing on him."

"I wonder who whispered in his ear," I said.

"I doubt he waits for the grapevine to provide him with news. He probably has ears and eyes on his payroll in every corner of this town."

"Was he angry?"

"Not at all. He wanted to know when we'd get around to actually interviewing *him*."

"Then he's willing?" For some reason that surprised me. I pictured him as an imposing figure, too busy to waste time on a B-level reporter and his sidekick.

"Yeah, he wanted to nail down a date right then," Travis said. "I told him I'd get back to him after we figure out what works for both of us."

"I know it's a great opportunity, but have you thought this through? What's going to happen when this story about Crawford doesn't air?"

"I don't know," Travis admitted. "I'll run it by my boss to see if he'd be interested in a piece about a local attorney with an impressive record of acquittals. Or I can get down on my knees and beg him to run it. Worst case scenario, I'll try to find an e-zine that's willing to take a free story. If Crawford is disappointed, he can blame us. To be on the safe side, you might not want to commit any crimes," Travis added wryly. "That way we won't need his services."

"Got it. I'll be sure to clamp down on my criminal tendencies. Seriously though, I'm interested to hear what he thinks of Epps."

"I got the feeling from five minutes on the phone with Crawford that he enjoys the sound of his own voice. If we can steer him with our questions, we may get an earful on a lot of subjects. We can't make the mistake of underestimating him though, or trying to play him for a fool. When I've asked people what they think of him, the one thing they all agree on is that he's sharp as can be and rabid in his devotion to his clients. He'll do anything the law allows to win them acquittals or minimum sentences."

I glanced at the clock above the kitchen table. "We'll have to finish this conversation later. If I don't hop in the shower in the next two minutes, I'll be late opening again."

"How about lunch at The Jerk?" he asked.

"Wait a minute—I thought you were in Albany. It's getting to be like *Where's Waldo?*"

He sighed. "Tell me about it. I'm needed back in the Glen for the evening news." All the traveling back and forth was clearly getting to him. "How's one o'clock?"

"You've got it. I think today's special is your favorite, turkey chili."

* * * *

After lunch Travis came back to the shop with me. He said he wanted to see me work. I told him he'd just be bored and he was welcome to wait at the house where he could take a nap or watch TV. "It sounds like you're trying to get rid of me," he said.

"I am, but for your benefit."

"Don't worry about me. I'll walk around and acquaint myself with your product line. Pretend I'm not here," he said as he disappeared down the first aisle. Less than a minute later, my mother's cloud appeared, white, tinged with red—something had her hackles up. And she clearly hadn't taken the time to make sure I was alone before barging in.

"Your grandmother informed me about your recent teleportation," she began. "I know we told you to practice the skill, but we certainly didn't suggest you break the law in the process."

Travis poked his head out of the aisle, perhaps thinking the new voice belonged to a customer. He and my mother saw each other at the same time. He jumped; her cloud bounced sharply, like a jet hitting an air pocket. I couldn't tell who was more startled. Although Travis had been treated to a similar experience with my mother and grandmother back in September, it had mercifully lasted only seconds, with no words exchanged. This time promised to be different, unless one of them skedaddled. But they both stayed where they were, each a shade paler than normal. What now? Acting the referee was pointless. Sooner or later they would have to reach an accommodation with each other if they wanted to be around me. I knew my mother and grandmother approved of Travis and he had given me every indication he wanted to accept me for who I was. I decided to sit back and see how things played out.

"Please excuse my barging in like this, Travis," my mother said, sounding properly contrite. "I'm sorry if you found it unsettling." Yay, mom. My mother rarely apologized, because, as she is quick to tell you, she is rarely wrong. The ball was in Travis's court.

"I appreciate that," he said. He seemed at a loss for something else to say, so I stepped in. I had plenty to say. I asked my mother if she understood the havoc she could have caused, and the difficult position she could have put me in, had someone other than Travis been in the shop. "I'll... I'll just finish browsing," Travis said, "while you two finish your conversation."

"So mom, what was it you wanted to say about my teleporting?" I asked sweetly.

"Don't gloat, dear, it's unbecoming. Besides, there was no chance I would be hauled off to jail for my error in judgment, whereas you might well have been." She did have a point.

"Okay, I will weigh the consequences of my actions more carefully, if you will agree not to barge in on me without first checking to see if I'm alone. The same goes for Grandma."

"I can hardly agree on her behalf. Have you forgotten to whom you're referring?"

"Well, at least agree to tell her about our pact and that I hope she'll abide by it too."

"It's a deal," Morgana said. "Please say goodbye to Travis for me. I suspect he's had enough discourse with me for one day." She lowered her voice to a whisper. "We told you he was a keeper."

Chapter 34

Three days later, on Wednesday the seventh, Travis and I went to dinner at the Grotto in Watkins Glen. It was touted as the best upscale restaurant in the county. The lighting was soft, Italian standards played in the background, and the waiters were dressed in black with gray ties and aprons. There were linen tablecloths and napkins and crystal wine goblets. The tables were set far enough apart that intimate conversation was possible if one spoke discreetly. But we weren't there for a romantic dinner.

When we arrived, Bradley Epps was seated at a two-top with a man I could only presume was Everett Royce, since I'd never met him. They both had untouched steins of beer parked in front of them and were deep in conversation. Unfortunately, the tables in their immediate vicinity were already taken. Maybe it was for the best that we were shown to a table some distance away. If the men were discussing business—the business of murder—seeing us there might cause them to change subjects. But we'd have to be creative if we hoped to learn anything.

The tuxedoed *maître d'* showed us to our table and presented us with menus that weren't laminated or sticky like the ones at The Soda Jerk. He was followed closely by our waiter, who introduced himself as Stephan, and asked if we'd like a drink. Some wine perhaps? I'd discovered back in college that alcohol can do serious damage to my magickal DNA. Abstinence was a small price to pay. I asked for water with a slice of lemon. Travis ordered a Coke. Stephan looked underwhelmed. After he left us to deliberate the menu choices, Travis recommended the lobster ravioli that he'd had on a previous visit as well as the *pappardelle* with duck ragout. All I could think about was how to find out what Epps and Royce were discussing. I'd been counting on sitting close enough to them that I could use a simple spell to amp up my hearing.

"Don't you have something stronger for this situation?" Travis asked when I explained the problem.

"I'm not Amazon, you know. I have certain abilities, not every ability under the sun. Give me another minute to think about this." I could try a spell to make our hearing acute enough to hear them, but we'd hear everyone in the restaurant—a muddle of overlapping voices that sounded like gibberish. If I cast a spell to make them speak loudly enough for us to hear, they'd be asked to lower their voices. But they wouldn't be able to comply. In the end, they might be asked to leave—the exact opposite of what we were trying to accomplish.

The waiter came back with Travis's Coke and my water, ready to take our order. I hadn't read the menu, being otherwise occupied. I looked to Travis for help. "To start we'll have the mozzarella and tomato?" he said as much to me as to the waiter. I shook my head, saying I'd prefer salad. The waiter noted the adjustment. "And we'll both have the lobster ravioli?" Travis continued. By then the waiter had the gist of how we worked and waited for my approval before noting it on his pad. He thanked us and promised bread was on its way.

"I have an idea," I said once he was gone. "It's a little unorthodox, but it may work."

Travis grinned. "A little unorthodox, huh? How would I even know the difference?" I loved his smile when he really let go.

I took off one of my pearl earrings while I worked out the spell. The warm Italian bread arrived with a dish of olive oil infused with herbs. I could smell how good it was going to taste, but first things first. Several minutes went by before I had a handle on the words:

Twixt pearl I wear and pearl I set
From ear to ear, pearls help me hear
The words of those you are most near.

"Wish me luck," I said, getting up to plant the earring.

"You don't need luck," Travis said. "If it's possible to do, I have no doubt that you can do it." His words were better than any romantic poem or love letter.

Fortunately, the door to the restrooms led past the table where Epps and Royce were eating their salads and speaking in undertones. If I walked behind their table, Epps's back would be to me. Royce might be able to identify my voice, but I wasn't planning on speaking. I didn't want to take a chance of just dropping the earring onto the hardwood floor as I walked by. It might make noise or roll too far away. I locked my eyes on it in the palm of my hand, and using telekinesis, set it down gently as close to Epps's chair as I could manage without pausing. Neither man appeared to have heard it. I kept on going to the restroom. The first part of my plan was complete.

Now to find out if the spell actually worked. I slipped into a bathroom stall to cast the spell where I wouldn't be seen. Closing my eyes helped focus my intent and at that moment I needed all the help I could get.

Twixt pearl I wear and pearl I set
From ear to ear, pearls help me hear
The words of those you are most near.

I said it three times and waited. Nothing. My heart sank. Maybe Travis's faith in me was misplaced. I left the stall and washed my hands, sure that even the door of the stall was germ central. I was drying them with the ubiquitous paper towels, when Epps's voice came to life in my ear as clear as the music that came through the ear piece of my iPod. I glanced quickly at the woman using the sink beside me, worried she could hear him too. She smiled. "Aren't these paper towels ridiculous?" she said. "I have to use three or four if I want to get my hands dry." I agreed with her, wished her a good evening and hurried back to our table, spirits high. Travis was digging into his appetizer; my salad awaited me. He put his fork down, looking a bit sheepish. "Sorry for starting without you. I'm really starving," he said in his defense.

"You're forgiven. I don't stand on formalities. A sorcerer has to be flexible."

"So, don't keep me in suspense. By the twinkle in your eyes, I'm guessing we're in business?"

"Yes, I'm just sorry you can't hear them too."

"I trust that you'll give me a recap," he said, attacking the mozzarella again. I picked up my fork, thinking I could chew quietly enough not to interfere with hearing their dialogue. I was wrong. The romaine lettuce was so fresh and crunchy it was as effective as a white noise machine. No salad for me. At least the ravioli wouldn't be crunchy. When I explained why I'd given up on the salad, Travis took a slice of his cheese and tomato and plopped them onto my bread dish. I mouthed a *thank you*. At the end of the meal, my plate was empty but I couldn't have told you what I ate or if I liked it. I'd eaten on automatic pilot. Travis pronounced it all excellent and promised to take me back there to celebrate after we closed the case.

On the trip back to New Camel, I gave him a rundown on the conversation between Epps and Royce. "They may have been playing it safe," I said, "using euphemisms for words that would be damning. They were in a public place after all and Epps is the County Prosecutor." Travis stole a glance at me from the driver's seat. "They didn't slip up at all?"

"Not that I could tell. They talked football and hockey. It seems Royce is a high school football coach and he works as a handyman on the weekends. They talked about his team and Epps's family. They traded opinions on movies and books. It was all very mundane. Here's an example. Epps said he was thinking of having his dining room painted. Royce said he'd be glad to give him a hand with it. Epps said his wife wanted it to be a standard dove gray. Could that have been code for murder? Sure, but was it? I don't know. They could just as easily have been talking about painting the dining room dove gray."

"Then we keep on going," he said, trying to sound upbeat, but unable to keep his disappointment from bleeding through.

"Eventually the killer is going to make a mistake," I agreed, "and we'll be there to catch them."

Chapter 35

Sam Crawford's office was also in Watkins Glen. That's where the similarities between his office and Epps's ended. Crawford had bought an old building in disrepair, had it razed to the foundation and rebuilt it to fit in with the surrounding structures that dated back to the late nineteenth and early twentieth centuries.

Travis and I walked into the lobby. It reminded me of a whiteout in a blizzard. The walls were white, the marble floor was white and the receptionist's curved desk was a stunning high-gloss white. The contrast between the historic exterior of the building and the modern interior was disorienting. Judging by Travis's expression, he'd also been knocked off kilter by it. That may have been Crawford's intent.

The woman behind the desk was Marsha Goodall, according to her nameplate. She looked up when the outer door closed behind us, but she didn't speak until we reached her desk.

"May I help you?" she asked in the hushed tones of a classical music DJ. Outdoor voices were clearly not appreciated in there.

"Kailyn Wilde and Travis Anderson to see Mr. Crawford," I said.

"Welcome. You are a tad early, so please make yourselves comfortable." She handed us little menus listing the complimentary beverages we could order while we waited. "If there's anything you'd like, please don't hesitate to ask. Mr. Crawford will be with you shortly."

Sleek white armchairs were clustered in groups of three around glass and chrome cocktail tables. We sat down, prepared to wait a while, but on the stroke of our appointed time a door off the lobby opened and Sam Crawford appeared. He strode over, introduced himself, and welcomed us to his office. There was so much good will oozing from him and Ms.

Goodall that the white walls were practically dripping treacle. Some people might call it graciousness and lament its demise in modern society, but it made me uncomfortable.

To my great surprise, Crawford was more down to earth than his reputation and trappings had led me to expect. He ushered us into his office, which had been done in earth tones and was decidedly warmer and more masculine than the lobby. If the lobby was intended to put you off balance, his office was designed to make you feel protected, cocooned. The wide-plank oak floors, the wainscoting, the rich Mahogany desk, the floor to ceiling bookcases with every volume as perfectly ordered as a crack army unit all reinforced the same theme—you'll be cared for and represented by the best of the best. Relax, I've-got-your-back, Jack.

His desk was remarkably free of papers and folders. He probably had enough staff to keep after the endless paperwork that computers were supposed to have done away with, but never did.

"I'm so glad you accepted my invitation to come straight to the horse's mouth," he said with a smile that seemed genuine. I was beginning to understand what his clients saw in him, beyond his outstanding record in the courtroom.

"It's our pleasure," Travis said. "If you're ready, we can get started."

"I'm surprised you don't have a cameraman with you," Crawford said.

"This was the only way I could get the network to sign off on the interview. They'll use stock footage. Everything's about the bottom line; you know how that goes."

"Only too well." Crawford leaned back in his chair and set his feet on the edge of the desk, legs crossed at the ankles. "Question away." Travis asked for permission to record the interview, which Crawford granted by way of a nod.

"To begin," he said, "let me tell you something you probably already know. You have far more devotees than detractors."

"Yeah, but somehow my fans are never as vocal as my critics. I imagine the CP did a hatchet job on me."

"Not really," I said. "He gave you credit for all you've accomplished and admitted that defense attorneys are a crucial part of the system."

"I'm shocked to hear that. Outside the courtroom he barely deigns to speak to me."

"Well, he's all about trying to protect the public from the same people you keep putting back on the streets," Travis pointed out. "It's not a great formula for friendship."

"Such is the nature of the justice system."

"Granted," Travis said. "But I for one, would have trouble sleeping nights if I kept people out of jail who were likely to go back to doing the things that got them arrested in the first place."

"Whoa, you come charging right out of the gate, don't you, cowboy? Look, you know how the law works. Not to denigrate Epps, but the formula is simple. If too many cases end up in acquittals or light sentences, maybe the County Prosecutor is not equal to the task." He spoke calmly and without rancor.

"Then you think Epps has failed to put enough effort into his work?" I asked.

"I can't speak to his level of effort, I can only speak to the results."

"It sounds like you might welcome a more challenging relationship with the CP," Travis said.

Crawford grinned. "Sure, maybe I'd sleep even better than I do now." I'd been on the fence about trying the honesty spell I'd used on Epps, since he'd had a little trouble shaking it off. But sitting there with Crawford and his expansive personality, I didn't think he'd have any such issue. If anything, he might slough it right off. For honesty's sake, it was worth a shot.

Let fear and caution leave your mind.
Fret and worry leave behind.
What is true may now be spoken,
What was hidden be now open.

"How does your family feel about your work?" I asked.

Crawford's smile faltered. "Interesting you should ask that question. I have three kids, two in high school. When they were little, they didn't care how I made the money to buy them what they wanted. Now they're at that rebellious age where they only see things in black and white. My eldest even accused me of being culpable in a distracted driving death, because…" He frowned for a moment and cleared his throat before continuing. "Because in his opinion my client should have been behind bars." I noticed the reset, but most people wouldn't have. That one honest anecdote was all the spell had bought. "Raising kids is definitely not for the faint of heart." He shrugged, not like he didn't care about what his children thought of him, more like he was prepared to be seen as the bad guy until they grew up and could see things in a more realistic light.

Merlin's wisdom popped into my head. "Life is lived mainly in the gray areas."

"Hey, that's good," Crawford said. "Mind if I use that line the next time my kids go for the jugular?"

"It's something a friend told me. I'm sure he wouldn't mind."

"I have a question for the two of you," he said. "I hear you've been looking into some deaths that took place over a period of years, true or not?"

"Where did you hear that?" Travis asked, sidestepping the question with his own.

"I have my sources," Crawford said with a sly smile. "There isn't much that happens in this county that I don't know about."

"Then you don't need me to confirm it."

"No, not really. But I would like to know if I'm right about why you're doing it. I like a mystery, a good brain teaser. You started your investigation right after your foster brother's death. When you were interviewed by the local paper at the time, you made it clear you didn't agree with the coroner's report that his death was caused by choking on a burger. I'm told that before he died, Ryan was snooping around, interviewing folks about the way their loved ones died. Knowing that, it wasn't much of a leap for you to believe Ryan's death had been staged to look like an accident, by someone who wanted to put an end to his inquiries. That's when you decided to take on his investigation. How am I doing so far?"

Travis's face was impassive. "It's an interesting tale."

"So interesting," Crawford said, "that I started looking into it more deeply myself. And you know what I discovered?" He didn't wait for an answer. "I discovered that a number of the deaths Ryan was looking into were my clients and that they died under what could be questionable circumstances. In a big city, it would be pretty hard to see the pattern, but up here there aren't a lot of trees to hide the forest. Statistically my clients have been dying in greater numbers than the general population. Greater numbers than probability can account for. My current theory is that someone is killing these people and making their deaths appear to be the result of accidents, disease, or criminal activity. Are we in the same ballpark?"

"I can't say."

"You mean you won't say," Crawford pressed him.

"I'm a reporter. I can't just give away my thunder."

"Okay, I can respect that. If I were asked to give away the strategy for defending my next case, I'd say the same thing."

It was time to get the dialogue back on track, *our* track. "Since you're not a reporter," I said to Crawford, "why don't you tell us who's on your list of suspects."

Crawford grinned. "You want me to do your job for you, huh?"

"No, just curious," I said. "No one can do our job for us."

"Sure, why not? My list would have to include anyone who suffered a loss at the hands of one of my clients, maybe someone with a superhero complex, or someone like Epps, making up for his shortcomings in the courtroom. Then again, I don't know if he has sufficient backbone to do it. I could probably come up with others if I gave it more thought."

"That's okay," I said.

"I bet if you gave Epps all the information and asked him for a list of suspects, my name would top the list."

"Why do you say that?" Travis asked.

"The man doesn't think further than the end of his nose. That's why he's so easy to beat in the courtroom. I would have nothing to gain and everything to lose by killing off my own clients. It would be the end of my very lucrative practice, one I worked hard to build. And I've become awfully fond of my lifestyle. So have my wife and three ungrateful kids. You know the saying 'A luxury once enjoyed becomes a necessity.'"

"Who said that?" I asked.

"A man by the name of C. Northcote Parkinson, a British naval officer in the early twentieth century. And now you know my vice—I'm a total history nerd."

We spent the next twenty minutes asking Crawford the kind of banal questions you see in most interviews. He was all over them. As Travis predicted, he loved to talk about himself. He regaled us with courtroom anecdotes that illustrated his prowess at defending his clients.

When we thanked him for granting us the interview, he asked when it would be aired, and Travis fed him some double-talk about the news director and needing to wait for a slow news day. He promised the attorney he'd get back to him.

We walked outside to clear skies and a calmer wind, but the cold air was as sharp as broken glass against my skin. I pulled up the collar of my coat and tried to convince Travis to let me drive him back to his apartment. He insisted he was fine, but with his hands stuffed into his pockets and his chin burrowed into his coat, he looked like a frightened tortoise. When I told him that, he caved.

Sitting in my car with the heat cranking, we held our little postmortem. "Crawford came pretty close to accusing Epps," he said.

"He definitely has a winning motive, but the vibe I got off him was of a bureaucrat putting in his time until retirement. I can't picture him sneaking around and murdering people."

"Did you try your spell on Crawford?" he asked. "I didn't notice anything different."

"I tried, but it didn't even last a minute."

"That's strange, isn't it?"

"Not really. Everyone reacts differently to that kind of spell. Or it could be my magick that's off today. It's far from an exact science." I pulled to the curb in front of his apartment building. "I bet I know what you're going to do now."

"What's that?"

"Use your persuasive wiles to talk your director into running the interview."

"Yeah," he said dryly, "wish me luck."

Chapter 36

Paul Curtis arrived for his reading in jeans, Timberlands, and a dark-plaid flannel shirt. He looked like a woodsman, a woodsman on his way to the dentist to have all his wisdom teeth pulled without benefit of Novocain or laughing gas. From my shop, I'd watched him park his Jeep at the curb and head next door to Tea and Empathy. I would have loved to be privy to his reading. I didn't understand why he found the prospect of it so unpleasant. Perhaps it was not only because he didn't believe in psychics and magick, but also because he didn't *want* to believe in such things.

I've seen a lot of men cling to the world they think they know with a sort of desperation. If they can't experience it with their five senses, it doesn't exist. Talk about the metaphysical and they are gone. Travis was one of them, until I made him a believer. And although Paul didn't appear concerned when he visited my shop in the past, it was probably because he'd convinced himself that it was all for fun. A psychic as talented and well-known as Tilly had the power to rattle his beliefs and provide hard evidence that as senses go, five doesn't cut it.

Paul had declined staying for the tea option upfront, and Tilly had promised him a quick reading, but being Tilly, she'd baked some scones and apple tarts with cinnamon and sugar anyway, hoping their warm, seductive smell would convince him to stay. The longer he stayed, the more she might glean from his words as well as his mind.

I watched the clock after he went in. When the half hour mark came and went, I knew he'd capitulated. Carbs: one, best intentions: zero. I even heard Tilly and him laughing. When I saw him leave after a solid hour and ten minutes, he seemed lighter of foot and spirit.

As soon as he was out of sight, I ran into the tearoom. My aunt was still sitting at the table, enjoying what I assumed was her second or third scone. I sat in the chair across from her. "Well—what happened?" She pushed the plate with the last scone over to me and followed it with the ramekin that held the last of the clotted cream.

"The dairy outdid themselves this time," she mumbled around a mouthful of the cream-topped scone.

"You know you say that with every batch they send, right?"

Tilly produced a blissful smile, too happy to take umbrage at my remark.

"What I really want to hear is what you found out from Curtis," I reminded her.

She wiped her mouth with a napkin. "He didn't even try to block me. Maybe he didn't realize he could. For an officer of the law, he's surprisingly straight forward and guileless. With Paul Curtis, what you see is what you get. That's a lovely trait in a man—in case you weren't aware of it."

"Is that a comment about Travis? I thought you liked him."

"I do. As do your mother and grandmother. I've never poked around in *his* head though. I suspect he's a lot more complicated—not that there's anything wrong with that. I, for one, always gravitated toward complex men. They're more interesting, even if they are a lot more trouble."

I already knew that Travis was multifaceted and complex and it hadn't sent me packing. But who was I to talk? We Wildes were nothing, if not complicated. "Can we get back to Paul Curtis?" I asked.

"Yes, of course. Duggan *did* interview Austin Stubbs. Curtis was there with him. But they never checked out his alibi, because the ME's report came out about that time and it was unequivocal—Axel overdosed on drugs that were self-administered. That was the end of the investigation."

"And the alibi? What was it?"

"I'm getting to it," she said. "I was just trying to build up a little dramatic tension first."

"I'm not a client, Aunt Tilly. You can dispense with the drama."

She chuckled. "What was I thinking? All that delicious, awful sugar must have addled me. Austin Stubbs claimed he was hanging out at the Longhorn Bar in Burdett, from seven o'clock that night until after midnight."

"Thank you, you did great," I said jumping up and kissing her on the cheek before I hurried back to my shop.

In order to scratch Austin Stubbs off our suspect list or elevate his standing on it, I had to see if his alibi held up. But first things first—I was going to Burdett to check out the motorcycle I'd seen in his yard. Tilly and I worked out the logistics of the trip to Burdett. I needed to have Merlin

with me in case something went awry with the spell. That meant that Tilly
had to come along to keep him in line. The more people involved, the
greater the odds that someone would make a mess of things. My money
was squarely on Merlin. For what it was worth, Tilly made him promise
to behave. There was some discussion about remuneration for his good
conduct and for keeping his mouth shut. I heard words like cake and pizza
being bandied about as part of the negotiations. I kept my nose out of it.

There was one party who was sure to be in a dandy snit by the time
we got home from our trip. Sashkatu had no patience for any deviation in
his routine. Having to stay home and nap with the riffraff all day was not
going to please his highness. He had me so brainwashed that I actually felt
pangs of guilt for a minute. Then my common sense returned and pointed
out that I was hardly abandoning him. He had a big warm house with lots
of comfy furniture to sleep on—poor baby.

* * * *

When we chose the day for our escapade, we made sure it wouldn't
conflict with the tour bus schedule. Neither of us could afford to lose the
revenue from a busload of holiday spenders. The next consideration was
the weather. I checked online and was relieved to see that the prediction
was for cold clear skies.

We decided to have Merlin glamour me right before we arrived at the
Stubbs farm so there would be less chance of the spell wearing off at a
critical time. When we reached Burdett, I stopped at the little café, where
Elise and I had bought the amazing Danish on our recent trip up there.
Since Tilly was always hungry when she was nervous and Merlin seemed
capable of eating whenever food was available, I thought it best to fortify
ourselves before the mission. Tilly took a bite of the muffin she'd chosen
and deemed it edible, a wild rave coming from her. Merlin didn't comment,
but he devoured his in record time, then half of Tilly's when she made the
mistake of going to the restroom. He was eyeing mine until I popped the
last piece into my mouth.

"Say naught to your aunt," he whispered to me, "but as muffins go,
these surpass the banana walnut ones she bakes."

"That might be because these are cranberry orange," I whispered back
with an edge to my words. We Wildes may be given to arguing among
ourselves, but the moment one of us is maligned or disrespected, we're
one for all and all for one. Merlin, who can be less than astute at times,
got the message in my tone and said no more on the subject.

We found a side road not far from the Stubbs's farm. No one was out and about, one of the benefits of cold weather. We parked where the homeowners weren't likely to see us if they peered out their windows, but it was hard to know for certain. We didn't expect to be there long in any case. Merlin began the spell, but suddenly stopped short. After all our planning and making sure Tilly had the spell reversal in her purse, this could not be happening! The one thing we'd overlooked was the possibility that Merlin might forget how to glamour me! My first instinct was to ask him what was wrong, but I talked myself out of it. *Give him a chance to remember on his own,* I told myself.

Tilly, who'd been riding shotgun, opened her mouth to speak, but I shook my head at her. The minutes ticked by with Merlin mumbling and muttering in the backseat. I was reaching the end of my patience when he finally spoke up. "My apologies for the interruption," he said. "I believe I'm ready to start over." Tilly and I shared a mutual sigh of relief.

I didn't feel any different when he declared the spell finished, but Tilly's face told a different story. She was agape. "What's wrong?" I asked her. What I'd meant to say was, "how do I look?"

She swallowed hard and tried to affix a smile to her lips, but it wouldn't take. Her face had gone a pasty white. I couldn't wait another second. I flipped down the visor to see for myself. It was my turn to be speechless. Behind me Merlin was bouncing up and down in his seat. "Superb! Magnificent!"

Had I not been going for anonymity, I might have been as pleased with my appearance as he was. But what were the odds that Austin Stubbs wouldn't recognize Elvis Presley?

Chapter 37

"Elvis?" was all I managed to sputter.

Merlin shrugged. "It would appear that the movies I watched last night were still fresh in my mind," he said without any discernible regret.

"It's true," Tilly piped up. "He watched *Girl Trouble* and *Blue Hawaii*. I would have changed the channel if I thought it would influence his glamouring today."

I peered at my image again. "I guess I should be grateful he wasn't watching *Young Frankenstein*." I turned to Merlin. "I don't suppose you could reverse this spell and reglamour me into an average guy?"

"It would be ill-advised. I might not be strong enough to reverse the second glamouring. Were I a younger man, it would not have posed a problem."

"Look at the bright side," Tilly said. "Stubbs may be so confounded by finding Elvis at his door that he might accidentally divulge something important." Maybe she was right. Besides, there was nothing I could do to change the circumstances.

"Wait a minute," I said, realizing I still sounded exactly like myself. "Won't my voice give me away as a woman? Not to mention, Elvis's voice was as famous as his appearance."

Tilly and Merlin burst into laughter. "You're the only one who will hear *your* voice," the wizard explained.

"I hear Elvis loud and clear," Tilly concurred. This whole experience was getting weirder by the second. I looked down at my clothes and found to my relief that I appeared to be wearing black chinos, a green wool sweater, and a leather jacket, circa 1960. Fortunately Merlin wasn't thinking of a beach scene when he glamoured me. A bathing suit in freezing temperatures would have been impossible to explain.

I circled back to the Stubbs farm and parked off to the side of the house where I could see the tarp-covered motorcycle. I debated whether to just sneak a peek and drive away or ring the doorbell and say I might be interested in buying the bike if he were of a mind to sell it. Ringing the bell won, but only because I stood to learn more about Stubbs that way. Plus I'd already created a whole cover story about a friend of mine in the area who thought Stubbs might have the kind of bike I'd been looking for.

When I suggested to Merlin that he and my aunt should wait in the car, he said he had to be right beside me in case there were issues with the spell. And once Merlin was going, Tilly would not be denied. "I can't very well keep tabs on him from the car," she said. "Isn't that why you brought me along?" Point taken. She might need to give him a swift kick to the shins or an elbow to the ribs.

We all piled out of the SUV and trooped over to the front door —Tilly in her down jacket over a flowered muumuu and sneakers, Merlin in an Arctic anorak and burlap pants, and Elvis. We must have been quite a sight to see.

I rang the bell and prepared to be gawked at. I was not disappointed. Stubbs opened the door and froze the moment he saw me. I don't think he even realized there were two other people standing there. "Mr. Stubbs, sir," I said, doing my best to use words Elvis might have used, "beggin' your pardon, but I wonder if I could get a look at your Harley?"

"You ever been told you bear an uncanny resemblance to Elvis Presley?" Stubbs said, his words dribbling slowly from his mouth as if he'd suffered a stroke. My question didn't seem to have registered at all.

"Yes sir, a time or two. Mind if I go have a look at your Harley?"

"And you sound just like him. Can you sing?" The gears in his brain must have started working again, because he was clearly hatching a scheme. Was he imagining himself a twenty-first century Colonel Parker to my reincarnated Elvis?

"I imagine most folks can," I said, trying to make light of the question. "Now about the Harley—"

"Yeah, yeah," he said. "I'll tell you what, I'll show you the bike if you agree to sing for me." I panicked for a moment, wondering if I'd be able to sing like the King or if I'd sound as off-key as I usually did. Then again, after I saw the Harley, it didn't matter what he thought of me.

"You got yourself a deal," I said.

Stubbs grabbed his coat off a hook near the door and led the way to the bike. He kept turning to look at me as if he was afraid I would disappear if he wasn't vigilant. It occurred to me, belatedly, that I should have done a little research on motorcycles, Harleys in particular. I probably could have Googled what to look for when buying a used one. As things stood, I'd have to adlib. When we reached the bike, Stubbs pulled off the tarp without ceremony. "There she is," he said. "By the way, are these folks with you?" He indicated Tilly and Merlin with a thrust of his chin.

"Yes sir, they most certainly are. This here's my aunt Tilly and the white-haired gentleman is my granddaddy, Mervin." Stubbs shook their hands, chatting them up like he was trying to ingratiate himself with my nearest and dearest.

The instant I saw the bike, I knew it was the one Lolly had seen the Biker Dude riding.

There was an intricate black and white pattern painted on the gas tank. She'd said it made her think of an abstract tangle of snakes, with their forked tongues extended. I could see what she meant. What now? I had the information I'd come for, but I couldn't just say *thanks* and *goodbye.* If he wasn't the killer, it would be rude, and if he was in some way involved in the murders, I didn't want him or any of his cohorts getting the idea we were on to them. So I took a slow turn around the bike, squinting at this and frowning at that and nodding to myself. When I came back to where Stubbs was waiting, I tried to sound like a shrewd buyer—a shrewd buyer who had no idea what the bike was worth. I was pretty sure if Nancy Drew could see what was going on, she'd be thinking, *You even have the internet, girl!*

"So—what would you take for her?" I said in a casual I-could-take-it-or-leave-it way.

Stubbs put his hand up to his chin and rubbed it back and forth over the stubble like he was doing some hard thinking. "Before you showed up, I wasn't of a mind to sell her. I have quite an attachment to her, you see." He gave me a sideways glance, no doubt assessing my reaction.

"You still ride her?" I asked.

"Not so much anymore, but my niece likes to borrow her, take her for a spin now and then."

"Give me a figure," I said.

"How about I get back to you? I want to give Lena a call and see how she feels about me selling it. Family—you know how it is."

"Yes, sir, I sure do. Might your niece be the Lena Halloway I met down in Watkins Glen the other day?" I had to make sure he wasn't talking about a different Lena.

"One and the same," he said. "Fine lookin' young woman, wouldn't you say?" Was he thinking of a little match making now? Hooking his family up to an Elvis reboot? Never mind that she was already engaged.

"Yes sir," I agreed. "I'll give you my number." As if on cue, Tilly pulled a torn envelope out of her purse and handed it to me along with a pen. I jotted down random numbers and gave it to Stubbs.

He accepted it with a sly grin, no doubt thinking he had the phone number of the next Elvis Presley. "Now," he said, "how about that song you promised me?"

"I never said I was Elvis," I pointed out, in case he took exception to my singing and hauled off and decked me.

"Yeah, yeah…get on with it."

"Love me tender, love me true, all my dreams fulfilled." I could tell by the way the three of them were cringing that the illusion didn't change the fact that I couldn't carry a tune.

"You're right. You ain't no Elvis," Stubbs said with disgust. "Go on, get outta here." He strode away in the direction of the house, muttering and cursing under his breath.

We climbed back in the SUV, laughing. The laughter would start to wind down, but then one of us would mention a different aspect of the encounter, sparking another round of hysteria. I even forgot to stop somewhere to have Merlin reverse the spell. None of us realized the lapse, until I pulled into a gas station outside Watkins Glen. The young man who pumped the gas didn't seem to notice that he was talking to Elvis, but the elderly woman walking back to her car from the station's mini-mart took one look at me and her eyes bugged out of her head. She toddled up to us as fast as her legs could carry her. "Elvis?" she said, her voice shaking, "that can't really be you?"

"Yes, Ma'am," I said. "Ya'll have a good day."

Chapter 38

By the time we were back in the New Camel city limits, Merlin had reversed the spell and I was mostly back to myself. My voice was still a little low and nasal, but he assured me that would soon fade. I dropped the members of my motley crew off at Tilly's house and went home. Five cats greeted me at the door. Maybe greeted was too strong a word. They locked eyes with me as if they were trying to send me a message. Although telepathy was not one of my talents, I had a pretty good idea what was on their minds. "I'm not late," I told them. They were not swayed. It occurred to me that they might be taking orders from Sashkatu who hadn't yet made an entrance. The wily old boy must have gotten to them, made them his puppets. It wasn't the first time. He probably convinced them they'd been neglected, forgotten, forsaken.

"Sashki, come out; come out wherever you are." When he didn't make an appearance, I went searching for him. I looked everywhere I could think of, before deciding that he must have found a new place to hide and nurse his snit. The other cats were waiting for me in the kitchen, so I fixed their dinner, even though it was half an hour early. I was hoping the smell of food would draw Sashki out, but he seemed determined to ignore me and his stomach. Worry feeds on worry, Bronwen used to say. I had no doubt that bit of wisdom was true, yet it never helped my mother or me to stop worrying. What's more, I couldn't recall it ever helping my grandmother either. "Wisdom is meant to be passed down to future generations," she'd told me when I brought up this failing. "Mark my words; someday down the line it will be needed. Maybe by your children." I should have known better than to question my grandmother. She was invincible, a fortress hard to storm.

I found Sashkatu an hour later when I was watering the plants in the living room. He was sleeping, curled around the trunk of the potted ficus, his black coat great camouflage on the dark soil. When the first drop of water hit his fur, you'd have thought it was hot oil by his reaction. He jumped up hissing, back arched, ears flat against his head. Admirable reflexes for a cat of his years. I felt bad about his rude awakening, but he had brought it upon himself. When he followed me into the kitchen looking for his dinner, I gave him some leftover salmon with his kibble. He took it as the olive branch I meant it to be and, after licking the dish clean, he climbed up on the couch where I was sitting. In his absence, the other cats had come to snuggle with me. He glared at the tabby in my lap, until she left, then took his rightful place in my lap with a grumble of contentment.

Travis was anchoring the evening news from Watkins Glen. Hearing about all the troubles and cross-purposes in the world didn't seem quite as bleak coming from him. I assumed no one else felt that way or he would be anchoring the news in a market like the New York City tri-state area. The few times he'd been afforded that opportunity, his demographics were high. Just not high enough to knock the competition off the ladder. I admit to being sorely tempted to use a little magick to smooth his way, but I always came to my senses before I did anything that foolish. Helping Travis would have meant derailing others in their career paths—black magick no matter which way you tried to spin it.

The news had barely faded to commercial when my phone rang. I didn't have to look at the Caller ID to know Travis was on the other end. I rolled out the story of my turn as Elvis Presley in great detail and he laughed until he was wheezing. I had to hold on while he went in search of water. "And the motorcycle?" he asked, back on the line.

"The same one Lolly described. But it gets better. Lena is Stubbs's niece."

"The CP's secretary?"

"The very same. And she must know Biker Dude, because Stubbs said she liked to borrow the bike now and then. No mention of any guy, though."

"Sounds like Stubbs doesn't know she's been lending the bike to a third party."

"That would be my guess. I'm planning to go back up there to check out Stubbs's alibi," I added.

"His bar cronies aren't the most reliable people to confirm his story. Odds are they were under the influence at the time, which makes their testimony worthless."

"But bartenders aren't allowed to drink on the job," I pointed out.

"Kailyn," he said with a laugh, "you're a little naive. We're talking about a hole in the wall bar in Burdett, off-season. I wouldn't be too sure about how strictly they comply with the liquor commission's regulations."

I stopped listening at *naive*. If I were a cat, my hackles would have spiked. "Is that how you win a point?" I said, not bothering to hide my irritation.

"Win? I don't follow." He sounded completely lost—men.

"Calling me *naive* is a putdown. It's a way to invalidate my opinion, my thoughts, me."

"I swear I didn't mean it that way, Kailyn." He was clearly taken aback.

"How *did* you mean it?"

"Like it's sweet that you trust everyone to play by the rules."

"You're not helping yourself," I said.

"Then please accept my apology, before I dig myself into a deeper hole." He sounded a little desperate, and I was finding it hard to stay mad at him anyway.

"Okay, apology accepted. But you might want to think about what you say before you say it in the future."

"Right, got it."

"Listen," I said, "do you want to hit that bar together?"

"I'm off tomorrow night if that works."

"Tomorrow night it is."

* * * *

We arrived in Burdett at a quarter past eight. In Manhattan, people were just getting ready for an evening out, but in Burdett most of the businesses were already shuttered for the night. The only places with their lights on were a pizza and pasta joint and the Longhorn Saloon—apparently the owner had a sense of humor. The name brought to mind old Westerns with honky-tonk piano music and corseted women in flamboyant dresses. Inside, this saloon was just a run-of-the-mill bar without pretensions. The sour smell of old beer and liquor hit us when we opened the door. The lighting was dim, possibly for ambiance, but more likely to mask the bar's deficiencies, like walls that needed painting. They were lucky most people don't have great vision. A few men were watching football on the flat screen above the bar. Two others were playing darts at the far end of the long, narrow space. They all looked middle-aged and older.

Travis and I sat down a few stools away from the TV watchers. The bartender came right over to us, blatant curiosity on his face. He was up there in years like the other men. I had the crazy thought that he might ask to see our ID and then demand that we leave, because there was a strict fifty and older policy. Travis ordered whatever beer they had on tap. I asked for tea. The cold damp of the day had left me chilled. The bartender wasn't sure if there was tea, but he went in the back to check. When he returned, he was carrying a mug of steaming water with a teabag afloat in it and Travis's beer. He found some sugar packets for me under the bar. "You folks visiting here or passing through?" he asked.

"I'm Travis Anderson and this is my partner, Kailyn Wilde. We're here investigating a murder."

His brow furrowed. "Are you now? There haven't been any murders in Burdett for as long as I've been living here." The TV watchers had turned their attention to us as soon as they heard the word *murder*. The bartender asked them, "Any of you guys know what he's talking about?" They all shook their heads.

"Axel Stubbs," Travis said.

"I'm afraid you've got your facts wrong. Axel overdosed on drugs. And that's gotta be three, four years ago by now."

"And good riddance," one of the TV watchers muttered.

"We have reason to believe the ME's report was wrong on one point," I said. "It's possible Axel didn't OD; someone just made it look that way."

The bartender shrugged. "What do you think I can tell you about it?" He sounded annoyed.

"We're not here to accuse anyone of anything," I said quickly. "We just want to verify an alibi."

"And whose alibi would that be?" the bartender asked.

"Austin Stubbs," Travis said. I watched the faces of the men and found it interesting that there was no push back, no how-dare-you from any of them. No one called us out for investigating a lifelong friend, a fellow townie. Apparently, Austin wouldn't win any popularity contest.

"Stubbs claimed he was here the night Axel died?" the bartender asked.

"When was that again?" This from a TV-watcher with a scruffy gray beard.

"July third, 2014," Travis replied.

"Kinda hard to remember a particular day that long ago," gray beard said.

"If it's any help," the bartender said, "Austin used to stop in most nights when Axel was alive."

"The more he drank, the more he'd ramble on about the hardships of raising a teenager alone," gray beard said with a grunt.

"And in the three years since then?" I asked.

"He doesn't come in that much anymore," the bartender said. It sounded like once Axel was gone, Stubbs senior no longer had much to vent about. "Hold on," he said, "I think maybe I *can* help you. It just struck me—the day before July fourth three years ago I had to close the bar for my dad's funeral. Austin couldn't have been here."

"Why would Stubbs have lied to the police, if not to cover up a murder?" I said to Travis on our way back to the Glen.

"Could be he was home alone the night his son died and he was afraid the truth wouldn't keep him out of jail. Seems like enough people heard him complain about Axel over the years, which gave him a motive. So he played the odds. According to the bartender, Stubbs was a regular there for a long time. Who would remember that he wasn't there for one night that long ago?"

"Except that he happened to pick the one night the bar was closed," I said.

"It wouldn't be the first time a little thing like that took down a criminal."

"I can see Stubbs killing his son in a fit of rage," I said, "but I can't picture him in the role of a caped crusader who suddenly feels the calling to eliminate other people who are potential threats to society."

"From everything you've told me about the man, I'm inclined to agree," Travis said. "He doesn't sound like an altruist. But facts don't lie. Lena is his niece, she borrows his motorcycle, the same one Biker Dude rides and you caught her sneaking into town hall and stealing Epps's files."

"Now if we could just connect the dots."

Chapter 39

New Camel was undergoing its annual holiday makeover. Town workers were draping green garland between the old-fashioned lamp posts that were already decked out with shiny red bows. Tiny lights were sprinkled throughout the garland. They were difficult to see in daylight, but at night they twinkled like reflections of the stars. Holiday music was once again coming from the speakers secured to trees and lamp posts. The weather had moderated enough for me to step outside without my coat to admire the full effect of the decorations. A half dozen other shopkeepers were outside too, all waving to each other. The cold made groundhogs of us. We hunkered down in our own little burrows. It took the holidays to draw us out.

Lolly was taking in the view and beaming with delight. She waved when she saw me and came across the street. "No matter how old I get to be, holiday decorations always make me feel like a kid again," she said.

"I know what you mean. I definitely need a little joy and this always does the trick."

"Is everything okay?" she asked. "I couldn't help but notice you've been away from your shop a lot lately."

"This investigation is a tough one," I said. "But we're all good."

Lolly put her arm around my shoulders and squeezed. "Hang in there — something's going to break soon, mark my words."

I laughed. "Are you trying to compete with my aunt?"

She looked stricken. "Heavens no, it would be a fool's errand at best. How *is* my favorite psychic baker these days?"

"Tilly's fine, probably in a baking frenzy for today's readings and teas." The cool air had made its way through my sweater and was nipping at my skin. Although the temperature was above freezing, it was miles from warm. When my shoulders quaked from the chill, Lolly sent me back inside with grandmotherly insistence and I obeyed. Up until my mid-twenties, I would have chafed at being told what was best for me. Maybe I was officially a grown-up.

The people on that day's bus tour were every bit as happy as we were with the moderating temperature and festive look of the town. Some of them had been to New Camel and my shop before, but many had not. It was easy to tell them apart. Those who were familiar with Abracadabra grabbed a wicker basket and made a beeline for their favorite products. The rest wandered in tentatively. Two women blocked the doorway, just poking their heads in, trying to decide it they wanted to venture farther. One of my more exuberant repeat customers saw the queue forming behind them and took it upon herself to go over to talk to them. "Don't be silly geese. Come on in. There's nothing in here to be afraid of. The beauty products Kailyn sells are better than anything I've ever tried and they don't cost an arm and a leg. Perfect for holiday gifts too!" Her last remarks did the trick.

I thanked her for her help. "I should hire you," I said.

She laughed. "I'm a city girl. No small town can contain me, but I'm glad to lend a hand when I'm here. If you're really grateful, maybe you could give me a little discount? I'm buying a ton of stuff today. With winter ahead, I need enough of everything to last me till spring." How could I say *no*?

When the bus pulled out of town three hours later, my coffers were full and my shelves were bare. It was going to take hours of work to restock the products before the next group descended upon us. That was the one problem with the holiday season—trying to keep up with the demand. I never had to worry about it when Morgana and Bronwen were alive. My spirits flagged from the loss of them in my everyday life and the weight of the work on my shoulders. How did Lolly manage all by herself at almost fifty years my senior? If only I could figure out how to clone her energy…. I was so lost in my thoughts that I jumped when the phone rang. I was surprised to hear Sam Crawford's voice and hoped he wasn't calling to ask *me* when his interview would be aired.

"Miss Wilde, I wanted to let you know that there was an attempt on my life last night," he said, dispensing with the usual pleasantries. His voice was tight as if he was still dealing with the emotional effects of the life and death situation.

"Are you all right? Did you call the police?" It was all I could think to say.

"I'm a little on edge, but otherwise fine. The police have all the details. I just thought you should know in case this person comes after you." Considering what already happened to us, Travis and I were always on alert.

"I appreciate the heads up," I said. "May I ask what happened?"

"I was attacked last night in my own driveway—a man in a ski mask. He must have been hiding in the bushes, because he lunged at me with a knife the moment I got out of my car. He went for my neck, but I managed to block him with my arm and I started shouting for help. That's when he ran off."

"You spoke to Detective Duggan?"

"Yes, for what it's worth. I've since hired bodyguards. I have to consider the possibility that this man is the killer you're after. He may have concluded that the most efficient way to eliminate future threats to society is to remove me from the equation. You may want to take precautions yourself."

"Did you recognize the man's voice?" I asked. "Did it sound like anyone you know?"

"He never said a word."

"I'm glad you weren't injured."

"Do you want the number for the agency supplying my security team?" he asked.

"Let me get back to you on that," I said. No way could I afford private bodyguards. Besides, my wards were better. They didn't sleep, eat, or demand overtime.

"No problem. And you might want to remind your partner not to sit on my interview too long or it might wind up being my obituary," he added without humor.

I couldn't contact Travis until after the evening news. He got to me first. "Did you hear about Crawford's close call?"

"From the victim himself."

"He called you?"

"He said he wanted to let me know so I could protect myself. Come to think of it, I really should place wards around you too. I don't know why I didn't do it before. When can I see you?"

"Tomorrow? I'm bushed and I'm anchoring the early news in the morning."

"No, tonight," I said, leaving no room for argument. In spite of how tired I was, it seemed imperative to protect him as soon as possible. If I ignored the sirens blaring in my brain and something happened to him, I would never forgive myself. Travis agreed, not that I gave him much of a choice. I packed up the items I needed for the protection spell and left the house to the sleeping cats. It wasn't the first time I'd thought that the Wilde cats had a better gig than we humans.

I jumped into my car that had been sitting in the dark for hours with the temperature dropping, and instantly started shivering. It was the kind of night when there is nothing better than curling up on the couch with a blanket, a book, a cup of Tilly's tea, and a cat…or six. I reminded myself that an entire winter season of such nights lay ahead, mine for spending however I chose. And once I placed the protective wards around Travis, he'd be more likely to wind up there beside me. I made it to the Glen in record time. *Probably because everyone else was at home, curled up on their couches,* my whiny alter ego said.

When Travis opened his door, I had no more reservations about having made the trip. He was wearing jeans and a T-shirt, no socks or shoes. His hair was tousled as if he'd been raking his fingers through it. He looked like a little boy up past his bedtime. "I can't believe you came all the way here tonight," he said padding after me into the living room.

"I had no choice. Nothing less than your life is at stake." I set the tote with the paraphernalia on the coffee table and told him to sit down.

"I think that's being a bit overdramatic," he said, dropping onto the small sofa.

I'd started arranging the symbols for the elements on the table, but my head shot up at his words. "How can you, of all people, say that?"

"I know what you're getting at, but I'm not Ryan. I'm not out there stirring up hornets' nests and provoking people."

"What do you think we've been doing, poking our noses into everyone's business—making new friends?"

He shook his head as if he was too tired to argue about it. "What's my part in this?" he asked, looking at the things I'd laid out on the table.

"You'll be happy to know that you don't have to move a muscle. You can watch TV or even fall asleep if you're so inclined," I added dryly.

"You're annoyed," he said.

"More worried than annoyed…maybe both. I'm worried that you're not taking the situation seriously enough and I'm annoyed that you have a different standard when I'm the one taking risks. It implies that I'm the weaker sex, less able to take care of myself. You will never find a stronger woman than a Wilde and that's before we even talk magick. Now shut up and let me get on with protecting you!" I started smiling in spite of myself and in seconds we were both laughing. "Okay, I admit that was a little over the top," I said, wiping away tears of laughter. "It's been a long day."

I explained what I was doing as I passed each of the elements around him. "The sand represents earth, the sea water stands for water, and the candle is both air and fire. The words of the spell are deceptively simple. They derive their strength from the power of the one speaking them:

Earth and water, air and fire,
Protect this man against all harm

After I was finished protecting Travis, I walked through his apartment to place protective wards around it too.

"Why not spend the night?" he said, coming off the sofa when I was repacking the elements. He put his arms around my waist. "You don't really want to drive back to New Camel, do you?"

"No, but I have to get up early tomorrow and start restocking my shelves. I'm out of so many products; my head spins just thinking about all the work. Besides, I don't want to bother my aunt to run over to my house in the morning to feed the cats. She had a busy day too."

Travis insisted on walking me down to my car. "I get it that you're strong," he said, "but I'm doing this so *I* can sleep tonight and if you have a beef with that, you'll have to take it up with my mother. That's how she raised me."

"Touché," I said. "But you might want to put on shoes first." He'd followed me into the hallway wearing a parka, his feet bare. "You really must be tired."

When we reached my car, he drew me into a crushing bear hug. "Thanks for worrying about me," he said. "Would it be too much if I asked you to call when you get home, seeing as how there's a killer on the loose and all?"

I said I was fine with calling him. Rapunzel-in-the-tower stuff is where I drew the line. As it happened, he had good reason to worry.

Chapter 40

I was moving along the road between Watkins Glen and New Camel at a good clip. There weren't many other cars around. At roughly the midway point in my trip, there was only one other car I could see—a small SUV in the left lane. I was in the right. The SUV passed me, then pulled into my lane. I assumed the driver was turning off at the next side street. He slowed down as if that was his plan, but he didn't turn. Maybe he wasn't familiar with the area. The street signs were so small they were useless at night, unless you had a pair of binoculars handy. We drove for a while that way, with the other car slowing at every side street and never getting back up to a reasonable speed. I wondered if he was one of those people you read about who enjoys messing with other drivers. I thought about moving into the left lane to get away from him, but what if he took it as an escalation of the game he was playing and tried to crowd me off the road? I stayed where I was, the memory of our run-in with the snow plow still fresh in my mind.

I was bone-tired though and my patience was eroding. I gave myself the sensible lecture I might have received from family and friends. What was my hurry? Five minutes one way or the other was not going to matter in the long run. Better safe than sorry.

The driver of the other car must have been enjoying himself, because the car slowed to a crawl. That's when the hatchback opened a few inches and a hand emerged holding a bagful of something, which it emptied onto the roadway directly in front of me. The hatchback was yanked back down and the car took off before I realized that the bag had been holding nails and spikes. They glinted in the headlights. It happened so fast I had no way to avoid them. That must have been why they dropped them when I was as close as possible. Even if I swerved into the left lane, I'd be driving over enough of them to put my tires out of commission. Just the kind of prank a carload of bored teenagers might try. I slowed and gripped the wheel hard in case the tires blew and sent the car into a tailspin. The wards held. But as I was congratulating myself, a light flashed on the dashboard with the words *Low tire pressure.* It showed that two tires were a problem, both on the passenger side. The wards had held, but not 100 percent.

A pair of headlights lit up my rear-view mirror while I was debating what to do next. The new car was quickly gaining on me now that I was limping along. Instead of switching lanes to pass me, the driver slowed to match my speed. If I sped up, he sped up. If I slowed, he slowed. After the attack on my tires, there was only one reason he would be doing that and it wasn't to strike up a friendship. He had to be in league with the people who dropped the nails. He was waiting for my tires to fail, so I would have to pull over. I wondered if the same person who'd planned the snowplow attack and the attack on Crawford had orchestrated this plan too. If he had, he was probably hungry for success after failing to kill any of us.

I pulled my phone out of my purse. I punched in 911, hoping either Hobart or Curtis would catch the call in the New Camel precinct. Hobart picked up and I gave him a quick rundown on the situation, adding that I couldn't be certain of my suspicions. Better to cover myself in the unlikely event that my fears proved groundless. If he arrived before the tires forced me off the road, the car following me would surely sail on by as if they'd never meant me any harm. Hobart couldn't arrest the driver for spooking me.

The uneven tire pressure was causing the car to list to one side. I debated the merits of pulling over before Hobart arrived, to see if the driver was really out to kill me. But it would be foolhardy to test the wards that way when they'd already proved to be faltering. Travis would never forgive me if I did something stupid and wound up dead. The silly thought should have made me giggle, but it didn't.

By the time Hobart arrived, siren blaring, the tires were making an unhealthy *wubba-wubba* sound. Another minute and I would have been riding on the rims. I pulled over with a sigh of relief and a knot of frustration in my gut. The other car drove by as the police cruiser joined me on the shoulder. "That the car you told me about?" Hobart asked, after making sure I was unharmed.

I nodded. "I memorized the plate number."

He grabbed a mini iPad from his car and took it down. "I'll run it as soon as I get back to the station. Okay if I call a flatbed for your car?"

"I don't think I have a choice. I only have one spare."

"You're shivering, Kailyn. You should go wait in my patrol car. I'll be there in a minute." I didn't argue. I was cold from the inside out. My phone rang as I was snapping in my seatbelt. *Travis.* He had to be wondering why I hadn't kept my promise to call when I got home. I took a deep breath, before calmly explaining what happened.

"That was no carload of teenagers," he said when I finished.

"Yes, in retrospect I realize that too. Officer Hobart is driving me home. Let me call you back when I get there."

"The moment you get inside," he said.

"Don't worry, I'll talk to you in about fifteen."

Chapter 41

Hobart got me home in twelve. On the way, he fielded a call from an elderly woman who was almost incoherent with fear, because she was hearing noises in her attic. Hobart was clearly torn between seeing me inside and rushing over to the woman before she had a heart attack. I assured him I was fine and sent him on his way. I climbed the steps to the porch, never so happy to be home. I groped around in my purse for the keys. *Where the heck were they?* My fingers finally closed around them. I unlocked the door and was turning the knob to open it when a large, gloved hand came from behind and clamped over my mouth. I was shoved inside, my assailant immediately slamming the door shut and relocking it. I felt the bite of a knife pressing into my back, right through my coat. *How had he breached the wards around my house? I definitely needed to strengthen them.*

"Screaming is only going to make me angry," he warned me as he withdrew his hand from my mouth. I was not by nature a screamer and this didn't seem like the best time to change course. The houses on my block were far enough apart that with windows and doors shuttered tightly against the cold, no one would hear me anyway. But my attacker wasn't the only one who was angry. I'd had enough for one night. I spun around to face him, the blade slicing across the back of my coat. I was not at all surprised to be looking at a black ski mask. He was a big guy. I'm five-seven and he was a good six inches taller. There was no way I could win a fair fight with him, let alone when he was armed with that knife. I reached up to unmask him, but his fist came down on my arm so hard I thought it might be fractured. "What do you want from me?" The question was a reflex; I knew what he wanted.

He laughed. It was an ugly sound I never wanted to hear again. "Your investigation stops now! If it was up to me, you'd already be dead, so don't tempt me."

I had no cards up my sleeve. But even if I'd had some, I was too mentally and physically exhausted to play them. It would have been helpful to have six big, overprotective dogs at that moment, but Merlin wasn't around to transmute my kitties. I knew Sashkatu would have come to my defense if he wasn't sound asleep and well on his way to becoming deaf. But I would never choose to put him in harm's way. I was on my own. The wards had prevented my tires from blowing out, I reminded myself. Maybe they could prevent the knife from killing me. At that moment two clouds popped out of the air, startling both me and my assailant.

"Oh," Morgana said, "pardon us. We didn't know you had company, dear." I'd never been so happy to see them.

"For goodness sakes," Bronwen snapped, "sometimes I think Matilda has more wits about her than you do. Can't you see that this man intends to murder your daughter?"

Morgana's cloud turned a bristling red. I wasn't sure if it was anger at Bronwen or at the knife-wielding masked man. Both their clouds crackled with lightning, jagged bolts of it shooting out in his direction. At first he'd been frozen in place as if he'd seen a ghost, which of course he had. But when the lightning hit his hand, he shrieked and dropped the knife. I immediately grabbed it. I'd seen too many movies in which the good guy doesn't pick up the weapon, and two minutes later he pays the price. But my assailant had no interest in his knife. He was at the door, trying frantically to open it. He finally remembered that he'd locked it and he threw the door open and fled. I thought about chasing after him to see where he'd hidden his car, but I didn't have it in me. Besides, odds were this was the same guy who'd been hoping to attack me when I pulled off the road, and Hobart already had his plate number.

I locked the door and went into the living room to collapse on the sofa. My mother and grandmother joined me, bouncing triumphantly through the air, their clouds a vibrant blue. I told them I was fine and thanked them for their timely help that may have saved my life. Scarlet smudges rose in the blue. I'd never seen either of them blush before. Maybe death was starting to have a salutary effect on them.

When the phone rang, I knew it had to be Travis. My mother and grandmother bowed out, Morgana reminding me to eat and get some rest—forever my mother. It tugged at my heart, this whole having her and yet not having her anymore.

"I know, I know," I said, answering the call. "I'm late getting back to you."

"Again! A guy could wind up with a complex." The words were light, but not the tone. I gave him a condensed version of the masked intruder, leaning more on the comic relief provided by Morgana and Bronwen than on the knife and threats.

"I don't like this," Travis said, choosing not to be amused. "You're going to call Hobart, right?" Despite the uptick in his voice, it was less a question than a demand.

"I will, although I wish I didn't have to. You know Duggan will have to open an investigation of his own now and he'll demand all the information we've worked so hard to come by. And if we don't comply, he'll charge us with obstruction of justice."

"After what almost happened tonight, that's the least of our worries," Travis said. "It seems we owe Crawford a *thank you* for the heads-up, even if it didn't help."

"Fine, you take care of that. I'll call Hobart. But we are not walking away from this case—not when we're finally making headway."

"I never said anything about giving up, even though I wish you would take a back seat."

"Good night, Travis."

"You'll call Hobart tonight? The sooner the police are aware this guy was at your house, the sooner they can start tracking him. If you delay, you could be putting other lives in danger."

"I said I would." But first I needed some comfort food. I grabbed an unopened pint of chocolate chip ice cream and a spoon and sat down at the kitchen table to make the call.

I told Hobart I had another crime to report. I offered to give him the details over the phone. He explained that as an officer of the law, he had to follow proper procedure. He couldn't make side deals with individuals. He had to take my report in person as soon as possible.

He arrived ten minutes later. We sat on the living room couch and I answered his questions the best I could. He seemed thrilled that I had the knife as evidence, even after I told him the assailant was wearing gloves. He explained that the ME would try to lift prints from it anyway. There was a good chance my assailant had handled it at some point without gloves. I told him my prints were already on file for purposes of exclusion. Duggan had taken them during the investigation into Jim Harken's death. Hard to believe that was two cases ago. Harder yet to believe there'd been so many murders in my little hometown.

"What happened to make the assailant leave?" Hobart asked.

I was tempted to tell him the truth, but I'd probably be carted off to a padded cell in a place with a name like Happy Acres. "I think he was only here to issue a warning," I said, which was also true and a lot less likely to breed consequences. Of course, Hobart wanted specifics about the warning. I admitted Travis and I were trying to find his brother's killer. I was treated to a lecture on why it wasn't safe to play detective.

When we finally moved on, Hobart asked if I remembered any identifying details about the man beyond his approximate height and weight. I reminded him that Ski Mask Guy, I was tired of referring to him as my *attacker* or *assailant,* had been covered from head to toe.

"But what about the color of his eyes? Or maybe you caught a glimpse of his hair?"

I shook my head. I tend to be detail-oriented, but when facing death, my first thought isn't generally, *Oh what beautiful baby blues the killer has.*

"Was his voice at all familiar?"

"No…maybe, I don't know. My head is spinning with everything that happened tonight."

"Okay," Hobart said. "I want you to close your eyes and try to recreate the encounter in your mind. Sometimes the subconscious remembers more than we're aware of." I did as requested and promptly fell asleep.

I woke to him saying my name. "I'm sorry," I said as a yawn ambushed me.

He got to his feet, smiling. "You did warn me you were tired. Look, I hated to wake you, but I want to be sure you lock up after me." I walked him to the door, covering another yawn with my hand. My brain felt foggy, as if part of it was still firmly ensconced in dreamland and had no intentions of making an appearance.

"Almost forgot," he said, turning back to me with one foot already out the door. "I ran the plate you gave me and as I suspected, it was reported stolen earlier today."

I nodded. I hadn't entertained much hope of a different outcome. No one clever enough to plan and carry out six homicides without being caught, and in some cases without even being pursued, would ever have used a car registered in their own name.

I went upstairs to my bedroom and found the cats splayed across the bed, a living pattern on the dove gray quilt. I didn't bother changing into a nightgown or brushing my teeth. I kicked off my shoes and crawled under the covers, doing my best not to disturb anyone. Sashkatu was lying on his private pillow that was pushed up against mine. When I laid my head down, he opened one eye and I swear he smiled to see me there.

Chapter 42

In spite of my fatigue, my eyes popped open at two a.m. I felt like I'd forgotten something important, but the harder I tried to retrieve it, the further away it slipped. After a frustrating hour of staring at the ceiling, I recalled the gentle spell my grandmother had taught me as a child when I was anxious before a test in school or a visit to the dentist. I hadn't used it in twenty years, but it came back to me in its entirety.

Oh sleep, sweet sleep, come nigh to me,
Make all my worries cease to be,
From now until the break of day
Bring only peaceful dreams my way.

The spell must have worked, because the next time I awoke the room was bathed in sunlight, a little too much sunlight for my recently shuttered eyes. That's what happens when you forget to close the blinds before falling into bed. Everyone else was awake too, stretching the sleep from their limbs.

Sashkatu led the parade down to the kitchen. I was dying for a cup of coffee, but I gave the cats their breakfast before putting it up to brew. I'd tried it the other way around, but found myself tripping over one cat after another as they milled about waiting for service. We all fared better when I saw to their needs first. Once their tummies were full, they left the kitchen for softer, cozier spots in which to nap or play. I sat at the kitchen table, sipping my coffee and craving a Danish or muffin from the Breakfast Bar. Cereal or eggs weren't going to cut it. After all I'd been through, I deserved something full of fat and sugar. Last night's ice cream binge didn't count. This was a brand-new day. I realized I was sounding a lot like Tilly. I tried to envision myself in one of her muumuus and vowed I'd get back to healthy eating at lunchtime.

I bumped into my aunt in the Breakfast Bar, with Merlin in tow. He had his nose pressed against the glass-fronted display case like an ancient toddler. One of the women behind the counter asked him to step back behind the red line. *Good luck with that,* I thought.

"Hi, Aunt Tilly," I said, tapping her on the shoulder. I could tell I'd startled her, because when she turned to face me she looked like I'd caught her doing something illicit. "As I recall, you once called me a traitor for frequenting this place."

She managed a lopsided smile, and I could almost hear the wheels spinning madly in her head as she tried to come up with a believable explanation for her presence there. "One has to check on the competition in order to stay ahead in the game," she said in a whisper that caused half the store to turn in her direction. "It's called industrial espionage."

When it was her turn, she bought half a dozen different goodies for her and Merlin to try. "You can't possibly judge a place by tasting one thing," she said as they passed me on their way out. Five minutes later, as I was leaving The Bar with coffee and a sticky bun, I bumped into Elise.

"You ruined my surprise," she said. "School is closed for parent-teacher conferences. Mine aren't until this afternoon, so I was planning to pop into Abracadabra for a breakfast visit."

"Surprises are overrated," I said, having had my share of them lately. "Breakfast together is the real treat."

I was already up on the counter sipping my coffee, when Elise walked in. She hiked herself up beside me. The counter had seen many a conversation between us over the years. She updated me on her boys, who were still coming to terms with their father's death. She said they were making progress—fewer down times, friends and laughter filling the house more often. I updated her on the investigation. She laughed so hard at the Elvis story that she spilled coffee on herself. But the events of last night changed her mood, even though I tried to minimize the danger.

She put her hand on my arm. "I'm sure your family and Travis have all expressed their concerns, so I'm not going to pile on. What can I do to help?"

"Thanks," I said. "You can help me think things through. This case keeps getting more confusing. With the exceptions of Biker Dude and Ski Mask Guy our suspects have good motives and reasonable opportunity. We just don't have enough evidence on any one of them to say definitively 'it's him or it's her.'"

"Okay, recap for me what you do know," Elise said in her getting-down-to-business tone.

"We know that someone has been killing off people who have either been acquitted of a crime or given a light sentence. Some of these fools have gone right back to their illegal behavior and wind up causing the deaths of innocent people. From my perspective, Epps has the perfect motive for the role of caped crusader, protecting the populace from potential repeat offenders. He's lost almost every case in which he's gone up against Sam Crawford. He can't find justice in the courts, so maybe he metes out justice after hours."

Elise swallowed a bite of sticky bun. "If he were the only suspect, it would be a slam dunk," she said, licking her fingers. "Where do you stand with the others at this point?"

"It's sketchy, but here's what we've dug up: Lena is Austin Stubbs's niece. He lets her borrow his Harley from time to time; she then lends it to Biker Dude, who's been keeping tabs on me and our investigation. We know that Lena stole papers from the CP's office on at least one occasion. We know that Stubbs lied about where he was the night his drug-dealing son was killed. We know that Everett Royce lost his wife to a man who'd been convicted of distracted driving once before, but was back on the streets in no time, courtesy of Sam Crawford."

"So lots of leads, but no hard evidence, except for the knife Ski Mask Guy dropped last night," she said. "Fingers crossed; maybe the ME will find usable prints."

I sighed. "Even if he does, it's not like Duggan is going to tell me whose they are."

"Now that he's on the case, you'll just have to go about the investigation in a different way."

I missed what she was saying, because my mind had just pieced together what had been nagging at me since last night. "The guy who attacked me was Biker Dude," I blurted out. "Ski Mask Guy is Biker Dude."

"What? Wow! Are you sure?"

"Ski Mask Guy's voice was a little familiar from the get-go," I said, "but I couldn't place it until just now. I'm kind of amazed that I made the connection at all. I only spoke to Biker Dude once, weeks ago. The voice last night was nasty, threatening, not at all like the one conversation I had with Biker Dude. But I'm still pretty sure it was him."

"I bet that's one of the reasons every bit of his skin was covered," Elise said. "He was hiding his tattoos!"

"You're probably right. But how do I connect everything? The next logical step is to find out whether or not Stubbs is aware that Lena lends his Harley to someone else. If he isn't, why has she been keeping it a secret? The fact I keep coming back to is that Lena knows Epps, Stubbs, and Biker Dude, but there's a good chance they don't know each other."

"Let's take one thing at a time," Elise said. "What if *I* call Stubbs? He's never heard my voice, so he'll at least give me a chance to talk. I can grab his attention right off if I say I *know* he couldn't have been at the bar the night his son was killed."

"That should keep him from hanging up on you initially," I agreed, warming to the idea. "When the police shut down the investigation based on the ME's report, Stubbs probably thought he was home free and no one would ever find out his alibi was a lie. It would also explain why he didn't want anything to do with me once I said I was reopening the case."

"I'm hoping what I say will unsettle him enough that when I tell him about his niece lending Biker Dude the Harley, he'll be too surprised to hide his true reaction."

"If he's not surprised, it's because he already knows about Biker Dude," I said. "But none of it proves he's the killer or if the three of them are in cahoots with Epps."

"You're right," Elise said, her exuberance fizzling. "I'm starting to understand your frustration."

"Look, your call to Stubbs will provide us with information we don't have and you never know which bit will be the key to finding the killer. I'd like to listen in on speaker phone. I've talked to Stubbs a few times now; I might have a better take on his reaction."

"Done," Elise said. "How's tomorrow night at six?"

"Pizza or Chinese?"

"You know my boys…. What do you think?"

"Mushroom and sausage it is."

* * * *

I poked my head in Tilly's shop at lunchtime and found her at her desk. Merlin was reading a book, not one of his usual pastimes when technology was available.

"No teas today?" I asked, after kissing her cheek.

"Today is inventory, reorder, and restock day—a pleasant interlude after weeks of nonstop baking."

"She calls it pleasant, I call it unfortunate," Merlin said, looking up from his book. His cheeks were a flaming red.

"Do you feel all right?" I asked him. "You look like you might be running a fever."

"Oh there's not a thing wrong with him," Tilly answered before he could. "I suggested he take time away from electronics and read a book, immerse himself in the arts of this era. The problem was that I let him choose the book." I had no idea what she meant, until I looked at the spine of the book he was holding.

"*Fifty Shades of Grey?*" I said, bursting into laughter. His enflamed face suddenly made sense.

"He already has the second and third books reserved at the library," Tilly said. "It's a good thing I can't be charged with endangering the welfare of a legendary sorcerer. Was there something you wanted, dear?"

"Yes," I said once I was able to stop giggling. "I need help restoring all my protective wards to full capacity. What do you say, Merlin?"

"Mayhap it can wait until this evening?" he asked. "I shall have finished this tome by then."

"That would be great," I agreed. It wasn't possible during the workday anyway.

Chapter 43

Duggan walked into the shop near the end of the afternoon. I'd been expecting a visit from him once he read Hobart's report. He roamed through the aisles while I rang up a customer's purchase. When the door chimes signaled her departure, he came out of the third aisle holding a jar and marched up to the counter "Hello, Detective," I said in the same pleasant tone I used with customers. No point in getting off to a bad start. I'd be gracious unless he treated me otherwise. "How may I help you?"

"What is this stuff?" he asked, setting the jar down hard on the counter. It was a good thing I didn't skimp on the quality of the jars I used.

"It's Arnica Montana, like it says on the label."

"This stuff approved by the FDA?"

"Everything in here is made from plants and herbs." I had no intentions of telling him about the secret ingredient otherwise known as magick. "The FDA doesn't regulate them."

"Figures," he said. "That's not why I'm here anyway. I came to talk to you about the incident last night."

"I told Officer Hobart everything I could remember."

"Anything else come to mind since then?"

I didn't want to tell him about my epiphany earlier in the day, but I'd promised Travis I'd be aboveboard with the police. And I don't take promises lightly. "It occurred to me just today that the voice of my assailant sounded a lot like the voice of a biker who dropped in here a few weeks back."

"Okay, I need you to come down to the station house to see if you can pick the guy out of a photo array."

"I need ten minutes to close up," I said.

"You've got it. Describe the guy for me."

"Under thirty, about your height, broad shoulders, dark eyes and spiked dark hair, stubble beard, tattoos on his arms and neck."

"Pictures? Words?"

"I don't know. They were mostly hidden by his clothes."

When I walked into the police station, Duggan was behind the desk, tapping away at the computer keyboard. Paul Curtis was fixing himself a cup of coffee from the old ten-cupper across the room. I declined his offer of one. Duggan pushed back from the desk and got to his feet. "Over here, Miss Wilde," he said indicating the chair he'd vacated. I sat down and found myself looking at four mug shots on the computer screen. "Click your way through all the photos, take your time. If you see the guy, tell Curtis. I'll check back later."

After Duggan left, the room instantly seemed bigger and airier. I started searching through the mug shots. Although I tried to stay focused on the faces in front of me, I couldn't help noticing Paul's movements. He seemed at odds over what to do with himself. I was using the only computer in the small sub-station and the precinct phone was silent—no one needed his help. I saw him glance up at the TV mounted on the wall across from the desk. It probably helped the officers on New Camel rotation pass the time in the days before our bucolic little town began hosting murders.

"It won't bother me if you want to put on the TV," I said.

"Thanks, I'm good. Anything I can get you?"

"No, but thank you." I realized that he might be worried Duggan would return and catch him watching TV. The detective didn't strike me as a man who would condone goofing off on the taxpayers' dime. But the TV was there for some purpose. Paul took out his personal phone and went into the back room to fiddle with it. He probably figured it would be easy to ditch when Duggan returned.

An hour passed before I reached the end of the file. I'd gone through hundreds of mug shots without finding a single one that came close to my memory of Biker Dude. Maybe he was a recent convert to the world of crime. If he didn't have a record, there wouldn't be a mug shot. Duggan was still MIA, so I told Paul I'd struck out, and he promised to pass that on.

"What will the next step be?" I asked. The detective might not tell me, but I had a shot with Paul. I could see the tug of war play out across his face. As much as he wanted to ingratiate himself with me, he didn't want to run afoul of Duggan. "I'm sure the detective won't just throw his hands in the air and give up on this lead," I said trying to draw him out.

"No, there are a lot of other databases, state and federal, where he can try to locate the guy, but you didn't hear that from me." I didn't have to; it was the kind of information you could learn from any number of television shows or a Google search. "The problem is that we don't have a name and he can't make you look through millions of DMV photos. Most likely he's going to ask you to sit down with a sketch artist. Then he can run the picture through facial recognition software. Not even that's a slam-dunk though. As much as half the adult population in this country can't be found on any databases."

"You're kidding? It certainly feels like Big Brother is watching each and every one of us."

"Yeah well, I'm sure it's only a matter of time."

"I'm surprised he didn't start with the sketch artist," I said.

"Having you ID a photo would have been more accurate than running a sketch that may or may not be good enough to find a match."

"I appreciate the info," I said. "The sooner you make detective, the happier everyone around here will be." I hadn't taken a poll, but I didn't want to lead him on by saying "the happier *I'd* be." Besides, I was pretty sure I spoke for everyone, except maybe Duggan's mother.

Chapter 44

Morgana dropped in the next morning and found me in the bathroom applying mascara. Her cloud appeared behind me in the mirror, looking a little deflated like a basketball with a slow leak. "Hi, Mom, how are you?" I asked, turning around to face her.

"Fine," she said in a gloomy tone, "well not entirely fine. It occurred to me that when you get married, I won't be able to come to your wedding."

"You can come if I have it here in the house."

She gave a little bounce. "You would do that for me and your grandmother?"

"Of course," I said, wondering how I would explain them to future in-laws. I might have to marry an orphan. "But I'm nowhere near thinking of marriage. I may decide not to ever marry." I'd hoped that announcement would end the discussion for now, but I should have known better.

My mother was clearly in shock. If her cloud had a mouth, it would have been hanging open. "What do you mean?" she sputtered. "You have to get married. It's up to you to continue the Wilde bloodline. It's a sacred obligation. Your grandmother will have a stroke if she hears about this."

"I don't think that's possible once you're dead," I pointed out.

"What's all this?" Bronwen's cloud popped up next to hers. The bathroom was getting crowded. Unlike Morgana, my grandmother appeared to be in fine mettle. Morgana launched into a recap of our conversation. I went back to my mascara.

"Is this true, Kailyn?" Bronwen asked calmly.

"I don't even know if I've found my forever guy. Can't we just table the subject for now? There's a tour group coming and I need to get over to the shop."

"What about Travis?" my mother said.

"I really like him, but I've only known him for a few months. We'll see."

"That's reasonable," Bronwen said. "We can revisit the subject at another time. Is that okay with you, Morgana?"

My mother ignored the question, choosing instead to pounce on me. "Aren't you and Travis still a couple?" Her voice rose three octaves; any further and only dogs would have heard her.

"We're dating, but we're nowhere near *forever* or *till death do us part.*"

"You're not getting any younger," she muttered.

I'm aging by the second, I thought, but I kept my mouth shut.

"She has plenty of time," Bronwen said. "Women today aren't marrying young the way we did."

"She is not just a woman of today," Morgana scoffed. "Like we, she is a woman of the ages. She is the last with the magickal bloodline. If she were to die without a child, it would mean the end of magick in the world."

"I'm leaving now, ladies," I said, edging my way out of the bathroom. "Why don't you talk this over and get back to me." They were so focused on each other at that point I'm not sure they even noticed I was gone.

I found Sashkatu dozing near the front door. I woke him gently and off we went to Abracadabra. They could have followed me there, but I was grateful they didn't. For all I knew, my nearly, dearly-departed remained in the bathroom for the rest of the day, thrashing out their eternal issues.

The tour group arrived at ten and within minutes, I was inundated with customers. Some of them had come to buy products for themselves, others came with gifts on their agenda, but all of them eventually left with both. It was a good day financially as well as socially, not a single sour note.

After the last shopper left to board the bus, I flopped down in the customer chair, exhausted from being on my feet all day and thirsty from talking non-stop. I'd left my water bottle on the desk behind the counter, but I was too tired and lazy to get up again. I went the easy route instead. I got a tight focus on the bottle and flew it over the counter into my waiting hand. At that exact moment, the door chimes rang. I jumped up like a kid caught cheating on an exam.

The newcomer was a big guy with a thick neck and wide shoulders like a football player. He had one hand in his jacket pocket. After my two recent brushes with death, I had to assume he was holding a weapon. I was on the verge of using magick to preempt an attack, when Sam Crawford appeared behind him. I stood down, relieved and a bit weak in the knees. The stranger had to be the bodyguard he'd told me about. They were dressed like twin wannabes—jeans, sweaters, Timberlands, and Canada Goose jackets, but Crawford had a good decade on the bodyguard. To the casual observer, they might have been friends who'd spent the day skiing and were just browsing around the quaint town. But knowing what I did, it was easy to see the differences between the protector and the protected. The bodyguard was alert and loose-limbed, clearly ready to spring into action at a moment's notice. His eyes didn't rest anywhere as he checked out the front of the shop. In that moment, I had the silly thought that I would never make it as a bodyguard. I'd be distracted by the first shiny, interesting thing I saw.

Crawford stayed near the door for a fast exit should that be necessary, while the bodyguard moved on to peer into each aisle, before disappearing down the hall to the storeroom. I prepared myself for a shriek of surprise or anger from my aunt if he barged into her shop and interrupted a reading. Everything remained quiet. The bodyguard returned and nodded to Crawford. My shop and I had apparently passed inspection.

"Sorry about all that," Crawford said, leaving the door and walking over to me. "My friend here goes by Mason." I decided not to ask if that was his first name or his last. Maybe Mason was a one-name wonder like Elvis, Cher, and Madonna. Mason acknowledged the introduction with a head-bob and took up a position at the front door.

"What brings you to my little town?" I asked the attorney now that I was breathing normally again.

"A yen for a burger at the Caboose. I've eaten burgers in the swankiest restaurants, made from the finest Kobe beef. None of them beats a Caboose burger. And as long as I was in town, I decided to stop in and see how you were doing after your ordeal at the hands of that creep."

"I assume you mean Ski Mask Guy. I'm a little shaken, but I'll be fine. Thanks for the warning."

"I guess after he struck out with me, he went looking for an easier target. I was hoping maybe you got a glimpse of his face."

"No, but it wasn't for lack of trying."

"Still not interested in having a bodyguard take the worry out of your life?"

"I'm okay," I said, "I'll give you a call if I change my mind."

"Fair enough, I just hope you're not depending on your attack cat over on the window ledge to keep you safe. He hasn't even bothered to open his eyes since we walked in."

"He's playing possum," I said. "He's very cunning."

Crawford grinned. "I like your style. Any chance you have a thing for older men?"

Chapter 45

I took one step outside the next morning, before unceremoniously landing on my butt. Everything was covered in a thin layer of ice, including my porch. That explained why Sashkatu refused to walk out with me. Until the sun could break through the heavy gray clouds and warm the air, moving about was going to be treacherous. Getting up from the ice wasn't easy with nothing to hold on to. My feet kept slipping out from under me. On my third try, I finally succeeded. I looked up and down the street to see if anyone had witnessed my debacle, but thankfully no one was out.

Since I'd fallen before I had a chance to close and lock the front door behind me, Sashkatu was able to watch my whole performance seated comfortably behind the glass storm door. The haughty expression on his furry face said it all—fools rush out, while wise souls first examine the situation. "Your highness might have given me a head's up if you were aware of the conditions outside," I grumbled. He must have seen the mailman or some other early bird meet with a similar fate and decided to let me test the proverbial waters before he ventured out. Sashki had always been a serious-minded cat who thought things through. When he saw that I was finally on my feet, he moved out of the way to watch my stumbling re-entry from a safer location.

Once I was inside, he cocked his head to one side as if to inquire, "What do you propose we do?" It was a good question. After considering my options, it seemed the most efficient solution would be an old spell of Bronwen's. It didn't require any props and we'd all used it often enough over the years that I knew it well. I just needed to be certain no one was around to witness the results. I poked my head outside again and looked up and down the block—no one in sight. I focused my eyes on the parameters of the melt I was seeking, in this case across my porch, down the steps that led to the flagstone path and from there across the road to the back of Abracadabra.

> Be gone the snow,
> Be gone the ice.
> I ask you once,
> I'll ask you twice.
> Be gone before
> I ask you thrice.

Before I completed the third repetition, steam was rising from deep in the earth. In seconds the ice was gone. Sashkatu must have recognized the spell, because he came to stand at my side, clearly amenable to leaving now. He trotted out ahead of me, hoisting his tail with a flourish.

Once we were inside my shop, he took the steps to his window ledge where he gave his paws a proper cleaning before falling asleep.

I peered out the front door, wishing I dared to melt the ice in front of my shop too. But there was a good chance the other shopkeepers were also looking outside, wondering if they would have any customers or if they should have stayed in bed. I found the bag of ice melt in the storeroom and spread it on the sidewalk. With tourism being our biggest industry, the town was always good about clearing snow and de-icing the walks, but I liked to add a bit of our magick-enhanced melt for extra protection. Next up was dusting. In a shop with dozens upon dozens of glass jars, dusting was a chore that never ended. By the time I finished the last shelf, the first shelf was dusty again. Years ago, my mother had come up with a spell to make the task easier, and it had worked like—well—like magick. But the last time she'd tried it, we'd already been having trouble with our magick and instead of cleaning off the glass jars, it dumped great clouds of dust all over the shop. We found out afterward that the incantation had drawn dust away from all the other shops in town in order to deposit it in ours. I had no intentions of ever trying that again.

After I'd dusted myself into a sneezing fit, I went into the storeroom to whip up a batch of my bestselling tummy tamer. I was well into measuring and mixing the peppermint, chamomile, and ginger when the door chimes jingled. I pulled off the latex gloves with a snap and hurried up front to see who'd been brave enough to ignore the elements.

"Travis?" I said.

"Uh oh, it's been so long you're beginning to forget who I am." He drew me close for a hug that escalated into a kiss.

"Why didn't you tell me you were coming?" I asked.

"I didn't want to get your hopes up," he said with a wink. "You know, in case the ice made me turn back. The roads in and around the Glen are in decent shape, but they got a whole lot worse the closer I came to New Camel. I almost turned back a few times, but then I thought about the prize at the end of my journey and it gave me the strength to struggle on."

I laughed. "Don't ever give up your day job to go into acting."

"Funny, that's exactly what my high school drama teacher told me."

I skewered him with my eyes. "As much as I want to believe you made the trip for the sole purpose of seeing me, what's your ulterior motive?"

"I cannot tell a lie, especially when you look at me like that. After I heard about the plot you and Elise hatched, I realized I wanted to be involved—it being about my brother and all. Besides, an extra pair of ears couldn't hurt."

We spent the day waiting for customers who didn't come, and talking. We still had so much to learn about each other that there was an endless supply of subjects. We braved the icy sidewalks to have lunch at The Jerk, picking our way there, arms intertwined like two old biddies hanging on to each other. If one of us fell, the other was doomed to follow, but we managed to reach the restaurant without mishap. We had Manhattan clam chowder with a hot cocoa chaser and a side of French fries, because they were Travis's weakness.

The afternoon was as bereft of customers as the morning had been. I closed early. Travis tried to talk me into riding back to my house in his car. I explained that it wasn't worth the effort of trying to get Sashkatu into the car when it was such a short distance to walk. In the end, Sashki and I went home by way of the path I'd de-iced earlier, while Travis drove his car around the block to meet us there.

We arrived at Elise's house promptly at six o'clock, bearing the promised pizzas. Before we left the car, I quickly de-iced the walkway to her front door to ensure that dinner didn't wind up on the ground. Zach and Noah opened the door before I had a chance to ring the bell. They were all over their famous new guest. I didn't even get a *hello,* until their mother reminded them of their manners. Even then it was an "Oh, sorry—hi, Aunt K." I relieved Travis of the pizza boxes, so he could talk to his groupies unencumbered.

I joked with Elise that I was insulted. I'd brought the boys hundreds of pizzas and other goodies over the years, but I'd never elicited that kind of excitement from them—not once.

She was putting slices of the pizza on a hot griddle to reheat. "You should feel honored. They treat you the way they treat me. We're always around; they know they can count on us. In a nutshell, you're family. Travis is a novelty, because they see him on TV. They can brag to their friends that they know somebody famous."

"Famous? Travis would find that very funny," I said.

"It's all in the eye of the beholder." She handed me a big bowl of salad from the refrigerator and asked me to put it on the table, then went into the family room to collect the three guys for dinner.

Half an hour later, we were all stuffed, except for Zach who was scarfing down a huge dish of ice cream. "Guys, remember what we talked about?" Elise said to them. "I need you both to go upstairs and be very quiet. It won't be for long." They nodded solemnly and then made a mad dash for the stairs, elbowing each other out of the way, Noah calling rights to the TV in the master bedroom. Elise looked at us and sighed. But a minute later, the house settled into silence.

We sat in the living room. To be anonymous, Elise blocked her number before she dialed Stubbs, and then hit the speaker button. After two rings, a gruff voice answered and she introduced herself as Gwen Jones.

"Yeah, so what do you want?" Stubbs demanded.

"Your alibi for the night your son died was a lie. I have proof that the bar wasn't open that night." There was only silence from the other end. The three of us were literally on the edge of our seats waiting for his reaction.

"You trying to blackmail me?" he snapped so abruptly that we all flinched, "cause you're barking up the wrong tree, lady. I have a mind to call the police on you!"

"You won't," Elise said evenly. "The police have reopened the case into your son's death and without an alibi, you want to stay as far away from them as you can. All I want is the answer to a question. Give me that and I won't bother you again."

"I'm gonna want to hear that question before I agree to anything."

"Are you aware that when your niece, Lena, borrows your Harley, she lends it to someone else?"

"Come again?" Elise repeated her words. "Hell no," he spat out. "Can't even trust your own kin these days. Who's she been lending it to?"

"A man who uses it in the commission of crimes."

"I want his name."

"I don't know that yet," Elise said. "But your niece does." She clicked off the call. I felt as if I'd been holding my breath for the duration of their dialogue. "What do you think?" she asked us.

"He didn't know about it," I said. "I'm as sure of that as I can be."

Travis nodded. "Me too."

"Okay," Elise said, "that makes it unanimous."

Travis smiled. "I imagine Lena is on the receiving end of a nasty tirade right about now."

Chapter 46

"Between the cold and how early it gets dark, all I want to do at the end of the day is go home, eat dinner, and put my feet up," Lolly said with a sigh. "I make only two exceptions—anything to do with my grandchildren and anything that affects my friends or this town." We were walking down to the New Camel police station. It had occurred to me that I wasn't the only one who could describe Biker Dude to the sketch artist. Lolly had seen him too.

I laughed. "I know what you mean. I think I'm becoming part bear. Find me a cozy cave and I'll see you in the spring. I don't remember feeling that way when I was a kid. I guess it means I'm getting older, huh?" I asked, half-jokingly.

"Talk to me in fifty years," she said.

Hobart was waiting for us with the sketch artist, a woman by the name of Libby. She was just shy of middle age and a few pounds beyond plump, with an upbeat personality that drew you right in and made you feel as if you'd known her for ages.

The large desk chair had been rolled around to the front of the desk to be near the two smaller ones. Libby already occupied the larger chair when we arrived. Lolly and I took the remaining ones. Hobart perched on the edge of the desk just beyond our circle like a kibitzer at a high-stakes poker game. Libby had a sketch pad turned to a clean page. "I'm hopelessly old-fashioned," she said. "I like holding real books when I read and I like sketching with pencil on paper. It's stood me in good stead for more years than I'll say and I don't see any reason to change now." She said all this in a good-natured tone, and I had the sense she'd used the disclaimer so often it had become part of her usual patter.

She led us through the process with succinct questions. Was his face round or long? High cheek bones? Weak chin or strong jaw? Ears close to the head or jutting out? And so forth. Lolly and I didn't agree on every aspect. At one point, I remarked that we seemed to be describing two different men. "It's not unusual for people to see things differently," Libby assured us, "I make allowances for it." When she showed us the finished sketch, we were both satisfied that she'd captured the biker. Whether we'd be told if it led to identifying the man was another matter. Duggan had nothing to gain and everything to lose by letting us know. Travis and I had solved two other cases before he could. Why would he help us outshine him for a third time?

Travis called the next day. I expected him to say that the police had arrested Biker Dude. "No, nothing yet," he said. "It could mean they still haven't been able to identify him, or they have his name, but can't find him. If that's the case, I'd expect them to go public with the sketch in the hope that someone will recognize the guy and come forward. So we're not out of the game yet. As long as there's any chance for me to catch Ryan's killer, I'm going for it."

I wasn't surprised. From the moment he'd found Ryan's body, he'd vowed to take down his killer. It was deeply personal. "There's one lead we haven't followed up on yet," I reminded him. We said Lena's name in unison. She'd been on my mind ever since I found out she was Stubbs's niece.

"If anyone can ID Biker Dude, she can," Travis said.

"I doubt she'll offer to tell us."

"I want to catch her at the end of the workday tomorrow. I'll tell her I know she's been lending Biker Dude her uncle's Harley without his permission. If she gives us his name, I won't tell the police she can ID the guy."

"That could work," I said. "What time do you want me at your place tomorrow?"

"I've got this one," he said. "No need for you to close early again."

"We're partners. Lena may seem like easy prey, but cornered she could be dangerous." He didn't have a comeback. "If she's armed, magick can even out the odds." A little reminder that it had saved his butt in the past.

"You drive a hard bargain, lady," he said. I could picture the wry smile on his face. "Tomorrow at four thirty." I agreed. State employees work until five. No point in taking the chance of missing her.

* * * *

It was nearly dark when I pulled up in front of Travis's apartment building. He'd been waiting in the lobby and came out as soon as he saw my car. He jumped in for the short drive to the courthouse. I parked at the curb and left the engine running to keep us warm. "We have to be careful," Travis said. "There's a fine line between citing a fact and accusing someone of a crime."

"I know. It can depend on a person's perception of an event. You say you were just giving her a friendly head's up. She says there was nothing *friendly* about it—you threatened her. For women, tone and body language have a lot to do with how we see things," I said.

"Translation please?"

"Keep your tone pleasant, conversational. Don't get in her face, it's an invasion of her personal space. Don't get between her and her car."

"Hey, where is all this coming from?" Travis asked. "You sound like you took a quick course in psychology overnight."

"Elise gave me pointers. She majored in psychology and social work, before she switched to teaching."

"Did she give you any advice on what to do now that I'm afraid to open my mouth?" he said dryly.

"Actually, she suggested I approach Lena first. Women are generally less wary of other women than they are of men."

It was after five by the time Lena left the building. We were beginning to think that she'd called in sick. When she did walk out, she was with Epps. They stopped close to my car to finish their conversation; then he went left and she headed for the small parking lot on the right. We had almost no time to approach her before she reached her car. I was worried that Epps might still be in screaming distance if she panicked.

We got out of my car after she passed us. Travis hung back, pretending to inspect one of the tires. "Hi, Lena," I called to her. She turned her head as I ran to catch up.

"Oh, hi," she said, coming to a stop. "You're Kailyn Wilde. You came to interview the CP, right?"

"Yes, the day of your shower."

"I'm sorry, but if you want to make another appointment with Mr. Epps, you'll have to call or come back tomorrow. The building is locked for the night."

"No, I was actually hoping you could help me with another matter."

"Oh...okay, if I can."

"There's a guy we've seen riding a motorcycle around the New Camel area and I was wondering if you knew his name."

"Why would I know some random biker's name?" she asked.

"Because you've been lending him your uncle Austin's Harley." There was an immediate change in her demeanor. She stiffened and had trouble looking me in the eye. She was probably trying to assess how much I knew and what she could say to put me off without digging herself into a deeper hole. "There's something else you may not know. The guy has a dark side. He forced his way into my house, wearing a ski mask and threatened me with a knife."

"If he was wearing a ski mask, how do you know it was the biker?" she asked, no doubt feeling like she'd cut me down and retaken the higher ground.

"Because his voice and the biker's voice are identical."

Lena seemed to be out of arguments. She glanced toward the lot where her car waited, maybe wishing she could summon it to her like cowboys once whistled for their horses.

Travis ambled up to us. "How are you, Lena?" he said pleasantly.

"What *is* this?" She backed up, fidgeting with the keys in her hand. It brought to mind the safety tip I'd heard years ago. If you find yourself out alone at night, make a fist with your keys between your fingers like spikes. You can rake them down an assailant's face to escape. I had to wonder if she'd heard similar advice and was arming herself against us.

Travis stopped where he was. "We're not the only ones who want his name. Kailyn filed a police report on the incident, so the cops are also looking to ID the guy. And their resources are a lot better than ours. If you're involved with this biker and his activities, you'd be wise to tell them before they come looking for you. If you give us his name and anything else you know about him, we'll even take it to the police and tell them you want to cooperate. You might still get out of this unscathed."

"Why should I believe anything you're telling me?" She sounded like she was on the brink of panic. "I've got to get home now. I have…things to do."

I took my business card out of my coat pocket and handed it to her. "Give me a call or come by if you want our help." She tossed the card into her purse without a glance, backing away toward her car. We didn't go after her, but she must have thought we would, because she kept her eye on us until she beeped her car open and jumped into the driver's seat.

Chapter 47

After our encounter with Lena, Travis temporarily moved in with me. We were agreed that if Lena didn't call or come by over the next three days, she probably wasn't going to. We had no idea if she was involved with Biker Dude beyond lending him the Harley. And even if she was, we didn't know if she would tell him about our meeting. All we did know for certain was that she wasn't above breaking rules even if it meant losing her job. And we knew Biker Dude could be charged with worse. If he wasn't the SCM killer, there was a good chance he was on the killer's payroll.

Travis explained our general plan to his boss so he'd be able to take the three days off with pay. The man didn't need convincing; the possibility that Travis might be closing in on the killer was enough to make dreams of a ratings bonanza dance in his head. He lobbied to send along a cameraman in case anything important went down, but Travis stuck to his guns. The circle had to be kept small. We couldn't worry about the safety of another person or a possible leak. If not for the protection my magick could afford us, I wouldn't have agreed to our sitting-duck plan myself.

When I'd invited Lena to visit me, I meant what I told her. If she wanted us to go to the police with her, we would. But we knew that if she came, there was a good chance Biker Dude would follow her. One way or the other, we hoped to learn the extent of their relationship.

We didn't tell Tilly what we were doing. Knowing would have been a burden to her. She would worry and work herself into a panic. I didn't tell Morgana and Bronwen either. As far as I knew, they weren't at liberty to pop in whenever they wished. There were restrictions. The night they'd scared off Biker Dude/Ski Mask Guy was pure happenstance, or so I'd been led to believe.

Day one dawned and Travis hung out in the shop with me. We put together a makeshift office for him in the storeroom. My work table stood in for a computer desk where he could get back to work on his much-delayed story about the latest corruption in state government. Since Tilly was bound to see him there when she walked between our shops, I made up a cover story about the wood flooring in his apartment being sanded and resealed, so he was spending a few days with me. Luckily, she wasn't that good at seeing through a lie, a little one anyway, especially when it came from me. In her loving eyes, I could do no wrong, which made me feel miserable about lying even if it was for her own good.

Sashkatu was the only one who suspected something else was afoot when I didn't crawl into my usual spot in the cat-laden bed. He went looking for me at two in the morning. When he found me in my old room with Travis, he planted himself between us. I awoke to his whiskers tickling my cheek while Travis was the recipient of his twitching tail. At breakfast the poor guy was picking cat hair out of his mouth. I couldn't resist a laugh and paid the price by aspirating a mouthful of coffee. I couldn't stop coughing for a solid five minutes.

When the three of us walked over to Abracadabra, His Highness climbed up to his sunny throne, but didn't fall asleep until Travis was settled in the storeroom and life seemed stable for the moment.

Aside from Sashkatu's displeasure over the changes in his realm, the day moved along in an orderly fashion. Business was sporadic, mostly locals stopping in. Lolly came by with a hefty slab of her new cranberry-pumpkin fudge for us to try. I accepted it as payment for a bottle of shampoo that was kind to dyed hair and, courtesy of Morgana's clever spell, made hair grow more slowly. Customers were nuts about the stuff. Instead of needing a touchup every four or five weeks, they could go a good eight weeks without seeing any roots.

I was ready to lock up for the night when Lena ran in as if she was being pursued. She immediately moved away from the door and windows. She grabbed my hand and pulled me into the first aisle, where we couldn't be seen from outside. Her hand gripping mine was as cold as ice and she looked as if she was on the verge of tears.

"Are you okay?" I asked.

"I need to talk to you. Can we go someplace else? Someplace safe?"

"Is someone after you?" Travis asked when he found us.

"Please, not here," she said. "I was hoping you'd be getting ready to close up and go home." I assured her we were. Whatever was about to go down, I much preferred it happen at home where Tilly and Merlin were a block away, instead of a few steps.

In less than ten minutes we were installed at my kitchen table. I put up water to make tea for Lena—Tilly's calming blend. It seemed to help. When she put the mug down, her hands were no longer shaking. "I came because I'm afraid to go to the police by myself," she said. "I'm afraid they'll throw me in jail. The man you asked me about—the one who was borrowing my uncle's bike—he's a friend of a friend who loves Harleys."

"Who is this friend?" I asked.

"She's a friend from high school, so I didn't see any harm in it. And the guy paid me a hundred bucks whenever he borrowed it," she added sheepishly. "I've been putting the money away for my honeymoon. I had no idea the guy was involved in anything illegal until the last time he brought the Harley back."

"Why, what happened?" Travis said.

"I went outside to put the bike in the garage and I overheard him on the phone. He said things were getting too hot and he had to lie low for a while. When he realized I was standing behind him, he cut the call short and accused me of eavesdropping. He was so nasty, like a completely different person. He warned me to forget anything I heard if I wanted to keep breathing."

"Did you mention this to your mutual friend?" Travis asked.

She shook her head. "I was afraid to tell anyone."

"But now you're here talking to us," I pointed out, "so what changed your mind?"

She took a moment to finish the last of the tea. "With or without my help, one day the cops are going to find out who he is and whatever it is he's done. He'll probably blame me for talking even if I don't." She started to cry. "I'd rather call his bluff then live with that threat hanging over me." I got her the box of tissues I kept on the counter. "His name is Kenny. Kenny Driscoll I think." She paused to blow her nose. "At least that's how he was introduced to me."

"Okay, Lena," I said, "tomorrow morning Travis and I will go down to the New Camel station house with you. You'll tell them you want to share what you know about this guy, but you want immunity."

"And protection," Travis added.

Lena looked more hopeful. "I can do that?"

"Yes," I said, "but you may have to negotiate a bit. We'll be there to support you and if you need an attorney, we'll help find one for you."

"I don't know how I can thank you," Lena said, tearing up again.

I put my hand over hers. "No thanks necessary." What I really wanted to say was *tell us why you copied those papers from Epps's desk.* Unfortunately I'd never be able to explain to her or the police how I knew about her afterhours return to the courthouse.

After I fed the four-legged members of my household, we humans dined on pasta with a pomodoro sauce and salad, the one Italian meal I could pull off without a hitch. We sat together in the living room to watch a few mindless TV sitcoms for distraction. By nine o'clock we were all tired enough for bed. Lena bunked down on the convertible sofa in my home office.

At three fifteen in the morning, I awoke as if I'd been roused by an alarm. I listened for it to happen again, but all was still. I was about to dismiss it as an emergency vehicle passing in the distance or the product of a dream, when I felt the house vibrate. The wards had been activated. Fortunately, Merlin had reinforced them all. My dreaming mind had interpreted the vibration as an alert. Everyone else appeared to be sleeping peacefully, unaware that a threat was at our gate. I drew my bathrobe around me, but I didn't want to disturb the cats by rummaging in my dresser for socks or a flashlight. Without turning on any lights, I padded down the stairs, the cold hardwood sending chills through my body like ripples of misgiving.

Chapter 48

The vibrations echoed through my body again as I made my way over to the living room window to look for who or what was disturbing the wards. I didn't want a would-be intruder to know he was being watched, so I stood to the side of the blinds and peered out between the slats. I expected to see Biker Dude or his alter-ego. But in the dull light from the street lamp, I didn't recognize the man standing at my fence line. He looked like an average Joe. But he was trying to gain entry to my property at three in the morning and that meant he was dangerous. I watched Average Joe take a run at the force field. He bounced off it like the ball in a rough game of handball and landed in the street with a thud that was loud enough for me to hear. He had to be frustrated and confused. I was willing to bet he'd never encountered protective wards before.

"What are you doing?" Travis whispered behind me. I jumped, letting go of the blind I was holding. It clinked back into position, sounding loud in the quiet house. At least he hadn't turned on any lights.

I told him about the man outside and when I peeked out again, he was still there, walking along the perimeter of my property, looking for a vulnerable spot he could break through. Although he couldn't know what he was up against, his resolve hadn't waivered, which reinforced my belief that he was more than just a common criminal. Any self-respecting burglar would have moved on to another house by now, possibly vowing to give up drinking and drugs. This guy was after bigger game, possibly Lena, more likely Travis and me.

"Let me have a look," Travis said. After a few seconds at the window, he turned to me. "Do you have a pair of binoculars?"

"Bronwen did—she was into bird watching." I found her binoculars in a drawer of the breakfront and brought them over to him.

"This doesn't make any sense," he murmured.

"What doesn't?"

"The guy out there is Darrell Flint, Lena's fiancé."

"Wait," I said. "How do you know that?"

"From Lena's bridal shower."

"Flint wasn't there."

"He kinda was," Travis said. "They had a big poster board covered with dozens of photos of Lena and him." Some detective I was turning out to be. I hadn't even bothered to look at it. But given the situation, any additional mental flogging would have to wait.

"Let me see." I took the binoculars back and we switched places again. Although I'd never seen the guy before, there was something familiar about his face. Maybe he resembled someone else I knew. It was just beyond my grasp. And then I made the connection. "Travis," I whispered, "he's the Biker Dude! And Ski Mask Guy." And Lord only knew how many other personas. Without biker duds, his hair combed conservatively and his face clean-shaven, he'd been almost unrecognizable.

"Why would he be trying to break in here in the middle of the night?" Travis said as much to himself as to me. "It's not like we're holding Lena hostage."

"I don't think he's here for her," I said, pieces of the puzzle beginning to fall into place. "She's here for him."

"What do you mean?"

"I think she's here to help him get inside. After we approached her yesterday, she probably went straight to Flint and they came up with a way to turn our little scheme against us. So today she came running to us for help like we told her to. Only now she's working with him, or maybe she always has been."

"Then he's here to kill us and make it look like a burglary gone bad," Travis said. "What about Lena?"

"I don't see her as a killer."

"No offense, but I'd feel a whole lot better if it was Tilly saying that."

"What's wrong?" Lena asked, making us both jump as if we were the ones sneaking around, plotting murder. She was at the top of the stairs, looking remarkably well-coifed for someone who'd supposedly been sleeping.

"There's a guy outside trying to break in," I said, playing dumb. Her hand flew to her mouth. "Are you serious? Did you call the police?" Her acting skills were top-notch.

"I'm about to," Travis said, going to grab the phone off the end table in the living room. He talked for less than a minute. When he hung up, he joined me back at the window.

"Are they coming soon?" Lena asked, her voice shaking, but for the wrong reasons.

"That's generally what happens when you dial 911," Travis said. I wished he would dial back the sarcasm or she'd figure out she'd been made. We didn't want her running off before the police arrived.

"Come down and wait with us," I said. "You'll feel safer if you're not alone."

"I'll just go to the bathroom first," she said. To call and warn Flint the gig was up, no doubt.

"There's a bathroom here too," I reminded her.

"Oh, right." She started down with a tremulous smile that still needed some work to look genuine. After she went into the powder room, I tiptoed around the squeaky floorboards to listen at the door. I didn't hear her voice, which meant she must be sending Flint a text. There was nothing I could do to stop her. I made it back to the window with only a second to spare before she opened the door.

One of the advantages of living in a town as small as New Camel—the cop on-duty wasn't often busy with other calls. Minutes later a patrol car rolled silently along the curb, no sirens or flashing lights to announce his presence. He'd even doused his headlights before turning onto my street. Flint was so focused on his mission that he didn't realize he had company until Paul Curtis jumped out of the cruiser, gun drawn, and identified himself. I turned on my outdoor lights to help him see. He shouted at Flint to raise his hands and drop to his knees. Flint reached for his waistband instead. I bit my lip, knowing what was about to happen. If I tried to warn Curtis, I'd only be distracting him.

"Hands up!" he shouted again, "do *not* give me a reason to—" Two shots rang out. Curtis ducked behind the open door of his patrol car. The bullets went wide, slamming into the grill, waking the dogs in the neighborhood, who in turn roused their humans. Lights flashed on in all the houses I could see from my window. The telephone rang, startling us like another gunshot. Travis had left it on the window sill. There was only one person it could be.

"We're fine, Aunt Tilly," I said, taking care to keep my voice at a normal cadence. I explained the situation as routinely as it was possible to explain a shootout. In the background I heard my aunt pulling out her baking pans. I raised my voice over the noise. "Promise me you'll stay inside until I call you back."

Travis grabbed my arm and pulled me down on the floor. I knew he was trying to protect me from a stray bullet, but our personal wards were still active. He didn't seem all that reassured when I whispered this to him. I compromised by getting up on my knees and peering outside between the bottom slats of the blinds. Flint fired two more rounds that dinged off the patrol car before he took off. Curtis shouted for him to stop. When he didn't, Curtis fired, taking him down with one shot. I watched Flint crumple to the ground. Curtis approached him cautiously, gun drawn. I couldn't tell if Flint was alive or dead. He didn't appear to be moving. I glanced back at Lena, who was standing behind us. She couldn't see what was happening, but she gasped at the sound of each gunshot, forgetting about the role she was supposed to be playing. Her eyes were filled with the horror of not knowing Flint's fate. All she could be certain about was that her future would never be the one she'd created in her mind.

There was a small emergency squad located right in New Camel, under the auspices of the fire department. Curtis must have had them on standby, because the ambulance arrived so fast it was like they'd been waiting in the wings for their cue to enter stage right. Two EMTs jumped out. They did a cursory assessment, placed Flint on a gurney, and loaded him into the ambulance. They took off with sirens blaring. Would they have bothered with sirens if the patient was already dead? I wanted him to live, at least until he gave up the name of the person paying for his services. Of course if he didn't make it, we still had Lena.

"What happened?" she asked in a barely audible voice.

"The would-be intruder was shot and is now being rushed to the hospital," Travis said, slipping into his reporter-speak.

I was at the window when I saw Paul Curtis walking toward the fence gate. I panicked. I had to shut the wards before he came in contact with them. His gun was holstered, but that didn't matter to the wards. *No weapons allowed* was one of the main principles I'd programmed into them. I never ran through the disarming spell as quickly as I did that morning. Talk about a close call. As Paul reached for the latch, the wards powered down. My heart was thudding as if I'd just missed being crushed by an eighteen-wheeler. It was a good thing no one else could hear it. As I went to open the door for him, I noticed that the deadbolt had been disengaged. If I'd had any lingering doubts about Lena, this obliterated them. She'd definitely come to help Flint get inside. I hid my reaction to the open lock.

Paul came in, looking both wired and exhausted. This could well have been his first shooting. He looked around the room and asked if everyone was all right. Travis and I said we were. Lena didn't respond. She looked shell-shocked.

"Is she okay?" Paul asked.

"I'm sure she will be," I said without much sympathy. Now that the drama was over, it occurred to me that Travis and I were still in our pajamas, he in a white T-shirt and pajama bottoms, I in a nightgown and robe. I felt a little uncomfortable, knowing how Paul felt about me. I wanted to tell him it wasn't what it looked like, but of course it was. I rooted around for something else to say. All I came up with was coffee.

"Thanks," he said, "but Detective Duggan should be here in a few and I'll be heading out. I just wanted to make sure you guys were okay." That's when Lena decided to make a run for it. While we were talking, she must have recovered enough to realize her predicament was about to get worse. We heard the back door open, thanks to the squeaky hinges I'd been meaning to fix. Procrastination has its benefits. Travis took off after her through the kitchen, while I flew out the front door with a baffled Curtis on my heels. As bewildered as Travis and I were about the morning's events, he was completely at sea.

We were all converging on Lena when she fled through the fence gate Paul had left open. In a commanding voice that left no room for argument, he told Travis and me to wait in the house as he pounded down the street after her. Although we were unaccustomed to obeying orders without some back and forth on the subject, this was one time we kept our mouths shut. We trooped back inside like good citizens and stood waiting behind the glass storm door. When Curtis returned without her, Travis grumbled to me, "I wouldn't have let her get away."

"You can't know that," I said, feeling the need to defend Paul since he wasn't there to speak up for himself.

By the time Duggan and the forensic unit arrived from the Glen it was four a.m., and we were sleep deprived and testy from too much coffee. He wasn't in much better shape, the circles under his eyes were as purple as bruises and the stubble of his beard was white. He asked us to describe exactly what happened between Curtis and Flint. I made it clear that Curtis didn't fire his weapon until after he was fired upon and that he'd narrowly escaped death by waiting. Travis concurred, although not quite as ardently.

"Tell me about this Lena," Duggan said.

"I don't know much," I said. "She works for County Prosecutor Epps and is engaged to Darrell Flint, the man who was trying to break in here."

Since there was no record of my nighttime journey into the courthouse, I wasn't going to incriminate myself by admitting to seeing Lena sneak in there. That would open a big old can of worms that included the concept of teleportation. Scientists would want to dissect me, any number of bad guys would want to kidnap and use me for their heinous purposes, and the good and decent people of the world would have one more thing to keep them up at night.

Duggan frowned at me, his bushy eyebrows cinching together over his nose. "Are you in the habit of inviting people 'you don't know much about' to spend the night?"

"It wasn't quite like that," I said. I explained the whole thing about Lena and her uncle's Harley and the various identities of Darrell Flint. "When I told Lena the police were trying to ID him, she was afraid she'd wind up in trouble for lending him the bike. We felt sorry for her, so we told her we'd go with her to the station house in the morning to help her explain it all."

"Wait a minute here. Are you telling me that the man who was trying to break in here was coming to silence her?" Duggan asked, trying to wade through everything I'd told him.

"That's what we originally thought," I said. "But now we believe he was coming to kill us, with Lena's help."

Duggan grunted as he pulled himself up from the couch. "I expect an immediate alert if Lena turns up again," he said, plodding to the door as if his legs had somehow doubled in weight since he arrived.

Chapter 49

Going back to sleep was out of the question with all the caffeine and adrenalin racing through our bodies. Travis offered to make breakfast for us, his one specialty—scrambled eggs. We agreed on the addition of mushrooms and cheddar. I was relegated to making toast. Travis watched me take my first bite of his masterpiece like a nervous parent watching his child's first recital. I gave him a thumbs-up with my mouth full. They were better than any I'd ever made for myself. Or maybe they seemed better, because I didn't have to make them myself.

While eating, we hatched a plan that might finally lead us to the killer. Travis insisted on cleaning up, with no argument from me. Then he headed back to the Glen and I dragged myself into the shower to get ready for work. Neither of us believed Lena would ever darken my doorstep again. Duggan might have better luck finding her in the wilds of Alaska than anywhere in Schuyler County. Bradley Epps was going to need a new secretary.

When Sashkatu and I arrived at the shop, we went straight over to Tea and Empathy, where Tilly was finishing up the baking she'd started in the wee hours of the morning. Merlin was perched on his stool eating a day-old carrot muffin, his beard catching most of the crumbs. He gave it a good shake, causing crumbs to rain onto the floor to Sashki's delight.

"So I missed all the excitement," Tilly said petulantly, after I gave her all the details of our harrowing night. She sounded as if she'd intentionally been left out of a good time.

"You couldn't have come over to my house with a gunman stalking the property. Morgana and Bronwen would have been furious if I was that thoughtless about your safety."

"I suppose," she said. "Between you and me, I'm not in any rush to join them over there. As dearly as I do love my mother and sister, I'm enjoying the peace and quiet for now."

"If you're seriously interested in helping us with the case, there *may* be a way you can," I said, stressing the iffy nature of what I was about to tell her.

Tilly's eyes lit up. "Of course, count me in! I'll be happy to do it, whatever it is."

"Hear me out first," I said. I might as well have been trying to keep the lid on a tween's enthusiasm after learning her pop idol is coming to dinner. "I don't know if it's something you *can* do or would even *want* to do."

"Oh I want to," she assured me. "Yes indeedy." If she were younger and more lithe, she might have managed a few back flips to prove her point.

"The guy Curtis shot isn't dead. I heard he's in a coma. Is it possible to read someone in a coma? And there's the issue of whether or not it's ethical."

Tilly's brow furrowed. "I've never been asked to read a person in a coma. If I had been, I probably would have refused. Without the consent of the person, it would be an invasion of privacy."

"What if the information in this guy's brain could lead us to the killer and save lives?"

"That's quite a mitigating factor," she said. "And the patient in question has already committed crimes. For all we know, he wanted to kill you and Travis." She gasped at her own words. "I'm in. If it's possible to collect the information you need, I will drill my way into his head and get it for you."

"Think about it carefully, Aunt Tilly. It won't be easy. We'll have to sneak you into and out of his room past a police guard."

"Pish-posh," she said. "That's the fun part."

"What about me?" Merlin demanded. "I'm more powerful than both of you put together."

"You'll have a role too," I promised. In spite of his propensity for making a muddle of things, we might need his help if the situation turned dicey.

When I called Travis to let him know it was game-on, he insisted on being included too, even if it was just to drive "the getaway car," as he put it.

"We don't need a getaway car," I said, "because we're not criminals. We're his family, come to say our final goodbyes."

"I still contend that with Merlin along, you might need a getaway car," he said with a chuckle.

Although we did our best to be prepared for any eventuality, there's only so much you can control in the kind of venture we were undertaking. One thing we could control—who was guarding Flint's room when we put the plan in motion. If Paul Curtis or Justin Hobart was there, we would scrub the mission and come back a different day. Other than Detective Duggan, they were the only cops who knew us and knew we were not members of the patient's family. We hadn't come up with a better ploy to be granted access to his room. Besides, who would be heartless enough to turn away the mother, grandfather, and sister of a man on the brink of death?

Everyone was pleased with their assigned roles, except Merlin. "Grandfather?" he'd sputtered. "Do I look like anyone's grandfather?" We all nodded.

"It's Grandpa Merlin or nothing," I said.

"Very well," he said imperiously, "then I will be the best grandpa you've ever seen."

It was Tilly who suggested we use a memory blocker to keep the cop on duty from reporting our visit to Duggan. For all we knew, Flint had no family, or conversely, he had one the detective had already met with. In either case, our cover story would quickly unravel. Tilly claimed to know the memory-blocking spell Morgana had created years ago.

* * * *

Schuyler Hospital was less than three miles from Watkins Glen. Since Travis lived substantially closer to it than we did, he became our scout. All he had to do was pop into the hospital and find out who was guarding the patient. If it was Curtis or Hobart and they saw him, he would say he was there visiting a friend. If it was a cop who didn't know us, he'd call and we'd pile into the car. Travis would meet us in the Glen and we'd head straight back to the hospital. Weather permitting, we could make the trip in less than an hour.

That first morning I must have checked my phone ten times waiting for Travis's call. "Hobart's here," he said when I finally heard from him. "Better luck tomorrow." We were all on edge for the rest of the day. When your adrenalin is pumping and you're psyched to go, it's hard to wind down to the pace of a normal day. Thankfully an unscheduled mini bus from the senior center in the Glen arrived at midday with eight women and two men who were spry enough to walk without assistance and every bit as sharp as my grandmother. Although I was a lot closer in age to the teenagers who came to New Camel, trailing behind their parents, glued to their phones, I much preferred the seniors. One elderly gentleman came into my shop with two women. While the women browsed, he came to the counter to flirt with me. He stated it right up front, said he needed practice; he was losing his touch. He had white hair and lively blue eyes and stood as straight and tall as a man thirty years his junior. We spent an enjoyable few minutes in playful banter until one of the women came up to the counter.

"George Neumann, you stop bothering this lovely girl right now."

"He's not bothering me," I said, "he's been charming. Besides, I'm not exactly a girl anymore." She wasn't listening. She threaded her arm through his and pulled him away.

"You old fool," she scolded him gently. "You're going to get arrested someday for trying to pick up girls." It seemed George had already made a conquest, even if he didn't know it yet.

When I saw Tilly at closing time, she'd also had a good day and Merlin was replete with leftover goodies. Lying in bed that night, I wondered how many more times we'd have to rev ourselves up for our little caper, only to stand down. I was worried we'd eventually lose our edge or whatever we had that passed for one.

The next morning, Travis called, and I could hear it in his voice when he said *hello.* The cop on duty wasn't anyone we knew.

Chapter 50

Travis let us off at the front door of the hospital. The plan was for him to park in the lot and wait there for my call when we were ready to leave. Tilly, Merlin, and I found our way to the corridor, off which Flint's room was located. The police guard was seated immediately outside his door, reading the local paper. We didn't see any doctors or nurses moving through the hallway, but they could be in any one of the rooms, including Flint's. If that was the case, we'd go down to the cafeteria on the basement level and have a cup of coffee before trying our luck again. If no opportunity presented itself over the course of an hour or two, we'd have to press *reset*. Compared to hospitals in larger, urban areas, Schuyler was tiny. Sooner or later someone on the staff was going to notice our ragtag little group and wonder why we were still hanging around.

Sometimes life hands you a lemon and sometimes it hands you a golden pass. We walked down the hall without seeing another soul. The cop didn't look up from the sports section of the newspaper until we were nearly standing over him. The name on his ID tag was Craig Boyd. When I said, "Hello, Officer Boyd," he dropped the paper and jumped up, looking as confused as someone caught napping on the job. He was young, fresh-faced, and most likely untried. It might work in our favor if we overwhelmed him with our distress, or it could work against us if he was gung ho to make his mark and get noticed by his superiors for being tough.

"How is my son doing, Officer?" Tilly asked in a voice tuned to a perfect pitch of anxiety and dread. She was wearing her gray and black muumuu under a black coat. It was her going to funerals outfit, minus even the jewelry she allowed herself at those times. She despised dark colors. Some people suffered from Seasonal Affective Disorder. My aunt suffered from wearing dark colors. She claimed they drained her spirit. Who was I to say she was wrong? Truth be told, even her usually sparkling red hair seemed less vibrant, as if it too were drained by her attire.

"Your son?" Boyd repeated. "I was told this man has no family."

"Oh no," she said, clutching at her heart. "Has something happened since I last spoke to his doctor?"

"No no, not at all," he said, taking her elbow and offering her the chair. Tilly stood her ground, refusing to move.

"I don't believe you. Something's wrong. I can feel it in my bones." She had worked herself into such a state that her breathing was erratic and actual tears were spilling down her cheeks.

"I swear to you, ma'am, nothing has changed. Come, come see for yourself." Way to work it, Aunt Tilly! He walked her into the room, but as we filed in behind her, Boyd's wits made a reappearance. "Wait, who are you two?"

"I'm his sister," I said in a choking voice that dared him to challenge me. "And this poor man is his grandpa. His hundred-year-old grandpa." Merlin opened his mouth to protest, but Tilly planted a subtle kick to his shin. "He's not supposed to be out in the cold," I said, "but he begged to see his beloved grandson." I couldn't have hoped to match Tilly's performance, but I must have done well enough, because I could see in Boyd's eyes that we'd won.

Darrell Flint looked considerably smaller and less threatening in the hospital bed with lines and tubes hooking him to various machines. "Officer," Tilly sniffled, "may we please have a few minutes alone with him?"

When Boyd hesitated, I said, "Look at him, look at us. We're not here to stage an escape. He'd die in seconds without the machines."

"May you never suffer anything this awful in your life," Merlin piled on. We were all looking at Boyd with teary eyes.

"Okay, all right. It's against regulations, but you can have a few minutes."

"God will bless you for your kindness," Tilly said as he walked out. "Please close the door so our sorrow won't be on display." The moment the door closed, Tilly sat down beside Flint and took his hand in hers. I dropped to my knees on the other side of the bed, so if Boyd peeked in, he'd think I was praying. Merlin took the one chair in the room and did his best to appear devastated.

I looked at Flint, trying to visualize him as the Biker Dude. Without his leathers and spiked hair, it wasn't easy. *Where were his tattoos?* His arms lay atop the blanket devoid of ink. So the tattoos were no more real than the Biker Dude persona.

Tilly was so still I couldn't tell if she was busy reading his brain or having trouble navigating it in his current condition. By my watch, ten minutes had passed before Boyd knocked once and opened the door. We presented the perfect tableau of a family in grief. He stayed in the doorway as if reluctant to intrude. "I'm sorry," he said softly, "but I have to ask you to leave now."

I rose slowly, my knees aching from the hard floor. In an effort to give Tilly every additional second he could, Merlin struggled to get up from the chair. I went to help him. It took three long attempts before I succeeded in getting him upright. Having run out of ways to stall, I walked around the bed and touched my aunt's shoulder. She let go of Flint's hand, but as she got to her feet, she started to sway as if she might faint. Her effort to read him had clearly taken a lot out of her. I grabbed her around the waist to steady her.

"Officer," I called, "if you could give me a hand?" Boyd rushed over to us and took hold of her arm, until she murmured that she was okay. He ushered us into the hall, where we all thanked him as profusely as our grief permitted.

"If you want to visit him again, ma'am" he said to Tilly, "you'll need permission from Detective Duggan. We're not trying to make things difficult for you, but you have to keep in mind that your son is under arrest for a number of serious crimes." Tilly assured him she understood. Merlin and I bobbed our heads to make it unanimous. I stayed near Boyd for an extra minute. Under the pretense of looking for my keys in my purse, I quickly wove the memory-blocking spell.

Be gone all thoughts you have of us,
As if they never were.
Forget our names and faces.
To you we never were.

I called Travis from the lobby and two minutes later we were on the road back to Watkins Glen. I was dying to ask my aunt what she'd learned, but first Travis deserved an account of our time in the hospital, which I supplied, with additional commentary from Tilly and Merlin.

"All right, Tilly," Travis said when we were done, "the spotlight is all yours."

"Well, he was a difficult read, at least partly because there was trauma and swelling from the bullet. It was like trying to drive from point A to point B with road blocks everywhere. When I finally reached a place with healthy brain tissue, it was like looking for a tiny needle in a giant haystack with the clock ticking."

"Consarnit, woman!" Merlin thundered. "I could expire by the time you get to the meat of the thing!"

"I'm getting there, old man. If I didn't take the time to properly explain the landscape of Flint's head, it would be easy to misinterpret what I found. Your impatience has only delayed the process." I was trying to tamp down my own frustration at that point, but I knew that interrupting Tilly was rarely a good idea. To pick up the train of her narrative, she'd been known to go back to the beginning, so I kept my mouth zippered.

"Now where was I," she muttered, making me stifle a groan. "Ah yes, I came across references to Sam Crawford often enough that they must have had more interactions than let's say, a neighbor or casual acquaintance. What troubled me was the odd mix of emotions Flint had about him."

"Like what?" Travis asked.

"I can't name specific ones, it's more of a general feeling I got. He gave me the creeps." I was beginning to think our trip to the hospital didn't net us anything of value. Tilly had done the best she could, given the twisted wreckage of his brain.

"What about Bradley Epps, Everett Royce, or Austin Stubbs?" I asked, holding out hope for something concrete.

"Epps, yes. He did seem more benign to Flint, but no one is completely dark or light. Oh, I did see Austin Stubbs," she added, snapping me back to attention.

"And?"

"Nothing much, I'm sorry to say. He didn't appear to have a big impact on Flint. I did feel darkness, but I think that was intrinsic to Stubbs."

"What about Lena?" I asked. The question was idle curiosity more than fact seeking.

"Well, of course," Tilly said. "I found her everywhere, as one would expect given their relationship. But his feelings about her were not as warm and glowing as they are for most couples about to wed. Of course that can be from the stress of planning a wedding."

"Or from being involved in illegal activities," I added dryly.

Travis dropped the three of us at my car, and I drove back to New Camel. Tilly had taken the day off, so after I deposited her and Merlin at her house, I stopped home to take Sashki with me to the shop. He groused a bit, but once I closed the door behind us, he seemed willing enough for a change of venue. There were times I was sure he came with me for no other reason than to rub his status in the faces of the other cats.

It was a short workday that began at one-fifteen. Only a few customers straggled in. I could easily have been closed all day with negligible loss of revenue. But a shop with hours posted on its door stood to lose a lot of customer loyalty if it wasn't open when it was supposed to be. Disappoint people often enough and they stop coming.

That night I didn't sleep well. I dreamed that Tilly and I were lost in Flint's mind, being chased by malignant emotions. Sashkatu must have sensed my distress. He wrapped himself around my head like a big, furry bandage. It must have helped, because when the alarm woke me at seven, it was from a sweet dream of my childhood.

Chapter 51

I was turning off the security system at my shop the next morning when Travis called. "The police found Lena and arrested Bradley Epps," he said. I felt like I'd been picked up by a tornado and set down in a stranger place than Kansas. A dazed "Wait—what?" was all I could manage.

"They tracked her down to her uncle's farm in Burdett." She might have fared better in Alaska, I thought, still reeling.

"Did they arrest Epps *after* they found her or *before?*" I asked, reasoning and logic seeping back into my brain.

"After. They brought her in for questioning, and then arrested him."

"In other words, she gave him up and took our advice to negotiate a deal with the police."

"Sure sounds like it," he said.

Epps had the right motive, the perfect motive. We should have taken the next logical step and confronted him about it. Why had we waited? Because you need more evidence than *it makes sense* or *it feels right,* when you accuse someone of murder. "Are you okay?" I asked Travis. "I know how badly you wanted to catch Ryan's killer yourself."

"Not so fast." He didn't sound as disappointed as I expected.

"I don't follow."

"I was thinking about Tilly's reading of Flint and I don't think we should dismiss it just because it doesn't jibe with the way we've looked at this case up until now. Duggan may think he has the killer, but what if he doesn't?"

"I'm listening."

"You saw how afraid Lena was when she came to us. I don't think it was all an act. I think she'd gotten herself caught up in something that scared the hell out of her. Who had the best shot of talking her into doing something she wasn't comfortable with?"

"The man she loved and was about to marry?"

"I bet Flint roped her into lending him the bike and helping him get into your house and who knows what else. He probably played up the money angle. Getting married comes with a lot of bills."

"But Epps doesn't have the money to pay him and Lena for extracurricular activities," I said. "Crawford is the one with the money to hire a killer. But there's still the issue of motive with him."

"The same motive we attributed to Epps."

"A guilty conscience? What about his practice and lifestyle?" I couldn't find a way around that mountain.

"True, he stands to lose everything, including his freedom, if he's caught. But the thing I finally realized is that Crawford is an arrogant man who believes he's untouchable. Failure is not in his vocabulary."

"Wait a minute," I said, "if you're right, why did Lena give the police Epps? Duggan is bound to see through the lie sooner than later."

"She probably wasn't looking further than the next five minutes. Flint is as good as dead. She's on her own; she has to be half crazy at this point. If I'm right, she was too scared to give them Crawford. He has the money to exact retribution. But she needed leverage, something she could use to negotiate a deal with the cops. Maybe she thought they'd release her and she'd have enough time to find a better place to hide before they realized she was lying."

"Or it really could be Epps," I said. "Maybe the deaths of those innocent people was the last straw for him. All he needed was someone willing to help out for free."

"A pretty tall order," Travis said dryly.

"Maybe not as tall as you think. Let me play devil's advocate for a minute. After Everett Royce's wife is killed, he goes to see Epps. Maybe he threatens to kill him for incompetency. Epps calms him down, says he has a better idea. They join forces. Epps supplies the expertise on how to avoid leaving forensic evidence. Royce does the deeds."

"I can maybe see Royce doing it to avenge his wife's death," Travis said, "but what about the others who were killed?"

"Okay, maybe Epps and Royce, his boy wonder, get away with the first one and it's cathartic for them—a kind of high. They're caped crusaders like their boyhood heroes. Well, maybe not caped."

"As scenarios go, it's not a terrible one. At least it's not any more far-fetched than believing Crawford suddenly grew a conscience and decided to give up all the trappings of his—Wait, listen to this—Flint's dead, possibly murdered."

Chapter 52

Flint's death weighed on my mind all day. I couldn't help wondering if our visit to him was the reason he'd been killed. But who would have leaked it? Officer Boyd was the only one who knew we were there, and the spell I'd used should have erased his memory of us. Maybe it was just a coincidence and Flint was eliminated because there was a chance, albeit a slim one, that he might wake up and start naming names. He'd gone from being useful to the killer, to being a messy detail, a liability to be dealt with once and for all.

When I spoke to Travis again that evening, he told me a man dressed like a doctor, down to the proper ID tag, was allowed into Flint's room by the officer on duty. He was in there for only a few minutes, during which time he must have introduced a lethal drug into Flint's IV line. When the nurse came to check on him thirty minutes later, he was dead. The ME's report was pending. My takeaway from this news was that the killer was erasing risk wherever it cropped up, leaving nothing to chance. I was worried that Travis, Tilly, Merlin, and I could be next on his list. Enough people who worked at the hospital had seen us walking around. Even if no one knew why we'd gone to see Flint, our being there was enough to raise the wrong eyebrows.

"I'm afraid you may be right," Travis said, after listening to my concerns. "It was bound to happen if we got close enough. I want you to lock up. Don't answer the door for anyone." I made him promise to do the same. But knowing that the wards were in place gave me some much-needed peace of mind. I called Tilly to make sure she buttoned up her house too, but she didn't answer. She'd probably taken Merlin out for dinner. If he nagged enough, she often gave in and took him to The Soda Jerk or the

Caboose. When I dialed her cell phone, it went straight to voice mail. My aunt always had her phone with her, but didn't always remember to turn it on—a problem with people of a certain age who'd lived without the convenience for the better part of their lives. I told myself she'd find my message when she got home.

I fed Sashki and his tribe. Watching them tuck into their dinners, I envied them their worry-free existence. They had a servant to prepare their food, clean their litter boxes, and make sure they had fresh linens upon which to lay their furry heads. I made a chicken salad sandwich and tea and took my dinner into the living room to distract myself with a TV game show. By seven-thirty the TV was no longer cutting it. I was really worried about Tilly and a certain wizard from long, long ago.

Not five minutes later the doorbell rang. When I looked through the peephole, I found my aunt and Merlin on my doorstep. If I'd given it any thought, I would have realized something wasn't right. Tilly had her own key and preferred to let herself in. She never rang the bell. She claimed she shouldn't need to as a member of the family. In my defense, I was so relieved to see her there that I suffered a momentary lapse in judgment. A big ol' double-wide momentary lapse as it turned out. When I opened the door, Tilly and Merlin were grim-faced. Before I could ask them what was wrong, Mason stepped out of the shadows with a gun pointed at Tilly's head. He jammed it against her temple, making her flinch for my benefit.

"Where are your manners?" he asked with a smile that chilled me. "Aren't you going to invite us in?" I stepped back from the doorway, my brain unable to communicate with my mouth. Merlin came in first, followed by Tilly and Mason, who looked like an odd pair of conjoined twins with the gun connecting them. The trick was going to be separating them. "We'll wait in the living room," Mason said. I had no idea what we were waiting for, but Tilly was my most immediate concern.

"Are you okay, Aunt Tilly?" I whispered to her.

"You do realize I can hear you," Mason said derisively. "You may as well speak up." He didn't wait for me to take the lead. He found his way into the living room and pulled Tilly down beside him on the couch, the gun still at her head. Sashkatu, who'd been on his perch there, climbed down Tilly and headed off, presumably to finish his nap in quieter quarters. Merlin and I were directed to the wing chairs facing the couch. I definitely preferred bodyguard Mason to killer-for-hire Mason, not that he was taking a poll.

"Might there be ice cream?" Merlin inquired.

"Shut up!" Mason said. "This isn't a party."

"It's not necessary to have a party in order to enjoy ice cream," he responded sullenly.

"I told you to shut the hell up or you can change places with Tilly here." Mason picked up the phone on the end table and tossed it to me. "Dial your boyfriend's number, then toss it back to me." Mason wasn't stupid, he knew that as long as he had a gun to my aunt's head, I wasn't going to try anything funny. "I'm waiting," Mason said tersely.

I tapped in Travis's number, and tossed it back as he'd instructed. If I'd been more certain of my accuracy, I would have thrown it back with a wallop of telekinetic energy and knocked him out. But I could just as easily have injured my aunt. Although I could only hear Mason's side of the conversation, it was enough for me to catch the gist of things. Simply put, we were his hostages and our lives would be forfeit if Travis didn't arrive within the hour, alone and unarmed. If anyone called the police, the clock stopped and the coroner could pick up our bodies.

I wanted to shout to Travis not to come, that he would just make the body count higher, but I didn't think our captor was bluffing about pulling the trigger. While we all might be dead soon enough, for the present we were alive and every additional second was a second in which one of us could come up with a brilliant solution to our predicament.

When the doorbell rang again, it was far too soon for it to be Travis, unless he also harbored the building blocks of magick in his DNA. I prayed for it to be the police, but it wasn't likely they were aware of our distress. In any case, they would never have rung the bell. Tilly and I exchanged anxious glances as Mason propelled her off the couch to answer it. I couldn't immediately see the newcomer, because he was blocked by the open door, but I heard Mason say, "It's about time."

"It couldn't be helped," the newcomer said, "there was a three-car pileup on 414." Something about his voice seemed familiar. I had the answer in seconds, when Mason, Tilly, and Everett Royce came into the living room. What the heck was Royce doing with Mason? Mason worked for Crawford, and I'd seen Royce huddled at dinner with Epps. Were they all part of some bad guy cartel?

Mason and my aunt took the couch again, leaving enough room for Royce on her other side. Tilly had gone from pale to ashen. I asked Mason if I could change places with her and was told to shut up. "All your problems will be over soon enough," he snapped.

Merlin had been remarkably quiet for some time. I had the feeling he was up to something and could only hope it involved saving us and not asking for ice cream as his last meal. Now that Mason had an accomplice, he was free to use the bathroom and raid my pantry for Oreos. As a captor, Royce wasn't as exacting as his partner. He kept his gun in the general vicinity of my aunt's head without pressing it into her skull. I watched Travis's hour count down on the grandmother clock on the wall.

The doorbell finally rang again, I wanted it to be Travis, but only if he had a plan to rescue us. I didn't want him to die with us. Since Royce was on guard duty with his own gun, Mason had his in hand when he went to open the door. Travis walked in and suddenly all hell broke loose.

From my vantage point, I watched five cats race into the foyer, where they wove in and out of Mason's legs like furry little rockets. They were a blur of motion. I'd had no idea they could move that fast. Mason was turning in circles, trying to get off a shot at them.

Before he could, he lost his balance and fell with a resounding thud. His gun spun away across the hardwood. Travis lunged for it like a base runner sliding into home. In one smooth move, he was on his feet again, the gun trained on Mason. We weren't out of the woods yet, but the odds were certainly improved.

The cats, who'd vanished when Mason hit the floor, reappeared, this time leaping from every high surface they could find. Since Travis and Mason were still in the foyer, one cat leaped off the steps onto Mason's back, ripping his claws down the base of his thick neck and across his back hard enough to draw blood and screams of outrage.

Another cat jumped off the china closet onto Royce, dragging his claws across his cheek and forehead. They were joined by three more of their brethren, leaping through the air like a team of mini ninjas. During the melee, I saw Royce's grip on his gun loosen as he tried to protect his face with his forearms. Before I could try to wrest it from him, Tilly had it in her shaking hands. She got to her feet and backed away from the couch, keeping the gun pointed squarely at Royce. When she reached me, she handed off the gun. We'd disarmed our assailants, but all the credit belonged to the cats. Sashkatu had resumed his place atop the couch. Looking straight at me, he winked. But I'd already deduced that he orchestrated and choreographed the brilliant attack of the familiars.

Mason and Royce were aghast. If the floor opened beneath them and Hobbits sprang up from Middle Earth, I don't think they could have looked any more stunned. I tried to calm my heart and mind, so I could think clearly. We didn't dare let down our guard; these were two extremely dangerous men who could overpower us again if we made the slightest mistake. Acrobatic cats notwithstanding, our lives were hanging in the balance until we completely incapacitated them.

Merlin, who didn't appear at all fazed by what happened, told Travis to bring Royce into the living room. Travis looked at me, eyebrows raised. I knew what he was thinking—it was a better idea to keep the two men apart. Although I shared his opinion, I suspected Merlin had a plan up his wizardly sleeves. I nodded back to Travis. I could see he wasn't happy about it, but he ordered Mason into the living room, staying far enough behind him, in case he should turn and try to grab the gun.

Merlin came to stand between us, facing our prisoners. He closed his eyes and began reciting a long string of words in a cadence that sounded something like a spell, but the words must have been in old English, incomprehensible to me.

"Wait," Travis blurted out, "damnit, wait!"

Merlin stopped and wheeled on him. "What is the problem?"

"I need to question them." He sounded every bit as ticked off as Merlin.

"And you believe they will answer your questions?" the wizard asked in a bemused tone. "Then by all means, proceed." He folded his arms, prepared to wait.

"You're both smart enough to know you can't get away with everything you've done," Travis said. "Answer my questions now and we'll tell the police you cooperated with us."

"Not going to happen," Mason sneered.

Royce echoed the sentiment. "Not a chance."

"You know how this works," Travis went on. "Even if you run, the police will catch up with you. First thing they'll do is separate you and put pressure on you to talk. Sooner or later one of you *will* break and he's the one who'll get the deal with the cops. You know we're not talking petty theft here. You'll be facing murder charges. Do you really want to torture yourself wondering if the other guy is spilling his guts to the police? Give up the creep you're working for." The two men stole a glance at each other, trust beginning to erode. Travis had gotten to them, but it wasn't enough. If we waited much longer, they would launch an attack on us. We might have the weapons, but we were rank amateurs and I was certain it showed. They had to know the odds were good that we would never actually fire at them and if we did, that we were likely to graze them or miss completely. I felt it in the marrow of my bones. Tilly must have felt it too.

"I've been doing a little neurological research," she said to Travis. I knew what that meant—she'd been snooping around in our prisoners' brains. "I have the name you want."

"You do? You're sure?" Travis asked, keeping his eyes and gun locked on our prisoners.

"Tilly wouldn't say it if she had any doubts," I assured him. "We have to let Merlin get on with…it." I didn't want to use the word *spell* out loud. Travis gave Merlin a reluctant nod to go ahead. The wizard repeated the incantation three times. Before the last words faded away, Mason and Royce were slumped on the couch, snoring.

"When will they wake up?" I asked.

"They will wake only if I repeat the spell backward," Merlin said on his way into the kitchen.

"All right, Tilly," Travis said, "let's have it."

Chapter 53

"Sam Crawford is the man responsible for all the deaths, including your foster brother's." Tilly spoke plainly, without the fanfare of which she was fond. No one said a word for close to a minute. We were all trying to make sense of her revelation. Questions bubbled up in my head, giving rise to other questions, with no answers in sight. Those answers would have to wait. We didn't have long to formulate a plan of attack. According to my aunt, snooper sublime, Crawford was waiting in his office until his two henchmen called to say the job was done. Surely there was a time past which he would assume they'd encountered problems. But he hadn't shared such a time with Mason or Royce. Tilly was certain the two men didn't possess that knowledge. She'd gone through their brains with a fine-tooth comb, as she put it. Any scruples she had about pillaging their minds had gone out the window the moment she and Merlin were abducted.

Travis and I agreed that Crawford wasn't likely to be a patient man. He wouldn't wait long before he ordered up some damage control. We had to assume he had at least one body guard or hired gun in his office with him. It seemed to me that the only way we could take on two of them was if we had the advantage of surprise. If I popped out of thin air, it was bound to startle and bewilder the most focused and stable of bad guys. People had certain expectations about how the world worked. Some things were possible, others were not. Appearing and disappearing were solidly in the *not* column. It was a dandy illusion for so-called *magicians,* but even if the audience couldn't figure out the mechanics of it, they recognized that it was only a trick—sleight of hand and misdirection, trap doors, smoke and mirrors. It wasn't real.

When Travis heard my plan, he vetoed it as being too dangerous. But the clock was ticking and when he couldn't propose a better one, he was forced to get on board with mine. We would drive to Crawford's office together. I would disconnect the security system with the spells I'd created for Epps's office and in a similar fashion unlock any doors that stood between Travis and the attorney. After he was well-positioned, I would teleport into Crawford's office and hopefully scare the stuffing out of the man and whoever else was with him. At the same time, Travis would burst in brandishing one of our newly acquired guns.

When I asked him if he had much experience with firearms, he told me he'd done some target shooting. I decided I didn't want to know how proficient he was or how long ago he'd participated in the sport. I was pretty sure I wouldn't be encouraged by his answers. Hopefully he wouldn't have to use the gun. Most people facing the business end of a gun tended to back off. Of course that probably didn't apply to bodyguards and hired guns.

I had my own misgivings about the plan, chiefly what to do after the initial shock of our entrance wore off. There was no way to prepare for it, since it depended on how many people Crawford had with him and how they reacted. Leaving Tilly and Merlin at my house in charge of the sleeping prisoners worried me too. What if Merlin was mistaken and the spell wore off on its own? What if Crawford had already sent a second team to accomplish what his first team failed to do? I made Merlin promise to do whatever it took to keep himself and Tilly alive. He promised around a mouth full of Oreos. I took it on faith that he said *yes*.

I had one more instruction for Tilly, before we ran out the door. "In forty-five minutes, I want you to call 911. Tell them Travis and I are being held against our will at Crawford's office. It's just a precaution," I added when I saw fear flare in her eyes.

"I'll set a timer this very minute," she said, heading to the kitchen. "And I'll make tea."

The drive from New Camel to Watkins Glen seemed longer than ever before. Fortunately the roads were dry and the traffic was light. I couldn't imagine racing there on icy roads. Travis parked down the block from Crawford's office and we hoofed it the rest of the way. Standing in the shadows, I recited the spell to disarm the security system, and Morgana's spell to unlock the front door and the door to Crawford's office. At the last moment I added a directive to make the locks move silently. There was still the possibility that if someone was looking at the door they would see the lock's position change, but in magick, as in life, you can't account for everything.

Peering through the front door, the lobby appeared to be empty. Light seeped from beneath the closed door to Crawford's office. I told Travis to go inside when I started the third incantation of the spell and to wait near Crawford's door until he heard evidence that I'd arrived. He leaned in to me and kissed me softly. "Thank you," he whispered, "for helping me make this right for Ryan."

"Don't get all mushy now, our minds need to be as clear and focused as possible for this to work." At least mine did. "Save it for celebrating our success." I sent a silent apology to Bronwen for breaking my promise to always do a trial run with an object before teleporting myself. There was simply no time.

From here and now to there and then
Attract not change, nor harm allow.
Safe passage guarantee to souls
As well as lesser, mindless things.

When I opened my eyes after the third repetition, I was standing directly in front of Sam Crawford's desk. The attorney installed behind it was turning a chalky white and his eyes were bugging out of his head. It looked like one good thump on the back would knock them out of their sockets.

"Ms....Wilde? How... How did you get in here?" he stammered.

"The only thing you need to know, Mr. Crawford, is that tonight you're going to give up your lavish lifestyle." My words would have had more impact if I'd had a gun to point at him, but Tilly and Travis needed the ones we'd confiscated more than I did.

"Hudson," Crawford bellowed, blood flow infusing his face again, turning it an angry red. "Get in here!" I listened for running footsteps, but there was only silence.

Crawford renewed his calls for Hudson as he opened a desk drawer and withdrew a handgun. "Make no mistake," he said, "I'm well-known for my proficiency with this weapon." It might have been a more believable threat if his hands weren't shaking so badly.

"It won't be long before you're just as well-known for your proficiency in murder," I said, locking my eyes on the gun. Success with telekinesis so soon after teleporting into the office was by no means a sure thing. *Where the heck was Travis?* I focused on the gun and pulled, but his grip on it was stronger than I'd expected. I summoned my remaining strength and tried again. I felt it give—just enough to encourage me. Crawford had felt the weapon move too. He frowned and readjusted his grip on it. I tugged at it once more, sheer determination making up for my flagging energy. I was almost as surprised as the attorney when the gun jerked free of his hand and flew over the desk into mine. I pointed it in his direction and hoped I wouldn't have to use it.

"What the hell are you?" Crawford snapped. The door burst open and Travis appeared, gun in hand and a wild, don't-mess-with-me look in his eyes. He threw the door closed behind him.

"What do you people want from me?" Crawford demanded. "Do you have any idea what I can do to you? Hudson!"

"We're here to get justice for all the people you killed or hired others to kill. By the time Ryan Cutler came on the scene, you probably didn't have a moment's hesitation arranging for his death too. But you should have. That was the single biggest mistake of your life. Ryan Cutler was my brother, and I will do everything in my power to see you rot in prison for the rest of your miserable days." Travis's throat had tightened with emotion, nearly choking off his voice. "Knowing that will give me some measure of peace."

We all heard the door click open. Travis had the presence of mind to slip behind it, probably hoping he could get the drop on the newcomer. I moved my hand with the gun behind my back, waiting for Travis to act.

"What's up, boss?" Hudson asked, holding a half-eaten slice of pizza. He glanced at me and gave me a head bob. Maybe it was normal for Crawford to have young women around after hours. I wouldn't have been surprised if he had an adjoining bedroom.

"Where the hell have you been?" Crawford thundered.

"I went to get a slice like you told me, remember? You said, 'I'm not hungry, but you should go grab some pizza. I'll be fine here for a few minutes.'" Crawford must have remembered, because he didn't pursue his argument.

I made a point of not looking at Travis in his hiding spot. He must have been waiting for the best moment to make his presence known, and I didn't want to direct Hudson's attention to him before then.

"Do you see this woman?" Crawford snapped, getting back to the business at hand.

Hudson frowned. "Of course I see her."

"Well she appeared out of thin air. She didn't come through the door, she didn't come through the window, she just *appeared!*" Hudson turned to me as if for verification. I gave him a *beats me* shrug and a little smile.

"Right, I'll definitely have to look into that," the bodyguard said in the tone of someone trying to calm a raving lunatic.

"Yeah, well while you're at it, you'd better look into that guy—"

As Hudson turned around, Travis threw the door shut and stood there with his gun pointed at the man's chest. "Hands up!" he shouted. I brought my gun out from behind me and aimed it at Crawford. "Hands up *now!*" Travis repeated.

Hudson took a moment to look longingly at his pizza, before letting it fall to the floor and raising his hands.

Crawford jumped to his feet. "What's wrong with you? I don't pay you to cower when there's danger. Take the damn guns away from them!"

Hudson ignored the order, directing his remark to Travis instead. "Okay, pal. I don't know what your beef is, but nobody's looking for trouble. Let's talk this out. What can we do for you?"

"Your boss is responsible for having my brother killed, along with five other people." I was amazed by how measured and calm Travis's words were. There had to be a whirlpool of emotions spinning inside him. Judging by Hudson's expression, he wasn't aware of Crawford's darker enterprise. He must have been hired for strictly legitimate bodyguard duties.

"Don't listen to them," Crawford raged. "They're the ones trespassing and threatening to shoot us." I could see that those words finally reached Hudson and he was struggling to decide where his allegiance belonged. Fortunately, he'd heard his boss sound like a lunatic minutes earlier.

"This man is a reporter," I said, indicating Travis. "Look at him, Hudson; you've seen him on the local news." I sure hoped he had. "There's no reason on earth for him to be here, unless he's telling you the truth." Hudson studied Travis and I thought I saw a flicker of recognition. But he was still clearly torn about what to do.

"Call the head of the news division," Travis said, "he'll vouch for me."

"We just want to hold Crawford here until the police arrive," I added. "They'll be here any minute." As long as nothing had gone awry back at my house where Tilly and Merlin were babysitting Crawford's henchmen.

"Let's talk money, Hudson," the attorney said, sweat beading on his upper lip. "Name your price to help me get out of here. These people are nuts. They have a vendetta against me. How does a million sound? Two million—you'll be set for life." If our plight wasn't so serious, I would have laughed at the absurdity of the situation. We were each lobbying to win the bodyguard to our side, even though Travis and I were the ones with the guns. We all seemed to have accepted the fact that Hudson could take the guns away from us any time he so wished. After all of Crawford's carefully planned murders, the thing that might undo him was hiring a bodyguard with ethics.

"I think I'll give it five minutes and see if the police show up," Hudson decided. "Do you think I can put my hands down?" he asked Travis. "My arms are really aching."

"Yeah, I guess so. Just don't do anything that's going to make me shoot you." I looked at Crawford who was still standing and ordered him to sit down and stay put. It felt good to be the one giving orders. A moment later we heard the wail of the police sirens.

"Travis, that money is yours if you let me go right now," the attorney said.

"You have got to be kidding," Travis said with a bitter smile. "What I would *really* like to do is point this gun at you and pull the trigger. But since I have no desire to be locked up, you'll get to live. From time to time I'll think about you in prison with your new best friends and your sumptuous new accommodations and I'll know that at least in your case, justice was served."

Chapter 54

Thanksgiving morning was sunny and cold, the sky an intense cerulean blue that looked like it could slice a bird's wing if the creature wheeled too sharply through it. Elise had asked us all to arrive at two, with dinner to be served around three. I was up early to prepare the side dishes I was bringing. This was the first Thanksgiving Tilly and I would celebrate without Morgana and Bronwen, the first Elise's sons would spend without their dad. Gathering together as one family promised to be healing for all of us. Travis had wrangled the day off, not that it was difficult after making headlines by bringing down Ryan's killer and his entourage. Like the rest of us, he'd suffered the loss of someone close to him.

Sashkatu and the other cats seemed to know it was not an ordinary day. After an early breakfast, the five younger members of my household followed me around as though trying to deduce how the difference would impact them. Sashkatu watched us from atop the couch, an old man who no longer understood the zip and zeal of youth. He'd lived through enough holiday celebrations to recognize the signs, even when the festivities were to be held elsewhere. I'd briefly debated taking him along, but with each passing year he had less tolerance for tumult. He'd be happier at home. Once I made the decision, Sashki closed his eyes and with a sigh of relief, fell asleep. The evidence was mounting that he had at least some rudimentary ability to read my mind.

Elise had asked me to find two new recipes to replace the standard casseroles of green beans and sweet potatoes. I searched the web and came up with one dish that combined butternut squash, quinoa, spinach, walnuts, and raisins and a second one for goat cheese and grape stuffed sweet potatoes. I made a few extra potatoes that I left in their natural state, in case Zach and Noah turned up their noses at the break with tradition. Tilly was also up early, baking for the occasion. According to Merlin's progress reports, there would be multiple pies and a tin of her crispy thin spice cookies. Travis had been charged with bringing the ice cream.

Elise's house was filled with the holiday aroma of turkey roasting in the oven. The boys were upstairs squabbling over some game—the beginning of a typical American Thanksgiving. I found Elise at the sink rinsing a package of fresh cranberries in a sieve. I set my two dishes on the stovetop. "They're still hot," I said, "but we'll probably have to reheat them before we sit down. Now, how can I help?"

"The table needs setting," she said. "Otherwise I have things under control."

"You're amazing," I said with admiration. "You're cool, calm, and collected even when there's a civil war raging overhead."

She laughed. "That's just white noise at this point. Look at you and Travis. You're actual heroes! Two days ago you could easily have been killed." She was tearing up, so I pulled her into a hug.

"But we're here and it's all good. Besides, don't you know there's no crying on Thanksgiving?"

When Travis straggled in fifteen minutes late, we were all accounted for. Although he'd had the longest trip, he confessed sheepishly that he'd lost track of time watching a football game. Elise forgave him. After all it was Thanksgiving and we had a lot to be grateful for.

When we sat down to eat, the boys called a truce in their dispute at their mother's request. Elise held up her glass and we all raised ours too. "To Kailyn and Travis," she said. "Congratulations and thank you. Due to your courageous efforts, Sam Crawford is behind bars where he belongs." We received a spirited round of applause. "And now," she went on, "I for one expect a detailed account of how it all went down—every why and wherefore!"

We passed the platters of food around the table as Tilly described how she and Merlin were snatched on their way from The Soda Jerk to her car. "When we got to Kailyn's house, they threatened to kill us if we didn't tell them how to breach the wards. They kept calling them a force field, like we were in *Star Wars* or *Star Trek* or something. I didn't know what to do. I just knew I couldn't let them kill Merlin. So I shut down the wards."

I took over to explain what happened once they were inside my house, and Travis carried on with the story from his arrival until we stormed into Crawford's office. I filled in the first few minutes when Travis was still in the lobby.

"What was Crawford's motive?" Elise asked.

"It seems the man had a conscience after all," I said, "and it finally caught up with him. His dilemma was how to keep earning the big bucks from clients and still live with himself after some of those clients wound up killing innocent people. The solution? Take their money, win their cases in court, and then kill them off. But Crawford didn't hit upon that solution until Everett Royce came on the scene and they put their heads together."

Travis picked up the thread of the story. "Everett Royce lost his wife to a distracted driver that Crawford had put back on the streets. Royce was devastated. He was determined to exact justice when the man stood trial for her death. He went to Epps and begged the prosecutor to pull out all the stops, cash in all his favors, and send the guy to prison for the rest of his life. Epps said he'd do his best, but maybe Royce should also talk to Crawford about dialing back his efforts, given the circumstances.

"Epps felt so awful about the whole situation that he started calling Royce to see how he was coping. That led to the occasional meeting for lunch or dinner. Epps became sort of a father figure to the younger man. Royce was a football coach at the high school and made extra money as a handyman. Epps sent work his way whenever he could."

"I'm sure a psychiatrist would have a ball sorting out that relationship," Elise remarked, passing the turkey platter around again.

"At some point," Travis continued, "Royce took Epps's advice and went to talk to Crawford about the upcoming trial. That's when things really started popping. When those two put their heads together, the solution was born. Royce had one stipulation—he wanted to take down his wife's killer himself. After that, Crawford hired Mason and Flint to help him with the others."

"Flint was the man we called Biker Dude and Ski Mask Guy," Tilly chimed in. "Can someone pass the stuffing and gravy?"

"How come they made some of the deaths look like accidents, but not others?" Zach asked.

Travis served himself a heaping spoonful of Elise's drunken cranberry sauce as he explained. "In order for it to look like an accident, the victim had to suffer from a condition that could be exploited, so their death wouldn't raise any eyebrows."

"I get it," Zach said, "you mean like giving a heroin addict an overdose of heroin?"

"Exactly."

"Or like killing someone who's depressed and making it look like a suicide." He was on a roll. "Or like—"

"You, young man, better forget about becoming a criminal mastermind right now," Elise said laughing. "Kailyn, I have a question for you. Were the murders committed months or years apart to keep the police from seeing them as a pattern?"

"That, along with the different methods of killing the people."

"Hey, Mom," Noah piped up, "no life of crime for you either!" Everyone laughed and Zach gave him a high-five.

"So was Lena involved in any of it?" Elise asked.

"Just lending Flint the bike and unlocking my door to help him get in. She claims she had no idea he intended to kill us. She thought he was still just trying to scare us into stopping the investigation."

"What about the night she sneaked back into the courthouse to photocopy Epps's papers?"

"That turned out to be nothing," I said. "She hadn't finished working on the papers and Epps needed them the next morning. Since she wasn't allowed to take the paperwork out of the office, she did the next best thing, figuring no one would be the wiser."

"What came of Austin Stubbs's fake alibi?" Merlin asked, finally putting down the turkey leg he'd been ripping into with his teeth. He looked more like he belonged at a medieval feast thrown by his pal, King Arthur, than at a twenty-first century American Thanksgiving. All that was missing was a wench or two.

"Travis called that one," I said.

"I might have done the same thing given the circumstances," he added. "Stubbs was afraid if he told the police he was home alone the night his son died, they wouldn't believe him. It was well-known in Burdett that he and Axel were always at each other's throats."

After everyone's questions were answered, the dinner conversation took a lighter turn, sprinkled liberally with compliments to the chef. I was accorded the honorary title of side-dish diva, and as always, Tilly's desserts won raves, making her blush almost as red as her curls.

We all helped clean up to give our hostess some well-deserved rest. Tilly and Merlin were the first to leave, both of them stuffed to the groaning point. Even so, the wizard tried to make off with the remains of the pumpkin pie beneath his parka, until Tilly caught him. "But you baked it—it's ours," he protested as she pulled it out of his hands.

"When you bring a gift to someone, it's theirs to keep," Tilly said. Merlin muttered something in old English, but made no further attempt to abscond with the pie. Elise stopped them at the door and handed the pie back to Merlin.

"Noah asked me to please give it to you," she said. "I hope you don't mind, Tilly, but I try to encourage generosity in my boys whenever I can." Merlin thanked Noah without prompting and left with a grin stretched across his face.

Travis thanked Elise for the wonderful Thanksgiving. Caught up in the spirit of the day, she made him promise to come again next year. I walked him into the foyer and found his coat in the closet. He pulled it on, lamenting the fact that he had to be in the newsroom early in the morning. We drew together in a lingering kiss that neither of us seemed willing to end, until Noah saw us and ran upstairs giggling.

When I got home, I fed my furries and collapsed on the couch. At first Sashkatu seemed miffed by my absence, as if he'd forgotten that he'd given me tacit approval to go without him. A full belly restored his good humor, because he climbed up beside me and rubbed his head under my chin like he used to when we were both younger.

"That's what I like to see," Morgana said, her white cloud appearing before me. "Happy Thanksgiving to my Earth-bound family."

"Wish you'd been with us," I said.

"Me too."

"Me three." Bronwen's cloud popped up beside my mother's. "I figured I'd find you here, Morgana. Have you forgotten? We're expected you know where." I knew better than to ask what she meant. They'd told me more than once that what happened on that plane was not for those of us still hooked up to flesh and bone.

"It's not tonight, Mother," Morgana replied. If she'd had eyes to roll, she probably would have rolled them.

"It most certainly *is* tonight. You should pay better attention."

"Ladies," I said, "it's Thanksgiving. Can't you let it go for now? It doesn't matter which one of you is right more often. No one else is keeping score. Besides, aren't you supposed to have left all that pettiness behind you?" Maybe that's why they were still stuck on the first rung of the heavenly ladder.

"She's right," they said at the same time, which started them giggling.

"Much better," I said. "Happy Thanksgiving!" They sent me their love and vanished together. Barely a minute passed before the phone rang.

"It's happened again," Tilly said in a fevered voice. I really didn't want to know what happened again. I just wanted to go to sleep. But that wasn't in the cards.

"There's going to be another murder," she said. And there it was— precisely what I didn't want to hear.

Acknowledgments

Special thanks to my daughter, Lauren, for her invaluable help whenever it's needed, and to my husband, Dennis, for shouldering more than his share. I promise to get back to cooking.

Don't miss the next intriguing book in the Abracadabra mystery series

MAGICKAL MYSTERY LORE

Coming soon from Lyrical Underground, an imprint of Kensington Publishing Corp.

Keep reading to enjoy a sample excerpt!

Chapter 1

"That infernal machine is naught but an instrument of torture," Merlin grumbled as he staggered toward us. "What possessed you to allow me on it?" With his long white hair that had come untethered during the ride and his rats' nest of a beard, he looked more like a wino than a legendary sorcerer from the kingdom of Camelot. He stumbled over his feet and pitched forward into the frothy layers of my Aunt Tilly's lavender muumuu.

"We tried to stop you," I reminded him. "You won't like it, Merlin, we said. Don't do it, Merlin, we said. Does that sound at all familiar?"

"Well yes, but you must admit that everyone on the ride seemed delighted."

"There are a lot of people who love rides like that," Tilly said.

"In that case, I can refer them to a beefy chap who works in a dungeon and is quite skilled in all manner of torturous devices."

Tilly held him away from her, hands on his shoulders. "Let's see if you can stand on your own without falling over." Merlin wobbled a bit before finding his equilibrium. "There," she said, letting go of him. "Are you at all queasy?"

"Not in the least."

"Count yourself lucky," I said, not having been as fortunate my one and only time on that ride. "I couldn't look at food for hours."

"You appear to be fine," Tilly proclaimed.

"I am not fine. The whole ordeal has left me famished," he said as we walked away from the Tilt-a-Whirl. We were in the thick of the forty-fifth annual New Camel Day Fair, elbow to elbow with a few hundred attendees. Moving from one attraction to another was largely a matter of joining the stream of people heading in the direction we wanted to go. If we weren't careful, we could wind up back on the line for Merlin's nightmare ride.

"I don't know how you can be hungry," I said. "You've already had three hotdogs, curly cheese fries, lemonade, and two root beers."

"And yet my stomach demands more."

"Does it have a particular request?" Tilly asked dryly.

"Cotton candy," he said without a moment's hesitation. "And a candy apple. I've never tasted either." There ensued a debate on the wisdom of Merlin eating the apple with its hard, sticky coating. A quick inspection of his mouth revealed he was missing a number of teeth and many of the remaining ones were chipped or broken. I explained that he could lose the teeth he had left with one bite into the apple. Tilly suggested replacing it with kettle corn, which proved to be a winner.

Two pounds of sugar later, we headed over to the booths where New Camel's merchants displayed their wares. My family had always participated, displaying our most popular health and beauty products. Tilly used our booth to hold a drawing for a free psychic reading and English tea. It was a lot easier when my mother and grandmother were alive and there were four of us to take turns manning the booth. Although Tilly and I had managed all right on our own last year, now that we had to oversee Merlin, we'd decided to forgo the booth this once. It was a difficult decision, because Abracadabra always enjoyed a nice uptick in its customer base when folks bought our products at the fair and decided they couldn't live without them.

I'd already been stopped by a dozen people who looked for our booth and were disappointed when they couldn't find it. When I offered to open my shop at three o'clock to accommodate them, they acted like they'd won the lottery. Tilly applauded the move as good business. Merlin contended it was a fool's errand to try to please everyone.

The Soda Jerk was the first of the booths we came to. They weren't serving sundaes and shakes on the spot, but two of the owners' great grandkids were there handing out paper menus with coupons to buy one sundae and get a second one free at their restaurant. Their line was long, but moved so fast that in no time we each came away with a coupon.

We walked past the booths that held no interest for Merlin—from vintage clothing to dollhouses, Victoriana to candles. Had it been up to Tilly and me, we would have stopped to say a quick *hello* to every merchant who wasn't busy with customers. But we'd learned the hard way that a powerful sorcerer with a failing memory could wreak all sorts of havoc if he grew bored.

When we reached the display of old-fashioned toys, Merlin was intrigued. He checked out the paddle ball, jacks, and kaleidoscope while we chatted with the owner, Nelson Biddle, a staple in the New Camel business community as far back as I could remember. He told us he'd been thinking of retiring, but his wife wouldn't let him. She didn't want him sitting around the house all day watching TV or following her around like a shadow. At that point, Merlin paddled the little ball into his eye and let loose a string of profanities, some in Old English, others that needed no translation. We apologized to Nelson and moved on.

"It's a wonder more children don't lose an eye from that thing," Merlin muttered.

"It's not meant to be aimed at your face," Tilly said.

"I possess a curious mind," he replied indignantly. "I was simply testing it from every angle."

Hannah Rose waved from the Busy Fingers booth when she saw us approaching. It would have been rude not to stop. She had a beautiful display of her handicrafts—knitted baby items, crocheted afghans, and embroidered throw pillows. She was also offering half price lessons in any of the handicrafts if booked during the fair. Like every merchant there, her goal was to entice fairgoers to visit her shop and become long-term customers.

While we were talking to Hannah, Merlin sidled over to the next booth. Since it was Lolly's, I didn't try to stop him. He'd be waiting in her line for a good fifteen minutes or more. Hers was always the longest line at the fair because she was known to be generous with the free samples of her satiny fudge. She believed if you wanted to hook a customer on your products, they needed to associate your shop with abundance and satiation. It was a philosophy that had served her well over the years. After scoring their free sample, most of the people in line generally bought a slab of fudge along with a box of her chocolates.

Tilly and I had just bid Hannah goodbye and were crossing over to Lolly's when a deep voice from the line shouted, "Hey, old man, no cuts." From what I could tell, Merlin had bypassed the line and marched straight up to Lolly who was in the process of handing him a number of samples. Lolly got to her feet, her cherubic smile stiffening. "Thank you, sir, but I'll decide on the rules and how to enforce them. There's plenty here for everyone."

Without missing a step, Tilly snagged Merlin's arm as she went by and dragged him away before he could turn the man into a slug. She made it less than thirty yards with her charge before he dug in his heels, bringing her to a hard stop that could have given her whiplash. "Don't you dare change him into some odd creature with all these people around," she warned him as I caught up to them. Merlin didn't move or show any indication he'd heard her. I followed his line of sight. He was glowering at No-Cuts-Guy in the line across from where we were standing.

"No dark magick," I added.

"Fear not, mistress," he said without shifting his focus. "I will do nothing untoward." I decided to give him the benefit of the doubt. It wasn't like I had much of a choice anyway. Tilly looked at me and shrugged, having apparently come to the same conclusion. Since the day the legendary sorcerer crash landed in my shop, we'd tried to keep him from drawing attention to himself and the fact that he hailed from another time and place. It was a losing battle from the start. On New Year's Eve, Tilly and I had finally caved. We resolved to continue giving him advice on spells and other actions he was considering, but we wouldn't penalize him for his choices. Unless they were likely to have a deleterious effect on our lives as well.

Merlin was still staring at No-Cuts-Guy. We waited anxiously for something to happen, something to change. I was half expecting the guy to turn into a frog right there in line. When the spell started working, I didn't immediately realize it. Two squirrels chased each other across the grass, coming to a stop near No-Cuts-Guy's feet. They were quickly followed by half a dozen more. Before we knew it, No-Cuts-Guy had an entourage of a dozen chittering squirrels chasing each other around him. The people nearby gave him and his squirrel circus as wide a berth as possible without forfeiting their place in line.

No-Cuts-Guy tried to shoo them away. He looked around for help, but since there were no squirrel containment officers at hand, he resorted to kicking at them. That was unacceptable to Merlin who instantly recalled his minions. Released from his control, they scampered off, except for the one Merlin charged with a second mission. That squirrel shimmied up No-Cuts-Guy's pant leg. The expression on his face was priceless. He broke into a panicked little dance, no doubt to dislodge the critter. When that proved unsuccessful, he ran off screaming in the direction of the first-aid station and port-a-potties.

"Doesn't he know you can't run away from your problems?" Tilly said with a giggle. Merlin had a grin from ear to ear. Everyone who'd witnessed the squirrel incident, as it was destined to be called, was roaring with laughter, until even I couldn't resist. But I never lost sight of the fact that there might be consequences for allowing the wizard such latitude in casting spells. Our resolution might need some editing.

Still in high spirits, we wandered into the part of the Midway where one could win a stuffed animal or a goldfish in a little round bowl. After scouting out the various games, Merlin opted to try his hand at darts. "All I must do is hit one balloon on that board," he explained as if we were the newbies at the fair.

"It's not as easy as it looks," I said.

"I'll have you know that back home I am considered the finest player of darts in the realm." I paid for three games with three tries each. The finest player in the realm failed to hit a balloon on any of his first eight attempts. However his last dart sailed straight into the heart of a sky-blue balloon that burst with a satisfying pop. I had my suspicions about how he accomplished that, but I kept them to myself. He picked out a gray stuffed bunny with a white fluff of a tail, after I nixed the goldfish. Too many cats in the family. The poor fish would die of a heart attack if it didn't wind up as someone's lunch.

When Tilly asked what he planned to do with the stuffed animal, he proposed giving it to Lolly's new great granddaughter. Silly as it was, I felt like a proud parent whose offspring has shown signs of thoughtfulness and generosity. From there we followed a crowd of people to what we hoped was the petting zoo. Merlin hummed a song as we walked. There was a familiar ring to it, but I couldn't immediately identify it. Once I did, I wasn't happy. He was humming the song "Camelot" from the Broadway musical. He must have seen the movie version of it on TV. Tilly chimed in with the words.

"I know what you're up to," I cautioned the wizard. "You're trying to send the subliminal message that New Camelot is the town's proper name."

"Oh dear," Tilly said, abandoning the tune. "If I'd realized that, I would never have aided and abetted."

The wizard looked wounded. "Why do you always think the worst of my intentions? Is it not possible that the song simply popped into my head on its own? Have you never had a tune take up residence in *your* mind?"

"Not such a convenient one." All the people passing around us were now singing the song too. Great, sooner or later someone was going to realize that by adding two letters to the odd name of New Camel, it became the much lovelier and more romantic New Camelot. From there it was a short leap to the fabled home of King Arthur and Merlin, the acclaimed sorcerer.

When we arrived at the petting zoo, we were able to go right in. Once inside the enclosure, Merlin's eyes lit up and he dropped his aggrieved expression as if it had come to the wrong address. Tilly and I knew how much he missed the animals that populated the forest near his home. But that was thousands of miles away and hundreds of years in the past. He folded himself down onto one of the low benches meant for children and within seconds the goats and piglets, lambs and bunnies left the children who were feeding them and surrounded the wizard, vying for his attention the way my cats did.

Children complained to their parents that he was hogging the animals. Parents complained to the animal wranglers that the old man must be feeding the animals unsanctioned treats—why else would they be acting this way? Before irritation could boil over into nasty words or heated actions, we told Merlin it was time to leave. He did not take it well. The animals seemed to share his disappointment and tried to follow him out. In the end, two animal wranglers and a maintenance man had to hold them back so we could leave without causing a mass exodus.

Poor Merlin was still reeling from his hasty expulsion from the zoo when he realized we'd come to the end of the fair. Of course no New Camel Fair would be complete without a couple of the town's churlish mascots stationed at the exit. Merlin took strong exception to their presence. "Thus the lie is perpetuated for another year," he protested at the top of his lungs. One of the camels spat at him. He spat right back. Before the animals' owner could add his two cents to the exchange, Tilly grabbed one of the sorcerer's arms, I grabbed the other, and we whisked him out of the fair, his feet skimming the ground.

I drove my aunt and our foster wizard to her house, stopped back home long enough to deposit my car in the driveway, grab Sashkatu, who was clearly miffed at being left for hours with the five other cats, and walked across the street to the rear door of Abracadabra. The moment we were inside, he ascended his custom-built steps to his padded window seat with its fine view of Main Street. He'd been my mother's familiar, and she'd spoiled him shamelessly. Not that I'd done anything to remedy the situation since he'd come into my keeping eighteen months ago.

I was turning the CLOSED sign to OPEN as my first customer reached the door. "I cannot tell you how grateful I am that you were willing to open for me on your day off," Lenore Spalding boomed. She was a petite woman in her fifties with the vocal projection of a stage actress. Whoever raised her had failed to teach her the difference between an outside voice and an inside one. "For a little bitty thing, she can sure rattle the timbers," my grandmother Bronwen used to say after each of Lenore's visits.

"I'm happy to oblige," I said. "Let me know if you need help finding anything."

"Thanks, but I know this shop like the back of my hand." She slipped one of the rattan shopping baskets over her arm and disappeared down the first aisle still talking. "I'm out of almost everything. If you hadn't opened, I was thinking of getting a hotel room and staying overnight." Her words carried back to me loud and clear. There wasn't a lot of *Excuse me?* or *What was that?* when you were dealing with Lenore.

She returned to the counter ten minutes later with her basket filled to the brim. "You have enough here to last you an entire year," I said, ringing up her order.

"Trust me, I'll be back in six months the latest. When I go without your amazing products for even a few days, gravity strikes." She let out a booming laugh that woke Sashkatu, in spite of his growing deafness. He opened his eyes, homed in on the source of the disturbance, and yowled at her. "Oops, sorry," she said. "I forgot how much he hates idle chatter." In all the years she'd been coming to my shop, she never figured out that it wasn't the chatter he minded, but the decibel of it.

After Lenore left, a steady stream of customers kept me busy until closing time. Word that I'd be opening must have made it around the fair. I was about to lock up when Lolly flew in the door, breathing hard, her face bleached a scary shade of white. "Kailyn, please," she said, her voice shaking, "would you—I mean, I need you to come with me."

"Of course. What happened? Are you okay?" Ignoring my questions, she grabbed my hand and pulled me out the door. By the time we crossed the street to her shop, she was bent over gasping for air. She allowed herself a few deep breaths, before leading me through her shop and out the back door to the small patch of weeds and dirt where she kept her garbage cans. That day a woman occupied the remainder of the space. She was on her back with her eyes wide open and one of Lolly's fudge knives protruding from the left side of her chest.

About the Author

Sharon Pape launched her acclaimed Abracadabra Mystery Series with *Magick & Mayhem* and its sequel, *That Olde White Magick*. *Magick Run Amok* is the third book in the series. She is also the author of the popular Portrait of Crime and Crystal Shop mystery series. She started writing stories in first grade and never looked back. She studied French and Spanish literature in college and went on to teach both languages on the secondary level. After being diagnosed with and treated for breast cancer in 1992, Sharon became a Reach to Recovery peer support volunteer for the American Cancer Society. She went on to become the coordinator of the program on Long Island. She and her surgeon created a non-profit organization called Lean On Me to provide peer support and information to newly diagnosed women and men. After turning her attention back to writing, she has shared her storytelling skills with thousands of fans. She lives with her husband on Long Island, New York, near her grown children. She loves reading, writing, and providing day care for her grand-dogs. Visit her at www.sharonpape.com.

SHARON PAPE

MAGICK & MAYHEM

An Abracadabra Mystery

SHARON PAPE

THAT OLDE WHITE MAGICK

An Abracadabra Mystery